The Keeper

By Nikki Moyes

Author: Moyes, Nikki

Title: **The Keeper**/*Nikki Moyes*.

ISBN: 978-0-6485149-0-9 (ebook)

ISBN: 978-0-6485149-1-6 (paperback)

For Melanie and Kellie.
Thanks for believing in my story.

The Keeper

I study the colour map of Terra Zoological Park and Research Centre. At two hundred and fifty hectares, it's the largest in the Tri-System. I swipe back to the conservation assignment uploaded to my school tablet screen: Investigate career opportunities in the preservation sector using a threatened species as an example and a zoological park keeper as your mentor. Due date: four weeks. I look at the map again. Cats of Terra, frogs of Atlas, reptiles of Triade.

"So, Cassie," Jayne studies me with her big blue eyes, her eyelids painted with ornate butterflies for the excursion, "the plan is to find the hottest keeper and do the assignment on him." She flicks her bright red hair from her face. It was purple last week.

"I swear Ms Barnett told us the project is about the animal." I attempt to keep the laughter from my voice as I roll my eyes.

"She said it's about the career, which as far as *I'm* concerned, makes it about the keeper, not the kept." She flutters her eyelids, giving the butterflies the appearance of taking flight.

"I was hoping for a mentor who knows more about animal conservation than his reflection."

People weave around us in the crowded zoo and I step aside to allow a large group to pass.

"Sometimes you're so boring..." Jayne trails off as she grabs my arm. "Oh My Governor Suri. That man is mine!"

I glance towards the cetacean pool where a dark haired, blue-eyed man stands in a tight wetsuit surrounded by a group of young women.

"I thought you wanted someone from our own Star System," I say.

"Atlas is renowned for its expertise with marine mammals." Jayne sighs before dropping my arm and skipping towards the enclosure.

"I'll catch up with you later then," I call out to her retreating back. She waves a hand over her shoulder.

I jog up the steps to the skyrail platform. The car arrives moments later and I squeeze into a window seat with my backpack perched on my lap while tourists pack in around me. From up here, the zoological park spreads out before me in a sea of greens and browns surrounded by the encroaching city buildings in the distance.

The skyrail car glides forward and I press my forehead against the glass to look down on the enclosures below. As we head towards the inter-planetary exhibits, I catch a flash of white feline below us. I lean forward and press the 'stop' button.

The skyrail glides to a halt at the next platform and I edge around the other passengers to get off. At the bottom of the platform stairs a cluster of signs point to various exhibits, but none mention what had looked like a Northern Snowy Panther.

I pull out my screen and search the park information database. According to the zoo, there are no panthers on display at the moment and the feline enclosures are several stations further along the skyrail track.

I pull up the map to work out where the enclosure I'd seen from above would be. The public paths detour past a variety of exhibits along a windy, indirect track. The dotted line of a staff access path creates a shortcut between my current location and the exotic animal enclosures. It's the only path heading in the right direction.

I look up from my screen. A small 'authorised personnel only' sign hangs from a chain across the pebbled staff access path. The area beyond the sign is quiet. A handful of families walk the public paths and I loiter, pretending to study my screen, until no one is looking in my direction.

I step over the chain holding the sign, careful to avoid the puddles dotting the dirt path. I walk casually, not looking back. My stride becomes confident when no one stops me.

I'm halfway along the path before I catch another glimpse of white fur in an enclosure not visible to the general public, if the general public stayed out of restricted areas. I edge closer and activate the recording function on my screen.

The snowy panther rolls on its back on a patch of grass. I shift slightly to the right to get a better view of the large beast.

"Native to Terra's northern continent, the Northern Snowy Panther can be unpredictable and is responsible for the deaths of several naturalists every year," I say quietly to the mic of the screen.

The panther rolls quickly to its feet and stands at attention looking towards the fence adjacent to where I stand. Its ears twitch and then it raises its long tail into the air.

A young man steps into my line of vision on the wrong side of the high perimeter fence, his beige zoo uniform nearly camouflaging him from sight. He runs a hand through his tawny coloured hair leaving several strands standing on end.

He creeps forward smoothly, blinking his eyes slowly at the beast. When he reaches the panther, he stretches out a hand and it presses its large head against his palm. The keeper squats and uses his hands to gently open the animal's jaws before removing something from his pocket to swab its mouth. The snowy panther towers over his squatted position.

I stand still so my movement doesn't spook the notoriously temperamental animal and slowly check my tablet screen, hoping the zoological park has an emergency contact for people about to be eaten by wild animals.

Before I can call for help, the man touches his forehead to the large feline's, before running a hand down its back. It butts its head into his shoulder in response. He stands as the cat prances away, and he backs out of the enclosure, locking the gate behind him. I step forward before I remember I'm not meant to be here.

"How did you do that?" I ask.

He spins around and a flash of guilt crosses his face before he resumes a neutral expression. I frown; I'm the one out of bounds.

With a quick glance at me, he turns away and walks off. I hesitate before running after him. After all, he hasn't kicked me out of the staff only area yet.

"I'm doing a conservation project for school." I mentally kick myself for mentioning school and sounding immature in front of a man who looks almost eighteen.

It's moments like these I wish I was more like Jayne. If flirting was a Tri-System sport, Jayne would win platinum for sure.

"I'm Cassie." I try another tack.

He glances sideways at me as he walks but doesn't speak. I follow until he stops by the door of a portable building and pauses to look at me, as though wondering why I'm still there.

"And your name is?" I ask.

I clutch my tablet in the silence. Maybe he doesn't speak to people who follow him through staff only areas.

"You've probably already been told, but I'm with the conservation class and we need a keeper to be our mentor for this project we're doing about working in the industry and I was wondering if you'd be interested in being my mentor?" I take a breath.

He pauses with his hand on the door. A wide, black band clings to his lower forearm. When the light hits it, silvery outlines reflect off the dark background.

He points to the pocket of the uniform shirt he wears, drawing my eyes away from his tanned arm. Not the most attractive coloured shirt, but he can pull it off. I wonder what he'd look like if he did pull off his shirt. I give myself a mental slap and stare at him blankly.

He repeats the action, this time running his finger back and forth. All the keepers I've seen today have the word 'keeper' stitched onto the pocket of their shirt. His has nothing.

"You're not a zoo keeper." Saying the words sounds so final. He shakes his head and opens the door.

My wristband beeps with a new message, but it's only Mum letting me know she and Dad will be home late tonight and I should stay at Jayne's. I look up and the man's gone, the door shut behind him.

I find my way back to the main path and wander back towards Jayne's location, watching the keepers as

11

I walk. That one looks too busy. She looks like a mad scientist. He looks like he just got out of prison. I'm not interested in a career with reptiles.

Back at the cetacean pool, Jayne introduces me to her mentor, Jamis, the dolphin trainer from planet Atlas. The crowd of adoring females around him has thinned since I left.

"Have you found a mentor yet?" Jayne asks.

"No." I sigh.

"Maybe Jamis can set you up with someone. Who works with the felines?" she asks. He rattles off a few names as he flicks water droplets from the railing.

"Do you have many staff here who aren't keepers?" I ask.

"Cleaners, vets, and a guy doing research." Jamis ticks them off on his fingers.

"Who's the quiet guy, dark blond hair, green eyes?" I hold one hand slightly above my head to indicate his height.

"That's Nobody." Jamis laughs.

"He must be someone. He was wearing a park uniform."

"No, I mean his name is the Atlasian word for nobody. Don't bother with him, he's mute."

"He's from Atlas?" I stare at Jamis in confusion.

"Of course not, he doesn't have our colouring." Jamis runs a hand through his black hair. I bite back a comment about my own brunette hair.

"What does he do?" I ask.

"Some sort of genetic research. He keeps to himself."

I step off the viewing platform. "I'll catch up with you later, Jayne."

12

"Where are you going? We have to leave soon," she calls after me, but I'm already gone.

I take the skyrail again, then jog back to the staff area. Once over the chain barrier, I glance down at my wristband to see how much time I have until the transport leaves.

I run smack bang into someone and land on my backside in the mud. I look up into the researcher's bright green eyes. He doesn't offer me a hand so I help myself up, my cheeks flushing. I brush at my denims, spreading the mud to my hands. He watches me.

"I'm fine. Thanks for asking," I mutter, looking at the ground.

His feet are bare. I glance up in time to see him raise an eyebrow before scooping my schoolbag off the ground. It has escaped most of the mud, unlike me.

He slings it over his shoulder and nods in the direction he was heading when I fell in the mud in front of him. He walks off, not turning to see if I follow. I sigh and run to catch up.

He pauses to put an empty bucket in the shed before heading to the same building as earlier. He holds the door open and waits for me to enter. After a moment's pause, I stalk past him. He drops my bag by the door and grabs a towel off a nearby hook. He tosses it at me and I catch it. He turns to his desk, ignoring me again.

I remove the worst of the mud from my faded denims, but the once white t-shirt is ruined. Streaks of mud pull at my skin as it dries on my face. I glance around the small room as I try to make myself presentable. The room is divided into several cubicle-type spaces with a kitchenette near the back.

My gaze falls on his bare feet. There aren't any stray shoes in the room. My eyes move from his feet up his lean body. I flush and turn to study the walls covered with sketches of animals. I look closer. They're hand drawn, extremely detailed and realistic, making each creature come alive on the page.

"Did you get these from a book?" I ask.

He looks up from the holographic display on his desk. He shakes his head and points at himself.

"Impressive," I say. Surprise flicks across his face. "I was thinking that even though you're not a keeper, my teacher would make an exception for a researcher..."

He leans back in his chair and folds his arms across his chest. He raises an eyebrow.

"...please." I beg. "I really need you to be my mentor for this project. I've never seen anyone handle a feline like you did. My teacher won't mind, honest." My chest tightens as I wait for his response. "You wouldn't even notice I'm here."

He considers me and my muddy footprints for a few moments. Finally, he shrugs.

"Is that a yes?" I bounce on my heels. I step forward to hug him but stop. He might change his mind if I cover him in mud. He glances up at the clock on the wall. It's nearly closing time for the zoo.

"Oh crap. I have to go." I grab my bag and run out the door. I've left the muddy towel on the floor.

Jayne gives me a look as I arrive dishevelled and sweaty from my run to the exit gate. She tilts her head to the side to get a better look at my dirty behind, before moving between me and the scanner's line of vision as we step aboard the transport.

"This better be a good story," she whispers in my ear as we take our seats.

14

"I slipped in front of a guy and then asked if he'd be my mentor."

"Was he good-looking?"

"Lord, yeah!" I grin. Jayne squeals. I cover my ears and wait for the other passengers to stop glaring at us.

"I need details." She clutches my arm.

"There's nothing to tell. He's going to be my mentor. End of story."

"What's his name? Is he a local? He'd better not whisk you away to some exotic planet on the other side of the universe."

"I guess he's from here. He doesn't have an Atlas or Triade look about him."

Jayne hums the wedding tune until we reach our stop. I give her a playful shove as we step off the transport. We take the elevator to her family's apartment and let ourselves in. Her parents are out, most likely still ferrying Jayne's two younger siblings to various after-school classes.

We kick off our shoes and throw ourselves onto Jayne's double bed. She turns the telescreen on to a current affairs program while I pull up my science homework on my screen, only to have Jayne toss it onto the floor out of my reach.

"Hey!" I make a half-hearted reach for it. Jayne leans over me and starts playing with my hair.

"You really should do something about this. I have plenty of colours in the bathroom," she says.

"You do anything to reduce my chances of snagging an eligible young man and Mum will report you to the Peace Keepers." I roll my eyes. Jayne sighs and flops onto her side.

"Has your mother run out of potential suitors for you, yet?"

"Lord, I hope so. I swear I've met the sons of every person she knows! You'd think having to move out of the city school district once I graduate is the end of the world, the way Mum acts." I rest my chin on my hands.

"I'll wait until I meet an astrogator or a wealthy space-pirate, but in the meantime Jamis is great to look at." Jayne smiles and stretches then sits up, looking at the image on the screen. "Hey look, it's a program on Governor Suri's visit to Terra. I bet the Governor of the Universe travels with plenty of eligible young men."

I shove her off the bed and she squeals as she hits the floor. A stock image of Governor Suri's sleek spacecraft in orbit around our planet, appears on the screen. The vessel is huge, capable of housing the delegates of Suri-governed planets. Two shiny dragons, one gold and one silver, decorate the sides of the spaceship. Below, the words 'United Federation of Humanoid and Intelligent Lifeforms' are displayed, with 'SURI' emblazoned across the bow.

'Vice Governor Jaarid will attend various meetings with Terra's leaders, with Governor Suri expected to make an appearance,' the reporter says as the image changes to the UFHaIL logo.

"Perhaps the Vice Governor has a son," Jayne says. I throw a pillow at her.

Assignment

Two days and a lengthy search of the zoological park later, I find my mentor at the lion enclosure, on the outside of the fence this time. He scribbles in a plastic notebook as he leans against a tree, shoes still nowhere in sight.

"What're you doing?" I glance at the page, but his writing consists of a series of scratch marks as though created by a race of clawed creatures instead of his marker pen. He looks up from his scribbles, pointing to his eyes, then the lions.

"Watching them? Well, this could be fun." I hover beside him.

He raises an eyebrow before returning to his observations. I mentally map out my project. *Today we watched the animals. Kind of like being a tourist only we get paid.* Yeah, I could do this job.

"I'm going to have to ask you a few questions for my assignment," I say after some time. His eyes flicker over mine as I hold a finger poised over my screen's record function ready for his answers. "What are you researching?"

He flips to a new page, his fingers long and graceful as he scribbles several words in Common. *Genetic sampling verification.* I wrinkle my nose as I try to understand his meaning. I record what he has written, but I'll have to Suri® the answer later.

"How did you get into research?" I ask.

He flips back to his previous page and returns to observing the animals. His writing reverts back to the language I've never seen before. I move into his line of vision, but he doesn't look at me.

"Hello?" I wave a hand in front of his face.

He steps around me, crouches down and places a hand against the fence. He stares intently into the enclosure until the lion approaches. He pulls a DNA sampling stick from his pocket and pokes it through the fence. I place a hand on my hip but am distracted by the way the animal responds, opening his mouth to accept the stick. I missed whatever command the researcher used to get the lion to do that.

He leans forward, revealing a leather necklace around his neck, but whatever hangs from it remains hidden under his shirt. He straightens and seals the sample stick in a small vial before returning it to his pocket.

"If you could be any animal, real or imaginary, what would you chose?" I try a different question.

He flips back to the fresh sheet and I wait for him to write something, but instead he quickly sketches a creature. It comes to life under his pen, a dragon soaring across the white page.

"Not what I was expecting," I say. "I picked you to be more of a tiger man."

His eyes widen as they dart to mine, making me wonder what I've said wrong. I change the topic before he decides to ignore me again.

"Care to tell me your name?" I ask.

He narrows his eyes slightly like I'm an unidentified specimen. I hold his gaze and after a moment he flips his notebook closed. The front cover is adorned with the initials 'DS'. It's not a name but better than nothing.

I type a few questions to ask him on another day if he's feeling more forthcoming. He doesn't respond to anything else I say and eventually I head home.

I don't have the time to make it back to the zoological park until later in the week. I head to the staff area first to see if DS is around. No one answers when I knock on the door of his building and peek my head around the door. I step in to see if he has a schedule to cut down on the time I spend searching for my mentor.

A simple sketch of a red tree-bear sits propped up on DS's desk. I open my screen to the park map and locate the correct enclosure in the hopes the drawing was left as directions.

After a short trip on the skyrail, I find him, still barefoot, playing a game with a little tree-bear using food hidden in different containers. The tree-bear keeps trying to peek inside DS's shirt, where a cloth sling sits against his skin. The bulge it makes is small and tucked close to his body.

"What have you got?" I ask when he pries the tree-bear away and steps out of the enclosure.

Sick monkey, he writes in his book.

"Should it be near the other animals?"

Not contagious. Malnourished, dehydrated, not eating, he writes.

"What happened to its mother?"

DS stiffens and closes the notebook. The tree-bear chatters away as though trying to talk to us and after a few moments of silence, DS responds to it with a similar chittering sound.

"Can you teach me how to interact with the animals like you do?" I ask.

He looks me over for a moment and then nods his head in the direction of a neighbouring enclosure. I follow after him and deposit my bag beside the gate as he directs. He places his own belongings beside mine, keeping back a handful of pellets. He gestures for me to hold out my palms and deposits half in my cupped hands.

He opens the gate and steps into the enclosure. I follow him through and he selects a flat grassy area away from the public view to sit down. He pats the ground beside him. I join him on the ground and rest my screen against one knee to film the lesson.

DS makes a clicking noise with his tongue and a furry, burrowing creature, the size of a rabbit, sticks its head out of its hidey-hole. He tosses a pellet of food towards the animal. The burrower edges towards the food and sniffs at it before gobbling it down.

DS mimes for me to hold out my hand with the food while he lures the animal over with a combination of pellets and clicking noises. I hold still as the animal hops gradually towards me. I try making the sound DS does and after a few goes it sounds fairly similar. The burrower clicks back at me as it rests its front paws on my hand and shoves its nose into the pellets.

I grin at DS and he smiles back. The little monkey in DS's sling sneezes and shifts its position. The burrower bounds away.

We develop a pattern over the week, as I pick up on my mentor's habits and non-verbal clues. I ask questions, but if he doesn't want to answer something personal, he ignores me until I change the topic.

His tactics change the more time we spend together and he reverts to scribbling interesting facts in his notebook until I get distracted and forget I still don't know what qualifications he has to allow him to work as a researcher, or who he works for. Other times he draws little diagrams and labels them in his own language of scratch marks which he doesn't explain.

DS introduces me to a few of the non-dangerous animals and teaches me to mimic their calls. The little monkey stays hidden in his shirt, although it becomes more active as the week progresses. A few times I catch DS watching me with a confused look on his face, but he glances away as soon as I look in his direction.

*

I lean back in my chair and subtly flip through the images on my screen to decide which will go best in my assignment, while my politics teacher drones on about something that may or may not be in the curriculum.

He flicks the classroom lights out so we can watch a televised program and I switch off my screen so the glow in the darkened room doesn't give me away.

On the program the host asks the next question to a balding man in the seat opposite. Across the bottom of the screen scrolls the words, 'Kerin Trenard and Murray Rivette - experts in inter-federation politics'.

"Are you suggesting the Keeper is unwell, or that Governor Suri is keeping vital information from the people regarding the state of the government's primary advisor?" The host reviews the screen resting across her lap before looking up to see the first expert's response.

"Look at the evidence in front of us," the man replies. "The Keeper hasn't been seen in months and the Temple Tigers have been. Everyone knows the Keeper banned those dangerous creatures after the incident with his eye."

"What a load of nonsense," the second man interrupts. "Atlas is currently preparing to celebrate the current Keeper's 110th anniversary. He's clearly not dead. It's not possible for anyone to hide the death of a Keeper. For those who don't know, the Keeper can't die until he has been replaced by an apprentice."

"I assume you're referring to the Takarna Trials?" the host asks. "Can you explain those for the audience?"

"Once the Keeper is satisfied that at least one apprentice is capable of completing the series of tests, he calls the Takarna Trials. Any young man bearing the mark of the Dragon Temple is eligible to compete. The winner becomes the next Keeper and is henceforth called Takarna–"

Jayne's head comes to a rest on my shoulder before she jerks up again in a pretence of waking. "Did I miss anything?" she asks. Someone behind us giggles while I attempt to keep a straight face.

"I hope you're all paying attention," our politics teacher says. "There will be an assignment after this."

I glance at the time on my wristband to see if I have enough time to make the next transport to the zoological park. The bell rings and Jayne and I quickly pack up our belongings and head to the station outside the school gates.

"Well that was boring." Jayne nudges my shoulder as we walk.

"The last class, or the whole day?" I ask.

"Today has been a complete waste of makeup."

The transport pulls into the station and I sink into the seat nearest the window. I balance my screen across my knees as I read through the outline of my report. Jayne holds up her screen to use as a mirror while she paints the finishing touches to a row of green ants marching up the side of her face to match the new green streak through her hair.

"Do you know what your mentor is researching yet?" Jayne swipes a layer of green over her lips.

I glance at my notes. "He's either attempting to use genetic testing to calculate the age of the universe, or he's collecting samples for a database in case the universe needs to be recreated."

"Which option do you think will sound less crazy in your report?" Jayne pulls her bag onto her shoulder as the transport pulls up to the zoological park.

"I haven't decided yet. Every time I try to find out what he's actually doing, he acts like he can't hear me." I step off the transport and Jayne follows. "I'll probably make something up. It's not like Ms Barnett will know the difference."

"Well, Jamis is much easier to get details out of. He loves talking about himself," Jayne says.

"I'd better go find where DS is today. See you back here in an hour?"

"Sure thing, Cass." Jayne prances off to find Jamis while I make my way to the portable staff building to find the day's sketch.

A short time later, with DS's latest sketch clutched in my hand, I head towards the golden bear enclosure. My mentor hasn't shown me how to interact with the more dangerous animals yet so I swing between excitement and anxiety as I walk.

When I reach the enclosure, I find him trying to pry a tiny monkey from the post of the outer fence. The baby animal sees me, stops its screeching, and drops to the ground before running at me. It's scrambled up my leg and clinging to my hair before either of us can react.

DS faces us with his hands on his hips and his eyebrows furrowed. The monkey cheeps what sounds like an apology but doesn't let go of me. I turn my head to study the little monkey that my mentor has been looking after for the last week. The monkey has the gangly limbs of a baby and is covered in three shades of fur; copper, blond, and ebony.

"What sort of monkey is it?" I ask.

DS steps forward and holds up three fingers before touching each colour of the monkey's fur.

"Three colours?" I guess.

He huffs out a breath and reaches for his notebook. *Tri-colour monkey*, he writes.

Depending on my mentor's mood, it's often easier to look up the basic information on an animal from the park's database than try to have a wordless conversation to answer common information.

"Does he have a name?" I pull out my screen and type the species into the search bar.

Zeke, DS writes.

The search on my screen comes up with basic information and one other important detail.

"There are no tri-coloured monkeys at this zoo and they're native to Atlas, not Terra." I hold up the screen for him to see.

The corner of his mouth twitches up and he holds a finger up to his lips.

"Does anyone know you have him? You didn't steal him did you?"

DS shakes his head and scribbles in his book. *Abandoned.*

Dozens of questions rush to mind, but while I try to organise them into ones DS may answer, tiny paws scramble at my buttons and try to burrow into my shirt. The little monkey settles for sucking on the material while staring up at me with big brown eyes.

"I think Zeke may be hungry."

DS rummages in a small satchel sitting by the gate and pulls out a bottle of milk. When he hands it to me, it's warm. I don't have time to ask how because Zeke grabs it and nestles into the crook of my arm to drink.

DS points a finger at him and looks like he is having a silent conversation with the monkey who stares back at him without stopping the suckling. My mentor grabs a couple of items from his bag and heads to the bear enclosure entrance.

"Wait, aren't you going to introduce me to this animal?" I ask.

Zeke lets out a horrified squeak at the same time DS shakes his head.

"Why not?"

DS holds up his hands like claws and makes a growling noise.

"But you're going in there."

He pauses before coming back towards me and writing in his book. *Alpha*, he points to himself. *Prey*, he points to me.

"What makes you an alpha and not me?" I demand.

He tilts his head to one side and studies me and Zeke for a moment before writing a single word in his book.

"Smell?" I say. "You smell like an alpha and I don't?" I lift an eyebrow. He nods his head. "What makes you smell like an alpha?"

His pen hovers over the page for a moment, then he changes his mind and tucks the book away. He points his thumb over his shoulder in parting and hurries off though the gate without me.

"Is he always like that?" I ask Zeke. The little monkey finishes his milk and scurries up onto my shoulder.

I sink to the ground and review my politics assignment while I wait for DS to return.

When he eventually appears again, he brings his bag over and sits on the ground a short distance from me. He pulls what looks like a crumpled, child's dress from his bag and drapes it over his shoulders.

Next he pulls a lock of what looks like tri-colour monkey fur tied together by a piece of string from his bag. DS runs it through his hands several times before offering an empty hand out to Zeke.

"Having a problem with your smell?" I joke.

The corner of his mouth twitches up into an almost-smile. I reach out to get a better look at the lock of fur, but he pulls it away. It disappears back into his bag, but not before I see that it's hair, not fur, although it's the same three shades as Zeke.

The little monkey sniffs the air for a moment and darts back over to DS. With a flick of his tail, Zeke disappears into the cloth sling inside DS's shirt, tugging the dress in with him.

My wristband vibrates when the hour is up and I hurry off to meet up with Jayne before heading home. On the transport, I Suri® a couple of details about necessary zoological qualifications. I've almost completed the assignment, but I haven't told my mentor yet. I enjoy his company and I've not yet discovered how he's developed such an affinity with animals. If I had his talent, I could become the best animal documentary maker this planet has ever seen.

My father sits hunched in his favourite armchair when I arrive home, the player churning out one of his old music recordings. *Dream, dream, dream.*

"You okay, Dad?" I pause on my way to my room.

"Sure, Sweetie, had a long day."

I glance towards the empty chair. "Where's Mum?"

"She's in the office, something about an application for a tele-program. I stopped listening when she mentioned Candice." He winks at me and I grin back.

I poke my head past the tiny closet space we call an office, to find my mother reading through several documents. A framed picture lies face down on one corner of the desk.

"Hi, Mum." I put the frame back up and turn it out so the old photo of Mum and her friend Candice in school uniforms can be seen.

Mum frowns at it. "Candice called to tell me Mark has secured a house in the central district. They're moving next week. You should see the images she sent me. The place is the height of luxury."

I shrug. "I guess she needs something to make up for being miserable when Mark's around."

"He's a very wealthy man. What else could she possibly want? Enough about them," Mum forces a smile onto her face. "We've been shortlisted by the tele-network for their new reality program." Mum waves the official plastic in my direction.

"That's great, Mum. Congratulations," I say, already creeping away from the doorway to save myself from a story about how she found this competition, what size house she and Dad will get to live in if they win, how the prize compares to

Candice's house, and who at work she thinks will try to steal the prize from her before it's drawn.

"Of course, we'll need to get you a whole new wardrobe, maybe new makeup," she says to herself. I dart back to the doorway.

"Why do *I* need new clothes?"

"You're going to be the star of the show."

'Marry My Teenage Daughter' is emblazoned across the page she hands me. My mouth drops open as I read the highlights.

"You can't be serious? I'm way too young to marry. You can't do this to me!"

"I'm trying to set you up for life. Where are you going to live after you graduate from school and housing control moves your father and me to the *outer suburbs?"* Mum asks.

"It's not the end of the world. I'll get an apprenticeship," I say with more confidence than I feel, my eyes drifting to the growing pile of rejected applications beside the commscreen on the desk.

"I sent the producer a copy of that mini film you made with Jayne. This could be your opportunity to become a presenter for that environment thing you're interested in."

"Animal documentary maker, Mum!"

"You're running out of options, unless you take an unskilled job and find a shared apartment in the city like that girl who was murdered in her sleep," my mother says.

"That happened last decade and Jayne's mum says we wouldn't have this housing issue if our planet accepted full governance from UFHaIL."

I glare at her, before storming out of the room, slamming doors as I go for maximum effect. My

28

bedroom door bounces back open and I have to slam it two more times before it closes to my satisfaction.

I ignore my father when he tries to talk me out of my room for dinner. He eventually gives up and leaves me alone. I spend the rest of the evening in a cycle of lying on my bed smothering my curses in my pillow, and standing by my door with my hand on the handle, trying to work up the courage to apologise to Dad.

In the morning, tired from a night of broken sleep, I break the news to Jayne. As soon as I mention the tele-program, she squeals loud enough for all our classmates to stare at us.

"OMGS! You're going to be a reality star!" She squeals again and I wince.

"It's the shortlist and I don't like being the centre of attention," I remind her.

"I know, but it'll be great practice for becoming a documentary maker and think of all the hot guys lining up to court you." Jayne places her hands over her chest and sighs as she stares off into the distance. I swallow the bile rising in my throat as the end of class bell rings.

"I really thought you'd be on my side for this." I walk away.

"Cassie, wait up. Think of the opportunity," she calls after me.

I avoid her for the rest of the day, even skipping our final class together. I catch the transport to the zoological park and locate my mentor, the animal drawing waiting on his desk even though I'm early. At least one person I know won't talk incessantly about how great it would be to make it on a reality program.

I drop my bag with a thud beside the enclosure and throw myself into a sitting position on the ground. I glare through the fence to where DS conducts a silent conversation with a family of small rodents.

DS stops what he's doing to look at me. He takes a step towards me, then pauses. He goes back to his notebook but glances at me continually. I hug my legs and don't ask him any questions, occasionally rolling my shoulders to ease tense muscles.

I don't notice my mentor leave the enclosure until he crouches in front of me. He hovers silently until I glance at him. His holds up an open hand and motions for me to do the same. I sigh and move to place my hand against his. He pulls back before our palms touch, then moves his hand until it's a fraction apart from mine. Zeke pops out of DS's shirt, dashes up my arm, around my shoulders, then back to my mentor.

DS's focus drops from my eyes to our hands. Warmth radiates from his palm and spreads along my arm. My eyes slide closed as I focus on the feeling. Tingling starts at my scalp and my muscles release one by one until my body relaxes all the way to my toes.

He leans towards me until his hair tickles my ear, giving me butterflies in my stomach. I breathe in his scent; a mix somewhere between a sweet evergreen forest and the musky smell of the animals he works with.

"My name is Dennian," he says, then he's gone.

I open my eyes to him walking away, my mind struggling to decide if I really did hear him speak.

"Wait. What?" I stumble to my feet, but he has turned a corner and by the time I catch up, he has vanished.

Obligations

"Hold up your hand," I say.

Jayne faces me across the table in the school library and does as I ask, her other hand swiping the page of her makeup e-zine. Neither of us mention the tele-program. I place my hand a fraction away from hers, but there's no warmth or tingling.

"Is something meant to happen?" Jayne asks.

"I don't know." I drop my hand back onto the table.

"How's it going with your mentor?"

"I still haven't found out how he got his job."

"Either he isn't actually a researcher and is secretly plotting to destroy the world, or he hasn't told you because he's mute," Jayne says. "Don't roll your eyes at me, young lady. I was going to invite you to Jamis' going away party."

"He's not – never mind. Why's Jamis leaving?"

"He's going back to Atlas for the 110th anniversary of something-or-other at the Dragon Temple."

"You weren't listening, were you?"

"I tuned out when he started talking about dragons as if they were real. Anyway, it should be fun, even if everyone there is a loony. I could colour your hair black and you'll fit in with the Atlas crowd." Jayne rests her elbows on the table.

"I'll think about it, but no to the hair." I push my chair away as I stand.

"You heading to the zoo again?" Jayne rests her chin on her hands as she studies me.

"I need to finish my assignment."

"What a work ethic you have, my dear Cassie. One might think your mentor is extremely attractive despite being mute."

"The project is about the career, Jayne!" Heat rises to my cheeks under her scrutiny.

"Sure, just don't forget you may soon have a dozen guys vying for your attention on this tele-program and Mr I-Don't-Speak won't be one of them."

"Gee, thanks for the reminder that my mother is trying to ruin my life." I walk out of the room.

By the time I find my mentor inside the lion enclosure with the mum and new cubs, I've pushed aside all thoughts of the tele-program. After all, Mum can't force me to participate. The producers will have to find someone else to degrade themselves on national television.

I reach for my screen to take a snapshot of the cubs with my mentor for the project only to realise I left it on his desk when I picked up the sketch of his location. I look back the way I came, but I don't need my screen that desperately.

"Hi, Dennian," I call out. He glances up and gives a small wave. I smile to myself. I didn't imagine him saying his name the other day.

He leaves the enclosure after a few minutes, detaching the cubs pouncing on his legs before joining me on the viewing seat. The day is overcast and the zoo is unusually quiet with only a few people standing by the fence and snapping pictures.

Dennian pulls his notebook and pen from a pocket and starts explaining in his neat handwriting how the new lion cubs are going. His sleeves are rolled up and the filtered light reflects off the silver outlines of mythical creatures on his armband. I stare at it until I can decipher the shape of a dragon and a unicorn. There appear to be other mythical creatures, but it's difficult to tell without getting a closer look at his arm. My cheeks heat at the thought of touching him to do so.

"Do you believe in dragons?" I watch his arm as he writes.

The pen drops from his fingers and he lunges forward to grab it as it rolls away between our feet. He fumbles picking it up, taking his time to sit back up. He finally looks at me, his expression carefully schooled. I watch his face, waiting for his reply.

When he starts to write on the notebook, I grab the pen and repeat the question. He sighs and glances around us. The visitors have drifted away to the tiger feeding presentation further along the path.

"They were real. They lived on Atlas, but they disappeared," Dennian says. I lean forward to hear him.

"Is that what the anniversary thing Jamis the Dolphin Keeper is going to is about?"

Dennian's face scrunches at the mention of the anniversary, but he nods his head. A solitary ray of sunlight breaks through the clouds making his hair glow a golden brown. I sit on my hand so I don't reach out to see if it's as silky smooth as it looks.

"How do you get an invite to the anniversary party?" I ask.

"You have to come from a pure-blood Atlas family." He stares at the enclosure fence. My hand goes numb and I pull it out from under me.

"Why does your armband have mythical creatures on it?" I reach out and touch the design, my fingers brushing the bare skin of his arm.

He leaps away; one moment sitting beside me, the next standing several paces away, his eyes wide and wary. I rub my fingers where they tingle from the contact with his skin. Dennian stares at me like a cornered animal.

"I should go," I mumble, glancing at the ground as I stand. One of my shoelaces has come undone and is dragging in the dirt. I don't stop to retie it. I start running as soon as he is out of sight. He doesn't follow.

*

"Don't forget to submit your conservation career assignment tomorrow," Ms Barnett says before dismissing our class the following week.

"I'm so glad that's over and we never have to go back to the zoological park." Jayne shoves her screen into her bag, reminding me I left mine lying on Dennian's desk.

"Jamis' party didn't go well?"

"It's about time you asked!" Jayne leans a hip against the desk. "It was dreadful. Nearly everyone there was from Atlas and they all acted like they were better than everyone else. Jamis didn't even acknowledge me for the whole evening. Talk about a waste of makeup!"

"Well, they do have a reputation for being arrogant. You won't catch me dating an Atlas-born guy." I hitch my bag onto my shoulder as we walk out of the school building.

"You want to hang out at my place this afternoon?" Jayne asks.

"You might be free of the zoo, but I left something there the other day and I need it back." I study the ground as we walk the short distance to the transport station.

"That's not an excuse to visit your mentor again?" Jayne gives me a nudge.

"I'd rather not run into him again."

"I thought you liked him?"

"He's not interested in me." The transport arrives and I step on, leaving Jayne to go home alone.

I arrive at the zoological park for the final time. I take a moment to memorise the surroundings before catching the skyrail to the staff buildings. The time on my wristband confirms it's feeding time for the animals and Dennian is likely to be occupied elsewhere.

I tap timidly on the door of his building. When there's no answer, I release the breath I'm holding, crack open the door and poke my head around the corner. I step into the empty room and head for Dennian's desk.

My screen lies beside his paperwork. I pause, my hand hovering over it as I stare at the sketch lying on his desk.

He's drawn a wall of books, each volume with the title clearly written on the spine; not that this helps my understanding, as none of the titles are in Common. One book stands out from the perfectly neat rows, as though someone was interrupted as they picked it up. There's an unusual mark on the floor; flat discs of amethyst in the shape of a dragon melted to the stone. A plush toy tiger pokes out from behind a heavy recliner chair. One of the toy tiger's horns hangs loose.

I shake my head, grab my screen and head for the door. I turn to shut the door behind me when someone touches my shoulder. I utter a surprised squeak and spin around to come face to face with Dennian. He drops his hand away.

"What do you want?" I hitch my bag onto my shoulder and narrow my eyes at him.

"I have to show you," Dennian says.

I raise an eyebrow and he looks intently into my eyes like he can read inside my head. I shift uncomfortably. He takes a step forward, closing the gap between us. Heat radiates from his body as he threads his fingers through mine.

The instant our skin touches, I experience the sensation of the ground dropping out from beneath me. I squeeze my eyes shut and grip his hand. My limbs are heavy, shackled to the earth before lightness spreads from our joined hands and flows through to our feet. The shackles fall away and I'm free, wrapped in the sensation of floating in warm water. Calm settles over my body and I open my eyes. Dennian stands before me, his hands by his sides and his eyes on mine.

"What was that?" I ask.

"How you make me feel," Dennian says.

"How did you do whatever you just did?" I wave a hand at him.

"I was trained." Dennian shrugs.

"By who? The Peace Keepers?" I tilt my head to one side as I study him.

Dennian presses his lips together and looks into the distance.

"Why do you pretend to be mute?" I blurt out.

He takes a step backward and is silent long enough I'm surprised when he speaks again.

"I don't *like* to communicate out loud."

"You're speaking to me now."

"You make me want to live," he says.

"Living is a good thing." I reach out and rest a hand on his arm.

He nods and this time he doesn't look at me like he's a cornered animal.

"I'd like to keep seeing you when my project is finished," I say.

"I'd like that too." Dennian smiles and brushes a strand of hair away from my face. My heart skips a beat.

"I'd better get going. Don't want to miss the transport home." I reluctantly remove my hand from his arm.

Dennian nods and steps away to let me pass. When I look back over my shoulder, he's still watching me with a small smile on his lips.

*

Back home, I pause on the steps and lift the limp leaf of one of Dad's potted plants. I collect the watering can and watch the water soak into the dry soil. My smile creeps back onto my face as I step into the house.

"We've received an acceptance letter from the tele-network." Mum stops me on my way upstairs. I halt with my hand on the rail as a fine sweat breaks out over my skin. I turn slowly and narrow my eyes at her.

"I can't do the show. I have a boyfriend," I say the first excuse that comes to mind. Her mouth opens in surprise, before she narrows her eyes back at me.

"What's his name?"

"Dennian."

"Does this Damien have a last name?"

"It starts with 'S'…"

"So does Suri. Doesn't mean he's the Governor of the Universe. How old is he? Where is he from?" she asks. I glare at her. "What does he do for a living?"

"He's a researcher at the zoo," I say with the speed of someone who has arrived at the first exam question they know the answer to.

"Where does he live?"

"Um…"

"You don't know much about this boyfriend of yours, do you?"

"I know more about him than the guys who are going to be on this stupid show." I wave a hand at the offending piece of plastic she holds.

"All of the young gentlemen have been vetted by the producer of the show. They will not be a second class employee at an animal facility."

"How dare you judge someone you haven't even met!" I stamp my foot then shuffle a few steps to cover the fact I succumbed to something so childish. "Dennian is smart and kind and really good with animals. You can tell a lot about someone by how they treat animals."

"If you were serious about this young man, you would have invited him for dinner to meet your parents, instead of hiding him away like a dirty little secret. This tele-program is an opportunity for you to meet suitable young men from good backgrounds who will take care of you as you grow old. Do you really think this Daniel fellow would actually ever marry you or just leave you homeless on the street?"

I open my mouth to respond, but with the end of the school year drawing near, I'm running out of options. I'm not willing to admit it yet.

"While you're under my roof you'll do as I say. No more excursions to see this young man. You will go to school and come straight back home. You don't go anywhere else without my permission, understand?"

I storm off to my room and activate my commlink screen. I tap Jayne's name in and wait for her to answer. Her face appears, her hair wrapped in a towel and a line of pink dye trailing down her neck.

"What's up?" She uses the screen as a mirror while painting a dolphin on one cheek.

"Mum grounded me," I say.

"Seriously! What for?"

"They want me for the tele-program –"

"Oh My Governor Suri!" Jayne squeals and I flinch. "My best friend's going to be a star!"

Jayne drops her paint pen, leaving half a dolphin on her face and starts tapping on her touch pad. I glance at my wristband, but it's too late to get a transport to the zoological park and find Dennian. I've never even seen him wearing a communicator.

"Do you think they'll let me come along too?" Jayne asks.

"Hey, why don't you do the show?" I suggest.

"I would, but I don't think they'd - oh, wow!" Jayne pauses her typing. "Part of the prize is a house for your parents and a house for you to live in with your husband. It's super flash and no interference from housing control. This is the answer to all your problems." Jayne looks at me with sympathetic eyes. I glare back.

"I'm not going to marry someone I don't know." I shut down the link and throw myself onto my bed.

*

My teacher calls my name several times throughout the class, but I have no idea what the question is, let alone the answer. Eventually he gives up and allows me to continue staring at my desk for the rest of the lesson.

Jayne slips me images of the prizes offered in the show, but looking at the houses only makes my stomach turn. I can see my life heading in two potential directions. Everyone I know wants to pull me one way, but I'm drawn to the other, despite the unknowns.

Tired of being the dutiful daughter, I skip my next class. This is my life. I should be able to live it without having to sacrifice what I want for my parents' financial security and Mum's competitiveness with her old school friend.

I won't make a decision until I speak to Dennian. We've only known each other for several weeks, but we have a connection that I've never felt with anyone else. I need to know if he feels the same.

I can always run away from home. Teenagers do that all the time, don't they? I fantasize about travelling the world with Dennian, him working with animals and me making documentaries.

My wristband rings as I wait at the transport hub. I hesitate at Mum's name, wondering what she'd do if I ignored her call.

"Hello?" Sometimes I wish I wasn't such a dutiful daughter.

"Your father's collapsed at work."

My mouth refuses to form the words I want to say. I adjust the receiver on my wristband.

"Did you hear what I said?" Her voice cracks. I wet my lips and try to form a sound.

"Is he...all right?"

"It's not good. The medics took him to the hospital. I'm there now. Can you leave class?"

I nod.

"Yes," I say when I remember she can't see me. She disconnects, leaving me standing alone staring at the transport pulling into the stop.

The next few hours pass in a blur. I meet Mum at the hospital. She doesn't comment on how fast I arrive. We stand by and watch a grey faced version of my father lying on the bed as doctors and nurses march through his cubicle conducting tests and administering drugs while muttering about complications. I hold his hand while they speak quietly to Mum. Dad opens his eyes and looks at me.

"I want to know you'll be okay when I'm gone, sweetheart. Your mother can't look after you forever and you can't survive on volunteer work at animal shelters."

"I'm going to be a documentary maker," I say.

"That's my girl, always optimistic even after all the rejections you've received." He gives a little laugh that turns into a cough. He continues when he gets his breath again. I want to ask a doctor why he's coughing, but I can't leave his bedside while he's like this.

"Consider the program for me, honey. It would put my mind at ease to know you and your mother were provided for. I never could match what Mark gives his wife. Maybe a husband will support your dream of travelling the galaxy to study animals. Or the tele-program could lead to your little documentaries being discovered."

"I can look after myself and you're not going to die," I tell him. "You're going to be around always. I need you here."

He smiles at me and squeezes my hand. The nurse comes in to give him his medication and he's asleep shortly after. Mum and I take turns at his bedside, but he slowly slips away from us.

On the third day, as we both hold his cool, clammy hands, he takes his final breath. Tears roll down my cheeks while Mum stares dully at Dad's motionless body.

*

Dad's funeral is the following week. Mum picks out his best suit while I compile a list of his favourite music for the funeral director. Time slips by as I sit on the floor beside his chair and flick through his list of songs. I play a few, but the words are intrusive in the otherwise silent house.

The house fills with boxes of Dad's belongings to be donated or stored while the documents on the office comm-screen steadily increase, all waiting for me to put my signature to the tele-program contract.

I walk into the house expecting to see Dad in the kitchen preparing dinner only to find the benches covered in gifted meals from friends and neighbours. In the bin, I find a cut up gift card from Candice and Mark.

By the front door, the plants wilt as I neglect to water them, a task that was always handled by Dad.

Empty dishes pile up in the kitchen and the weeds creep through the garden pots. We move quietly through the house, Mum's weeping my only company.

On the day of Dad's funeral, I stand by the tomb, as his wrapped body is lowered into the hole, and ignore offers of sympathy from people I hardly know. Mum stands stiffly beside me.

"He asked me to marry him first." Mum says softly. I glance up to find her eyes on Candice and Mark, who came over to offer their sympathies before finding seats away from the grave.

"Mark?" I look over at the couple seated beside each other while still maintaining as much distance as possible. Sunlight glints off the massive stone set into the ring on Candice's finger and the matching dangling earrings.

"I turned him down because I was in love with your father. I could have had the house and jewels instead of burying my husband too young. Love doesn't last, Cassie. Money does. Don't make the same mistake I did." Mum moves away to greet a newly arrived mourner.

Jayne slips her hand into mine like we're little girls again. Her hair is mauve to match her dress and tiny teardrops fall in painted rows down her cheeks.

"Don't you have your art camp to go to?" I ask as I stare past the crowd of people here to witness our grief.

"No," she says. "I have nowhere else to be other than here with you."

I rest my head on her shoulder and let the tears slide down my cheeks.

Zoo Keeper

Dennian

I wake unexpectedly from sleep, lying perfectly still on my bed of grass as I assess my surroundings. Zeke rests against my chest, his tiny chest rising with each breath. For a moment I'm disorientated by the arrangement of the few lone stars peeking through the orange glow of the surrounding city. I'm not accustomed to viewing the galaxy from this planet.

The faint scent of fresh charcoal and violets fills the air as Star appears silently beside me. She leans against the side of the zoological park staff building. My pupils widen in the darkness to follow her movements.

"Lucei and Thylace are concerned you'll miss Takarna's anniversary celebrations," Star says.

I shrug. The planetary alignment between the Atlas capital and its moon won't occur for another two hours. The worshipers can't arrive on Takarn Island until the teleportation portal opens. I still have time to make it to the Atlas star-system.

"Niko Shen has a last minute report to submit to the governor. He won't be able to make the celebration and his wife won't go alone," Star says.

The sick feeling growing in my stomach over the last few days eases slightly. Star studies me for a moment.

"Something else bothering you, brother?"

I'm waiting for Cassie. She hasn't visited since she said she wanted to keep seeing me and I have no indication as to why. Cassie fascinates me. She sees through me in a way others don't. The last time she came to watch me work, she'd asked me about my lack of shoes. No one else has ever noticed my bare feet. I didn't know how to tell her the truth, so I hadn't replied.

My childhood guardian, Carlen, always said it was a waste to provide me with items I wouldn't live long enough to use. My clothing consisted of items left behind by the previous apprentices when they died, and being younger, I was too small to wear their shoes. By the time the shoes fitted, I'd become used to bare feet.

Star squats beside me and brushes the back of my hand with her fingers. "Ah," she says. "I hope you've still had time for research?"

I reach for the book beside me and hand over my notes. Star flips through them, staring up at the sky as she does the complicated mathematical adjustments in her mind.

"Approximately 41.99999996," she says.

That's pretty close to my guess, confirming her original calculation was accurate. Time is nearly up. As soon as we hit the magic number, the world will end. A wolf howls in a nearby enclosure.

"Kllrarn it to hell!" Star throws my book to the ground and stands. "We need a sign! Surely Aurumargent has alluded to a solution by now." Star paces back and forth. She stops suddenly as she catches my hesitation. She narrows her eyes and I blank my mind to hide the name I promised I'd never speak.

"Whatever information you have obtained, provide it to me now." Star holds out her hand.

I sigh, reaching for the drawing I made of the library. I find myself wishing I hadn't drawn the dead amethyst dragon scorched onto the floor, but when an image is in my mind, the need to recreate it as I see it is undeniable.

Star takes the sketch from me and I hold my breath as she folds back one half of the drawing so only the bookshelves are displayed. I lean forward at her unconscious action. She has never ignored a part of a drawing before. She tilts her head as she reads the titles.

"What do you suppose the difference is between 'Creation of Evolution' and 'Creation of Myth'?" Star asks, reading the book titles.

My mind flashes to the intensely lit, white corridor with the overlapping realities and the doors leading from it, the ones I wasn't meant to be able to see. I'm pretty sure evolution refers to our universe, so maybe myth is a different one. The dragons had to come from somewhere. The early murals leading up to the Dragon Temple depict them arriving on Atlas. Maybe it's where they went after they left our world several millennia ago.

"You could be correct," she says. "What's the location of these texts?"

Not here. I take the drawing back from Star and trace a finger over the Temple Tiger toy abandoned behind the chair by the dead dragon.

Star sighs. "I'll stop by later, Dennian. Alert me to any issues with the ceremony." Then she is gone.

I take a final look up at the stars and move to gather my belongings. Zeke shifts in the sling but doesn't wake. The Atlas nobles will be queuing at the portal to take them to Takarn Island and I need to be there before they arrive.

My sketchbook falls open at my feet to the drawing I made the day Cassie ran into me and fell into the mud. The girl's face is obscured by her hair and the evening gloom, as she crouches among headstones in a graveyard face-to-face with the Temple Tiger I know as Myaa. I'm becoming more certain that the girl is Cassie.

"You will always be alone in this world," Carlen took pleasure in informing me. "You will live alone and you will die alone and there is nothing you can do to change that."

I wonder who is right; Carlen or the drawing. I won't find out by continuing to wait here. I have obligations to meet.

Reality

My teachers are sympathetic when I return to school the week after Dad's funeral. I have no issues with missed school or extensions for my overdue assignments. I grow tired of all the 'How are you?' and 'If you need to talk…'. If I'm going to talk to someone it won't be with my slightly eccentric maths teacher.

I return to the zoological park one last time before I hand my project in. Somehow, the fact I'm grounded is forgotten with everything else going on. It's been nearly three weeks since I was here last, but it feels like a lifetime ago.

The heaviness in my chest eases as I board the skyrail to take me to Dennian's building. Everything that has happened makes me curious about his parents. Are they both alive? Does he visit them regularly? Do they miss him when he's away? Are they happy together?

I knock on the door of the staff building. When no one answers, I ease the door open and step inside. Dennian's desk is bare and his drawings have disappeared from the walls. The breath leaves my body and I hold onto the edge of the desk to keep myself upright. He's gone.

My eyes are dry as I leave the building although numbness has settled over my mind. A man in the brown uniform of a keeper, so similar to the one Dennian wore, heads towards the building. My legs move until I find myself standing in front of the man.

"Excuse me? I'm looking for Dennian the Researcher. Can you tell me where he is?" I hold my breath as I wait for his reply.

"He left several days ago. Think he went back home."

"Do you know where that is or if he left any contact details?" I ask.

"He's mute. It's not like he ever told us anything about himself or even wore a wristband. Sorry." The man shrugs and walks away leaving me and my bleeding heart all alone in the busy zoo.

I sink to the ground beside the path and allow the tears to fall. Several weeks ago I had both parents, a crush on a fascinating boy, and dreams of a career as animal documentary maker. Now I've lost Dad and Dennian. The end of the school year is fast approaching, leaving Mum anxious about where Housing Control will move us, and the impact it will have on her social status.

When I get home that evening, I sign the paperwork for the tele-program and give it to Mum. The contract requires two immediate family members to participate, but with no close family, I nominate Jayne to help my mother choose my future husband.

My mother manages a brief smile before returning to her glass of port. I shut myself in my room, with only my tears for company. Sometimes it feels good to have a cry. This is not one of those times. I'm like a boat drifting forgotten in the ocean with no land in sight and no one knows I'm even out here. My life will now be directed by other people.

The last day of the school year comes and goes. My graduation day is spent packing a bag for the six-week tele-program. I hide away not wanting any of my former classmates to know what I've signed up to.

*

The chauffeur directs the black stretched-transport onto the long, gravel drive and Jayne makes a strangled noise as the mansion comes into view. She leans across me to peer out the window.

The building stretches out in both directions, disappearing behind rows of trees. Stone columns and floor-to-ceiling windows with balconies dominate the façade of both storeys. Steps lead up to a path that winds towards the front entrance.

Big metal gates swing closed behind the vehicle. I wipe my hands on the clingy red material of the dress that had been sent for the program and tug at the plunging neckline.

The transport comes to a halt at the front stairs and the driver steps out to open my door. I twist sideways, focusing on climbing out of the car without flashing too much leg or cleavage at the hover-cams zipping around.

Jayne and Mum follow a pace behind me as we approach the hostess of the show standing at the top of the steps. As she begins to introduce herself as Sara, a man standing off to one side, steps forward waving his arms.

"Cut!" he yells. "What the hell was that? You weren't smiling. You're getting married!" He waves a hand at me before ushering a pair of makeup artists forward. "Who did their faces? I can't have the star of the show being diminished by whatever is going on with her friend's face."

Jayne reaches up to touch her carefully applied miniature bells and ribbons painted across one cheek. She rushes back to vehicle and twists her face in all directions to check her design.

"What's wrong with my face?" she asks her reflection.

One of the artists sets about wiping Jayne's face clean before reapplying basic makeup. The other opens his bag and grasps my chin with one hand while he attacks my face with various brushes.

"Get back in the vehicle, do a lap and when you get out, look happy to be here," the director orders when the artists are finished.

"You're kidding?" I say.

"This show will be a success. My career is riding on it." He steps forward, takes me by the elbow and bundles me back into the vehicle.

I clench my fists as the chauffeur directs us on a lap of the driveway.

"They gave you my bells." Jayne looks at me sadly. I lean forward to see my face in the centre console mirror. A set of tiny bells tied with a ribbon mark my left cheek.

"Yours looked better." I reach over and squeeze her hand.

When the chauffeur opens the door this time, I give a sarcastic smile for the hover-cam. I get two steps before the director points us back to the vehicle. Two more failed takes later, he grabs my arm and pulls me aside.

"Your mother signed a contract. You play the game or we get another girl. How long do you think your lovely mother will last in the *suburbs*? She'll never live down the humiliation. She was born for greater things. You can have the luxuries of life too if you cooperate."

He lets go of my arm and I stumble in my heels on the steps, catching myself before I do any damage.

"Final take!" he yells.

Mum and Jayne slide back into the car after me and my mother takes my hand in hers.

"I really need this," she begs. "I've already told Candice you're getting married."

I glance away not wanting to see the tears forming in Mum's eyes. I take deep breaths, but despite the chauffeur driving slowly, we're back at the steps too quickly. I close my eyes for a moment and pretend I'm Jayne. I picture her blonde streaked hair and her bells now painted on my cheek.

I slide gracefully from my seat after the driver opens my door and stare in wonder at the front of the mansion as though this isn't the seventh time I've seen it today.

"Oh My Governor Suri, it's stunning." I squeal and wave a hand in front of my face.

"Cut! What in Kllrarn's Hell was that?" the director demands.

"You wanted me to be enthusiastic." I put my hands on my hips and glare at him.

"Not you, them. What were you doing?"

I turn to look at Mum and Jayne to find them staring at me as though expecting me to tear my clothes off and run screaming through the grounds.

"It's okay, Trev," Sara says. "We can splice Cassie's reaction into the first shot with the other two."

"Fine. Get them in the house before we lose the rest of the day," Trev, the director says. I've passed the first test.

Sara hands me a stack of re-writable plastic cue cards that fit into the palm of my hand and leads us into the mansion. I wobble on my heels as they sink into the plush carpeted hallway. Gilded mirrors and landscape artwork line the walls.

Jayne falls into step beside me. "Have you ever wondered where that expression came from?"

"What?" I look up from the stack of cards containing lines the director recommends I say for the camera, along with hints on how to act.

"Kllrarn's Hell," Jayne clarifies. "Haven't you wondered who he was, why he has his own hell and what he had against vowels?"

I come to a stop in the hall and stare at Jayne, my cards momentarily forgotten.

"No," I say.

I glance back at the cards in my hand. *Never appear to know more about a topic than the man you are speaking to*, it says. When no one is watching, I slip the card under a potted plant perched on a side table in the hallway.

"Okay, just me then." Jayne steps away from me, suddenly distracted by the opulence of the bedrooms.

Sara points me to one of the rooms and I peek inside briefly. My faded brown bag sits on the plush cream carpet, brought up during one of the many takes of me exiting the vehicle. The bed dominates the centre of the room with its thick patterned covers giving it the appearance of needing a step ladder to climb on top.

A large, abstract painting hangs above the head of the bed and a mirrored makeup station with various cases sits beside the bed. A wardrobe takes up the opposite wall. The wide window looks out over the gardens and on the other side of the room, a door leads into a luxurious ensuite.

Sara hurries us along. I trail after Mum and Jayne while reading the cards as Sara gives us a brief tour of the house.

I laugh out loud as I read the next card. Jayne peers over my shoulder to read it.

Questions to consider if there is a lull in the conversation: What big muscles you have, do you work out? What stunning eyes you have, have they always been that colour? If you were to take up a shirtless hobby, what would you choose?

Jayne grins at me. "All great questions. I can't wait to see what their replies will be." She winks at me as I roll my eyes and we step out into the garden.

"Over there is where the wedding will be conducted in six weeks' time at the completion of the show." Sara points to a stage with a bare arbour set up in the middle of a grassy area. Several large trees provide shade to the flower beds that circle the lawn.

I look at the empty stage and my stomach turns. When I try to picture myself standing up there, I can't see the face of the man beside me. Jayne clutches my arm in excitement.

Trev meets us as we head back into the house and starts throwing around orders. We all need to change before meeting the men this evening and I need my dark brown hair up instead of down. Jayne and Mum are whisked away, while the two artists from this morning lead the way back to my room.

They introduce themselves as Lori and Carter. Lori flicks through dresses on hangers in the wardrobe before pulling out a different red dress to wear. I slip into the bathroom to change.

The new outfit is a deeper red with a full skirt, plunging neckline and floaty gauze sleeves that reach to my elbows. Lori taps on the door and enters before I can speak. She quickly zips up the back before steering me into the bedroom as I focus on not tripping over the reams of fabric around my feet.

I sink into the seat by the makeup station and stare at my reflection while Lori begins brushing my hair and twisting it up onto the top of my head. Carter spreads out his various brushes and after wiping my face clean from the previous colours, begins on a new look.

"All done." Carter flicks the final brush over my cheek where a large red heart matches the deep red of my eye shadow. He hands me a pair of red shoes with heels high enough for me to not need the step ladder to get into bed.

"Head downstairs for final instructions from Trev," Lori says. "We'll be nearby in case you need any touch-ups between takes."

I slip the shoes on which give me enough height that the skirt now sweeps the floor instead of tangling my feet. I leave the two of them to pack up while I walk carefully downstairs in the heels.

"Oh, no." Jayne greets me at the bottom of the stairs in a pale pink slimline dress and bare makeup. "That is tacky." She reaches into her small bag and pulls out a face wipe.

"They've only just done my makeup," I say as Jayne wipes my cheek clean.

"Don't worry, I'll fix it for you." Jayne pulls out a tiny brush and a deep red colour and starts painting my cheek. When she is finished, she holds up a mirror. A curve of tiny hearts wind their way up my cheek and side of my face.

"That looks lovely, Jayne." Mum smiles at both of us.

"Ready, ladies?" Trev steps through a doorway followed by Sara and hands me a new stack of cue cards. "I'll be out of sight for most of the evening, but Sara will be there if we need someone on camera. She knows what's needed this evening." He taps Sara on the cheek and heads outside.

Evening approaches as Sara directs us out into one of the gardens lined with candles leading off the main drive. She positions me by a fountain while my mother and Jayne wait further back towards the house. I can hear my mother repeating 'so nice to meet you' to herself. I take one last look at my cue cards and then hold them obscured from the cameras by my hand as Sara directed. I square my shoulders, take a deep breath, and imagine I'm about to present a wildlife documentary.

Gravel crunches as the first vehicle approaches. I scrub my free hand against my thigh and force my face into a smile as the first young man walks towards me. He wears a black suit with a pale blue shirt and his hair slicked back.

"Wow, you look gorgeous," I recite the first of my cue phrases, my smile still in place. He leans in to air kiss my cheek.

"Hi, I'm Phil. I'm twenty years old and I'm a fitness instructor." He flexes one bicep and smirks at the hover-cam as he hands me the bunch of flowers he holds.

"I can't wait to get to know you." I take the bouquet from him.

I keep the smile on my face as I step aside. His smile falters as he moves past me. I stare ahead until the director catches my eye by waving madly from the bushes and indicating I should turn and watch the guy walk away. I do so in time to catch him also turn and give me a wave. I wince.

When he reaches my mother and Jayne, I turn back to wait for the next guy. An assistant leaps out from behind a hedge to take the flowers and disappears from scene.

The next young man comes at me in a dark blue suit with a slight variation on the hair style.

"Wow, you look gorgeous," I say.

"Hi, I'm Rick and I'm nineteen." He kisses my hand and when he releases me, I wipe it on my dress. He pulls a small box of chocolates from his back pocket and I try to look grateful as I accept the slightly crushed and melted offering.

"What do you do for a living?" I ask the second cue question.

"My parents are wealthy. I don't need to do anything."

"Oh." My mind goes blank and I glance at the cards in my hand to remember what I'm meant to say next. "I'll see you at the drinks party."

He leans in close and whispers in my ear. "You sure will, Darling. I'm going to win this game."

"Great to meet you." I sidestep him and position myself to receive the next man. After a few moments, I hear Rick move away from me and I let out a breath. I toss the chocolate box into the hedge, roll my neck, and stomp my feet, catching myself from toppling in the high heels shoes I forgot I was wearing, and wait.

"Next one is strategic placement," Trev leans out from the bushes to hiss at me. "Keep him talking for as long as possible."

I give him a thumbs-up and face forward as the next contestant approaches. They've given him a striped jacket, probably so he will stand out among the others.

"Hi, I'm Prince. I'm 20 years old and I'm going to make you my princess." He places a tiara on my head and leans in to kiss me. I turn my head and his lips land on my cheek. I catch the eye of the director encouraging me to get him talking.

"Why thank you kind sir." I drop a curtsy and take a subtle step back as I rise, nearly tripping on my dress as I do so.

"I will fight wild animals and dragons for your love." He thumps his chest and my smile sticks in an awkward position.

"Haven't seen any dragons near the house, yet," I say.

"I will find one for you," Prince declares.

"I look forward to it," I manage, stepping to one side so he can proceed on to my mother and Jayne.

I stop remembering names, ages, and occupations as the next few men greet me and I repeat the same lines to each one. The important points, name, age, occupation, place of birth, headshot are listed on my cards for reference.

"Last one," the producer calls out as the car approaches.

"You can do this," I mutter to myself. "Mum needs you to do this."

The young man approaching me wears a dark suit like the rest, but he has matched it with a galaxy print tie, the stars sparkling in the path lighting.

"That's an awesome tie." I improvise my lines.

"Thanks, I'm Nathan. I'm eighteen and I've been accepted into an apprenticeship at SuriTech."

"Oh, thank the Lord, you're not another crazy." I grasp his hand that he holds out in greeting.

"Rough evening?" he asks.

"You have no idea!"

"Maybe I should go meet your parents before all the other guys get jealous." Nathan winks at me and I release his hand.

"I'll see you inside." I step to the side to let him pass. He grins and waves as he walks off.

"Cut," Trev calls from the bushes.

Lori and Carter appear from behind me and attack my face with a makeup brushes while adjusting my hair. A third person steps forward and hands me a glass of sparkling water. I lift it to my lips.

"Ah! No drinking. You'll smudge your lipstick." Trev waves a finger at me.

"I'm meant to hold a glass that I'm not allowed to drink from?" I frown at him.

"Yes, and try to look happy. We don't want to be here all night with the filming." Trev says.

He positions me by the bushes to do a little spiel about my thoughts. I quickly review the speech on the screen he hands me.

"I feel so lucky to be standing here with all these eligible guys. There are very different personalities but some really good ones. Ha, ha, ha," I say, facing Sara.

"Tell me what you think about the young men here to win your heart." Sara smiles at the hover-cam before it turns its lens on me. I nod and glance at the cards again before looking up at the camera.

"Phil, what a good-looking man." I wave a hand in front of my face to appear flustered. "I've always had a weakness for blue eyes," I add. I think that one is meant to be added in for Rick, but half of them had blue eyes so who knows where they'll use it.

"Nicely done," Trev says. "We'll have your mother in her own house in no time."

I glare at him, re-take the glass of water I'm not allowed to drink, lift my skirt away from my feet with my spare hand, and pick my way carefully over the paving stones in my ridiculously high heels. I make it to the door without tripping and have to pause for the camera to get into position inside the room. Sara counts down on her fingers and we step into the room.

The boys cheer as if I've produced a miracle. I curtsy and smile as per my cue cards.

"I'm sure you're all eager to spend time with Cassie this evening," Sara says to the room. "Remember that one of you will be leaving the mansion at the end of the evening."

After a pause for the camera, Sara rests a hand on my shoulder. "We've briefed your mother. She'll lead the introductions this evening. I'll be back for the elimination." She walks out, leaving me smiling numbly at the room of men.

My mother sends one of the young men to escort me into the courtyard. He takes a seat beside me as Mum join us. Jayne hovers nearby.

"So Elliott, tell us about yourself," Mum says.

"I'm a road marker. It's a pretty difficult job, you know. All the lines have to be straight…" he pauses to consider his statement. "Unless the road curves and then they aren't straight."

Elliott takes a sip of his drink, while I clutch mine for a quick getaway.

"This has ice in it." Elliott places his drink on the table and stares at the condensation forming on the glass. "Where do you think the water on the outside of the glass comes from?"

"Ah…" I glance away hoping he didn't catch my alarmed expression. From where I sit on the edge of the couch, I can see the guys inside. Several of them lean over each other to watch us. Nathan browses a bookshelf. My mother nudges me and I look back. She raises an eyebrow at me.

"Oh," I say. I flip through the cue cards in my hand to find the questions I have to ask.

"What are your plans after this show?" I ask.

"Oh," he picks up his glass again and watches the water running down the outside. "There's a big highway project starting in a few weeks. I really hope this competition doesn't take too long. I'd hate to miss it."

"I'm pretty sure that won't be a problem." I throw a worried look at Mum, but she is focused on smiling at the hover-cam.

"I need to steal Cassie away for a moment." Jayne sneaks up behind me and rests a hand on my shoulder.

"Sorry, have to go." I clutch my glass to my chest and bolt out of there as fast as my heels and long skirt will allow.

"Thanks," I say as we escape into the garden.

"Don't thank me yet. Trev isn't happy with your reactions. There are eleven men here all wanting to get to know you." Jayne waves a hand at the doors leading back to the sitting room. "Enjoy the experience."

"They're not here for me. I bet every single one of them wants something out of this competition that has nothing to do with getting to know me," I say.

"So? If they're playing the game, then so can you. You want something out of this? Blow everyone away so people remember your name and next time you submit a demo documentary to someone, they offer you a job on the spot."

I turn the idea over in my head.

"Make them perform for you," Jayne whispers in my ear.

I laugh. "Fine, but if this goes badly, I'm blaming you."

"Go get them, girlfriend." Jayne claps her hands. I take a rebellious sip of my water and head back inside.

Mum has moved to a different seating arrangement in the expansive lounge room. One of the young men already sits opposite her. He twists in his seat making facial poses at the hover-cam.

I flip through my cards until I find his; Eric. I fix a smile on my face and imagine he's a rare breed of monkey that I need to capture for a documentary. I take a seat beside Mum.

"So Eric, tell us about yourself," I say.

"I'm an international model so I travel a lot for photo shoots."

"That must be exciting," I say. "Do you have to learn different walks and poses?" I lean forward as though I'm interested in his response and his face lights up.

"Let me show you a few of my best moves." He jumps to his feet and moves to a clear section of floor to demonstrate his walk.

"See what I did there?" He turns to look at me. "It all depends of the quality of fabric, but if you wear a shirt like I'm modelling this evening, the cloth clings in the right places."

I dig my fingernails into my palm and nod my head.

"Sorry to interrupt. I was hoping to have a word." A different guy approaches us. Eric looks momentarily put-out but quickly schools his face into something less likely to cause wrinkles. He stands and heads back inside. We repeat the process with – I check my cards – Merron and then several others.

Trev stalks the perimeter of the room occasionally tapping one of the eleven guys aside to speak to Sara and the camera about their first impressions of me and the expensive house we are in. I smirk when I catch Sara attempting to prompt them until Trev gets red in the face and storms off.

Sara calls the evening to an end before I have a chance to talk to Nathan. The guys are left to mingle while Sara takes my stack of cards and leaves me in a room further down the hallway. Lori and Carter stop by to touch up my hair and makeup and let me know that I look dehydrated which is bad for my skin. I resist the urge to toss my nearly full glass of water at someone.

I stalk the room barefoot for some time, while trying not to make any facial expressions that may damage the paint on my face, until Sara steps into the room. I quickly tuck my feet under my skirt and ignore her pointed look.

"Your mother, friend and Trev have discussed which ten men will be staying in the competition." Sara hands me a set of cards. Eric's is at the top of the pile. "Read them out in that order and remember to pause for the camera to capture the reactions. Each man will approach to thank you for selecting them. We'll give you a cue when it's time to read out each name. As you get to the last three cards, aim to look like you've had a hard time deciding who to pick."

"I haven't picked anyone," I point out.

"The audience doesn't need to know that. They're the ones who need to be invested in your journey."

I roll my eyes and quickly flip through the cards. Nathan is in position eight so he'll have a long wait to know if he's staying especially as I didn't have time to speak to him further this evening. I do another quick scan of the cards, but I don't know the guys' names well enough to work out who is missing.

I put my shoes back on and follow Sara to the staged location off the living area of the mansion. The young men arrange themselves in front of me while Sara and Trev stand off to one side. Mum and Jayne aren't present so that it will look like the choices are all mine.

As I call each name, the guy steps forward and kisses me on the check before moving to one side. Nathan grins when I finally reach his name.

"Thank you, Cassie. I'm really looking forward to getting to know you better." Nathan beams at me before joining the others. I give him a genuine smile in return.

Two guys remain before me; the road-marker, and another who I vaguely remember speaking to but couldn't recall any details about without checking my cards. Trev doesn't give me the next cue so I stand there getting more uncomfortable with each moment. My expression morphs into something vaguely pained to match the feelings produced by my high heels. Trev finally gives me the cue to read out the final card.

"Elliot," I say.

The road-marker steps forward as though genuinely confused that I've read out his name. Once he has joined the others and one man remains standing alone on the other side, Sara steps up beside me.

"Merron, you were not selected this evening. Please say goodbye," she says.

Merron says a quick goodbye to the guys and then me, maintaining a smile the whole time. Maybe they weren't paying him enough to play this game.

First Dates

I wake in the massive bed with makeup smeared across the pillow and people piling into my room to prepare me for the day. I escape to the bathroom and lock the door so I can shower in private. When I emerge, Lori and Carter do my makeup and fix a new hairstyle, while another pair flutter around the room laying out clothing and shoes. Sara arrives with a hover-cam in tow as I finish dressing.

"Today we will be choosing your wedding dress," Sara announces.

"How exciting!" I exclaim for the camera. At least today's pale blue dress is loose fitting and something I'm able to get in and out of without assistance. Sara nods approvingly. I drop the smile from my face.

"It's a twenty minute drive to the store. Catering will have your breakfast ready in the transport, although you might not want to eat it. You'll need to look slim in your dress. We leave in five." Sara sweeps out of the room.

I head downstairs to find Jayne waiting for me in a deeper blue version of what I'm wearing.

"Where's Mum?" I ask.

"She's not coming with us today. I think Trev is going through the programming with her. Just you and me today, babe." She grins.

I glance at Sara, Lori and Carter who have joined us on the steps and raise an eyebrow, but Jayne takes no notice.

Exactly five minutes later, the vehicle sweeps onto the driveway. As this isn't a camera scene, we open the doors ourselves and get in. As soon as I've slid onto the seat, I reach for the food tray. I spend the drive deliberately eating in front of Sara while she purses her lips and Carter mutters about me ruining his hard work. Jayne sits with a screen across her knees flipping through various images of wedding apparel.

The transport halts in front of a high-end dress store and the five of us hop out of the vehicle. Trev waves an arm from his position in the store window where a closed sign is illuminated. Lori inspects my teeth for evidence of breakfast before she, Carter, and Sara disappear into the store.

"Makes it start to feel real, doesn't it?" Jayne stares at the window display as though her fingers are itching to touch the clothes.

"Perhaps I should have outsourced this task to the model. He would have known exactly which fabric is best." I hide my nerves behind the sarcastic comment.

After a few minutes of watching Sara and Trev speaking to an older woman in the store, Trev waves Jayne and I forward. We walk towards the door which Sara opens as we approach.

"Welcome." The owner greets us with a nervous smile.

"Hi. I hope it's not too much bother having your store closed for the day," I say my first cue.

"Oh, no bother at all," the woman gushes.

At a nudge from Trev, the woman recites a series of lines that I have to respond to, such as what sort of look am I going for and did I know the history of this building. According to my cue cards, I'm a traditional wedding dress girl and am fascinated by the building I've never seen before.

Trev makes us do two more takes before he has the desired reactions and dialogue. Once finally done, I can take in the expansive store with row upon row of dresses I may be forced to try on. Queasiness settles in my stomach. Sara comes up beside me.

"We're here to select five dresses for promotional images. The audience will vote on which one you'll wear for the ceremony," Sara says.

"I don't have any say in what I wear?"

"Of course not," Trev interrupts. "Women take weeks to make decisions like that. We need to do it in a couple of hours."

I roll my eyes and flip through the dresses on the rack nearest to me.

"First we need to see if she looks best in the virginal pink or green of new beginnings." Lori holds up two dresses in both pale shades and I wrinkle my nose at the pink.

"Have her try on both," Trev says.

"I know you're a busy man," Carter interrupts. "How about you let us handle the initial selection?"

Trev nods his head and immediately pulls out his screen to organise destroying some other element of my life. He walks out the door and leaves us alone. I let out the breath I was holding.

The shop owner ushers me to a seat by the accessories while Lori and Carter stalk the rows of dresses for items to try on me. Jayne joins Sara in trying various headwear and jewellery on me. They flitter around me while I stare at my reflection in a floor-length mirror to make sure it's still me staring back. As my image blurs into something I no longer recognise, Jayne snaps her fingers at me.

"Come on, Cass. It's time for the dresses."

I glance over to where Lori and Carter have hung a mountain of dresses on a rack by the change room.

"The first one is in the change room," Lori says. "I'll give you a hand getting into them."

"I can do that!" Jayne drags me into what would have been a spacious room if not for the monstrosity of fabric seeming to stand up of its own accord in one mirrored corner.

Before I have time to protest, Jayne has closed the door behind us.

"It's a bit…" I stare at the first dress in horror.

"Hmm, not exactly your look, but we may as well try it on." Jayne claps her hands together and grins at me.

"How do you suppose I get into it?" I eye the pale green creation as one might an animal that may attack at any moment.

"Perhaps, you should crawl up under it?" Jayne suggests.

A giggle escapes my lips, but after a closer inspection, stepping into it doesn't appear feasible. I strip off my blue dress and hang it on a hook.

"If I don't reappear in the next five minutes, send a search party." I burrow my way under kilometres of fabric. The layers go on forever. "You could clothe half the city with this." My words are muffled by the dress.

When I find the centre, I stretch my hands above my head and wriggle my way up.

"Surprise!" I yell as my head emerges from the corseted detail of the bodice.

"You have it on sideways," Jayne points out.

I twist around until the dress is lined up properly. I have to stand on my tiptoes for Jayne to lace me into it correctly. She leans over at an awkward angle to reach over the skirt.

"I think I like this one after all. None of the guys will be able to get close to me," I say as Jayne steps back and we study my reflection. "I wonder what would happen if I let my legs slide out from under me. Would the dress keep me upright or would I disappear forever in waves of green fabric?"

"I dare you to try." Jayne grins at me.

"How are you girls going in there?" The shopkeeper knocks on the door.

"Be out in a minute," I say.

Grinning back at Jayne, I allow my legs to slowly slide out from under me. For a brief moment the corseted top holds me upright and then the dress collapses and I vanish into a sea of material with a squeak.

"Help." I don't know if anyone can hear me although hands grope near mine. Eventually Jayne's laughing face appears closely followed by the concerned faces of the shopkeeper, Sara, Lori and Carter.

"Perhaps we should try a different design," Carter says.

The shopkeeper and Lori help me out of the dress, while Carter selects the next dress. They reluctantly leave me alone again with Jayne as they cart the first dress away.

Sara and the owner pull dresses off racks and pass them to Jayne who helps me into each one. They pass in a whirl of greens and pinks, each a different design, most long, some knee-length.

I step out in a short, ruffled green design with a gazillion tiny hooks down the back and pause in the centre of the store to see if spinning in a circle before a mirror will make the reflection appear more like me. It

70

just makes me dizzy. I lean against a mannequin dressed in a wedding suit.

"So – you feel like getting married?" I ask him. Unfortunately, he has about as much personality as many of the contestants and continues staring at himself in the full length mirror. As I pull away, one of the two tiny metal rings on the chest of my dress catches on his suit and I spend a frantic moment trying to untangle myself before anyone notices.

"Cassie, will you come over here? We need to have these images completed by the end of the day," Sara calls out to me.

I sigh and make my way over to the drop screens set up against one wall. A pair of tele-program employees toil over changing the scenery for each outfit I try on. I plaster a smile on my face and get ready to pose for the camera.

The shopkeeper rushes up as I step onto the small stage area. "Wait. You forgot the tassels." She holds up two bright pink tassels to my chest and it suddenly occurs to me why this dress has the two metal rings on the front.

"No way." I back up a step.

"But you'll need them for the wedding dance," the woman says.

"I'm not doing any wedding dance that involves nipple tassels."

"Can you imagine your mum's face if you showed up in a dress with tassels?" Jayne doubles over with laughter.

"Pull yourself together, Jayne, and help me get out of this stupid thing." I stomp off the stage and head back to the dressing room.

After what seems like hours and two dozen dresses later, Sara starts arguing with Lori and Carter over the photos and which five combinations should be used in the promotional shots. I edge away down the aisles hoping they don't notice me.

I emerge from the racks to discover the back of the store is set up as a museum exhibit of wedding costumes. I gravitate towards the glass case in the centre of the space.

Two mannequins pose together inside the case. The dress on the female is a simple but stunning floor-length tunic with cap sleeves and a split up to the hip that reveals the flowing trousers underneath. The white of the ensemble is broken up by pale green embroidery depicting a forest and an assortment of animals and birds.

The male outfit has a traditional Atlas look about it with the cape hung over his white shirt and loose trousers. A gold and a silver ribbon wind around the mannequins' left arms as though binding them together.

"Wow!" Jayne says from behind me. "That's a bit different."

"It's beautiful," I say.

"It also belonged to a royal couple and cost a million credits at auction." Jayne points to the placard mounted at the base of the case.

"Maybe someone could make a replica?" I say hopefully.

"Cassie, that thread-work would take forever to do. Best we go see what the team has picked out for you. I'm hoping they go with one of the green dresses and then my dress can be a deep green." Jayne tugs on my hand, leading me back to the front of the store. I look over my shoulder to catch a final glimpse of the white outfit as we leave.

By the time we get back to the others, five boxes sit on the counter. The storekeeper takes a scan of my body for the dress adjustments. She assures Sara her team will be up all night until the adjustments are finished.

"You'll be a married woman in six weeks," Jayne points out as the transport pulls up at the front of the shop.

The queasy feeling returns to my stomach. I wonder if I can get out of the wedding if I come down with something terminal.

*

After breakfast the following day, Jayne appears with a stack of cards in her hand.

"First group date. You, outside now." She bounces with excitement.

I follow her out to the patio where the guys lounge casually displayed by the outdoor pool. Trev points us both into position for the cameras. My eyes scan the group. Once again, the guys appear to have been dressed by the same person from the same store, except for Nathan who rebels with a t-shirt saying, 'Gravity – I fall for it every time'.

"Good morning, boys," Jayne begins. "Today some of you will be going on a group date with my beautiful friend, Cassie." She pauses for them to cheer and the hover-cams to reposition. "If Cassie reads your name out you will have ten minutes to get ready and meet us on the driveway." She slips me several cards and then steps away.

I look at the card on top and start reading out the names, pausing after each one for the guys to quiet down. Some get more cheers than others.

"Christopher. Nathan. Phil. Eric. And Zak."

Our job done, we back away while the pods zoom in to get the reactions of those chosen and those left behind.

"Have fun." Jayne leans in to hug me. "I'm off with the crew for my own dress fitting."

She leaves me and I go wait by the driveway having already been dressed for the morning in an old-fashioned pleated skirt and blouse with puffy sleeves.

I flip the cards over and read the guys' details on the back. Zak is an actor planted to create drama, but the other four men are all possible contenders.

Two vehicles arrive and I enter the first one with Mum and Trev. The five guys take the second vehicle and we all head out of the compound towards an elderly persons' residence.

"Zak isn't a serious contender. You can spend the date between the other four and he'll do his own thing. Game face on, girl," Trev says as we step out of the vehicle and head up the steps towards the building.

I take a deep breath and smile as I walk through the front door. The five men join me and a woman steps forward to introduce herself.

"You are the entertainment for the residents today," she says. "We have several classes that they attend so I'd like a couple of volunteers to help out there. Otherwise, go get to know the people here. Some of them don't get many visitors so it's nice for them to have a chat with someone new."

Mum edges up behind me. "I hope you're taking note, daughter. Without this program, I could be looking at life in a place like this." She glares moodily at the brightly painted walls.

"Thanks for the pressure, but you're hardly old enough for a place like this," I reply. She huffs and wanders away.

The woman ushers us into the main living area to introduce us to the residents. Some look up curiously at the hover-cams, but others ignore us, more interested in their various recreational activities.

"We've got others lined up for their fitness class." The woman points us towards another corridor that leads to an exercise room.

"I've got this one, boys." Phil steps forward. "Let's get the music started and I'll show these old people how to move."

"Perhaps a competition would make this more interesting." Zak leans casually against the doorframe in view of one of the hover-cams. "You start and I'll take over. Winner is the one who's more interesting."

Phil frowns at Zak, and Trev tugs on my arm.

"Hang out with these two for a bit and then move on to interact with the other men," he says. "Make sure you join in all the activities."

"I'm hardly dressed for a fitness class." I wave a hand over my current ensemble.

"Join in and look happy about it. I'll be watching." He stomps away.

I follow Phil and Zak to the room, choosing a section of floor closest to the door and join in with the elderly residents as Phil gets the music playing and starts them moving. Every now and again Zak steps in with the most ridiculous moves he can come up with and confusion ensues as the class tries to follow both instructors. I use one of these moments to slip out the door.

Back in the main living area, Nathan chats with several elderly women who laugh at whatever he's saying. Eric prances around demonstrating his more elaborate modelling walks while several residents lean around in their chairs to see the telescreen behind him. I join a card game with two old men and Christopher.

"Shush everyone. The governor has arrived," one old lady calls out reaching for the volume control.

I turn in my chair to watch the news story as someone shoos Eric out of the way. On screen, Terra's leaders assemble to greet the Governor and Vice Governor of the Universe.

"I remember the last time the governor was here. Thirty years ago it was," the old man beside me announces.

"Thirty-three years," the other card player corrects. "I was a supplementary Peace Keeper. Got to be in the same room as him once. Tall fella he was. Piercing brown eyes."

A tall female, with silvery hair braided around her head like a crown, steps forward. It's impossible to tell her age due to the silver and gold dragons painted on each side of her face. She's flanked by an older man who I've seen in images – Vice Governor Jaarid. Three Peace Keepers in their blue uniforms make up the rest of the group.

"I thought Governor Suri was a man," Phil says.

"The last one, Aden Suri, had a male body, although they tend to be gender fluid. Best not to call the governor male or female as you can never be sure which they'll be. Rumour has it Aden died under mysterious circumstances. No one even knew there was another Suri until this one appeared," the old lady pipes up. "Incredible isn't it? There's a thousand years of accumulated memories in their head. It's enough to send a normal person insane."

"What do you mean?" I ask.

"The Suris have genetic memory, born knowing everything their parents did. That's why there's only ever one at a time. They don't like having too many of themselves all with the same mind."

"How do you know all this?" I ask.

"I dated an Atlas man in my younger days," she says with a fond smile. "They like to keep their hand in politics."

"Did you marry him?" Nathan asks from across the room.

"Oh no. The people of Atlas like to keep their bloodlines pure, especially if they're from the capital, Atlia. They don't marry foreigners."

The news program moves on to other topics and we drift back to what we were doing before.

Trev approaches from wherever he's been loitering and slips a card into my hand. I scan it quickly and tuck it away.

"What do you think the key to a successful marriage is?" I ask the men at the table.

"Lots of sex." Zak appears behind me.

"I didn't know you needed to be married for that," Christopher jokes.

"What you want is someone to share your secrets with," one of the old men says.

Once the conversation is going, I slip away from the heated discussion. I've got three more questions to ask in front of the other guys.

I flop down in a seat near Nathan and his companions. Once the hover-cam joins us, I quickly glance at the next question, before leaning in to engage the residents.

"Tell me about the love of your life."

The ladies are keen to tell long-winded stories about husbands and boyfriends. Nathan remains fairly quiet, admitting to one previous girlfriend when pressed, but insisting his focus has been on his studies. Eventually I have to excuse myself to ask questions for Eric and Phil.

By the time Trev reappears to tell us we're leaving, I'm mentally exhausted and don't feel like I know any of the men better than I had that morning.

When we finally make it back to the mansion, Sara lines the five men up to inform them their next challenge is to write an essay on the values of marriage and commitment.

"I hope you listened to your elders today on the topic," she says, amid numerous groans from the men.

Once the guys are set up with their task, Sara leads me up to my room where the five different wedding dresses are laid out across the bed.

"Get dressed, we're doing the opening sequence of the tele-program and promotional photos as soon as you are ready."

"Which dress do you want me in?"

"It doesn't matter. We'll be doing all five." Sara pauses to answer the knock on the door. She opens it to let in Lori and Carter. "Send Cassie to the rose arbour when you're done," she tells them as she walks out.

The rest of my day is spent changing dresses, hairstyles and makeup before acting out walking down an aisle, throwing a bouquet in the air, and pushing away a stand-in man in a tuxedo. Several scenes are repeated because I don't have the right expression. The men will be added in later with their promo shots. The ones who stayed behind this morning have already done theirs.

By the time we're done, I limp back to my room to kick off my high heels and change into an evening dress in a deep blue. The skirt sweeps the ground, so I refuse to put shoes back on.

I check in with Trev, Sara, and Mum on the winners and losers of the essay competition. Jayne, having begged Carter to allow her to be 'in charge of my face', paints a row of blossoms up one of my cheeks.

Once she is done, I take my stack of cards into the elimination room. Sara announces that Nathan won the essay competition. His prize is a single date with me tomorrow. A smile creeps over my face as he steps forward to thank me.

He steps back into line as I read through the names of the other contestants. Christopher remains standing alone once I run out of cards. Sara tells him to say goodbye and he departs the house, leaving nine behind.

*

The next day, I wait in the garden dressed in a yellow sundress with my hair hanging in perfect ringlets about my face and a picnic basket hanging from one arm. A pair of hover-cams follow my every movement.

I grin when Nathan walks out of the double glass doors and heads towards my position.

"Ready to get to know each other?" he asks.

"Sure," I reply.

He takes the picnic basket in one hand and holds my hand with his other. His hold is firm and warm. It's kind of nice, not awkward like I thought it would be, but it lacks the weird electric sensation of Dennian's touch. My smile slips from my face.

We walk across the mansion lawns with the camera pods hovering in front of us.

"How about here?" Nathan gestures towards a sunny patch of finely manicured grass. I glance at the blanket already spread out on site.

"Looks great," I try to sound enthusiastic. Nathan tugs me down onto the blanket.

"Upset about having lost two potential husbands already?" he jokes.

"Oh definitely," I say. "I only have nine boyfriends left and I only get to keep one of them. It's a sad, sad day." I sigh dramatically.

Nathan laughs. "Well, all in all I think it has been a good week. I've managed to eliminate my hottest competition and we're about to enjoy a very generous picnic in the grounds of a property that none of us could ever afford to own ourselves. I've certainly had a good week."

I glance out over the grounds. A row of trees obscures the view of the mansion. The hedging plants closest to our position rustle as Trev shifts in his hiding spot. I turn back to study Nathan who is busy positioning the picnic contents across the blanket.

"Why are you here?" I ask.

"My parents are really close. I feel like I'm ready for a serious relationship. I want what they have and I'm here to see if that one person could be you." His response comes across as practised, like one of my cue cards.

"Why are you really here?"

Nathan glances at the cameras, then back to me. He places a hand over the mic clipped into his collar and I do the same to mine.

"Honestly? My SuriTech apprenticeship depends on me being married. My supervisor nominated me for this show," Nathan says.

"So our relationship would be one of convenience?" I roll the idea around in my mind. Would a relationship with Nathan give me my freedom and still give Mum what she needs? Why does it feel like a betrayal to what I had with Dennian?

"That sounds terrible." Nathan scrunches up his face. "You seem like an awesome person and I'd like to get to know you better. I think we could be good friends and maybe one day that could become something more."

"We'd be honest with each other? No lying for the camera?"

"Yes." He nods.

"I'm only here because my mother will be forced to live in the single women's accommodation in the outer suburbs if I don't participate. She thinks that is the equivalent to the world ending. I met someone I really like a few months ago," I say.

"Oh." Nathan fiddles with the edge of the blanket. "Where is he?"

"I don't know." I bite my lip. "My father died just before we got accepted for this program. With everything going on, I never had the chance to tell him what was happening."

Nathan reaches over and takes my hand. A hover-cam zooms in on our clasped hands.

"Hey, don't cover your mics," Trev calls out from the bushes. I remove my hand from my mic, blink back tears and direct a big smile at Nathan.

"Do you believe in love at first sight?" I ask one of my cue questions.

"Do you? Or should I walk past again?" He moves to stand and grins at me.

"I'm being serious." I smile and he sits down again.

"Hmmm, that sounds like a bit of a loaded question to me. I believe in attraction at first sight, but I think love needs to grow and develop between two people. How can you truly love someone until you know if you can put up with all their bad habits?" He grins again.

"What are your bad habits?"

"Ah, the first step towards love. I leave the toilet seat up and I hate washing dishes," he says. "And you, future wife?"

"I believe in love at first sight, I moult, seriously like hair all over the bathroom no matter how many times I clean it up, and I'm not fond of the dishes either."

"Damn it, we're going to have to hire a housekeeper," Nathan jokes.

"How will you spend all your housework-free time?" I select a piece of cheese from a plate and pop it in my mouth.

"I love astronomy." Nathan glances up at the sky as though he can see all its secrets. "Did you know that many of the stars we see at night have already died? It takes so long for light to reach us, we're actually looking into the past. I should bring you out here in a few weeks to see the formation of the Lordinia Black Hole nine hundred and eighty two years ago."

"How was it created?" I lean forward watching the excitement on his face.

"There was an accident at the original SuriTech Laboratories. It set off a weapons dump, destroying the whole star-system. Part of the SuriTech induction is about the dangers of experiments. They don't want a repeat of Lordinia. On the positive side, that's what created the power vacuum that allowed Governor Suri to form government."

"What do you mean?" I ask.

"The explosion happened during a gathering of feuding warlords. Killed them all. The original Governor Suri stepped in and united everyone left behind," Nathan says.

"Well that's more interesting than anything my politics teacher taught us," I say.

Nathan laughs, but his response is cut off by Trev approaching. He sends Nathan over to where Sara now stands with another hover-cam to discuss the progress of the date with a camera.

Trev hangs around to hand me new cue cards with hastily scribbled phrases for me to repeat to another hover-cam. Once I'm done, Trev sends me back to the house. I give Nathan a quick wave before leaving him behind.

Jayne meets me inside. "How did it go?" She clutches my hand and bounces on her heels.

"Good," I say.

"But…?" She frowns at my less than excited tone.

"He's not Dennian." I slip my hand from hers and disappear into my room to be alone.

Alpha Male

Jayne and I stand in the living room, surrounded by the contestants. I wear a simple thigh-length dress that I can move around in so I'm hopeful we'll be doing something active for this group date.

"Reveal your true nature," Jayne says playfully, as she hands me the cards. "When Cassie says your name, join us for the next group date."

"Prince. Rick." I suppress a sigh as the two guys yell loudly and thump their neighbours on the back. "Elliott. And Guya."

I lower the cards and smile in what I hope is a believable manner. I hold the expression for the required camera shot then walk out with Jayne.

"This is going to be a nightmare," I say once we're outside. "Rick's creepy, Elliot could make a snail look interesting, and Prince is crazy."

"Prince is another paid contestant like Zak. He stays as long as he brings in viewers," Jayne says. "And Rick has good social connections, so you'll have to put up with him a bit longer."

"What happened to you and Mum making the decisions?"

"Yeah, right. It's all about money and influence. Trev says whoever can bring in the most, stays the longest."

I stop suddenly and turn on Jayne. "There is no way I'm marrying Rick. I'd rather be out on the street."

"I doubt your mum feels the same way," Jayne says. "You haven't even got to know most of the guys. Give them a chance."

I roll my eyes at her as we slide into the first vehicle. The guys arrive minutes later, and Mum joins them to ask the real contestants various questions about family, friends, and job aspirations.

The transport comes to a stop some time later. I bound out of the vehicle and look out across the car park.

"A zoological park?" I hug Jayne as she comes up behind me. "You know me too well."

"Happy birthday, Bestie. There's going to be cake later." Jayne hugs me back.

"You can hold me like that anytime." Rick, having exited his transport with the other three guys, reaches his arms around me. I give him a shove and he goes sprawling.

I step around him and head inside the gates to where Sara and the cameras wait for us. Mum stays in the transport ready to leave again now her task is complete. Jayne stands to one side while the guys arrange themselves on either side of me, Rick brushing dirt from his clothes.

"Hello, Cassie, gentlemen. Today you will be participating in a variety of activities to reveal your true nature. Firstly, one of the keepers will introduce you to some of the animals. Then you'll be divided into two groups to raise as many credits as you can from the public in one hour." Sara waves a young keeper forward.

"Do you think the keeper was chosen to look good on camera?" Jayne whispers in my ear. "He doesn't look old enough to be an expert in anything."

A small laugh escapes my lips as the man in question quickly checks his appearance in Carter's portable mirror.

"Don't be mean," I tease. "He's at least as old as Jamis was and I've never met anyone better with animals than Dennian." My voice trails off as I swallow the lump trying to form in my throat.

Jayne squeezes my arm. "You're right. I'm sure this guy's not just a pretty face." She winks at me and follows it up with kissy noises.

"Whatever," I shove her away. "I'm here for the animals." I manage a grin before I head over to the keeper.

"My name's Glen and today I'm going to show you behind the scenes in one of the marsupial enclosures," the man says as we gather around.

"Boring," Prince says. "How about you show us the water-bulls?"

"Wild animals are unpredictable. We'll stick with safe ones today." Glen turns away and leads us towards an enclosure with a small burrowing creature similar to the breed Dennian had introduced me to.

Glen passes out a handful of chopped vegetables and lets me through the gate. Rick and Guya follow me in. Rick also has food in his hands, but Guya holds a hover-cam controller.

"Are the other two coming in?" I ask.

"Road-boy is scared of the animals," Guya says, not taking his eyes off the controller. "Prince said he'd rather wrestle a bear."

"Fine with me." Rick edges closer to me, but I side-step out of the way and put Glen between us once the keeper joins us.

Glen leads us around the side of the exhibit to where several burrow entrances are partially obscured under bushes. He points out the dishes for us to leave the food and begins a monologue about the creature. I edge away from the group and sit a short distance from a burrow.

I mimic the sounds Dennian taught me and when a furry head pokes its head out, I toss a small piece of food in its direction. I tune out my surroundings and Guya's hover-cam, and focus on the animal.

It hops closer and a smile spreads across my face. I imagine Dennian sitting beside me issuing silent encouragement. I stretch out with the final slice of vegetable between my fingers. The creature reaches out towards my hand.

Rick throws himself at the animal which squeaks and disappears back into its burrow.

"Damn it, I missed." Rick pushes himself up onto his elbows from where he's landed beside me.

"What is wrong with you?" I demand. "You scared it away!"

"I was going to catch it for you."

"Don't. Just don't." I push up to my feet and stalk away.

"Perhaps we should start the next activity?" Glen ushers us out of the enclosure and points us back towards where Sara and Trev wait.

"All credits will go towards renovating the primate enclosure and the winning team will be safe from elimination. Cassie, you will be with Prince and Guya." Sara hands each of us a collection tin.

"Which animals are the primates?" Elliott asks.

I scrub my hands over my face as I discard my first response as being too sarcastic. Before I come up with an alternative, Rick butts in.

"Why aren't I in Cassie's group?"

"Don't want to bore the girl to death by spending time in your company," Prince replies.

Rick takes a swing at Prince. I pull a 'see-what-I-mean' face at Jayne and walk away from the group. Guya wanders over to me still fiddling with his controller. Two other hover-cams follow us while another pair hang around Jayne, Rick, and Elliott.

"We'll probably get more interest if we start near the primate exhibits," I say.

"Whatever you say, princess," Prince says. I roll my eyes and fall into step beside Guya.

"How come you have a controller?" I nod at the device in his hands.

"This one's mine," Guya says. "My uncle's a big movie producer, but he won't give me any camera time. Says I need to 'make it on my own', so here I am, making a name for myself. Ever used one of these?"

"We could ask people to pay us to take our clothes off." Prince sticks his head between ours.

"I've only used hand-held cameras," I reply, ignoring Prince.

"You can have this one when I leave. I'll tell Dad it broke and he'll get me a new one," Guya offers.

"You'll show me how to operate all the features?" I ask.

"Sure. I heard Jayne say it was your birthday. Consider it a belated present."

"Thanks." I grin at Guya.

"We should set up a kissing booth." Prince jumps in front of us as we near the primate enclosure. Behind us, a lion roars for the crowd.

"Stop it," I demand.

"Say my name, sweet Cassie and I will do as you command." Prince sweeps a bow in front of me.

"What's your name again?" I tilt my head to one side and study him as though I don't recall having been introduced.

"It's Prince." He frowns at me.

"Okay, go away Prince." I turn my back to him and walk over to a group of mothers with their children and begin my spiel about raising credits for the enclosure.

When I look around, Guya is talking to an old man nearby and Prince is surrounded by a bunch of teenage boys. I turn back to my group.

"Your credits will be supporting a great cause," I say.

"Oh Lord! What is that boy doing?" one of the women exclaims as she is about to transfer me ten credits. I glance over my shoulder.

Prince clings to the wrong side of the high wire fence of the lion enclosure. This park is old. Where Dennian worked, no one could have scaled the electronic partitions.

"Cassie!" Prince calls out.

"What the hell are you doing?" I yell.

I'm dimly aware of someone racing off towards the park entrance, hopefully to get the veterinarian and a tranquiliser gun; for Prince with any luck.

"I'm the man!" He yells, before slowly climbing down to the ground, on the lions' side of the fence.

He faces me, oblivious to the fact he has attracted the attention of the enclosure's occupants. I count three massive beasts, one male and two female, eying the intruder.

"Get out of there!" I march towards the enclosure. The tall fence, garden bed, and timber railing prevent me from getting closer.

"Kiss me and I will," he says.

"Don't be stupid. There's a fence between us. Those lions will tear you to shreds – Look out!" I yell as the alpha lion creeps forward, its tail swishing.

Prince spins around at the panic in my voice. The lion sinks into a crouch. People shout around us. Hover-cams circle like vultures. Somewhere, a television producer rubs his hands together with visions of impressive show ratings.

I glance around for something I can toss to distract the lions, but I hesitate, not wanting to hurt the animals. Would eating a person upset their stomachs? Out of the corner of my eye, I catch a flash of movement. I hope it's the vet or at least a keeper.

A man springs off the timber railing and leaps at the fence, reaching the top before I can blink. He jumps from there, landing neatly on the ground in front of Prince. He wears a zoo uniform, although I doubt this is standard procedure for idiots trying to feed themselves to the lions.

The lion lunges at this new intruder. I suck in a breath and squint my eyes, not wanting to see someone torn apart, but unable to look away. A terrifying growl rips through the air and the lion halts mid stride, hesitating at the challenge. Relief flows through me that the tearing of limbs, and blood and guts has been postponed momentarily. Where is a tranquiliser when you need one?

Prince, white and shaking, chooses that moment to run to the fence and start climbing. The lion feigns a lunge, but the man stands his ground, growling once again.

Prince makes it half way down the fence before he's grabbed by several keepers, who arrive sprinting like they're being chased by lions themselves. They pull

Prince to the ground beside a keeper's bike that now lies abandoned on the ground.

Prince cowers on the ground, pale and shaking. By the wet patch on his pants, he could use a change of underwear. The veterinarian arrives in a vehicle, having had to collect his equipment first, and starts lining up a shot at the lion, but the man still in the enclosure and crowd gathering outside, hamper his view.

I bite down on the knuckle I hold to my mouth as the man faces off with the lions. For the moment he is the alpha, but if he runs or backs down, he's dead.

The two lionesses wander off now the prey has escaped. In a blur of movement, the keeper spins out of his crouch and throws himself at the fence. He vaults over the top before the lion's half-hearted attempt to swipe its giant paw at him can reach its target. The man stands up and glances in my direction.

I gasp as the green eyes meet mine. For a moment, his face lights up with recognition, then he takes in the hover-cams. Before I can move towards Dennian or say anything, irate zoo personnel surround him.

"What the hell were you thinking?"

"You could've been killed!"

"I don't care what kinds of stunts you pull wherever you come from. You can't get away with that kind of recklessness at this zoo!"

The keepers argue with Dennian who responds with hand signals. The hover-cams whiz around the scene. Dennian ignores them, glancing occasionally in my direction.

Prince remains quiet. Perhaps he realises how stupid he's been. The poor lions nearly got shot because of him.

Dennian slips out of the circle of zoo personnel who have turned their attention to Prince. I hear Peace Keepers mentioned. The teenage boys bolted long ago, so Prince won't even get his credits for the dare.

Dennian approaches me, angling himself to stand with his back turned to the cameras. I throw my arms around him and press my face into his shoulder.

"Where's Zeke?" I ask.

"Home." He surprises me by speaking out loud.

Standing encircled by his arms, I'm swamped by the possibilities of what could have been, before I lost Dad, before I sold myself for Mum's comfort. Tears begin to fall until I'm sobbing uncontrollably into Dennian's shoulder. He holds me as I cry until calm settles over me.

"You left," I mumble into his shoulder.

"You left first," he says.

"Not by choice."

He turns his head, glancing at the cameras and back to me, raising an eyebrow when I look up into his face.

I try to work out how to tell the man I'm falling for that I'm on a tele-program where the winning contestant will marry me.

"Mum's making me participate in a reality tele-program." I pull away and brush at the makeup smeared onto his beige collar. I don't mention Dad. It's too raw for me to speak out loud.

"You're getting married?" Confusion crosses his face as though he's trying to make sense of the chaotic thoughts in my mind.

"It's not my idea. I didn't want to do this."

"I thought..." he pauses, "...there was something between us?"

92

My stomach twists in a not-unpleasant way. I have a sudden vision of myself in the white embroidered tunic-dress walking down the mansion garden path towards Dennian.

"You hardly know me," I say.

"I see you." He reaches out and brushes a tear from my cheek.

"I have to marry one of the contestants on the show."

I think I step closer to him. His green eyes lock with mine and I drown in them. The corners of his mouth turn up into a grin. His eyes flick over to the hover-cam that focuses on us.

"If I was an option, you'd choose me?"

"Yes." It comes out as a whisper. If I'm going to get married, I want it to be to this man standing in front of me.

He fingers entwine with mine then his lips are pressed against mine. My eyes slide closed as my mind is swamped by foreign sensations; uncertainty, comfort, desire. I'm no longer me, but both of us. I press against his chest to stay upright. Dennian's pulled roughly away and my eyes fly open.

"Hey, get your hands off her." Rick takes a swing at Dennian.

Dennian blocks the punch with his arm and Rick falls to the ground with a confused look on his face. Dennian plants a quick kiss on my lips again before disentangling himself.

"See you soon." Dennian's lips brush against my ear as he speaks before he strides past the cameras as if they aren't there.

"Wait…" I move to follow him, but someone grabs my arm.

"What's going on?" A puffed Jayne asks. "I heard someone was in the lion enclosure or something. Why is Rick sitting on the ground?"

"She was kissing that keeper," Elliott says.

"Seriously, you guys couldn't have waited for me?" Jayne glares at Elliott and Rick.

"Hey, check this out." Guya pushes into our circle. "I got a close up of that guy in the lion enclosure and Prince wetting himself."

I shake Jayne off, step over Rick, and run in the direction Dennian took. I round the corner, but he's nowhere in sight. I turn in a slow circle.

A young woman leans against a fence, her sleeveless, collarless blue shirt showing off athletic limbs. Her brunette hair, several shades lighter than my own, hangs in a plait down her back. She doesn't drop her gaze when I meet her grey eyes.

Jayne catches up with me, dragging my attention away. When I look back, the woman has disappeared. I crane my neck to see down the paths, but she's vanished.

"He's gone." I turn in another slow circle as I search.

"Who's gone?" Jayne asks.

"Dennian…" And the girl.

"Your mentor for the school project?" Doubt fills her voice.

I nod. Suddenly her arms are around me in a big hug.

"I'm sorry, Cassie. I knew this was a bad idea coming to a zoo again so soon, but your mum thought it might help you move on with one of the contestants."

I pull away. "He was here."

94

She tries to hug me again, but I slip from her grasp and stalk away. Away from her. Away from the men in my life. Away from the cameras. Hopefully not away from Dennian.

Back at the house, Lori and Carter whisk me away for an outfit change and to repair the makeup I smudged on Dennian's shirt so we can go straight into elimination.

Downstairs, I poke my head around the door to check on the eight men standing in position. Prince is missing.

"They sent him home," Jayne whispers as she slips me seven name cards.

"Why are we doing an elimination, then?" I don't look at the names.

"Apparently that's what the audience wants. It adds tension." Jayne shrugs.

"The rescue from a lion wasn't good enough?" I mutter.

Sara waves me into the room. I put my serious face on, step into position, wait for Sara to say her lines, and start reading the names one by one. Nathan and Guya are fourth and fifth and I breathe a sigh of relief. Eric and Elliott are the two left standing as I turn over the last card.

"Eric."

The model steps forward to thank me for choosing him. Elliott remains behind with a confused look on his face as though unsure why the others all left.

"Elliott," Sara says. "You haven't been chosen. Please say your goodbyes."

"Looks like you'll get to be part of that road project, after all," I say when he reaches me. He leaves the mansion with a smile on his face. Mine slips away once the cameras turn away.

*

I wake early, having barely slept during the night. I sit in the bedroom window seat, staring out over the garden as the mist dissipates under the first rays of sunlight.

When I go down to breakfast fully dressed in another impractical gown with Carter's makeup hiding my sleepless night, there's a note propped up on the counter. Mum and Jayne aren't around and I open the card warily.

"I have a surprise waiting for you in the garden. Come join me after breakfast," I say out loud for the benefit of the camera.

I nibble on a piece of toast before making my way to the garden. Best to get the surprise over and done with. I reach the courtyard garden with its vine-covered walls and strategically placed bench-seats. Sara, beautifully poised as always, awaits me halfway along the path.

"Cassie...." She pauses for effect, as I remember I have to smile or do the scene again, "How are you feeling?"

"I'm excited. You know how much I love surprises." I put as much enthusiasm into my voice as possible. I haven't had to repeat a scene for days.

"We lost Prince unexpectedly yesterday..." Sara adds a dramatic pause and I stifle a laugh at her wording. "So let me introduce you to his replacement."

The door in the far wall opens and my heart stops for a second. Dennian steps through the doorway, smiling his shy little smile. I freeze in place worried that if I move or blink I'll wake up from this dream.

"Dennian is the youngest contestant at seventeen years and works as a zoological researcher," Sara says the lines Dennian should be saying.

Dennian walks towards me, pausing to brush his lips against my cheek. He steps back and offers me a piece of dark cloth wrapped around a small object. I take it in my hands and peel back the edges. Nestled inside lies a sparkling, multi-coloured stone, the size of my thumbnail, hanging from an intricate silver chain.

"It's beautiful." I hold it up and the sunlight reflects rainbows off it.

Dennian takes it from my hand and steps forward to fasten it around my neck. It nestles out of sight under the neckline of my dress.

His lips brush my ear. "It's a dragon stone. It absorbs and stores energy." He steps back.

"Cassie, I'll let you introduce Dennian to the other contestants. They're waiting by the pool." Sara backs away, leaving us momentarily alone with the cameras.

"How did you do it?" I ask.

Dennian shrugs, but a small grin tugs at his lips. "They wanted someone to replace the boy who annoyed the lions. They thought I was interesting."

"We'd better go find the other guys before Trev comes looking for us." I slide my hand into Dennian's and keep hold of it until we reach the pool.

Seven young men fall silent as I approach with Dennian following behind. I pause while Mum and Jayne join us from the house. Mum's face turns into a frown at an unannounced man, while Jayne raises her eyebrows at me.

"This is Dennian. He's our new houseguest," I say to the group.

"What do you do, Dennian? When you're not competing for time with our Cassie," Phil asks.

Dennian looks at him, makes a sign with his hands and glances briefly at me. Mum's frown deepens.

"Dennian works at the zoo we visited yesterday," I say.

"Is he deaf?" Zak says to no one in particular.

Dennian flicks his hand in what appears to be a rude gesture.

"No, he's not deaf." I grit my teeth in an attempt to be politer than I believe Dennian was.

"Weirdo," Rick mutters under his breath. Dennian ignores the comment.

"You're the guy who saved Prince from those lions," Guya says and suddenly the guys are all talking again.

"That was awesome the way you leapt..."

"I thought you were both going to get torn to pieces..."

Trev waves to me from the house and I back away quietly leaving the guys to get to know Dennian.

Fears

Jayne and I walk into the open plan room where the guys already sit at tables. My eyes come to rest on Dennian sitting at the edge of the group.

After we say our hellos, Sara steps into the room with a casually dressed man. Mum's away again doing behind the scenes stuff with Trev.

"Good morning, ladies, gentlemen," Sara says. "Today you will be facing your greatest fears."

"What?" Zak leaps up from his chair and paces. "I didn't sign up for this," he mutters.

Dennian stares intently at Sara as though trying to read a tricky document. Two chairs along, Nathan's face pales and he scrubs his hands against his legs. I'm not really sure what my greatest fears is; maybe being powerless or having to marry someone I don't like to protect my mother's future.

"Mr Turro is here today to teach you several creative techniques to lead you in a journey of self-discovery. I'll leave you in his very capable hands," Sara says.

"Who here has drawing experience?" Mr Turro asks. Rick's hand shoots into the air and Dennian's follows more hesitantly. Mr Turro walks over to where Rick sits. "What do you draw?"

"Cartoons and caricatures mostly." Rick glances around the room to see who is watching and puffs out his chest for the close-up camera shot. Another hover-cam focuses on me but turns away again at my crossed arms and unimpressed look.

"And you?" Mr Turro asks Dennian who looks back at him without speaking.

"Dennian does realistic drawings, mostly of animals," I say.

"How do you know?" Rick glares at me.

"Dennian was my mentor for a school project at the zoo," I say. "I saw a lot of his art. He's really good."

"Must have got a great mark with a mute mentor," Phil mutters.

"Actually, I earned a great mark." I stare Phil down until he looks away.

"Focus people. Today I will demonstrate various drawing techniques. You will use one to depict your greatest fear. You will be awarded points for artistic ability and clarity of your fear. Cassie and Jayne will be guessing what your fear is. Rick and Dennian, you may use your own drawing techniques if you prefer."

I tune out as he hands out sheets of drawing paper and pencils, and demonstrates different styles of drawing. Dennian starts sketching over the whole sheet of paper. I can't see what it is from where I stand.

"He didn't even stop to think about his fear. What do you think it will be?" Jayne whispers in my ear.

"I can't imagine him being afraid of anything." I shrug, watching him draw.

"It's probably something embarrassing like having to stand in front of a crowd and give a speech," Jayne says. A snort of laughter escapes before I can stop it.

"I'm just glad they're not making me do this," I say.

Rick starts drawing while the others try to copy what Mr Turro has drawn on the board at the front of the room.

"I heard Trev say they're going to use these in the challenges. Make the guys face their fears," Jayne whispers.

"That's horrible!"

100

"Makes good programing if they freak out. Do you think any of them will cry?"

"Depends how honest they are today," I say.

"Done." Rick waves his drawing in the air. Mr Turro takes it from him and places it upside down on his desk, so I can't see who had done which drawing.

Trev steps into the room and taps me on the shoulder motioning for me to head outside. He passes me a stack of cards and I flip through them quickly before standing in front of the camera with the guys in the background of the shot.

"I'm beginning to see connections with several of the young men now," I recite. "This challenge will be very telling. What are their greatest fears and will it affect our relationship if they can't overcome them."

We do two more takes before I have the lines fluent and I can head back into the room where the guys are finishing up. Mr Turro collects the drawings and the men file past us silently on the way out of the room. Dennian studies the floor with a furrowed brow as he walks out and doesn't look at me.

Mr Turro shuffles the drawings before handing me the pile. Each one has a number stuck to the top corner for identification. Trev slides an evaluation sheet onto the bench and moves around us to make sure the cameras get the best shots. Once satisfied, he steps back and I turn the first drawing over. It's a cartoon spider with big eyes and long eyelashes.

"I don't particularly like spiders, but this one's kind of cute," Jayne says.

"Too cute to be Rick's greatest fear, don't you think?" I say.

I write 'spiders' and 'Rick' next to box 1 on our evaluation sheet and pass the drawing to Mr Turro for artistic assessment.

"Someone's afraid of heights," I say looking at the next one. A roughly drawn person teeters at the top of a cliff as they windmill their arms. I write the fear in the box and move on. It's followed by what we guess are drowning, bugs, and snakes. We leave the names blank for the moment, unsure who belongs to each fear.

"How bad do you think these fears are? Because they're looking more like dislikes to me." Jayne flips over the next drawing. "Kllrarn in Hell! He's terrifying!"

I look over at the drawing. The detailed accuracy encompasses the entire sheet of paper.

"It's Dennian's," I say.

"Well, I don't know what it's about, but that's got to be my new fear." Jayne shudders while I study the drawing.

An ageless man stares at me through a single, crazy, pale blue eye. His dark silvery hair is long and unkempt, with small twigs and leaves giving the impression he has hiked through the surrounding forest. By the sweat marks under his armpits, it hasn't been a gentle stroll. The right side of his face is scarred by five long claw marks, leaving his left eyelid sunken and closed. His mouth is turned up in what could be a grin but looks more like a sneer. His left hand is raised in a beckoning motion. The right, a shiny pink stump, rests against a tombstone above an inscription:

TARLA SHEN

FIRST CHILD OF

NIKO SHEN AND LARI SHEN

AGE THREE MONTHS
CAUSE OF DEATH UNKNOWN.

Dried flowers and children's toys lie scattered at the man's feet, where the removal of the stone grave cover exposes the gapping darkness below. To one side of the drawing a second stone stands, although most of the words are lost to the edge of the page.

ZETH
SECON
NIKO SHEN
AGE SEV
CAUSE OF DE

Toys lie on the second grave as well, although this one remains sealed.

"Who do you think the man is?" I ask.

"Probably a figment of his imagination. I'm calling this one a fear of death," Jayne says.

"Wouldn't it be Dennian's name on the inscription then?"

"Good point. How about fear of being buried alive?"

"I guess so," I concede although I feel like I'm missing something in the detail and I doubt Dennian will tell me.

"Ok, process of elimination. Who do the rest belong to?"

"Guya is afraid of confined spaces." I drag over the drawing that reminds me of a movie director's sketch.

Jayne and I spread out the remaining five drawings and randomly guess who drew which. When we're done, we leave Mr Turro adding in the artistic score and calculating the total.

We meet up with the guys in the living room although none of them push for my attention preferring to stay lost in their own thoughts. After some time Sara and Mr Turro join us with the results.

"Today's winner is Guya with his fear of confined spaces," Mr Turro announces.

"Guya, you have a single date with Cassie," Sara says as Guya is thumped on the back by his neighbours. I grab Mr Turro as he leaves the room.

"Why didn't Dennian win? He's the best artist."

"Your description of the fear didn't match his." Mr Turro walks off.

After lunch and another outfit and makeup change, Sara taps on my door before poking her head around the corner.

"Guya's ready for your date," she says.

"That was quick."

"He requested something locally. Meet him down at the West Wing Media Room when you're finished here." She nods to Lori and Carter and leaves.

I make my way downstairs and across to the West Wing. I haven't been this way before, but a hover-cam loiters in one corridor and I follow it to a door marked 'Media'.

Guya swings the door open and grins at me. "Welcome to my domain."

He waves me forward and I step into the semi-darkened room. Rows of screens and controllers line the walls. Two older men stand up from their chairs and introduce themselves as the camera operators.

After the introductions they make themselves scarce in one corner of the room, although one of the screens they monitor is of Guya and me.

"Your mum said you're interested in making documentaries, so let me show you how all this works." Guya waves a hand at the screen displaying the other guys lounging around in one of the outdoor areas.

Dennian sits on the ground away from the others with his hand outstretched towards a garden bed. As I watch, a large green frog leaps onto his palm.

"One top-rating movie, or in your case, documentary can have you set for life. No need to sell your soul to these people for a few credits."

I turn my focus back to Guya.

*

I wake in the morning to the most practical clothes I've seen since I've been in the house. I dress in the stretchy leggings and fitted designer top and head downstairs to find Mum and Jayne.

"What's the plan for today?" I ask.

"They haven't told us yet. We'll be meeting the boys offsite," Jayne says between bites of toast. I glance at Mum who's also dressed for outdoors.

"Trev wants to get them to start facing their fears," she says. I put down the piece of fruit I was about to eat.

"Has anyone worked out what Dennian's fear is?" I ask.

"Apparently it's a childhood nightmare." Jayne shrugs and brushes crumbs from her fingers.

"Still trying to work out what to do for him," Trev says as he steps into the room. "You ladies ready to get this show on the road?"

I trail behind the others as we get in the vehicle. Mum and Jayne have a folder between them and discuss the various contestants.

"I don't know what you need to debate so hard," I say. "Dennian wins and Nathan's runner up."

Mum snaps the folder shut and studies her hands resting on top. Jayne glances between her and me.

"Dennian's not a serious contender," Jayne says. "He's only here to replace Prince and he'll go as soon as he has no entertainment value, which probably won't be long seeing as he doesn't speak."

"He can talk and he's the one I choose."

"Well you better hope he does something interesting," Mum says as we drive down a remote road and come to a stop near where the guys stand.

Sara stands beside a woman dressed in khaki. Marker cones line the ground between them and us. Mum walks over to Trev while the rest of us gather around the newcomer and Sara in a loose circle. Covered crates sit by her feet. I move in beside Dennian.

"What do you think's in them?" I whisper.

He makes a wavy motion with one arm and I grab his hand in my own, tugging him closer so the others won't hear.

"If you don't talk, you'll be eliminated."

Dennian runs his tongue over his lips. He glances at the hover-cams, Mum, and back to me. He opens his mouth twice before any words come out.

"Snakes," he says.

"What?"

"Crates full of snakes. Eric's fear."

I lean forward to see Eric at one end of our semi-circle. Sara has stopped talking and the older woman

106

lifts a lid from the nearest crate. Eric curses and backs away, but Rick grabs his arm.

"Scared of a harmless little reptile, are you, Eric?" Rick laughs.

"You'd be scared of them if you'd seen a fellow model strangled to death during a photo shoot. The guy's face turned the most hideous shade of purple while they tried to pull it off him. I still can't bring myself to wear anything that colour." Eric shudders.

"Leave him alone," Nathan says. "You wouldn't like it if we were facing your fear."

The woman lifts one end of a huge snake from a crate. "I can assure you, there is nothing little about these pythons. Today you'll be racing around the cones in pairs while carrying a snake. If your reptile touches the ground, you must go back to the start."

"Eric, as this is your fear, you get to start," Sara says. "Who would like to be teamed with Eric?"

"Hell no! I'm not going to lose." Rick backs away from Eric.

"Me." Dennian steps forward.

"It speaks!" Zak exclaims.

"Shut your mouth." I glare at Zak.

"First pair: Eric and Dennian. Come get your snake," Sara says.

"I can't." Eric stands rooted to the spot with tears welling in his eyes.

Dennian walks over and places a hand on Eric's arm. Eric closes his eyes, his chest heaving, but his trembling slows. Dennian nods towards the woman. An assistant runs over to her, and the pair lift the snake out. They drape the head over Dennian's shoulders and the tail over Eric's. The model keeps his eyes closed and doesn't flinch. The snake's tongue flicks out tasting the air around Dennian's face.

"Who's next?" Sara asks.

Jayne drags me forward while the boys pair up. By the time we're all ready, Eric still hasn't moved, but he hasn't panicked either. Dennian's hand remains resting on Eric's shoulder. Dennian manoeuvres them around so they face the start line. The rest of us move into position.

Sara holds up a horn and on the signal Jayne and I stagger forward with the heavy snake over our shoulders. Rick and Phil run past us yelling at each other to keep pace as Rick edges ahead of his teammate. Nathan and Zak stride past keeping in time.

"Oh My Governor Suri! It's getting in my hair!" Jayne squeals. We pause at the turn-around point so I can untangle the snake.

"Don't drop the thing!" Jayne yells as the snake slithers off one shoulder.

"I've got it." I heave it back up. It coils its tail around my neck and I tug it loose so I can breathe.

Dennian and Eric reach our position. Eric's eyes remain shut and he moves like a sleepwalker.

"Hurry up," Jayne says.

In front of us, Rick trips, bringing Phil and their snake down. They struggle for a moment to get free as the reptile handler and assistant run forward to rescue the snake.

Nathan and Zak cross the line first, with me and Jayne not far behind. Dennian walks Eric across moments later and hauls the snake off him. While Dennian puts the snake back in its crate, I check on Eric.

"You all right?" I touch his arm. He jumps and opens his eyes.

"Where's the snake?" He backs away from me.

"It's okay. Dennian put it away."

"It's over?" Eric rubs his hands over his arms.

"Yeah. You did good."

"I'm going to go sit down." Eric walks away and sits some distance from us, his arms wrapped around his middle. I turn back to the group. Trev frowns at Eric.

I go to sit on the grass where the snake lady packs up, but Trev directs us up a track. I stand, brush off the back of my pants, and walk between Nathan and Zak. Jayne pushes ahead, trying to get Dennian to speak.

"What do you think we have to do next?" Zak asks.

"Probably another fear." Nathan glances over at Eric. "Not sure if I'd be as brave about mine."

"Arrgg. I should have made something up. I didn't think they were going to put us through this."

"What's your fear, Zak?" I ask.

"Lightning." He shudders.

I glance up at the cloudless sky. "I think you're fine."

Up ahead, the rest of the group come to a stop. Three people wearing harnesses stand by the edge of a cliff. Nathan stops walking.

"Fear of heights – this is mine," he mutters.

I reach for his hand. It's cold and clammy.

"Come on. Eric managed the last one. We'll get you through this too."

Sara calls us over and Nathan follows meekly after me. He stops well back from the cliff. Zak walks up to the edge only to be halted by one of the tethered assistants placing a hand on his arm. Zak leans forward to peer over the drop. He whistles.

"Damn, that is high."

Nathan gulps beside me, his face draining to a sickly white. I squeeze his hand. Sara steps forward to give her spiel.

"This next challenge is abseiling down the cliff-face to a cave system where you can hike back up to the meeting point. I'll let these people fill you in on safety."

"Caves, don't like the sound of that," Guya mutters.

Sara steps aside and a fit young man steps forward to take her place.

"You'll each be given a harness and instructions on how to abseil. As the lady said, there's a cave system you need to reach. One of the instructors will be down there to assist. The cliff has a lip near the bottom. Do not go past this. There are sharp rocks below and if you fall they will kill you. Understood?"

Our group nods, some enthusiastically, others more nervously.

"Good. Go get your gear on."

Phil, Zak and Eric get kitted out first and while they set up on the cliff edge, Dennian helps Nathan into a harness. I'm about to join them when Trev steps over to the head instructor. I pause, bending to fiddle with my shoe fasteners while I listen.

"The last trial was boring. I need screams this time. These are meant to be their greatest fears," Trev says. "Show me terror or you're out of a job."

"It's rock climbing, not skydiving. Short of letting them free climb or dropping one of them, there won't be a whole lot more action than what you see here," the man replies.

I stand and collect my harness.

"Have you done this before?" One of the assistants asks as I join the boys.

"I've climbed small cliffs," I say.

"What on Terra for?" Nathan moans.

"Jayne helped me make a documentary on rock frogs. Most disappeared when they heard us coming though, so it wasn't very good."

Dennian laughs and the instructor turns to him. "Any experience?"

Dennian shrugs and I nudge him.

"Not with equipment," he says.

"Okay then, let's get you settled," the man says.

"I don't know if I can do this," Nathan says.

"Of course you can. I've had seven-year olds on this cliff," the man says.

Dennian places his hand on Nathan's shoulder. "Breathe," he says.

Nathan takes several deep breaths and the colour slowly returns to his face.

"Fear is in the mind," Dennian says. "It can be turned off."

"That easy?" Nathan asks.

"No. It takes training."

"Why aren't you scared of falling?" Nathan asks.

Dennian shrugs. "I've fallen before. Still here."

"How about Dennian goes first and I'll be right beside you the whole time?" I say.

"What's Dennian going to do? Catch me if I plummet to my death?"

"Yes," Dennian says.

"Promise? Because if I die, you'd have less competition," Nathan says.

111

"Cassie wouldn't want someone who let her friend die," Dennian says.

When the spotter indicates that the first three have reached the caves, Dennian and I guide Nathan to the edge of the cliff and the instructor clips us into the safety lines. Nathan's trembling returns as Dennian removes his hand from Nathan's arm and leans back into his rope, his feet resting on the cliff edge. I copy Dennian's position and wait for the instructor to help Nathan into position.

The equipment is simple – a single switch controls the stop and go. The longer you hold it on, the further you drop. Dennian leans further back and releases his switch, taking several controlled bounces down the cliff. The instructor pushes Nathan out. For a moment Nathan sinks lower, his legs bending as he refuses to take his feet from the edge. The instructor nudges Nathan's feet off and he drops several metres. I swing down beside him.

"That wasn't so bad now, was it?" I joke.

Nathan moans in response with his eyes closed and white knuckles clenched around his tether line.

"Keep moving!" The assistant above us shouts. Beside him, Guya and Rick wait for their turn. A pair of hover-cams zips around us.

"Can you take another jump?" I bounce across so I can reach out and place a hand on his trembling arm. He shakes his head.

"You just need to get down to the cave and it will be all over," I assure him.

Warmth spreads through my body, bringing a sensation of incredible calm. Nathan's breathing slows and his fingers ease from their cramped grip. I glance down at Dennian to see if he feels the same thing. His intense stare is focused solely on Nathan.

Nathan's hand creeps up to the switch. He hesitates for a few more moments before pressing it briefly. He drops jerkily and swings into the cliff face.

"Keep your feet on the rock and sit back like you're on a chair." I bounce down to his level.

Nathan gets his feet in position and even opens his eyes. Without looking up or down, he executes several small bounces down the cliff. I keep level with him.

"You're doing great…"

Something small and furry hits my shoulder and I shriek before realising it's a stuffed toy attached to a rope that's been thrown at us. Nathan freezes, his fingers turning white again as they grip the tether. Two more toys swing at us. Another reaches Dennian below us, the rope hitting my leg as it passes. I shake it off.

"Ignore it," I say to Nathan. The calm feeling has disappeared and with the hover-cam by my face, I want to be down at the cave already.

I'm afraid Nathan is going to hang there again, but he hits the switch and makes a series of sudden drops.

"Nathan, stop!" Dennian yells.

"I've got to get down. I've got to get down," Nathan mutters. He drops again.

"Stop. Ropes are tangled," Dennian calls out. I glance up to see one of the stuffed toys wrapped around Nathan's tether.

"Nathan. I need you to stop. I'll go up and untangle you." I switch the reverse on and begin ascending.

The sound of line whizzing through a switch, has me glancing down in time to see Dennian make a sudden extended drop. His hand remains on the switch as he drops towards the cliff lip.

I reach for the tangled ropes as Nathan makes another jump lower. The friction of Nathan's line descending past the other rope, slices through the tether like a knife. It rips through my hand, tearing skin as Nathan falls, the rope dropping in a loose coil after him. His arms flail as he opens his mouth in a silent scream.

Dennian lunges sideways, catching Nathan's wrist as he falls. Dennian's tether snaps taut, vibrating as it takes both their weight. Nathan screams as his shoulder twists into an odd position.

"Help! Help!" I yell up to the instructor above us.

I fumble to lower myself. My hand stings, slippery with blood and torn skin. A camera pod hovers between me and the boys.

On the cliff edge, people hurriedly haul the stray ropes clear while the instructor gets ready to descend. I'm halfway to the boys, when Dennian looks up past me and winces. He wraps his legs around Nathan and throws both hands towards the rock face as his tether snaps from their combined weight.

A scream rips through me as the pair disappear over the lip. I hang in my harness, frozen with indecision. The hover-cam drops past me and I'm about to curse the operator for their insensitivity, when it pulls up suddenly in my line of sight, slightly below the lip. I scurry down the rock face, banging my knees and elbows in my haste. I reach the lip moments later.

Dennian hangs to the underside, his fingers jammed in two sets of gouge marks on the otherwise smooth surface. Nathan has his legs and one arm wrapped tightly around Dennian. The arm Dennian caught him by, hangs loose by his side. I edge towards them carefully, keeping an eye on my own tether line.

114

"One of the instructors is coming," I say. "I should be able to hook you both to my line until he reaches us."

"Won't hold three." Dennian's voice is strained. "Clip Nathan to you."

"What about you?" I'm beside them now. My bloody hand keeps me off the rock face, while the other reaches between the two guys to find Nathan's harness clip.

"I'll be fine without the extra weight."

My hand brushes Dennian's hip as I fumble for Nathan's harness. To distract myself, I glance at Dennian's hands. His fingers are splayed across the gouges and I can't tell how he is still holding on to the cliff. The marks on the rock remind me of those on the face of the man from Dennian's fear drawing.

"Cassie." Dennian's words come out strained and I shake the thoughts from my mind. I grasp the broken tether line through the buckle. Nathan still hasn't moved.

I edge closer, careful not to bump Dennian and his precarious hold. I use my knees to brace myself against the rock, while I tie Nathan's tether through my buckle as close as possible. I give it a tug to check the hold.

"Nathan, I need you to let go of Dennian."

"Can't." Tears stream down Nathan's face, soaking the front of Dennian's shirt.

"Sure you can." I reach around and grab Nathan's good arm, twisting him to face me. Shards of rock fall from his hair when he moves. Losing his grip on Dennian, Nathan lunges for me. Our legs tangle and for a moment I'm terrified Dennian will fall, but his fingers remain locked into the gouges. I push away from him, taking Nathan with me.

Dennian's right hand slips from the rock face. His fingers brush over his broken tether line and the remaining rope falls to the ground. Once free of the tangled lines, Dennian swings his hand back up to the ledge and tucks his feet up. Using his toes as leverage, he climbs up over the lip. I hold my breath until he is over.

I change the switch back into ascension mode, but it struggles to edge our way up. The instructor appears above us and quickly hooks Nathan into a new safety line, but my knot has pulled tight and we can't free Nathan from my set-up. The two of us crab climb as we guide Nathan up and across to the cave entrance.

Nathan collapses to the ground grasping his shoulder the moment my feet hit solid rock. I tumble down on top of him trying to avoid his injury. The instructor pulls out a knife and cuts Nathan's broken tether. I roll away so Dennian and the instructor can pull Nathan away from the edge.

As adrenalin drains from my body, the throbbing of my shredded hand increases. I clutch the bloody appendage to my chest.

Several people run down from inside the cave with a stretcher and medical supplies. Jayne pushes past the guys to get to me.

"Oh my Governor Suri! I thought you were all going to die!" She squeezes the air from my body. My legs start to tremble and I sink back to the cave floor.

"Damn, that's a nasty dislocation." The instructor winces at Nathan moaning in pain.

The medical team descend on Nathan. One of them places a Pain Numb patch on Nathan's tongue while the other repositions his injured shoulder. With a sudden pop, Nathan's shoulder shifts back into place.

"Holy Twins, that hurt," Nathan curses, cradling his arm to his chest.

The medics check me next. One of them sprays something brown on the torn skin of my hand before wrapping a bandage over it. When they turn to Dennian, he waves them off. They turn their attention back to getting Nathan out of the cave.

"How are your hands?" I reach for Dennian. Tiny spots of red mark the tips of his fingers, but otherwise no one would be able to tell he fell down a cliff.

"I'm fine."

"Let me guess. Pain is also in the mind?" I say.

The corner of Dennian's mouth turns up and he reaches for my bandaged hand. He holds it loosely between his and the stinging stops immediately, replaced by tingling. I run my good hand through his hair to remove the tiny shards of rock stuck there.

"If everyone has had enough excitement for the day, we should get walking back up to the top," the instructor says.

I nod my head and Dennian, Jayne, and I follow him through a series of torch-lit caves leading back to the surface. Jayne remains unusually quiet as she walks by my side clutching my good hand.

We emerge into the sunlight to a vehicle waiting to transport Nathan and me to the medical facility to be checked over. A paramedic tries to get Dennian to go too, but he refuses. As he has no obvious injuries, he is allowed to stay behind.

Mum pushes over and presses me to her chest. Tears well in my eyes as the danger of the situation finally hits me. Trev jumps in the back of the vehicle with us, leaving no room for Jayne. She gives me another hug and then waves as we drive away.

At the medical facility, Nathan is taken off for a scan on his shoulder. Mum sits beside me as a doctor removes my bandage and uses a cloth to wipe down my hand.

"Good news," he says. "There's barely any damage to your hand. As long as you keep dirt off it, those grazes will be healed in a day or two."

"Grazes?" I say numbly. I look at my exposed hand. Sections of skin are red and chafed, but there's no hint of the torn skin and blood from the incident.

The doctor sprays a protective coating over my hand and we go wait for Nathan.

"Where's Dennian?" I step into the private waiting room and nearly walk into a hover-cam.

"Cassie, can you tell me how you felt watching the rope break today?" Trev asks.

"You've got to be kidding me?" I clench my fists and step forward. "Is this some kind of game to you? Nathan and Dennian could've died. I can't imagine that would have been good for your precious ratings."

I say several other things before Nathan appears with his arm in a sling. His face turns a sickly colour when asked to recount his experiences. I drop in a few curse words that will need to be edited out, before the medic from the caves appears. Between him and Mum, they usher me outside and Trev makes himself scarce.

Nathan sits beside me in the transport as we head back to the mansion. The others take a different vehicle to give me time to 'regain my composure'.

"I guess if I'm going to lose the competition and my place at SuriTech, it may as well be to someone who can keep their promises," Nathan says.

"What?" My mind was back at the cliff face.

118

"Dennian promised to catch me if I fell," Nathan replies. I reach out and squeeze the hand of his good side.

"Do you think there's a way for us to survive this program without ending up in a worse situation than we were previously?" I ask, but Nathan doesn't have the answer either.

The elimination is a sombre affair that evening. My only consolation is Dennian's name is listed on the second card. Saving Nathan's life must have been considered interesting enough to keep him around a little longer.

When I reach the final card, I struggle to read out the name. These choices aren't mine. How many lives will be damaged in this process? A lump forms in my throat as I look up at Rick and Guya waiting for the final name. My pause isn't staged this time.

"Rick," I finally say. Below the camera frame of our faces, I scrunch his name card into a little ball and toss it to the floor. I tune out his words and Sara's standard lines.

"I'm sorry," I say when Guya steps forward to say goodbye. I flee the room before the tears start to fall.

Intruders

Two days later, Trev summons Jayne, Mum and me into the garden where Sara waits for us. I glance at the others, but Jayne shrugs and Mum is focused on Sara, a small frown creasing her brow. I force a smile onto my face, but my eyes are blank and my body numb.

"Cassie, I have a surprise for you." Sara pauses while the cameras zoom in on our faces. I focus on holding my expression while I wait for her to continue. "Let me introduce you to the Intruders."

"What?" My smile drops from my face.

"Who are these people?" Mum interrupts. "Not more actors or random people off the street, I hope. Cassie is already infatuated with that mute boy."

"He can talk, he chooses not to and he is way more interesting than the other idiots that have been picked for me," I snap.

"Everyone needs to calm down. Mrs Brooke, the young men being introduced to Cassie today are from three noble families of the Tri-System. They are all potential finalists. Now if you can get ready again, the first car is here. Smile," she says.

I shake myself, pull my shoulders back, and try to look happy about meeting whoever is about to show up. Mum and Jayne take up positions several steps behind me as a tall, blue-eyed, dark haired man strides towards us.

"Prince Stev, from the Atlas System, is the son of Governor's Delegate, Glar Shan," Sara announces.

Stev strides up the walkway to place an air kiss near my cheek. A pair of Peace Keepers with the Atlas trident mark on the shoulders of their uniforms, loiter at the edge of the camera scene.

"Hi, I'm Stev, I'm twenty-one years old and one day I'll be King of Atlas."

"Impressive," I say although my voice lacks enthusiasm.

"Not as impressive as my gift to you." Stev reaches into a pocket of a coat of wool so fine Eric is likely to be distracted all evening. Stev pulls out a dull brown rock and drops it into my hand. "This is an extremely rare dragon stone. The stones were magicked by the dragons to store energy. They were given as gifts to important Atlas nobles and now I offer it to you."

The rock is twice the size of the one Dennian gave me but without the iridescent colour.

"Magicked by dragons?" I raise an eyebrow. "Why is it dull?"

"All its power has dissipated, but it's still a valuable stone. I can tell you the entire history at the party, save you being bored further by your current company in this little house."

I bite my tongue and allow him to continue as I slip the rock into my pocket. Stev walks inside after a brief introduction to Jayne and Mum. I turn around to watch the interaction.

"He is sooo hot!" Jayne hisses at me after he walks off.

"What happened to people from Atlas not marrying outside their race?" I say.

"Don't be judgemental, Cassie. You have lovely blue eyes and your hair is almost dark enough to be Atlasian. Now turn back around so we can meet the other two," Mum says.

I frown at her before turning back to Sara. When I'm smiling again, she introduces the next man.

"Farray hails from a noble family of the Triade System," Sara says as the next young man arrives. His muscular bulk fills the traditional black and yellow robes of Triade.

"Good Morn, I am Lord Farray. You are here to serve me. We will be much happy," he says in broken Common.

"Lovely to meet you," I say.

"Yes." He moves off. Whatever he says next has Jayne in giggles and him looking confused. Trev waves him onto the house to meet the other men.

"Last but not least is Prince Saul of Terra from the Main Continent. His father is in the city with the local delegation for the meetings with Governor Suri," Sara says.

Saul approaches in a crisp white suit.

"Hi, I'm Saul, I'm nineteen years old and I'm a legal trainee." He glances at me briefly and then studies the garden surrounding us.

"Great to meet you." I suspect Trev picked up on the sarcasm in my voice, but he doesn't make me repeat the scene, so maybe Saul isn't a serious contender or Trev still feels guilty about the abseiling incident.

"I'll see you inside," I add to appease him anyway.

"Yes, I'm looking forward to meeting the other men." He flashes me a smile and walks past to meet Mum and Jayne.

I wait for a few minutes in the garden for the guys to size each other up. When Trev gives me the signal, I make my way into the sitting room.

122

I pause on the threshold and scan the room. Nathan sits on his own with his arm in a sling. I head over to him and slide into the vacant seat.

"Not happy with the current quality of candidates?" Nathan jokes.

"I didn't ask for more." I pull a face. "How's the arm?"

"Good, actually. The med team say I have to keep it in the sling, but Dennian put his hand on my shoulder earlier and it didn't even hurt. Not sure how I'll ever make it up to him for saving my life."

"Where is he?" I scan the room.

Zak tries to have a conversation with Farray, but the newcomer ignores him, choosing to stare moodily at the carpet. Stev stands in a group with a drink in his hand.

I sweep the room, finally landing on Dennian outside the camera range, loitering behind a large plant. His eyes are fixed on the group standing together.

"I should go check on him," I say.

I sidle over to Dennian. "Hiding, that seems a little introverted even for you."

He glances at me then back at the group across the room. I slip the rock from my pocket and hold it up for Dennian to see.

"One of the new guys gave me this. He said it's a dragon stone, but it looks nothing like the one you gave me."

Dennian reaches out a hand to the stone, but stops before touching it. His expression darkens.

"Dragon stones turn dull if taken from the true owner. Stev must have stolen this one during the Keeper's anniversary celebrations."

"What should I do with it? Won't the Keeper be mad?" I hold the rock away from me.

Dennian closes my other hand around it. "Keep it. It may be useful one day."

"What are you doing hiding over here?" Mum walks over to us. She grabs my arm and steers me away from Dennian as though she hasn't seen him standing there. "Come meet Saul," she says.

I slip the rock back into my pocket and take a seat beside Saul who watches the room's occupants with interest. Mum pulls over a spare armchair.

"So, Saul, you're a prince? Do you have any siblings?" Mum asks.

"Two younger sisters." Saul takes a sip of his drink then looks at me. "You know Stev isn't a real prince?"

"What do you mean?" I glance over at the black-haired intruder.

"He's the current king's nephew. He had four cousins, but they all died of unknown causes according to my father. Around here, Stev is known as the Faux Prince."

"You must know a lot about the ruling families of the Tri-System," Mum says.

Saul nods his head and points to Farray. "Not sure why he's here though. His family's been invited to the meetings with Governor Suri, but they've never put in an appearance before. My father says they didn't accept UFHaIL and thought the Warlords were a better option for the universe."

"Have you ever met the governor?" I ask.

"Nah. It's a big universe. They don't stop by our little planet very often. Enough of dull politics. Tell me which of these strapping young men have caught your eye?"

My eyes flicker over to Dennian's hiding place. He hasn't moved, but his eyes follow Stev. The Atlas prince strolls away from his group, having caught sight of the artwork pinned along the wall.

"What's with these?" Stev peers at each drawing.

"They're the things we fear." Nathan rubs a thumb against his shoulder.

"Bonus for me. Know thy enemies' fear." Stev smirks. "I hope Cassie wants her husband to have artistic skill because you're all terrible." He stops in front of Dennian's picture and laughs.

"Who's afraid of Takarna?" Stev turns to look at us.

Dennian moves suddenly, bolting towards the door, but Trev steps into the doorway blocking the escape. Dennian stops, his back to the room, as Rick points towards him. Stev stalks toward Dennian with the smirk still on his face.

"What could possibly make someone afraid of the Keeper of the Dragon Temple?" Stev asks.

Dennian curls his fingers into the side of his legs, his back still to us.

"Look at me when I'm speaking to you!"

"Leave Dennian alone." I stand up at Stev's bellow, but Mum jerks me back into my seat. Saul leans forward to watch the interaction.

"Dennian?" Stev laughs. "Do you know what your name means in my language, *Orphan Nobody*?"

Dennian turns around after a prod from Trev. Stev's eyes settle on Dennian, who keeps his gaze on the floor, his hands curled by his side. Stev sticks his face right up into Dennian's – an easy thing to do considering they are both a similar height and build.

"Don't worry, a nobody like you is unlikely to ever meet Governor Suri's chief advisor."

"What's that supposed to mean?" I stand up again and step out of Mum's reach.

"No offence, darling. The Keeper is almost always picked from Atlas. Only those from noble Atlas families and the governor's delegation ever meet him. I met him at his 110th anniversary as Keeper of the Dragon Temple." Stev scans the room to see who is impressed by that. "Two of my uncles have been selected to train as Takarna's apprentices."

Dennian darts past Trevor and disappears into the garden.

*

The day begins with me meeting Dennian, Saul, Rick, Phil, and Farray at an offsite location.

"Know what we're doing today?" Phil eyes the non-descript, grey bunker at the end of the hall with suspicion.

"It can't be too physical in this outfit." I indicate the flowing sleeves of my green full-length dress.

"I bet it's more fears." Phil wraps his arms around his body and gives a mock shudder.

"There are five of us, not counting Cassie. They better not makes us go through everyone's fears," Rick says.

"Don't know why we're putting ourselves through this," Saul says. "It's not like we can win against Faux Prince Stev with his uncle to become the Keeper and his father a delegate."

"His uncles are dead." Dennian leans against a wall of the room we wait in. They're the first words he's spoken since he ran out on us last night.

"How do you know?" Rick demands.

"All Takarna's apprentices have died." Dennian stares off into the distance.

"How do you know?" Saul asks.

"Takarna lives until someone replaces him. He kills them to live longer." Dennian shrugs.

"You could get in a lot of trouble for saying things like that." Saul walks up to Dennian and stares into his face. Dennian stares back.

"Interesting," Saul says. "You're not afraid of me, so your problem with Stev isn't about royalty. Do you have an issue with people from Atlas? I wouldn't be bothered if you did. I'm not fond of the snobby bastards myself."

Saul places a hand on Dennian's arm and Dennian jerks away from the contact.

"Ready for the next challenge?" Trev step into the room followed by Sara.

"Your challenges are weaklings to me." Farray thumps his chest.

"Anyone else want to see this guy crying in a corner?" Phil mutters.

Trev leads us into the bunker room and makes the guys stand in a loose semi-circle around me. The space is not much bigger than the luxurious bathrooms at the mansion. The walls and floor are smooth except for four small circular indents by the doorway. Sara steps into the doorway followed by three hover-cams and Trev steps out of view.

"Today is a team challenge. In each scenario, you have a token to retrieve and place in a slot. This door will only reopen when all four tokens are in place," Sara says.

She steps out of the room leaving the hover-cams with us as the door slides closed. There's no handle or opening device on our side and I can't see the door seams once it's closed.

A beeping sound has me looking up as hundreds of spiders drop down on top of us. Someone screams. I think it might be Rick, but I'm too busy trying to flick the spiders from my face to see. The spiders' legs tangle in my hair and dress as I try to shake them loose.

"Get them off me!" Rick shrieks.

He backs into a corner and stomps his feet at any spider even looking in his direction. "You're not paying me enough to do this crap!" he shouts at the nearest camera.

"Can anyone see the token?" Saul calls out, ignoring the few spiders crawling over him. Dennian stands perfectly still with his eyes closed as spiders cling to his clothes. Farray brushes furiously at his hair.

"There." Dennian opens his eyes and points to a corner where dozens of spiders scurry around.

"Where?" I creep cautiously towards them.

"It's tied to one of the large ones," Dennian says.

"You mean we have to touch it?" Phil's voice comes out high pitched.

"There it is!" I lunge towards a large spider with something round and black on its back, but it scurries away.

"Where did it go?" Saul asks. Dennian points above our heads.

"Kllrarn it!" Phil curses. "How are we meant to get it now?"

"Cassie's the lightest. Two of us can lift her up and she can grab the thing," Saul suggests.

"I'm also the one in a dress and heels."

128

"Tuck your skirt up. We won't look – promise," Saul says. "Want to get up close and personal, good-looking?"

Dennian steps back at Saul's look.

"Fine, Phil it is then," Saul huffs.

The two boys get into position while I pull my shoes off. Dennian reaches out and takes them from my hand. I tuck my long skirt up and step onto Saul and Phil's thighs.

They wrap their arms behind me so I don't wobble, but the spider is just out of reach. At least it hasn't scurried away while we got into position.

"Now what?" Phil asks.

One of my shoes flies over my head, hitting the wall slightly above the spider we're after. The critter drops suddenly and I lunge forward with my hands out.

"Ah!" Saul squeaks as I topple forward.

The spider lands in my hands as something snags the back of my dress slowing my fall. A seam rips as I land lightly on my shoulder with Saul, Phil, and Dennian landing on top of me. Dennian releases his grip on my clothing and crawls off me.

"Did you get it?" Saul asks.

I open my cupped hands to find the spider is still alive after our fall. I quickly untie the cloth fastening around him, grabbing the token and dropping him to the ground. The spider scurries away as I weave my way through the critters to the door and slot the token in place.

A small gap appears at floor level and the spiders scurry away.

"Arg!" Rick brushes his hands over his body in case there are any left.

As the last spider disappears, the sound of wings begins. A small square box is lowered towards us, stopping just out of reach. Bats hang from it, while others fly around the room.

"Hell, no!" Saul grabs Dennian's shirt and backs them up against a wall, using Dennian to shield him from the airborne creatures.

"I take it this is your fear, Saul?" I look up at the device above our heads. "Lift me up to the box, Phil."

Phil bends down so I can climb onto his shoulder. I grip his head as we wobble upright.

"Step to the left," I instruct.

We stagger sideways and I grab the edge of the box. Bats go everywhere, disturbed by the motion. I shriek as one flies into my face. Behind me something hits the floor. I twist around to see Saul has dropped to the floor still holding the back of Dennian's shirt. The two boys have ended up in a heap on the floor as Saul tries to avoid the bats.

I turn my attention back to the box. It has handles on either side that look like they need to be held in to open the box.

When I try to press the handle in, it takes both hands. I can't do both sides at the same time.

"This looks like it will need a few of us to open," I say. "Rick, Farray, get over here."

"I carry no one," Farray says.

"Well, I can't hold you up, you great monster," Rick retorts.

Dennian pries Saul's hands from his clothing and joins us. With a lot of grunting and a few curse words, Rick gets under one side of Farray with Dennian supporting the other side.

"Great look, Cassie," Rick grins at my bare legs and skirt hitched up around Phil's ears.

"Just hold the handle in," I growl at Farray.

We both manage to hold them in at the same time and a token falls out of the bottom, rolling along the floor until it stops at Saul's feet.

Rick drops Farray on the floor, while Phil lowers me a little more gently. I manage to dismount without flashing my underwear at Rick.

Dennian grabs the token and places it in the wall. The instant it's in place, a load of snow dumps on us. I gasp at the sudden chill.

I shake myself only to discover I'm chest deep in the stuff. Several flakes sneak down the inside of my dress sending icy trickles down my spine. Screams start from the location I last saw Farray, as Dennian and Saul emerge above the snow.

I move towards the noise as Dennian throws himself in the same direction. He reaches Farray's location first and drags him to his feet.

"Help! I die not willingly!" Farray wails.

"It's just snow," I say through chattering teeth. My thin dress doesn't provide much protection from the cold.

"I freeze in death." Farray lunges at Dennian as though he can climb onto his shoulders. Dennian falls backwards and disappears under the snow.

"Dennian!" I wade towards him.

Farray grabs at me, but Saul and Phil manage to restrain him. Dennian surfaces holding a white token in his hand.

"Found it," he says

"Are you going to put it in the wall?' Rick demands. "I want to get the hell out of here."

"What's Phil fear?" Dennian asks. Phil's face pales as he continues to hold a struggling Farray.

"Just put the thing in the wall," Saul demands.

"Phil's fear is last. I want to know what to expect," Dennian says.

"What about you? You haven't had a fear yet," Phil replies.

"They haven't worked out mine." Dennian glances at where the door should be.

"Drowning," Phil mumbles.

"What?" I ask.

"I can't swim." Phil shakes uncontrollably. He releases his grip on Farray who throws an elbow at Saul. The royal yelps and backs away.

"So are we expecting water next?" Saul holds his nose. "If the token is underwater, we'll need someone who's comfortable underwater to search for it."

"Me," Dennian says.

"All right. Dennian gets the token and the rest of us keep Phil afloat," Saul says.

I make my way towards Phil and Saul as Dennian heads towards the indents in the wall. I rub my chilled arms as I wait.

"You're on your own." Rick backs away from us.

Dennian places the second-last token in its slot. A blast of hot air passes over us, scorching my face while leaving me shivering in the quickly melting snow. Cold water falls like rain from above and Phil hunches up beside me. I huddle next to him and Saul for warmth.

The lights go out as the rain increases to a torrential downpour. The water swirls, tangling my legs in my skirt and making it heavy, as Phil clutches my arm.

A flash of artificial lightning reveals Dennian ducking beneath the now waist-deep water. Splashes make me jump as fish fall from above us. They bump into our legs as the water rises quickly to my chest. My heart rate increases.

"Dennian had better not take long to find that token," Saul shouts over the sounds in the room. Lightning flashes again. Rick and Farray huddle against a wall, but I can't see Dennian.

"Has he come up yet?" I yell.

"I can't see," Saul replies.

My feet lose their grip on the floor and my dress drags me under the water. For a moment Phil still has hold of my arm and then I'm swept away in the swirling water. A fish hits me in the face before I resurface briefly. I cough up the water I swallowed.

I kick my legs to try to stay afloat in the rising water, but my skirt tangles around my legs dragging me under again. I've lost sight of the guys in the dark.

I didn't get a proper breath before going under. I fight my way back to the surface, but I don't know what direction is up anymore. I tug at the laces on the back of my dress, but I'm tied in tightly and can't rid myself of the weight. The pressure increases on my lungs as the last of my air escapes.

I surface briefly, but as I snort the water from my stinging nostrils, I'm dragged under again. I fight the water and my dress in a panicked frenzy. My head aches as I fight against breathing in the turbulent water.

Hands grab at me. Lips press against mine and air fills my lungs again. I can't see Dennian in the dark water, but calm flows through me. He runs a hand down my back and my dress loosens. With a final breath into my lungs, he shoves me up to the surface.

My dress slips from my body as I break the surface of the churning water. I cough up water and wipe a hand over my eyes, struggling to see through my wet lashes. Shivers rack my body as I suck in deep breaths.

The rain has stopped, halting the rise of the water. Lightning illuminates several of the guys clinging to the box hanging from the ceiling after the bat challenge. I tread water, spinning in a circle searching for Dennian.

"Has anyone got the token?" I think the voice belongs to Saul, but I'm not sure.

If anyone had an answer, it's drowned out by a gurgling suction sound. The water pulls at me and I draw in a breath before going under once more. My arms flail as I fight the suction. Fish hit me as they're sucked away. Water fills my ears and someone's leg hits my side. My feet connect briefly with the floor before they're pulled out from under me again.

The rush of swirling water continues and I'm dragged towards a wall. I have no idea how long I've been under the water, but I need to take a breath. I break the surface before I hit a wall with a thud and I'm sucked down to the floor.

My fingers scrabble at the gap in the floor that opened for the spiders. My lungs burn, but I can't break the suction holding me to the floor. I'm going to die on a stupid reality tele-program.

Hands reach out, pulling me upright. The water has receded to chest height and I gasp for air. Several bodies slam into us and we all go under again.

I press against the wall and struggle to my feet as Dennian pulls Phil up. The water is now waist height

134

and the lights flicker back on. My whole body trembles and I can't tell if the water running down my face is from my dripping hair or tears.

I do a head count as we press against the wall for balance, water swirling around our legs. Saul, Rick, and Farray stagger to their feet beside us.

I shake my wet hair from my face as my dress washes up against my legs. I clutch it to my body. My fingers brush against the ends of the laces that had held me into the dress, now cleanly sliced through.

Phil sinks to the floor and cries. Beside him, Rick coughs up water, thankfully too distracted to notice I'm in my underwear. My legs give way and my bare legs connect with the cold wet concrete floor.

Dennian's hand brushes my arm, his eyes asking if I'm okay. I nod my head, although I'm not really sure if I am. Dennian wraps his arms around my shivering body.

"Is Phil okay?" My words are muffled against Dennian's soaking shirt.

"He's alive, but I might have to make him forget too." Dennian brushes his thumb against my cheek. Fatigue washes over me. I want to lie down. The fear of the near drowning is becoming fuzzier in my mind.

The last of the water drains away, leaving six of us dripping in the tiny room with four tokens stuck in the wall. I'm not sure if I fall asleep or not, but when I open my eyes I'm alert again and no longer cold. Dennian places a butterfly kiss against my forehead and turns his attention to Phil who rocks quietly back and forth. The door slides open.

"Congratulations on great teamwork," Sara says from the dry corridor.

Just out of camera sight, crew stand by with blankets, hopefully so we can get dry and warm. Trev lurks in the corridor and anger washes over me. I snatch a towelling robe from an outstretched hand, wrap it around my wet, nearly-naked body and confront the director.

"Are you trying to kill us?" My voice is surprisingly calm.

"We had you monitored the whole time," Trev says.

"I nearly drowned!" My voice rises this time.

"But you didn't and we got great footage."

I clench my fist, but Dennian appears behind me and grabs my arm.

"Transports will be here in five minutes," Trev calls out as he makes his escape.

Rick and Farray bolt for the door wrapped in their towels, but Saul steps in front of Dennian before we can follow out into the sunshine.

"I can't work you out," Saul says to Dennian. "The guys say you're a researcher, but I've seen Peace Keepers with less talent than you. Who do you really work for?"

"Is there a problem?" I ask when Dennian refuses to speak.

"My point is, last night our friend Stev talked incessantly about how great he is and about his father's role in the Government as though he's already won this competition."

Saul pauses to glance at me before addressing Dennian again.

"I don't like people like that to get their way. You seem to have your own special little skills and I suspect you may have your own government connections – you certainly know who Stev's family are, don't you, Dennian? What I don't get is how someone who can calmly go through four of our greatest fears completely unruffled while saving our lives, would back down to an upstart like Stev. I think you have the best chance of putting the Faux Prince back in his place and I'm willing to back you on that."

Beside us, Phil gives a thoughtful nod. His arms are still wrapped around his body, but his eyes have lost the haunted look they held moments earlier. Dennian's gaze rests on each of us briefly before he pushes past for the door.

"I'll let you think about it, shall I?" Saul calls after him.

The ride back to the mansion is quiet. I try to remove the water from my ears, but sounds remain muffled. I remember struggling to breathe in the water, but it already feels like it happened a long time ago. Occasionally Rick glances over at my bare legs, but even he stays quiet about my state of undress.

The men are dropped off at their wing of the house before the vehicle pulls up at the front steps for me to exit. I head straight to the living room.

"What on Terra happened to you?" Jayne lifts a damp strand of hair from my face before pulling a face wipe from a pocket and sets about removing the remains of my makeup.

"They nearly drowned us! That's what happened!"

"It was only meant to be another fear challenge." Mum steps forward to check that I'm still in one piece.

"The first fear challenge went so well, you thought I'd be fine with another one?"

"Trev said it would be perfectly safe." A slight wobble enters Mum's voice as she takes in my damp towelling robe over my equally damp underwear.

"Trev wants the highest tele-program ratings. If Dennian wasn't here, I'd be marrying the last man left alive." My voice rises as tears start to form again. Jayne wraps me in a hug and Mum wipes away one of my tears.

"I'll go speak to Trev." Mum frowns at the door.

"There's no point," I say. "He won't listen."

"Pity you can't sell an expose to a rival channel," Jayne says.

I stare at her. "Guya left me his hover-cam. What if I can film something of value? Give us a back-up plan in case Trev tries something else?"

"We signed a contract," Mum says. "If we don't do as directed, it'll all be for nothing."

"What if I earned enough credits that we didn't need this contract?" I say.

Mum nods her head. "I'll see what I can do. This show was never meant to put you in danger, Cassie." She gives me a brief hug and leaves the room.

I pace my bedroom until late that night in an effort to tire myself sufficiently to keep the dreams at bay. They come for me anyway once I've slipped beneath the covers and closed my eyes.

The nightmares try to take hold of me, dragging me beneath the dark surface of the churning water, but every time the panic rises in my chest, Dennian is there reaching for me. He presses his lips to mine and my weighty dress slips from my body leaving me pressed against Dennian's chest, clad only in my underwear. Heat rises through me and I eventually drift into a restless but dream-free sleep.

*

"Today we'll be playing a quiz. In honour of Governor Suri's visit, the questions will have an interplanetary theme."

Sara stands in front of the men with small tiles under her feet to prevent the heels of her shoes sinking into the lush grass. Mum, Jayne, and I stand to one side. I'm the only one in flats.

"Take your places," Sara says.

Several of Trev's assistants step in to position us in the garden. Sara, Jayne, and Mum remain standing on their little squares. I end up perpendicular to Sara and facing the men in their row. Finally an assistant hands me and the guys a Touch Slate each. Trev darts around checking our positions.

"Ready, and smile," he calls out as he steps out of scene.

"The rules are simple," Sara says. "I will ask a question and you each write the answer on your Slate. Men, if you get a correct answer, you can take a step towards Cassie. Cassie, if your answer is wrong, you take a step backwards. Ready for the first question?"

"Yes," we all say at different times.

"Cut! I need you all to speak together," Trev calls out. "Take it from the question, Sara."

"Are you ready for the first question?" Sara smiles at us.

"Yes," we say at roughly the same time.

"What astronomical event will occur this week?" Sara asks.

I use my finger to write 'creation of black hole' on the screen. I look up to see if everyone else has finished.

"Show your answers," Sara says.

139

Dennian, Nathan, and Stev have all written the 'creation of Lordinia Black Hole'. Two others have written the same as me. We all step forward.

We continue with questions about the meeting with Governor Suri and when the last ones occurred. I get some answers right from watching the newscasts. Twice I have to make a small step backwards. Stev, Saul, Nathan, and Dennian consistently get the answers correct.

"Who is the most powerful person in the universe?" Sara asks.

For a moment I hesitate, about to write Governor Suri, but maybe their adviser is the correct answer. I write 'The Keeper' on my Slate. I look up to see Nathan has written the same thing and Stev wrote Takarna. Dennian, along with the others have written Governor Suri.

"The correct answer is…the Keeper." Sara pauses, "Stev and Nathan may step forward."

"Takarna is only a conduit for knowledge from the dragons Aurum and Argentum. Governor Suri makes the decisions," Dennian says.

"Don't be a sore loser, Nobody," Stev says. "If Governor Suri and Takarna had to fight to the death, Takarna would survive."

"Only because Takarna can't die until an apprentice replaces him," Dennian replies. The hover-cams zoom in closer to capture the argument. Sara stays quiet to let it play out.

"He can't die, so we're right and you're wrong," Stev says.

"If I'm wrong, how did Takarna lose his hand?"

My mouth drops open as Stev takes a step towards Dennian with his fists clenched by his sides. Nathan, several paces behind the lead three, moves to block Stev's path. Trev waves frantically at Sara.

"The answer I have recorded stands. Moving onto the next question," she pauses for Stev and Nathan to step back into place. "Every Keeper of the Dragon Temple has been descendant from which legendary figure?"

I glance at the guys, but only Stev and Dennian are writing. Everyone else looks at each other and shrugs.

"That was a difficult one. Stev would you like to share the answer?" Sara says.

"That would be my ancestor, Mellakai the Dragon Slayer." Stev flips his Slate around to show the words. Dennian has also written Mellakai.

"Why would a relative of a dragon slayer be picked as guardian of the Dragon Temple?" I ask.

"That would be a family secret. I'll tell you once we're married." Stev winks at me.

"Mellakai drank the blood of the dragons he killed to gain their powers," Dennian says.

"Shut up, Nobody! He did no such thing!" Stev says.

"I don't understand," I say.

Dennian locks eyes with Stev. "The Keeper mimics dragon skills. The dragon blood makes Mellakai's descendants more likely to succeed as Keeper."

"Final question is worth triple points and the winner gets to pick who goes on the next group date," Sara interrupts.

Stev, Nathan, and Dennian are all within three steps of me. I meet Dennian's eyes and he smiles reassuringly back at me. A moment later, the smile slips from his face and his eyes go blank. He looks down and moves his finger rapidly over the screen.

"Where might I find Mellakai's sword, Slayer?" Sara asks.

Dennian's hand still moves over the Slate. If I get the question wrong, I'll be out of Nathan's reach. Stev knows a lot about the guy so I write 'Atlas' on the screen and hope for the best.

"Show us your answers," Sara says.

Nathan has also written 'Atlas' while Stev writes 'Governor Suri has it'. Dennian is still drawing. I take a step forward to peer at what is on the screen as both the guys either side of him do the same. He's drawn a medallion made up of connected mythical creatures.

"Freak!" Stev grabs the screen jerking Dennian out of his trance. Dennian grabs it back, swiping his hand over the image to clear it.

"As Dennian hasn't answered, Stev wins," Sara declares. "You have until tomorrow morning to pick another two guys to go on the group date with Cassie."

I try to catch Dennian's eye, but he won't look at me. He leaves as soon as they are dismissed while I'm held back to discuss the quiz with a camera.

Keep Silent

Dennian – age six

The frog leapt onto my palm and I stared into its eyes. He smelled like algae and damp places. I closed my eyes and concentrated. His thoughts were simple, revolving around where to find the tastiest insects and the hollow tree branch he found that amplified his singing in a way he was sure would attract the females.

A hand grabbed my shoulder and I leapt to my feet, tensed to run. The scent of pepper and decay filled my nose. I should have known my trainer was near if I hadn't been so focused on my little frog.

Master Carlen released me and seized the frog that had leapt to the ground when I jumped. He smashed his hands together, squishing the frog between them. My eyes opened wide as goo dripped from his fingers. I could no longer hear the frog's thoughts.

I waited for him to make it a lesson – how to put a creature back together. Master Carlen never missed a chance to show how powerful he was. But he didn't. He shook the frog bits from his palm and it splattered across the grass, all the life gone. I edged a step backwards and placed a hand on my rolling stomach.

"How dare you speak to Governor Suri!" Master Carlen grabbed my shoulders and shook me until my teeth knocked together and I bit my tongue. A metallic tang flooded my mouth.

His unprotected mind swamped my own. His thoughts swirled in a chaotic tornado, never quite settling on one thought or action. Aurumargent whispered into his mind, urging him to release me, but he didn't notice.

"I didn't know who she was," I whimpered.

His thoughts gained focus for a moment. The new Governor Suri came to our island. Master Carlen was caught by surprise by her appearance. He had known Governor Aden Suri was dying but didn't know there was a daughter.

"The portal is closed. Who else did you think would be arriving on our island, stupid little boy?" he hissed.

"I thought she was the dragon."

"What dragon?" Confusion swirled around fury and his thoughts skipped again. I pulled back, shielding my mind from his before they made me sick.

"The little blue one that came to Aurumargent's temple several suns ago," I stammered. Sapphia – Aurumargent had called her Sapphia and spoken directly to her.

I hadn't meant to speak to the governor – that was Master Carlen's job. I'd only wanted to know if she was the one I'd seen at the temple who made me promise not to say the other dragon name. Her scent had been a mix of the black from fire and little purple flowers, same as Sapphia. I wanted her to be the dragon so she could save me. If the dragons returned, I didn't need to be here and I could live with the tigers again.

"Useless child! Can you not tell the difference between a large scaly creature and a thin-skinned human?" Master Carlen shook me again. "The dragons are dead. They are never coming back."

"But...but we're meant to wait here...look after the temple, until they return." I blinked back tears forming in my eyes.

144

"No." Master Carlen's eyes flashed with a crazed light. "*I* am meant to wait here. And I will live forever, because the dragons will never return."

I shrunk back from his maniacal laugh, but his fingers dug into my shoulders preventing my escape. He glanced up over my head to where the satellite planet of Atlas hung in the sky and then grinned at me. The fabric of existence tore open and we tumbled into the dark nothingness.

It lasted a fraction of a moment, but my insides clenched when I landed on the undergrowth at the edge of the forest. I lifted my head. In the distance, Atlia City lay beside the ocean. Between the city and us sat the grassy hill of the Children's Cemetery.

Master Carlen grabbed my wrists and dragged me towards the headstones. I sucked in a deep breath. The smell of decay and pepper almost masked that of the ocean and the faint warm fur scent from the forest.

Master Carlen threw me down in the dirt by my headstone – the one with my other name on it. Old flowers littered the ground around me. There would be freshly cut ones tomorrow.

Master Carlen waved his hand and the stone covering the grave slid to one side. He pushed me and I tumbled into the hole. I twisted onto my back in time to see Master Carlen wave his hand again. The stone slid back into place and blocked out the sun.

I screamed at the top of my lungs and beat my fists against my stone coffin, but other than the sounds I made and the occasional scuttling insect, I was in complete silence.

I stopped when I became too hoarse to continue. I flopped back onto the stone floor and cried for a long time. The air became heavy as I lay in the cold, damp darkness of my grave.

My name was on the stone above me. This was where I belonged. The realisation brought on fresh tears. I didn't stop until the air began to run out. I tried to slow my breathing – small, shallow breaths. Dizziness overcame me.

I slipped into unconsciousness.

*

A bright light appeared and I drifted towards it. I had no recollection of why or how I arrived here. I narrowed my eyes against the light.

The tunnel led towards a brightly lit room. Hidden doors shimmered at the edge of the light. I reached towards one, but my fingertips tingled against an invisible barrier before I could touch the next door. It was as though each door led to an identical corridor all taking up the same space as every other corridor but never quite interacting. Someone called me, the voice somehow familiar.

"Tarla, you're not meant to be here. You need to go back." The woman's shimmering silver gown clung to her body like scales. Her yellow eyes narrowed into slits like those of the Temple Tigers. She took my arm and led me back through the door. I fell into darkness.

*

The stone grated above me. I wasn't sure when I'd regained consciousness. Maybe it was only in that moment. I drew in a deep breath of fresh air but was too terrified to move. Decay and pepper mixed with a dozen tiger scents.

My hand flew to the back of my neck. My fingers clawed at the slightly raised pattern of my tattoo. I'd hoped death would remove it from me. I was still trapped, unable to run from Master Carlen.

A hand reached down and dragged me from my tomb, tossing me to the ground beside the next headstone. Fresh tiger prints circled the graves. I kept my head down as my fingers stretched out into the dirt, smearing Lucei's tiny paw prints, before Master Carlen noticed they morphed into footprints.

My heart pounded in my chest, but several tigers loitered by the forest edge, watching over me. Master Carlen leaned down, putting his face close to mine.

"You're lucky I'm looking out for you. If you ever speak again, I will return you to your parents." He jerks my face towards the palace at the edge of the city. "You wouldn't want to face the same fate as your brother, now would you?"

He forced my head back to the headstone beside mine. Zeth's name filled my vision.

Single Dates

It's late afternoon by the time Stev, Phil, Zak, and I return from our dance instruction class. Stev's dance style is unique and I struggled to follow the movements he expected of me, possibly because I kept trying to put more distance between us. Phil has no concept of rhythm, and Zak has sweaty hands.

As the day wore on and my frustration grew, Trev made me repeat more and more takes. I'm not even talking to the guys on the way back to the mansion and the camera control man turns the cameras off for now.

When we arrive back at the mansion, I storm off to my room where I get half an hour of privacy before Lori and Carter show up to prepare me for the evening party.

Mum knocks on my door as they put the finishing touches in place. She ignores the crew as they pack up and leave. Mum closes the door once they depart.

"I spoke with the other network," she says when we're alone.

"What did they say?"

She pauses for a moment. "They're not interested in an expose on this show..."

I sink back into the chair, my insides twisting as my backup plan vanishes.

"But I told them you like to make animal documentaries. They said they'd be interested in a deal if you got footage of Temple Tigers."

My mouth drops open. "How am I meant to do that? They're native to Atlas..." I trail off.

Trevor has mentioned I will meet the families of the final four guys. I've never been to Atlas, but I've heard the faster vessels only take a couple of days to get there. Once there, I'll have to find time to sneak off and find the elusive tigers.

"When do they want it by?" I ask.

"They didn't set a time frame. No one from their network has been able to get footage. They suggested having a relationship with a local may be beneficial."

I screw up my nose for a moment. Would Stev know where I could find the tigers?

"Thanks, Mum. I'll figure something out. Make sure Stev stays long enough for the family dates." I give her a quick hug and walk out of the room.

I pause on the staircase leading to the reception room, fixing my smile in place before I step through the doors to greet the remaining men.

My eyes automatically seek out Dennian. He glances up briefly from where he sits with a sheet of paper resting on a side table. A smile pulls at his lips before he returns to his drawing.

I walk slowly past him glancing at the sketch. An angel statue looms at the end of cramped rows of shelving stacked with crates and boxes. As I round the small table, my eye is drawn to a chest on a lower shelf of the drawing with a rusty lock hanging from the latch.

I drag my eyes away from the sketch and scan the room for Stev. He sits on a couch on the other side of the room. I take a deep breath and approach, taking a perch on the edge of the seat beside Stev. I avoid looking in Dennian's direction again, although I catch him pause momentarily as I sit down.

"Tell me about your home planet, Stev. Do you have many native animals where you live?" I flutter my eyelashes.

"Atlas has some of the most unique fauna and marine life in the galaxy," Stev says. "We have more marine mammals than the rest of the tri-system put together –"

"What sort of land animals do you have?"

"Father's cousin, he's the mayor of Atlia City, that's the capital of Atlas, he has a small menagerie. His last acquisition was a pair of tri-colour monkeys –"

I wince, thinking of little Zeke. My eyes briefly go to Dennian before returning my attention to my target.

"Temple Tigers are native to Atlas, aren't they?" I interrupt again before he can go off on a tangent about monkeys.

"Of course, that's how they got their name. They live near the Dragon Temple."

"Do you live near the temple?"

"As close as anyone else does," Stev replies. "The Dragon Temple is on a magical island. On a clear day it can be seen shimmering in the ocean off Atlia City, but you can't reach it."

"Why not?"

Stev glances around the room quickly to make sure no one listens to our conversation. Besides the hover-cam, no one else appears to be observing us.

"The island is protected by dragon magic," Stev whispers. "There's a portal in the ocean to reach it, but it's only active during a full moon."

"Right." I nod, trying to keep my expression neutral. "The tigers live on the island? Does your father's cousin have any tigers?"

"Well, no. Grandfather caught a cub once, but..." He glances around the room and leans towards me. "There have been reports of the adults vanishing."

"Vanishing?" I try to keep the scepticism from my voice.

"Whenever someone came close to catching one, it disappeared. It's like they can turn themselves invisible." Stev keeps his voice low.

"What happened to the cub?"

"The whole tiger streak showed up and slaughtered Grandfather's servants. The cage was found with the bars sliced clean through and the cub missing. An adult tiger's claws can cut through any material," Stev continues to whisper.

I sit back for a moment assessing my options. I wasn't sure how to get footage of a deadly animal without risking my life. My thoughts are interrupted by Sara entering the room holding a white envelope.

"I have a card here with the name of the person who will be spending the day with Cassie tomorrow. I'll leave it here." She places it on the table in the centre of the room and walks out the door.

Nathan is the first one to stand and take the envelope. He slides the first card out and reads what it says. "Help me choose the perfect gift."

"Maybe we're going jewellery shopping." Saul grins at me.

"Or lingerie," Rick says.

"And the lucky person is…" Nathan glares at us until we are quiet and then he pulls out the next card, "Stev."

I suppress a groan and focus on maintaining my smile. I need Stev to reach the finals, but I don't know if I can continue to act like I like him if we have to spend time alone together. After all, I'm considering pursuing a deadly tiger to avoid spending the rest of my life with the guy.

"Naturally. I am the most sophisticated one in this room," Stev replies.

"What makes you so special?" Saul demands. "My father is part of the Government Delegation as well and I'm a real prince."

"The people of Atlas have always been special. That is why nearly every single Takarna has originated from Atlas. Those descended from the dragon hunter, Mellakai, have developed special skills," Stev says.

"Such as?" I ask before Saul can.

"Telepathy," Stev says.

I raise my eyebrows. Dennian stands abruptly, folding his piece of paper and paces across the opposite side of the room.

"I'm sensing disbelief. Allow me to demonstrate. Think of a number between one and ten," Stev says.

"Okay," I say.

Stev moves to sit beside me and takes one of my hands in both of his. I force myself not to pull away from his touch.

"Now focus on your number," he says.

Four, four, four. He stares at me intently as I repeat the number in my mind. A bead of sweat breaks out on his forehead as he places his free hand on both of ours. I'm about to pull away when he finally speaks.

"Your number is … four," he says. I blink several times and open my mouth, but nothing comes out. "Would anyone else like to try?"

"Sure." Nathan stands and walks over to us. I shuffle over so Nathan can squeeze onto the couch between us. He holds out a hand to Stev.

"Six," Stev says after several long moments holding Nathan's hand. Dennian rolls his eyes.

"Anyone can do a party trick," Saul says.

"Fine, I'll think of a number and you can guess," Stev says.

"Sounds boring. What's in it for us?" Saul yawns.

"If any of you get it right, you can have my date card for tomorrow."

"How do we know you're not going to cheat?" Rick sits forward in his chair.

"I'll write the number on my hand."

Several people nod in agreement to this, so Stev leaves the room to find a marker. He returns with his left hand clenched shut and places the date card face up on the drinks table in the centre of the room.

"It's a number between one and ten. Who's first to guess?" He smirks.

"I'll give it a go," Phil says.

Stev walks over to him and offers a hand. Phil takes it and squeezes his eyes shut. His mouth moves several times before he speaks.

"Seven?"

"Wrong!" Stev crows. "Who's next?"

Saul leans over the back of the couch to whisper in Nathan's ear. "If we each pick a different number, odds are one of us will get it, right?"

Nathan grins and waves Stev over. "My go," he says. After a moment of holding Stev's hand, Nathan chooses three.

"Wrong again," Stev says gleefully.

I watch each of the others line up to take his hand and guess a number. Saul picks eight. The guy from the medic team goes with six before leaning over to check Nathan's shoulder injury. Farray refuses to participate so I step in and say nine. Eric and Zak select four and five.

"Looks like I'll be keeping our date after all," Stev says to me, his left hand still closed.

"Damn it," Saul mutters. "His number must be two."

"Hang on a minute," I say. "Dennian hasn't had a go."

I hope he's been listening to our guesses and comes to the same conclusion as Saul who's not very subtly resting two fingers against his cheek. Stev holds out his right hand to Dennian.

Dennian stops pacing and glances at me. He rounds the furniture and swoops the card off the table.

"It's nine point three four," Dennian says, before striding out of the room with the card. Stev's mouth drops open as shock spreads across his features.

"Hey! I never said that was correct," he yells after Dennian's retreating back.

Stev takes a step forward, but I grab his left hand. Saul leaps over the couch to assist me with the struggling Atlas prince. We drag him to the ground and as Nathan sits on his chest, Saul and I uncurl his fingers. The number nine point three four is written in black on his palm. Stev glares at us.

"Get off me," he growls. The three of us back up.

"Looks like you're not the most special in the room." Saul grins at Stev who brushes imaginary wrinkles from his clothes.

"He obviously cheated," Stev says.

"How?" I demand. "Dennian was on the other side of the room the whole time."

"Exactly. He wouldn't be able to read the number in my head from over there even if he does have some telepathic skill," Stev says indignantly. "I've been training since I was twelve years old. It takes years to learn this trick."

Nathan snorts. "You're just jealous he beat you at your own game. Never mind, maybe you'll get another opportunity to go on a date with Cassie."

I bring a hand to my mouth to hide my grin and make an apology as I back out of the room. I need to get to sleep. I'm going on a date with Dennian tomorrow.

*

I step out of the front door in a figure-hugging royal purple dress. The skirt sweeps the ground as I walk and I focus on each step so I don't trip on the hem.

Dennian appears silently beside me, having walked through the garden, and takes my hand. Before we reach the waiting vehicle, Trev steps in front of us.

"Where's Stev?" he demands.

"He lost a bet last night. Dennian's taking his place." I smile sweetly at Trev. "Haven't you watched the camera edits yet? It's going to make for great ratings."

I tug Dennian's hand and climb into the vehicle before Trev can respond. Gravel crunches under the wheels as we pull away from the house.

"How'd you get Stev's number correct?" I ask.

"Lucky guess." He looks out the window, not meeting my eyes and ignoring the seat-mounted camera.

Being used to Dennian going silent when he doesn't want to talk about something, I change the topic. "You've worked at a few zoological parks. Have you ever seen a Temple Tiger?"

"None in captivity. They can't be contained," Dennian replies.

It takes me a moment to realise he didn't actually answer my question. I sigh and take Dennian's hand in mine and we sit silently through the rest of the journey.

The vehicle pulls up in front of the National Museum. A woman wearing tailored trousers and a light tan shirt with the museum logo stands on the top step to greet us. Trev scrambles out of a second vehicle and checks the scene before a crew member opens our vehicle door.

Dennian slides out first and I follow, arranging my skirt around my legs as I step onto the pavement. The museum lady frowns at Dennian.

"We were told an Atlas noble would be coming," she says. "We were hoping the young man would help choose the gift we're to present to Governor Suri tomorrow."

"We can choose," Dennian says.

The woman continues to frown, but at Trev's urging she leads us into the museum. Light pours into the entranceway through the glass door and walls.

"This building was erected in 746 AG..." the woman rattles off the information like she has said it a thousand times before.

"Do you think she's going to hang around and tell us boring facts the whole time?" I mutter to Dennian.

"I can add irrelevant facts if you want." The corner of Dennian's mouth twitches up.

"Please do. I'd love to see her face."

"We have an exhibit on loan from Atlas in honour of the Keeper and Governor Suri's visit," the woman continues.

"Do you know any facts about Atlas?" I whisper. Dennian purses his lips together for a moment.

"Yes," he replies shortly.

"If you'd like to step this way?" The woman gestures towards a set of frosted sliding glass doors. The door opens automatically as we approach and I step through followed by Dennian.

I walk forward, scanning the room with its path winding through various exhibits, some interactive and others behind glass cabinets.

"Step forward if you seek to know the future." A man appears beside me triggered by a sensor plate under my foot. I let out a small shriek as I step backwards.

"It's a hologram," the woman says. "The Keeper startles everyone."

Two eyes stare arrogantly at me from behind an unkempt mane of grey-black hair. He holds out both hands as though reaching for us. The hairs on my arms stand on end. The Keeper's face is as ageless as in Dennian's fear drawing although this image has both his hands and eyes. I wave a hand towards what looks like a living person, but my hand passes through it.

"He's the man from your drawing." I turn towards Dennian, but he's no longer behind me. "Dennian?" I call out. I make my way back through the door.

Dennian leans against the wall, his forehead pressed against it as his arms cradle his head.

"Are you okay?" I ask. Dennian thumps a fist lightly against the wall and straightens up.

"Yes. Shall we go in?" Dennian ushers me towards the door as though he didn't bolt moments ago.

"Are you sure? Do you want to tell me why you're afraid of the Keeper?" I rest a hand against Dennian's arm.

Dennian shakes his head quickly and steps forward. He pauses for a second at the door to take a deep breath and mutters something under his breath that sounds like 'he's dead, he can't kill me'.

"There you are," the woman says. "I thought I must have bored you already."

I laugh uncomfortably. "Of course not."

I walk forward and the hologram appears again. "Step forward if you seek to know the future."

Dennian's slips his hand into mine and our fingers entwine. His palm sweats despite the air conditioned room.

"Takarna is the current Keeper of the Dragon Temple of Atlas," the woman says blandly.

"Any fun facts for me or shall I make some up?" I ask softly.

"You first." Dennian swallows as though the words are difficult to speak.

"Okay." I squeeze Dennian's hand and attempt to copy the dull drone of our guide. "The Keeper, also known as the advisor to the Governor of the Universe, spends his free time sampling hair product to maintain his luscious locks."

Dennian bursts out laughing, the nervous look leaving his eyes.

"Your turn," I say.

"The 198th Takarna is Governor Suri's least favourite," Dennian says. "Takarna used to be right handed, but Governor Suri cut it off after a heated argument."

158

"Where did you hear that nonsense? Takarna is the governor's most trusted advisor," the woman interrupts.

Dennian looks the woman in the eyes but speaks to me. "Another fun fact; all Keepers are cursed with dragon magic, unable to pass to the Otherside until an apprentice is successfully trained to take his place. There must always be a Keeper, although the name, Takarna, is only given after the successful completion of the trials."

Our guide hurries us on as though afraid someone might hear Dennian's blasphemous comments. We move on through the room.

An old painting of a mountainous island hangs on the back wall. A lake dominates the centre of the island and a craggy peak is thrust into the middle of the lake as though anchoring the island to the ocean floor. Gold and silver dragon statues entwine around the peak. A crescent moon hangs large in the bright sky and a Temple Tiger crouches on the sandy bank of the lake.

"Is that the Dragon Temple?" I point at the dragon statues. Dennian nods.

"Here's a fact your young man may not know," the woman says. "Takarn Island, where the Dragon Temple is located, can only be reached on a full moon despite being visible from Atlia, the main city of Atlas."

"Why is that?" I ask. Stev had mentioned something similar.

"No one knows for sure," she replies.

"The island isn't actually there," Dennian says.

"What do you mean?" I ask.

"Two thousand years ago, when Mellakai was hunting dragons to extinction, the first apprentice suggested the island be relocated. The boy assumed if the dragons were as powerful as they claimed to be, they should be able to move an island," Dennian says.

I laugh. "And people believe that?"

Dennian shrugs. We move on, skimming over the display of Atlas history and their role in the Government, until another hologram appears. With brown hair and grey eyes he could be the twin of the girl I caught watching me at the zoological park the day Dennian rescued Prince from the lions. I step onto the marked plate to see what this one has to say.

"You must unite the universe under one rule. The fate of the world depends on it," the young man says.

"Takarna Ritash," Dennian says. "Keeper when the Government was created."

"There was a girl watching me who looked just like him." I stare at the young man's hologram.

Dennian gives me a curious look. "Star."

"Sorry?"

"The girl you saw is my sister, Star," Dennian says.

"You have a sister? Is she older or younger?"

"Older," Dennian says after a moment's pause.

"Are you related to Takarna Ritash? Because she looks like she could be his twin." I wave a hand at the hologram.

"Star is a descendant of Ritash's sister."

"Is that how come you know so much about the Keeper?" I ask. Dennian shrugs, avoiding the question.

The woman waves us along. "It's time to choose a visiting gift for Governor Suri." She leads us to a storage room. "You're free to browse through here."

I turn in a slow circle taking in the rows of shelving. Dennian stares to our right. He walks in that direction,

160

peering quickly down each row as though looking for something.

"Dennian?"

He pauses at one row near the end as I catch up to him. I look down the aisle. An angel statue looms between the rows. I blink several times trying to rid myself of the déjà vu.

"Have you been here before?" I ask.

Dennian shakes his head, but heads directly towards the items by the statue. The sign above one shelf says, *Items belonging to Space Pirate Kanack.* Dennian reaches out to touch the lock on an old treasure chest. It sits in the same location as the drawing he made the day before.

"We don't have a key for that one." The woman has followed.

A click echoes in the aisle and I turn to see Dennian with the open lock in his hand.

"Must have been stiff," he says.

He lifts the lid and we all peer inside. Dennian reaches in and pulls out a stone tablet covered in scratches. The marks resemble the language Dennian wrote in when we first met.

"What is it?" I ask. Dennian run his finger over the text like a blind man might do.

"It's a record, written by Takarn," Dennian breathes reverently.

"You mean Takarna?" I ask.

"No, Takarn was the first Keeper. All those after him are Takarna."

"Can you read what it says?" the woman asks.

He runs his finger across the scratches, pausing at one consisting of two entwined marks. "The symbol of the Dragon Temple. This is the gift you should give Governor Suri." He holds it out to the woman.

The guide fetches two workers to move the chest. I wander down the aisle, but before I can study any of the stored items, Trev appears like an annoying stalker.

"I hear you've completed your task." He nods his head, agreeing with himself. "As this time was meant to be Stev's date," he glares at Dennian, "I've arranged for you to have a private dinner with the prince."

"Faux prince," I mutter. *Who you need to find the Temple Tigers.*

"Off you go. Lori and Carter are waiting for you back at the house." Trev shoos us from the room.

"Sorry." I reach for Dennian's hand.

Two hours and one outfit change later, I walk out to the pergola in the garden wearing a long dusty-green dress with flowing sleeves. My hair has been coloured black and arranged artistically on top of my head. I blow a few stray wispy bits out of my face in disgust. Pebbles dig into my feet protected only by flimsy black ballet flats as I follow the path where Stev waits.

Stev stands as I approach, smoothing a hand across his black suit jacket over his dusty-green shirt. We look like a matching pair of dolls.

"You look good," Stev says, "the colour brings out your blue eyes."

I force a smile and take a seat opposite him. "You mean I look an Atlas native."

"I'm hardly going to marry someone who doesn't."

A waiter appears silently beside us and deposits plates of food on the table, before disappearing back down the path.

"You were born on Atlas?" I ask.

162

"Of course. My family live in the capital, Atlia City, and can be traced way back to Mellakai's second granddaughter on my mother's side –"

"Why would you want to marry me?"

Stev opens his mouth then closes it again quickly. He narrows his eyes at me and signals Trev who loiters in the bushes.

"Delete that," Trev says to the camera before turning to me. "How about you ask Stev about his relationship with his father, Planetary Delegate Glar Shan?"

"I don't care about his father. I want to know why he's here." My voice rises.

"We're moving on. Put that smile back on your face and we can continue," Trev says.

"Any other questions you'd like me to not ask?" I glare at the man.

He waves his hand impatiently to get me to face Stev again. "Smile!" Trev darts back into the bushes.

I squeeze my eyes shut briefly and remind myself that I need to get to Atlas to film the Temple Tigers if I want any control over this situation.

I take a deep breath, open my eyes, and fix a smile on my face. "Tell me about your father."

I pick at my food while Stev rambles on about his grandfather who was a twin. The Shan and Shen families are the descendants of the two brothers, but despite a strong emphasis on inheritance, Stev has no living siblings or cousins. With Trev hovering nearby, I don't ask him any questions about the cousins Saul said had died.

When I reach my limit on the amount of Atlas political structure I can handle, I place a hand to my stomach and groan quietly. Stev pauses his dialogue briefly.

"What's wrong with you?"

"Nothing," I add in another groan and clutch the tablecloth with my free hand. "Maybe I should go." I drop my voice to a whisper.

"Yes, yes, perhaps you should." Stev shoves his seat back from the table putting more distance between us.

"I can stay…if you want me to…?"

"No need to do that," Stev replies quickly.

I nod my head and lean on the table to help me stand while still clutching my stomach with one hand. I stagger from the pergola and don't straighten up until I'm out of sight. I hike my skirt up and dash back to the house and up the stairs to my room, grinning the whole way about my getaway.

My evening is spent in the shower watching charcoal trails of water flow down the drain as my hair slowly returns to a lighter shade of brown.

Fitness

The ten men stand in the mansion's spacious gymnasium, clad only in identical black jockey shorts as a ripped fitness instructor paces in front of them. Dennian is the only one still wearing a t-shirt.

The instructor pauses in front of him. "Take it off."

Dennian stares back at him with his best mute expression.

"Does this guy understand what I'm saying?" The instructor turns to ask the crew standing in the background. Trev marches over with a frown on his face.

"Of course he does." Trev turns to Dennian. "Unless you want to be eliminated right now, you'll take your shirt off."

Dennian glances over at me with a pained expression. I give him a nod of encouragement. All the others are already half naked and he's seen me in my underwear. Dennian looks away and finally pulls his shirt over his head.

He lifts his arms over his head, revealing a jagged scar across the left side of his ribs. He doesn't look at anyone as he stands beside the others with his back to the wall.

A dragon stone, like the one he gave me, hangs from the leather strip around his neck. His multi-coloured stone is larger than mine and it's clutched in a metallic dragon claw. My eyes travel down his toned body. Beside him, Rick sucks in his stomach.

"How long do you think he can keep that up?" I mutter to Jayne as I nod in Rick's direction.

165

"Oh, at least until the camera moves off him." She giggles. "Damn, there are a few good-looking bodies there."

My eyes drift back to Dennian's toned abs as Sara steps forward to give us the rundown on the group activity.

"Cassie, today the boys will be tested in a range of health and fitness activities to test their suitability as a husband. Nathan says his shoulder has recovered, but the doctor has advised him to take it easy, so Nathan won't be ranked on a couple of the activities."

I nod my head, my eyes on Dennian as he continues to study the floor. The instructor steps forward while his two assistants hover nearby.

"We're going to start with a few warm-ups before we get into the testing phase of today, so I'll get you all to line up in two rows."

The guys step into the centre of the room arranging themselves in the rows. Dennian hesitates for a moment before stepping into place. As he turns to face the instructor, I catch sight of his back. His skin is criss-crossed with faint lines and he has a tattoo in silver and gold between his shoulder blades.

"What happened to your back?" Phil asks.

Dennian narrows his eyes at Phil but doesn't speak. Phil glances away first. The other guys stare at Dennian's back, but none of them say anything to him.

After a few dynamic stretches, the instructor splits the guys into two groups. Trev steps forward to place Dennian in the same group as Stev, perhaps hoping their on-going conflict will translate into more competitive drama.

One assistant sets Dennian, Stev, Rick, Farray, and Nathan up on running stations. He starts them out slow with a gradually increasing speed. Another assistant monitors the others doing a variety of tests such as sit-ups and push-ups.

The instructor leads Phil over to a screening station and Trev waves me over to join them. I walk over as Phil steps into the scanning area marked as a square on the floor surrounded by three transparent walls.

"This scans the boys and highlights any previous injuries, broken bones, that kind of thing," the instructor says.

I nod my head as the machine scans Phil. The instructor shows me his screen where a bright spot appears on the representation of Phil's right arm. He flicks on a pointer and shines it on Phil's arm in the exact same location.

"Broken arm when he was younger," the instructor says. He flips through other information on the screen. A blood test shows on one of the pages, but there is nothing unusual about Phil's details.

Trev comes over to have a word with Phil who heads off to an adjacent room. Through the door, a pair of stools are set up. Trev scribbles a few notes on cards and hands them to me.

"Time for a one-on-one chat with Phil." He points me towards the room then moves off to arrange for Eric to be scanned.

I glance at Dennian as I walk from the room. He runs with a long easy stride. Rick rests against a wall, bent over with his hands on his knees. Stev wipes a hand over his brow while glaring at Dennian and trying to run at the same time. Stev stumbles briefly but regains his footing. Dennian's eyes are closed, ignoring the rest of the room as he runs. Farray's pace is slow but steady, without Dennian's graceful gait.

Phil sits on one of the stools in the next room and I join him on the other. I glance at the cards in my hand then look up and smile at Phil. The hover-cam moves into position while I hold my expression and ask my first question.

"How did you break your arm?"

Phil begins telling me an elaborate story that will probably be edited out of the footage. Eric gets sent in to replace him shortly after and Trev slips me new question cards. I'm not given anything to ask of Farray or Saul so I head back into the room to watch the testing.

Stev steps out of the scanning area and walks over to a bench to watch the others for a moment. The trainer shows me the screen.

"Nothing much of interest. I'd say he's had a pretty easy life, although the people of Atlas tend to have a naturally high level of fitness anyway."

"Why are there no blood test results?" I look at the blank spaces on the screen.

"Both Stev and Dennian have refused a blood sample."

"What?" Stev demands from behind us. "What reason did Nobody give for refusing?"

"Same as you," the instructor says. "Cultural reasons."

Stev grabs the small torch the instructor had been holding and marches over to where Dennian completes a series of push-ups.

"What are you doing?" I call after him.

Dennian gets to his feet as Stev approaches and eyes him warily.

"What cultural reason could you possibly have, Nobody?"

Stev whips the torch up and shines it in Dennian's eyes. Dennian flinches but doesn't look away.

"Just checking," Stev says.

"Concerned we might be cousins?" Dennian replies.

Stev takes a swing at him, but Dennian blocks it with his arm and the instructor steps between them, placing a hand on each of their chests. Dennian backs away from the contact.

"You're in the scanner next," the instructor says to Dennian. "Stev, it's your turn on the weights." He grabs the torch from Stev's hand.

Stev shoots a final glare at Dennian before turning on his heel and stalking off towards the weights corner where Rick watches us. Rick sucks in his stomach again as the camera swivels in his direction.

"What was that about?" I ask.

Dennian shrugs and steps past me into the scanning area. The instructor activates the scan and waits for the information to appear on his screen. He points to Dennian's scarred side with the torch.

"I'm betting he's had a couple of broken ribs," he says.

We both watch the screen as it lights up with dozens of bright spots from head to feet.

"Oh, Lord," the instructor whispers. "He's broken a lot more than his ribs."

He swipes at the screen to hide the previously broken bones data leaving several other injuries marked, the brightest being on one lung in the same area as Dennian's scarred side. The instructor waves him over to us.

"How old were you when you punctured your lung?"

"Ten." Dennian glances at me.

169

"Take a deep breath in then release it." The instructor holds a small measuring device in front of Dennian's mouth as he breathes out. "Hmmm, hasn't affected your lung capacity."

He runs Dennian through a series of exercises to check for range of motion and flexibility, but the reading from the scanner is the only indication of Dennian's past injuries.

"Okay, you can go into the next room for your interview." Trev approaches having watching the whole process.

Dennian heads straight through, but Trev grabs my arm halting me for a moment.

"Ask him about – "

"I think I can work out what to say." I shake Trev's hand off and follow Dennian into the room.

Dennian ignores the stools, preferring to stand in the centre of the room. He looks up when I enter, but I can't decipher his expression.

I walk up to him and place a hand on his bare chest. His heart beats rapidly beneath my fingertips as I look into his eyes to see if he is okay with the contact. His green eyes stare back into mine as he remains still beneath my touch. A camera hovers nearby, but we ignore it.

"What was that about, with Stev?" I ask.

"He was concerned we may be related," Dennian says. I raise my eyebrows, but Dennian doesn't elaborate.

"You don't look like you're from Atlas."

"Not all of them have dark hair and blue eyes, just the ones they allow to live," he says.

"What do you mean?"

"Nothing."

When he doesn't continue, I trace my hand across to the scar on his side. Its jagged edges are slightly raised against his warm skin, but it's fully healed like it's been there for some years. Dennian moves his arm out of the way so I can see it clearly.

"How did this happen?"

"Training accident."

I look up into Dennian's eyes again, the question unasked.

He sighs. "I was distracted."

"By what?"

"The remains of the last boy who failed the training course." The way he says it makes me hesitant to ask further questions regarding that incident.

"How did you break all your bones?" I haven't removed my hand from his skin and his muscles ripple as he turns slightly to watch me.

"Fell off a cliff."

Trev won't be happy with Dennian's brief responses, but I know better than to push him when he's talking. I duck under Dennian's arm and trail my hand around to his back. Dozens of faint lines criss-cross his back. They appear to have been made by some kind of whip. Before I force the words out of my suddenly dry throat, Dennian answers my unasked question.

"My training master did that."

"Why?" I whisper.

Dennian tenses slightly under my hand. "I challenged him."

His muscles are tense under my fingers so I trail them up to the mark between his shoulder blades.

"You have a tattoo."

Two dragons face each other with wings outstretched. One is gold, the other silver, the same colours as the Dragon Temple from the painting in the museum and the dragons on Governor Suri's spaceship. Dennian stays silent, but then I haven't actually asked a question.

"Mum hates tattoos. She says people always regret them when they're older and want to have them removed."

Dennian makes a noise that sounds a bit like an amused snort that lacks humour.

"It can't be removed. I've already tried."

Dennian pulls away from my hand and turns to face me. His lips are pressed together in the way he does when he's done talking. I reach up and press a kiss to his cheek.

"Let's head back in," I say.

Dennian nods and leads the way. I watch his back as we walk, the muscles clearly defined beneath the scarred skin.

"How about we make this next test more interesting?" Phil says as we step back into the room. He stands between a pair of weight benches.

"Such as?" Eric asks.

"Whoever lifts the most weight, gets a kiss from Cassie," Phil says.

"Not going to happen." I glare at him.

"No, we make good prize," Farray says.

"How about the winner has no chores for a week and losers do a nudie lap of the room," Saul wanders over to suggest.

"Fine with me." Phil flexes his bicep.

"Count me out," Zak says. "I'm not going up against a fitness instructor."

"I'm out too. The medic won't be happy if I hurt my shoulder again," Nathan says.

"So who's up for a nudie run when I win?" Phil asks.

"I crush little man," Farray says.

"Not everything is about bulk, you know. Strength is also about muscle optimisation." Phil puffs out his chest.

"I'm just here to watch." Saul leans against the wall as the instructor comes over to set the weights on the bar.

"You and me then, big boy." Phil settles onto the first bench and Farray on the second. An assistant steps in to spot each of the boys with the weights.

Both lift the first weight and the instructor adds extra plates to the ends of each bar. On the third lift, Phil struggles to lift the bar from the cradle. Farray adds a final weight to demonstrate his superior muscles. His arms tremble as he lowers it back onto the cradle

"I better lift," Farray says. "No better lift than Triade Prince."

"Best of three tests?" Phil asks. "I'm not running around the room on my own."

"Dennian hasn't had a go yet," Saul says. "I'm sure Cassie wouldn't object to him running around the room in the nude."

"He no better lift like Farray." The Triade prince thumps his chest.

"One hundred credits says Nobody can't lift half that weight," Stev says.

Dennian steps forward and I place a hand on his arm. "You don't need to do this," I say.

Dennian walks over to the bar and slides an additional weight on each end.

"Don't hurt yourself," Nathan says. "You don't need to compete against these guys."

"No worry your face," Farray says. "He no get this off rack."

I glance at the instructor, but his casual stance suggests he agrees with Farray. Dennian lies down on the bench, rests his hands on the bar and closes his eyes. He takes a deep breath and lifts the bar smoothly upwards.

The instructor lunges forward to spot him, but Dennian lowers the bar back slowly and unassisted. The bar clanks into its cradle and Dennian sits up. We stare at him.

"How did you do that?" the instructor asks.

Dennian shrugs. "It's all in the mind." He stands and moves onto the next testing station.

"You cheat." The Triade prince steps towards Dennian with a thunderous look on his face and muscles rippling.

"They're weights. How could he possibly cheat?" I say.

The two guys eye each other, but when Dennian doesn't cower before him, Farray mutters something under his breath and punches his fist into the weights bench. The bar jumps out of the cradle and falls to the floor with a thump that I feel through my feet.

"Strip off, then." Saul grins at Phil and Farray.

I take a small step away from Saul, but Farray drops his shorts on the floor and strides casually around the room with his nakedness on display. Phil hurries to drop his own shorts before dashing quickly around the room with his hands over his crotch. He's dressed again before Farray finishes his lap.

"Enough playing around, boys. We have work to do." The instructor ushers everyone on to their next task while Farray pulls his shorts back on.

"Nice package. Pity about what it's attached to," Saul whispers as he slinks past. "It's almost disappointing Dennian won that contest."

"Get your mind out of the gutter," I reply with a grin. He gives me a wink as he backs away.

By the end of the day, I feign interest while Mum and Jayne pore over the results. Farray is strongest if Dennian's effort is discounted as a fluke, Phil has excellent cardio fitness, Dennian is a born athlete but loses marks in Mum's eyes for previous injuries and the dragon tattoo, Nathan and Eric are fit, Rick isn't.

None of it matters, because Trev arranges for Zak to stage a dramatic walk-out during the elimination ceremony. I'm warned beforehand so I have time to practice my surprised expression. The evening ends with nine men still in the mansion.

Dragon Keep

Dennian – age ten

I jerked awake to a loud thump and a grunt of pain nearby. My hands flew up defensively, before falling back to my sides. I lay still on the grass bedding as a wave of pain and dizziness washed over me at my sudden movement.

The sounds came from outside the room, so knowing my life wasn't about to end in the next few moments, I paused to block the pain receptors in my brain. Relief came quickly although the dizziness took longer to subside.

I touched my fingertips to the bandages on my back and they came away damp. I didn't like large amounts of blood. It reminded me of Zeth.

I rolled to my knees carefully, stiff from lying on my stomach half the night. I breathed deeply through my nose as I stood. Hints of decay, pepper, violets and charcoal reached me over the coppery tang of my own blood. I paused in the shadows of the doorway as I assessed the threat.

"We warned you never to lay a hand on him again." Governor Suri's voice had a deadly edge to it.

"I'll do as I please. Your precious government relies on me holding this position. I fall, so do you," Master Carlen hisses.

"You think too highly of yourself, old man. I guarantee I could arrange it so no one noticed your disappearance for years."

"You already know you can't kill me," Carlen replied.

I sucked in a sharp breath, my eyes glued to my master arguing with the ruler of the universe.

"I've only tried once." Governor Suri reached out and traced a small cross over Master Carlen's heart where I'd once seen a scar as he changed his shirt.

"You would never win a battle against me." He pulled himself up to his full height and looked down on the governor.

"That would sound more convincing if you hadn't recently lost your eye."

Governor Suri's hand lashed out and grabbed Master Carlen's right wrist. A small gasp escaped my lips at the blade she held against Master Carlen's skin.

I edged out of my room and escaped the cavernous dwelling where I'd lived since the second anniversary of my birth. It wasn't safe to be near Master Carlen when his power had been challenged.

Despite my weakened state, I made it up to the temple and lay on the stone floor behind the broken crystal orb. Dampness spread across my damaged back, but there was nothing more I could do for my injury other than block the pain. Exhaustion claimed me and my world turned dark.

*

I was ripped from a nightmare by a hand gripping my shoulder. My body was rigid from lying prone on the cold stone. Carlen yanked me to my feet and the skin pulled on my back. A wave of dizziness passed over me although I still had a firm grasp over the pain.

"She took my hand!" Carlen shook his wrist stump in my face. "You'll pay for this."

My eyes opened wide at the red and blistered skin that had already formed over his missing hand. He wouldn't be able to draw without his dominant hand.

I was too stunned by his missing hand to react when he jerked me backwards and we transported to the main Atlas continent. The planets were not quite aligned so he had to make a second jump to appear on the far edge of the tiger forest.

The scenery blurred as he dragged me through the undergrowth behind him. I could have tried to fight him, but that was what got me into this situation in the first place.

A chill ran through me as we reached the edge of the Children's Graveyard. Master Carlen dragged me forward, holding me at arm's length, his remaining eye watching my hands warily. We stopped in front of the grave he'd buried me in several years earlier. The headstones stood in a row as they had always done; Tarla, Zeth, Lucei, and Tryce Shen.

Still grasping me with his left hand in a way that made blood trickle down my back, he waved his stump at the stone grave cover. It slid to one side, throwing aside bunches of fresh flowers in a reminder of my recent tenth birth anniversary. It was the same every year: flowers for the birthday and toys for the death-day. I averted my gaze from the stuffed toys covering Zeth's tomb beside us. Carlen beckoned me forward.

"You didn't think I would let you live, did you?" he asked with a crazy look in his remaining pale blue eye. I didn't answer. I hadn't spoken any words out loud for four years now.

A loud snarl sounded from the tree line and I jerked my head up. Early morning light glinted off the tips of Myaa's horns. She took a slow step towards us while maintaining her crouched hunting position, her tail flicking from side to side. Fear spores flooded Master Carlen's scent as he held me between him and the Temple Tiger. I ripped my shoulder from his grasp.

I ran, heading in Myaa's direction. My mind whirled faster than my legs. I slipped past Myaa and she held her position.

Master Carlen would be able to track me down via the mark on my back as he had every time before when I'd tried to run away. I needed somewhere he wouldn't follow.

I headed for the Dragon Keep – the one overlooking Old Atlia City. He was afraid of the deadly tunnels. I was never sure why. He would have had to complete the tasks at the end of his apprenticeship.

I paused inside the cavern entrance, my pupils adjusting to the dim light. I reached a hand above my head, but I still wasn't tall enough to reach the ceiling. Nausea swept over me as my body reminded me of the injury to my back. I walked forward until the cool water lapped at my bare feet. The watery entrance to the underground caverns was the first obstacle to prevent locals from entering the Keep.

Once I entered the water, I'd be unable to pause again until I reached the end of the tunnels, or died. I touched the scar over my ribs from the last time I entered the tunnels. I wasn't drugged this time although the urge to throw up was the same.

I lowered myself into the water and focused on fission – separating oxygen from the water so I could breathe. Myaa had taught me after the first time I'd drowned. The underground tunnels were too long for anyone to hold their breath.

I emerged from the other side of the underground lake and negotiated the first objects. Dodging the next obstacles, I reached the chasm that confused me last time I came here.

This time, I didn't hesitate at the decomposing flesh hanging from Goyer's skeleton slumped against the wall, beside a pool of dried blood. I did glance at the curse he'd written in blood as I prepared to take on the chasm. A curse upon Carlen: his death on an apprentice's sacrifice.

I appeared on the far side of the chasm as the stone blade swung through the location I'd stood moments earlier, leaving only a scar and the memory of my broken ribs and collapsed lung. The cuts on my back started to bleed again. I kept moving.

I skidded to a stop when my deadly passage ended in a huge cave system. Thousands of sparkling gems lay strewn about the cavern floor. The waterways of Takarn Island were littered with similar stones. I breathed in the musty charcoal scent of the long departed creatures and stumbled over a yellow dragon scale.

The cave opened onto a cliff face, wide enough for several dragons to take-off and land at the same time. I walked to the edge and looked out over the calm ocean. The edge was so high I could see the illusion of Takarn Island in the distance. As the sun set, the final rays of light appeared to flash off the Dragon Temple on the highest point of the Island in a blaze of silver and gold. The crescent of the satellite planet hung low in the sky behind it.

My bare toes gripped the edge of the shelf, scores from ancient dragon talons cutting into my soles. I placed my hand against the edge of my bandaged back.

I'd been fighting to stay alive my whole life. I'd died and been revived on four separate occasions. When Master Carlen caught me, it would be my fifth journey to the Otherside. I wondered if the ones who guarded the brightly-lit corridors would let me pass this time.

My mind drifted to Goyer. Myaa had told me an apprentice was not completely dead until another had replaced the Master. Did that mean Goyer's spirit waited somewhere? Would he be summoned for the Final Trial?

I considered Goyer's curse. If I sacrificed myself, Master Carlen would die. I peered forward and contemplated the distance to the rocks far below. A fall from here would break every bone in my body.

I spread my arms wide like dragon wings and leaned forward, letting the wind support me, until I was at the point between living and dying. For the first time in my life, the decision was mine to make. One of us was about to die.

Revelations

An early morning ray of sunshine falling across my pillow pulls me from sleep. I'm tempted to stay snuggled under the blankets until Lori and Carter arrive, but someone taps softly on my door. I sit up, checking what I'm wearing – sleep shorts and a singlet – and throw off the blankets.

Dennian stands at the door, his brow furrowed. I poke my head into the hallway to check for people and cameras and quickly wave him in. I close the door.

"What's wrong?" I ask.

He wanders across the massive room and sinks into the chair at the makeup station. I sit on the edge of my bed facing him. His eyes scan the room as though searching for inspiration. They eventually settle on me.

"Tattoo is a brand. Ties me to my training master so he can always find me," Dennian says.

"What kind of training are we talking about?"

"It's forbidden to discuss."

"Okay..." I reach out and squeeze his hands, pulling him closer to me, but he glances away.

"The marks on my back..." His eyes meet mine again, "I was punished for trying to kill Carlen."

My mind goes blank for a moment as my brain tries to determine if my ears heard him correctly. Several questions try to force themselves out of my mouth at once.

"Your training master?" I guess and Dennian nods.

"Why?" I ask.

"I was looking after..." he pauses, choosing his words carefully, "a Temple Tiger cub. He tried to kill her."

My breath catches in my throat. Dennian has seen a Temple Tiger.

"Why would Carlen do that?" I try to focus on Dennian's words instead of my own need to find the tigers.

"To teach me I was powerless," Dennian replies.

"What happened to the cub?"

"He never found her. Lucei's grown up now."

"Hang on a minute, this isn't a recent thing?"

"I was almost ten," Dennian says.

"You tried to kill someone when you were ten years old?" I shove Dennian's chest lightly. "Stop scaring me! I thought you were confessing something you did recently."

I let my hand drift to his side. Now I know it's there, the scar across his ribs is noticeable through his shirt.

"I hope the Peace Keepers dealt with him harshly for scarring you like that."

"He died…unexpectedly…not long afterwards," Dennian says.

"Thank you for trusting me, Dennian."

I lean forward to hug him, resting my head on his shoulder. He wraps his arms around me but doesn't relax.

"Are you happy?" I ask.

"I am when I'm with you."

Knuckles rap on the bedroom door and I leap up.

"The hair and makeup team are here," I hiss.

Dennian glances at the door then makes his way silently to the bathroom. As soon as he is out of sight, I open the door and let Lori and Carter into my room.

183

Lori heads straight to the wardrobe and starts selecting outfits while I take the seat by the dresser that Dennian occupied moments earlier.

After picking an outfit, Lori tugs my hair into an elaborate up-do while Carter spreads an array of makeup across the dresser. He grabs one of my hands to study the damaged polish on my nails.

"This won't do. Where's the polish, Lori?"

"I left a range of colours and remover in the bathroom," Lori replies.

"I'll get it." I try to stand, but Lori still has hold of my hair and forces me back into the chair with a hand on my shoulder.

"You need to stay still so we can get you ready."

I glance nervously at the reflection of the bathroom door as Carter enters. He emerges several minutes later with a couple of small bottles in his hand as though nothing is amiss. He takes hold of my sweaty right hand and begins removing the nail polish. I keep my eyes fixed on the bathroom door in the mirror.

My heart rate has slowed by the time Lori and Carter walk out leaving the bedroom door slightly ajar. As soon as they are out of sight, I dart into the bathroom.

The room is almost half the size of the bedroom with a large tub, shower behind a clear glass screen, toilet, basin, a row of large cabinets and a mounted first aid box. Dennian isn't in the room.

I saw him enter and I kept an eye on the door the whole time. I tap my foot on the floor tiles, but they're all firmly in place. I run a hand along the walls, rapping my knuckles against them in places. Eventually I look up and stare at the ceiling.

"Lost something?" a voice asks from the doorway.

I jump and place a hand to my chest as I glare at Jayne leaning against the doorframe. "Don't you knock?" I demand.

"What are you doing?" Jayne glances at the ceiling.

"How would someone get out of this room?" I ask out loud, casting my eyes around the room once again. Jayne gives me her best 'you're acting crazy' look.

"Well, I don't know how they do it where you're from, but on my planet we generally use – The Door." She runs a hand over the doorframe.

"You'd be *seen* if you used the door." I ignore Jayne's sarcasm for my own chaotic thoughts.

"Okay.....a hidden door," she suggests. I spin around and point my finger at her.

"There isn't one. I've already looked," I sound slightly crazy even to my own ears.

"You know what? I think it's time you and I go for a little walk. Get some fresh air. I think this competition is getting to you." Jayne takes my arm and leads me from the room.

When we arrive downstairs, Dennian sits on a couch beside Nathan, waiting alongside all the other men to find out what we will be doing for the day. For a moment I consider whether I'd dreamed our conversation, but he wears the same dark grey shirt he had on in my room. Jayne and I sit on the vacant couch and Sara enters the room.

"Today we'll be looking into your family trees," Sara announces. "You will each have the opportunity to work with an ancestry consultant and contact family members if need be."

Trev steps forward to send the guys off in different directions and assign the three consultants to those who want the assistance.

A fourth consultant spends some time with me and Mum, but there is nothing particularly show-worthy in our history. Once that is determined, Trev drags me off to do spiels about the boys for the cameras. He hands me cards, focusing on the three royals, as well as Nathan and Eric. The others, including Dennian, we barely discuss. Uneasiness settles in my stomach.

After picking at my lunch, Jayne and I sit in a pair of comfy chairs by a solid table. Stev enters with a large sheet of paper. He takes the seat opposite and lays his family tree on the table between us.

Jayne gives me a quick puzzled expression. Stev's family history is laid out like an actual tree with branches and relatives' names drawn like to look like leaves. Not all the people are named and plain leaves mark their place. The base of the tree trunk bears the name Mellakai, the dragon hunter.

"Tell me about your family." I smile at Stev and hope this will be less painful than I expect.

"This is me here." Stev points to his name at the tip of one branch.

I study the tree while Stev talks and Jayne asks various questions about his relationship with his father, Glar Shan, and his uncle, the king of Atlas. My eyes are drawn to a set of familiar names: King Niko Shen and his wife Lari Shen – the names on the gravestone of Dennian's fear drawing.

The branches, particularly on Stev's side of the tree entwine about each other in what appears to be several marriages of cousins.

According to the tree, Stev is an only child. His aunt has a child marked as deceased and Niko Shen has four children marked as deceased. Niko and Glar's fathers are twin brothers, marked on the tree above two crossed branches of family. Several other relatives have no surviving children.

If I'd been seriously considering a future with Stev, I'd question why all his cousins died as babies, but with Trev hovering nearby I keep my mouth shut.

Rick, Eric, and Phil take turns next. Their family trees are drawn in a more familiar format, but I don't spend much time with any of them before Trev moves them along.

Farray's drawing focuses on the direct family line of royals without spending time on any offshoots, except for one branch going back over nine hundred years. He includes angry red marks over several members of the family. Farray's family are descendant from the surviving younger brother all those years ago. By the looks of it, his family rules due to the deaths he has marked.

"What is the significance of these people?" Jayne points to the red marks.

"Destroyer kill them all dead." Farray glares at us.

"Who's the Destroyer?" I ask.

"You see star of Lordinia explode? Destroyer does this. Kill much my ancestor!"

"Black holes happen at the end of a star's life. You can't blame a person for that," I say.

"I not have in my home, silly girl." Farray rips his drawing from the table and storms out of the room.

I clench my jaw but manage not to say anything offensive on camera.

"Right, well I don't think he's going to be the one for you," Jayne says. I burst out laughing.

Trev ushers Nathan in while we try to regain our composure. He slides into the seat Farray vacated and places his page in front of me.

"Good afternoon, Cassie, Jayne," he says.

"How's the shoulder?" I ask.

"It actually feels great, normal even."

"That's good." I nod and smile back at him.

"Enough with the flirting, you two. Tell us about your family, Nathan," Jayne interrupts.

"We weren't –" Jayne places a hand over my mouth to prevent me from finishing.

"This is me here." Nathan points out his name on the standard family tree design.

His family is small, or at least what he has chosen to share with us is, without the complicated entwining branches of Stev's family.

"I have a younger sister and brother," Nathan continues.

We chat for a few minutes, but Trev doesn't consider there to be much of interest in his family, so Nathan leaves and Dennian enters.

Dennian takes the vacated seat and places the drawing in front of me. Jayne reaches out and pulls it closer before looking up at Dennian with a frown on her face.

"This is a tree," she says. "We need a 'family tree'."

"It is," Dennian replies.

I tug it towards me and study the tree covered in yellow blossoms. One flower on the main trunk has a red centre with red spreading out towards the edges. Each flower after this one also has a red centre although the red portion grows smaller the further from the original bud.

A narrow thread of rot twists along several branches. The blossoms following it have a purple edge to each petal. The band of purple is thicker on every flower with a red centre.

188

One rotting limb has been hacked off, its mauve buds dying in the sun. Small twigs litter the ground beneath the tree with the dead mauve-edged flowers.

"Each flower represents a person?" I ask.

Dennian nods and Jayne looks at me like I'm crazy.

"Stev also drew a tree," I say.

"But his involved names, not flowers," Jayne says.

"Which one is you?" I look at Dennian.

He points to a blossom lying on the ground under the tree. The centre is red and the edge has a thick band of purple. Near it are two joined buds – one a dead brown, the other with hints of the red and purple like his own. A couple of other buds are scattered nearby, but the further from Dennian's flower they are, the more blossoms on the ground are dead.

In the tree above, the tips of the entwined branched are stripped of their buds. The branches with flowers lacking the purple mark have maintained their recent buds, but on the branch directly above Dennian's flower, only one bud remains. It has a narrow band of purple and only a hint of a red centre.

"What about your parents? Which flowers are theirs?" I ask.

"They're still on the tree." Dennian doesn't move to point them out.

"What about your sister, Star?" I ask.

"Not her tree," Dennian replies.

"She's adopted?" I guess.

"Me," he replies.

"Well, I've learned absolutely nothing about your family from this," Jayne says.

Trev sends Dennian out and calls Jayne over for some thoughts in front of the camera. I stay seated, trying to make sense of Dennian's tree.

I study the branch above his flower. Several smaller branches entwine around each other and twin blossoms sit near the junction.

I pull out the discarded family trees from the other boys. Stev's is at the bottom of the pile and I pull it free, laying it on the table beside Dennian's.

"What are you doing?"

I jump at the sound of Jayne's voice beside me.

"They're the same tree." I point out the twin buds in the same location as Stev's grandfather and great-uncle.

"That's a bit far-fetched, don't you think?" Jayne leans in and studies the two drawings.

"I think Dennian may be related to Stev," I say.

"Their trees are kind of similar, but that could be the way they drew them and Dennian's is missing the kids." Jayne points out a variety of names of children marked as dead before they reached the age of one.

"I think they're the flowers on the ground," I say.

"Where's Dennian on Stev's family tree, then?"

I study the branch I thought Dennian's flower had come from. Tarla, Lucei, Zeth, Tryce, and Lyri are all cousins of Stev's. I scan further, but his name isn't there.

"I don't know," I say.

"You forgetting one important detail," Jayne says. "Dennian has fair hair and his eyes are green. He's clearly not from Atlas."

"I guess so." I take one last look at the two trees before Trev calls me over for some camera work.

*

"How do I look?" Jayne spins in a circle as I stare at her with an open mouth.

Her hair hangs in natural honey brown curls which match the hazel contacts in her eyes. Her carefully applied makeup gives her a grownup appearance.

"Well the boys certainly won't recognise you," I say. "You don't look like you at all."

"But I'm still beautiful, right?" Jayne frowns at her reflection in the mirror.

"Stunning." I grin at her.

"I feel naked," Jayne replies.

"Well that dress is a little…" I pause.

"Low-cut? Short? Red?" Jayne rattles off a list of adjectives.

"Yes." I agree.

"Well I am trying to see which one of your men are willing to be tempted by another woman. Trev said he'll be giving them all something to make them completely truthful and lose their inhibitions. Any bets on who will cave to temptation?"

"You have no chance with Saul, Stev, or Dennian," I say.

"What makes you so sure?"

"You're not Saul's type, Stev wants someone who looks like they're from Atlas, and Dennian doesn't like being around people."

"What do you mean I'm not Saul's type?" Jayne places her hands on her hips.

"Never mind," I say. "Shouldn't you be heading off to the club before the guys arrive?"

"Right." Jayne leans in to kiss my check then rushes out the door with a small clutch bag.

"Have fun," I call out after her.

I head downstairs to meet Mum and Trev in one of the living spaces in the mansion. Trev has folders of information about each of the remaining nine men.

"I think we can do a double elimination after tonight." Trev lines up four folders; Rick, Dennian, Phil, and Eric.

My pulse drums in my wrist. "There's been a lot of tension between Stev and Dennian lately," I say. "What do you think that's about?"

"A bit of friendly competition, I imagine." Trev shifts Dennian's folder back into the main group. "We'll see how the boys go tonight with Jayne and Sara."

"You said Cassie and I'll meet with the families of the top four contestants?" Mum eyes the remaining folders.

"Yes, obviously we need to plan ahead, especially with the foreign Princes," Trev says.

"Farray is weird and Saul is more interested in the other guys than he is in me," I say.

"Don't be silly, Cassie. Of course Saul likes you." Mum makes a note on her screen.

"Why is Farray even here?" I ask. "He doesn't like me and he certainly doesn't act like he wants to be here."

"His family contacted us shortly after we arranged for Prince Saul to come. Didn't want much in turn, just a visa for his security team and orbit approval for their spacecraft during programing."

"What security team?" I ask. "Stev and Saul both have Peace Keepers loitering around the grounds. I haven't seen any for Farray."

"It doesn't matter. I'm not sure if Farray provides the best viewing. He lacks audience appeal," Trev says.

"I want to meet with Nathan and Dennian's families," I say.

"We don't know anything about where Damian comes from or who his family are," Mum says. "Now, Stev comes from royalty. Don't make the same mistake I did in rejecting Mark for your father."

"Dennian has a sister called Star and he's related to Stev," I say.

Mum stops doodling on her tablet screen. "What?"

"Dennian's family tree is exactly the same as Stev's," I say.

"Nonsense." Mum flips open Dennian's folder and jabs a finger at his drawing. "This is a tree. There aren't any names on it."

"Could be interesting to meet his family, see if we can dig up some juicy details." Trev tosses Dennian's file to one side.

"We're going to meet Stev's family." Mum grabs the folder and tosses it in the keep pile on top of Dennian's.

"Wouldn't it be great if we got to see Stev's home city...?" I leave the question hanging in the air.

"The viewers would love that." Trev taps furiously away on his tablet before reaching into the folders and pulling out the two drawings. Even from the other side of the table I can see the same pattern in both.

"They're probably cousins of some sort," I suggest. "I bet there's some sort of scandal involving Stev's relatives. Maybe one of them had an affair with someone from Terra, which is why Dennian doesn't have Atlas colouring..." I sit back waiting for Trev to

193

call me out for trying to play him, but he traces a finger over the branches of Dennian's tree ending at the flower I believe represents Stev.

"Let's see what happens when Jayne returns," Mum says. "Some contestants may not be suitable."

"Fine. I'll be in my room." I stand abruptly and walk out. Trev continues to stare at the two family trees and I smile to myself.

I flop down on the spacious bed and glance at the time on a small ornamental piece on the dressing table. I doubt the guys will be back for some time yet. I expect Jayne will fill me in on the juicy details as soon as she returns. I imagine Dennian sitting in a corner trying to avoid everyone.

To distract myself, I pick up the screen Sara left so I could 'have input' into the wedding preparations. I flip through the pages without paying much attention.

A thump and a crash outside my door have me sitting bolt upright. I discard the screen and make my way cautiously to my closed door. I pause for a moment with my hand on the handle, but the sound has stopped. I pull the door open and look out.

Dennian sprawls across the floor with a large picture frame on top of him. I dart forward to pull it off him, leaning it against the wall it fell from. He looks up at me with unfocused eyes and a face drained of colour.

"Have you been drinking?" I glance down the hall, but I can't hear anyone else in the mansion.

'Cassie.'

My name sounds in my head, but his lips didn't move.

"Did you just…" I'm not sure what I mean to ask.

'Going to be sick…'

He lurches off the floor and through the door to my ensuite. I give him a minute before checking on him. He's slumped against the sink, one hand gripping the edge.

"Have you always been telepathic?" I grab a glass from the counter and fill it with water so he can rinse his mouth out.

'Not always, I had to learn so I could communicate with the dragons when they return,' Dennian replies as though his response is completely logical. *'If they return. Carlen said they won't, but I saw one once when I was six. She was little and blue.'*

He must be drunker than he looks. I once had to sneak Jayne home after a very big night out. She was so drunk she kept falling over. The whole walk home she talked nonsense about packing her suitcase and putting it in her back pocket.

I hand him the glass and his hand slips off the edge of the sink leaving a trail of pink foam.

"Have you got something on your hand?" I ask.

He opens his eyes and lifts his arm in front of his face. One of the silver-outlined creatures on the black armband has changed colour. The strange pony-like creature with two horns, like a rhinoceros crossed with a unicorn, is now yellow. He stares at his hand as though only now noticing it. Blood foams from a deep gash on his hand and drips down his wrist.

"Your hand is bleeding!" I gasp. What had Jayne told me about this evening? Something about a drug to make the guys truthful and lose their inhibitions.

'My blood is full of tiny spikes. I don't feel so good.'

"Dennian, are you allergic to anything?"

He looks at his hand like he doesn't recognise it. I grab hold of it for a closer inspection. His palm is sliced open and blood foams from it in tiny bubbles.

'What they gave me doesn't like my blood. It fizzes in my body.' He slumps against the wall clutching the glass of water in his good hand then he laughs. *'Stev is going to feel terrible.'*

"I'm going to get the medical team."

'Don't leave me.' He puts the glass on the floor and reaches for my hand. *'I can fix me. Carlen used to poison me all the time.'*

"I'm beginning to understand why you wanted to kill the guy," I say.

He frowns at the medical cabinet on the wall for a moment. A look of annoyance crosses his face and he raises his hand as though reaching towards the cabinet. The door of the first aid cabinet swings opens and the contents crash to the floor.

I crouch down to gather up the items but can't find any disinfectant or bandages. I turn back to find he already has the items. I frown in confusion at the contents on the floor and the items now beside Dennian.

He holds his wrist and focuses on the gash. I creep forward. His eyes slip closed as more bubbles seep from the wound.

"Dennian, I really think you should go to hospital."

He pushes up to his knees and runs his hand under the water. When he pulls his hand back, blood seeps naturally from the wound with only the occasional micro-bubble forming.

He pinches the edges of the cut together for a moment, his lips moving silently. He then bandages his hand.

"That's not going to work," I object. "It will need stitches."

'It'll be fine.' He's not overly coherent, so I nudge him when he slumps into the corner. He opens one eye.

"How did you get back here? You were meant to be gone for hours."

I wonder if he would have answered if he wasn't throwing up in the toilet again. When he looks slightly better, I give him back the glass so he can rinse his mouth out.

'My head's fuzzy. I need to lie down.' He struggles to his feet and I offer an arm to help him up.

'If you won't let me fetch a medic, you can stay here where I can keep an eye on you." I direct him towards my bed.

Once he's as comfortable as possible with his feet hanging out from under the blankets, I take advantage of his talkative state.

"How did you guess the number Stev wrote on his hand?" I ask

'He thinks loudly.'

"You read his mind from across the room?" I ask and Dennian nods his head. "I thought a telepath had to touch someone to read their thoughts?"

'Not if you're any good. Although it helps to touch the first time to tune in to that person.'

"Is that why you flinched away from me when we first touched?"

He nods his head again.

"Where were you born?" I ask.

'Atlia, the new city. The old city flooded long before I was born.'

"Why don't you look like you're from Atlas?"

197

'Can you keep a secret?' He leans up towards me, resting on his elbows to whisper, forgetting he isn't speaking out loud. I nod.

'They all have the chimaera gene, even the ones that don't look like they do.' Dennian flops back onto the bed and presses a hand to his temple.

"What's the chimaera gene?"

'Can't talk about it. They kill the chimaera.'

"Who do?"

'The parents. I don't want to talk about them.'

"What do you want to talk about?" I lie down until my body is pressed against his.

'I think I love you.' He reaches out his good hand and brushes a strand of hair from my face. *'And it hurts because I'm scared it can't be.'*

"I think I love you too, so don't be scared." I press my lips to his and lose myself in his kiss.

I rest my head on his chest listening to his breathing become even. Eventually I drift off to sleep.

*

'Who are you?' In my dream I'm still lying with my head and hand resting against Dennian's chest. I think Dennian's addressing me until another voice replies.

'We demand you release us from this prison, dragon-pet.'

I notice Dennian's furrowed brow even though I'm not able to move my body in my sleep induced haze. A patch of white glows from the dragon on his armband.

'I don't know what you're talking about. You should not be addressing me like this. You should direct your words to the Temple of Aurumargent,' Dennian replies.

198

'Who holds the key to Myth?' another voice demands.

'I know nothing of a key,' Dennian replies.

'Do not lie to us!'

'Perhaps the dragon did not tell him, Griffin. Nasty manipulative creatures they are.'

'How would you know, if he knows or not, Phoenix? I say we set a boggart on him. Can't trust a sabre horn. Teach him not to mess with the creatures of Myth.'

There appear to be multiple voices in my dream although none of them make sense.

'You will pass on a message to the dragon...' the first voice says.

'There are no dragons.' Dennian doesn't sound like he believes his own statement.

'You will tell the blue hatchling that if she and her kind do not free us, we will destroy them....'

*

I wake to early morning rays streaming across my face. The bed beside me is empty. I sit up and toss the blankets aside. Dennian sits on the floor with his back against the wall and a sketch book across his knees. His face is a better colour although still not back to normal.

"How do you feel?" I ask.

"My head hurts," Dennian says.

"Using your words today, I see." I grin at him. He looks up at me with an alarmed expression. "Don't worry, I won't tell anyone you're telepathic."

"Last night is a little fuzzy," he says.

"Well, I had the weirdest dream last night." The details are already becoming vague in my mind.

I climb out of the warm bed and slide down the wall next to him. I lean over to see what he's drawing.

I stare at a black hole feeling like I'm being sucked into the page. The lines swirl into a vortex in the centre of the page. Stars and planets are drawn into the centre, followed by much larger galaxies. Dizziness washes over me and I have to look away from it for a moment.

"Is this meant to be the Lordinia Black Hole?" I ask as Dennian puts the finishing touches to the page.

"No." He traces his finger over to a smaller dark spot on the drawing. "This was Lordinia."

"It looks like the whole universe is being sucked into that thing," I say.

I gently tug the book off Dennian's lap and flip through the pages. The first one I come across is the medallion he started drawing on the quiz day, the one with the dragon in the centre and other mythical creatures surrounding it.

Some of the pages appear to have been added to the book after they were drawn. I catch sight of the one I'd seen once before of all the books and the amethyst scales melted into the floor.

"Where do your ideas come from?" I ask.

"I draw what I see in my head. It helps me work out what they mean."

"What does this one mean?" I tap a finger against the books.

"I think there is important information in that book."

"About what?"

"The creation of the world," Dennian replies.

I flip back several pages to see what else Dennian's drawn. The girl in one drawing is crouched among headstones in a graveyard face-to-face with a Temple Tiger.

"That's me," I say.

"I thought so too," Dennian said.

"You don't know?"

"Not always."

"Do you know where this is?" I ask.

"The Children's Graveyard. Outside Atlia City, near Stev's uncle's house," Dennian says.

"You know where Stev's uncle lives?" I raise an eyebrow.

"Everyone knows where the palace is." He shrugs.

"Stev says the tigers are dangerous. You only taught me how to handle the non-dangerous ones."

"They won't harm you if they recognise my scent," Dennian says.

I drop his sketch book on the floor and straddle his lap before threading a hand through his hair. The strands are soft almost like a fine fur.

"Will this work?" I lean into his body and press my lips to his.

'Yes.' He moans as he kisses me back. His hands slide up my back holding me closer.

I glance up at the time displayed on the device by my bedside.

"You better get out of here before Lori and Carter arrive." I pass the sketch book back to Dennian.

I suddenly remember the cut to his hand although the bandage is gone. I take his left hand in mine and look for the wound. There's only an angry red line and an older thin-line scar. I check his other palm to make sure I have the right one.

"How did you do that?" I ask.

"I should go." Dennian deposits me on the floor and stands before walking out of my room. The door closes quietly behind him.

Politics

Jayne bounds into my room ahead of Lori and Carter. She plonks herself on the edge of my mattress while my team sets about prepping me for the new day in front of the cameras. I'm beginning to forget how I used to look.

"Okay, quick recap of last night," Jayne begins. "I arrived at the club and Sara welcomed each of the guys in with a pat on the shoulder, which was actually her administering the truth drug."

Carter grabs hold of my chin and turns my head to look at him while he applies my makeup.

"Farray started ranting about something being destroyed. Saul was flirting with the guy serving the drinks, who in Saul's defence was super-hot. I set about flirting with the guys to see how they'd react. Rick got super-creepy and kept trying to touch me and then Stev started screaming and scratching at his skin. I had to accompany him to the hospital while Sara kept an eye on the others."

"Stev had to go to hospital?"

Carter tuts at me and turns my head back to him again. I look at Jayne through the mirror.

"Remember how Dennian mentioned the descendant of the guy, Mellakai, having traces of dragon blood? Well apparently that's true and the drug reacted badly to it. Stev's been in hospital all night having his blood cleansed."

"How is he now?" I ask.

"You'll get to see yourself. We're heading there as soon as you're ready.

I stand from my chair to allow Lori to pull today's dress up over my hips and lace me into it.

"All done," she says with a final tug.

"The transport's out front." Jayne pulls on my hand.

Half an hour later, a driver drops us at the front of the hospital. Jayne leads the way to a private room with two Atlas Peace Keepers stationed by the door.

"You poisoned me!" Stev's voice carries into the corridor, but I miss the reply of whoever he's yelling at.

Jayne taps on the door and the Peace Keepers step aside to let us through.

"Look who I brought to see you," Jayne says.

Stev rests against a pile of pillows stacked behind his back. A tube runs from the inside of his elbow to a machine beside the bed and then disappears under his bed-gown. Blood flows through the loop cleansing his blood.

"You should have seen it last night," Jayne whispers in my ear. "His blood was bubbling."

"I can imagine." I step towards the bed and smile at Stev. "How are you feeling?"

"Violently ill." Stev wipes a hand across his pale, clammy face and shoots a filthy look at Trev.

"Keep him happy," Trev leans in to whisper in my ear before escaping from the room.

"It's lucky I'm the only one with dragon blood," Stev says to the room. "Anyone else would never have survived the ordeal."

"I'm sure you've been very brave about the whole thing." I force my face to maintain a concerned expression.

A doctor enters the room to check Stev's vitals. "You're doing much better this morning. We should

204

have you out of here shortly." The man makes a few notes on Stev's medic-screen and walks out again.

"Looks like you'll be back in time for the elimination party," Jayne says.

"My name had better be the first one you read out," Stev says.

I glance over my shoulder to where Trev disappeared. "I'm sure it will be. We better let you rest. We'll see you this evening." I back out of the room and Jayne follows.

We head back to the mansion. The guys have a free day to do as they please, while Mum, Jayne, Sara, and Trev go over details of the family dates and wedding preparations. I interrupt their conversation a few times but am mostly ignored.

I nap on a couch for a while until Lori comes to fetch me for another outfit change for the pre-elimination party.

I enter the room in a short, dark blue dress. Several of the guys stand as I enter but most remain slumped in their chairs. Stev sits in the centre of the room telling whoever will listen about his ordeal.

"Looks like everyone had a big night," I say.

"We think so, but honestly, none of us remember much." Nathan shuffles over on his couch and I sit carefully between him and Saul keeping my hands over my lap to ensure my dress remains covering my underwear.

"At least Dennian handled it better than the faux prince," Saul says.

"What do you mean?" I ask.

"That guy has dragon's blood in his veins or I'm not a prince," Saul declares.

We glance over to where Dennian sits alone drawing in his sketch book. The colour has almost returned to his face.

At Trev's signal, I stand and move around the room, making sure to speak a few words to each of the remaining nine men. I only have a couple of moments to check on how Dennian is feeling before I have to move on to Stev.

It's a relief when Sara calls us to the open space used for the elimination. She hands me the cards while the guys step into position.

"Gentlemen, today two of you will be leaving the house. If Cassie says your name, you'll be safe until our next elimination." Sara holds her smile for the camera then backs out of the scene.

I glance at the cards. The first name is Stev. I read out each name until only Phil and Rick remain behind. Phil bows his head, composing himself before approaching to say farewell.

When I look over at Rick, anger reddens his face. He says goodbye to a few of the guys before stepping over to me.

"You have no idea what you're missing. You'll regret turning me down when you're stuck sleeping beside one of these losers."

"Goodbye, Rick." I clench my teeth and wait for him to storm off.

There are seven men left in the program and I'm impatient for it all to be over.

*

After breakfast Sara collects me from the kitchen and we head to one of the living areas where Stev,

Saul, and Farray stand around in the princely garb of their respective planets. I wear a floor-length gown trimmed with tiny sparkling gems. The tri-system symbol marks both my cheeks thanks to Jayne's handiwork.

"We have a special surprise for you today," Sara says. "Stev's father, Atlas Delegate Shan, has arranged for you to attend the meeting with Governor Suri today. You will be witnesses to this historic gathering."

"We'll be in the same room as the Governor of the Universe?" I stare at Sara in shock.

Stev snorts with laughter as though this is a normal event for him and he can't understand why I may be nervous. Saul looks like he already knew what was happening and Farray has a gleam in his eyes that sends a shiver down my spine.

After a few moments of prompts and filmed responses, the four of us head outside to a waiting hovercraft with Atlas government markings along the side. My eyes widen at Delegate Shan's transport.

I hitch up my skirt to climb into the craft. Three remaining guys wait by the entrance of the building to see us off. Dennian isn't among them. Saul catches me looking and glances in the same direction as he takes the seat beside me. Stev and Farray settle in opposite us.

"Does Dennian train with Tristen?" Saul asks me.

"Who?"

"He trains the Perceptive Peace Keepers," Saul says.

The craft lifts silently off the ground. I hold my breath and dig my nails into the seat as the ground falls further away.

"Why would Nobody know a Peace Keeper trainer?" Stev sneers. His face has returned to its normal colour after the poisoning incident and with it his attitude.

I take a deep breath and shift my gaze away from the window. I focus on Stev in front of me as we fly swiftly through the air. Beside him, Farray glares at the passing scenery.

"I figured the guy is a Peace Keeper," Saul replies. "He's clearly Perceptive."

"It takes dragon blood to be a Perceptive," Stev says. "And if he had the blood he would have been sick too."

"He looked pretty off-colour to me yesterday. Don't you agree, Cassie?"

I glance at Saul but don't reply.

"It takes decades to become a Perceptive and they don't start training until they are eleven. You don't know anything," Stev replies.

"I bet you a thousand credits that Dennian will be at this meeting today," Saul says.

"The guy's an animal researcher," Stev replies.

"Actually he isn't," I say. The boys look at me. "He's never actually said what his real job is, but he trained with someone called Car-something."

"Hmmm, might be one of the governor's trainers. I still say he'll be there today," Saul says.

Stev and Saul eye each other for several long moments while Farray continues to stare out the window. I squeeze my eyes shut and pretend I'm back on the ground. It's easy enough to do. With my eyes closed in the silence, I can convince myself we aren't in the air.

An almost unnoticeable bump alerts me to our landing at the National Conference Centre. As soon as the door-lock releases, Farray jumps out, his mouth twisted into a sneer. A second hovercraft lands and Stev and Saul's Peace Keeper entourage join us at an unobtrusive distance.

A middle-aged Atlas man approaches, flanked by two more Peace Keepers in their distinctive mid-blue uniforms with trident symbols on their shoulders. Stev bows slightly to him while I try to manoeuvre out of the transport in my long skirt. Saul holds out a hand to assist me and I take it gratefully.

"Father, this is my future bride, Cassie."

I wrinkle my nose at Stev's statement but aim for a smile before anyone notices. I still need to get to Atlas to negotiate my freedom.

"Cassie, this is my father, Glar Shan, Atlas Delegate to the Governor of the Universe."

"Pleased to meet you, Delegate Shan. Stev has mentioned you a lot," I say.

"I'm sure he has. Young Stev Shan has a promising future ahead of him. Come, come. I've arranged for you to be seated with a view of the proceedings. I, of course, will be seated with the other delegates."

Glar Shan claps his hands together and looks us all over with his blue eyes.

"Awfully good of you to arrange this for us, Father. It's important for Cassie to see what my future will look like before we marry." Stev falls in beside the delegate as we head towards the security checkpoint. Farray and Saul trail behind.

"Is that a dragon stone?" Delegate Shan glances at my necklace and I reach up to touch the stone Dennian gave me.

"It was a present," I say.

"It wouldn't be appropriate to wear that in the presence of Governor Suri. Dragon stones are reserved for officials and Perceptive Peace Keepers. I can look after it for you until after the meeting," Glar Shan offers.

I hold the stone for several moments before unhooking the clasp and handing it over. Delegate Shan slips it into an inside pocket of his official jacket.

Peace Keepers flank our group and as we get closer to the entrance more Peace Keepers stand guard. Two hooded figures stand by the entrance while others, our personal guards among them, scan the crowd.

"Perceptives have their hoods up." Saul falls into step beside me. "They're trained to see people's emotions and outer thoughts to prevent any incidents. They hide their faces to protect their identity and help their focus without visual stimulation. The other Peace Keepers are Protectors, trained to use violence if necessary to keep the peace."

"Doesn't seem like it fits with the government's pacifist reputation," I say.

"Only the strong can afford to be passive – Governor Suri's moto," Saul says. "That elaborate circle on the uniform means they work for Governor Suri instead of one of the planets. Terra's symbol is a bit lame in comparison." He nods his head towards a Peace Keeper with a twig and leaf on his shoulder.

We cross the open courtyard in front of the building. A ring of curved sculptures circle the area. Each pair balances over channels cut into the ground

"What's with the weird art?" I nod my head at the ones nearest the building entrance.

"They're blast absorbers," Delegate Shan says.

210

I trip over my feet. "Are blasts…expected?"

"Of course not. Stick by me and you'll be well protected," he replies.

We enter the building through a scanner and Delegate Shan leads us up a set of stairs to a gallery overlooking a massive meeting hall. I peer over the rail at the two large semi-circle tables facing each other. Several seats are already occupied while other people mingle in small groups.

"I'll be down there with the other delegates during the meeting," Glar Shan says. He nods his head at Stev and heads back down the stairs with his Peace Keepers. Stev's and Saul's take up position along the wall behind us.

Clusters of seats are arranged along the length of the gallery area. We have a small balcony to ourselves, although several other groups of well-dressed people sit nearby.

Stev takes a seat in the front of the two rows, while Farray throws himself down in one at the back. Saul joins me at the rail.

"Can you see him?" he asks.

"Who?" I ask.

"Dennian."

I scan the room below us. The Perceptives all stand with their hands clasped lightly behind their backs and heads lowered under their hoods as though their focus is outside the room. The Protectors' hands cross in front and their eyes scan the room.

"That's him there." I point to the hooded figure standing below us with the elaborate circle on the shoulder of his blue uniform.

"How can you tell?" Saul leans out over the edge.

"He's the only one not wearing shoes."

"Excuse me, sir, madam?" A serving man steps towards us with a tray of steaming hand cloths. Saul and I hold out our hands and the man uses his tongs to hand us each a cloth before moving on to the next people.

"I will not tolerate their presence." A voice bellows from the doorway below. I lean forward over the rail still clutching my cloth.

Several people step into my line of sight. The first is a huge man dressed in yellow and black clothing that resembles Farray's outfit. A metallic crown circles his head and is smeared in a bright green gel. His men have the same substance smeared across their foreheads.

Beside him stands a woman almost as tall, although she wears blue fabric trousers and shirt similar to the Peace Keepers. Her silver hair is plaited around her head like a crown, and a gold and a silver dragon paint her cheeks making it difficult to determine her true appearance.

"That's Governor Suri," Saul whispers in my ear.

"The Peace Keepers are present for the security of everyone at this gathering." Their voice is calm but carries across the room.

"My personal guard have been forbidden from attending me. I will not have these…witches getting into my head," the man bellows.

"We can assure you, they are not witches, and you appear to have already taken precautions against mind-readers. However if you are uncomfortable by their presence, they can remain outside." Governor Suri waves a hand and the hooded figures step away from their positions and head towards the exit in an orderly file.

Below me, Dennian tugs his hood off and changes his stance so his hands are at his front like the Protectors. Two others across the room copy his actions.

The big man runs his eyes over the remaining Peace Keepers. He waves a hand towards one of his men who steps forward holding a jar of glowing green gel.

"I hope you don't mind if I check that they all left?" The Triade lord grins evilly at the governor.

"Dragon's bane is really unnecessary," they reply.

The lord, who I'm beginning to suspect is Farray's father, dips a finger into the gel and touches it to the forehead of the nearest Peace Keeper. No one reacts until he reaches the first man who removed his hood like Dennian did. The instant the gel touches his skin, the man screams and claws at the air in front of him. The Perceptive beside him, hauls him from the room before he too can be touched by the substance.

"It must react to dragon blood," Saul whispers. Below us, Dennian hasn't moved.

My heart pounds in my chest as his turn approaches. Beside me, Saul holds his breath. The lord reaches out and smears a line of gel across Dennian's forehead.

"Satisfied?" Governor Suri asks drawing the man's attention away from Dennian's rigid body.

"Humph," the man mutters as he turns away.

I drop my hand cloth over the rail. It lands on Dennian's shoulder. He flinches before realising what it is. With a quick glance around the room, he wipes the gel from his face and drops the cloth out of sight behind him.

Governor Suri leads the way towards the seating arrangement. As they approach, two horned tigers stand from where they'd been lying out of sight.

I gasp. "Temple Tigers."

"They go too." Farray's father waves a hand in the direction of the two tigers. Governor Suri laughs.

"Temple Tigers do as they please. If you wish to attempt to remove them, by all means, go ahead." They extend a hand to the animals in invitation.

The man growls and marches towards his position at the table. Several more massive men with green smears on their foreheads follow him to their seats.

"Takarna must not be attending today." Stev leans over the rail between me and Saul for a better look at the two animals.

"What makes you say that?" I ask.

"The Keeper hates the tigers. Banned them all after he lost his eye to one," Stev says. "Glad I'm not down there with them."

Governor Suri strides over to the centre of one semi-circle and stands by the chair while everyone finds their allocated seat. A grey haired man takes the seat beside the governor.

"That's Vice Governor Jaarid," Saul whispers, as we sit back in our own seats. "The woman wearing the crown on the governor's other side is my mother."

Saul's mother is younger than the two rulers, her hair still a deep brown.

"What happens when they get too old to rule?" I ask.

"Mother says Governor Suri is actually quite young. She met the previous Governor Suri and says this one can't be older than twenty-five. They apparently change their appearance so people aren't uncomfortable if the current Governor Suri is too young. This governor has ruled for the last twelve years," Saul explains.

"But that would have made them around thirteen when they became governor," I say.

"Age doesn't matter to the governor. They might even be younger than that," Saul says.

Governor Suri and Vice Governor Jaarid take their seats, leaving Saul's mother standing. She claps her hands together and scans the room.

"It has been many years since a government gathering was held on Terra and I wish to extend a warm welcome to Governor Suri for gracing us with their presence. I also wish to acknowledge Vice Governor Jaarid, Delegate Glar Shan of Atlas –"

Delegate Shan stands abruptly and bows to the room. "King Niko Shen gives his apologies. He was unable to spare the time to leave Atlas."

"Yes, thank you," Saul's mother says. "Now where was I? Ah yes, I also wish to extend the welcome to our guests from Triade. It's been too long since they joined our table."

"I wonder why they're here," Saul mutters with a brief glance over his shoulder at Farray.

I look too. A man dressed in Triade yellow and black approaches the prince. Stev's Peace Keeper takes a step forward but allows them to speak to Farray. Their native language is guttural and I don't understand any of the quiet conversation. I turn my attention back to the room below.

"It's an extra special week for us here on Terra as we'll finally witness the creation of the Lordinia Black Hole," the Queen of Terra says. "Governor Suri, I imagine you would have seen this astronomical event on multiple occasions. Do you have any words for us?"

Governor Suri stands abruptly and spreads their hands on the table in from of them.

"May Aurumargent guide us to salvation. May our actions, however wrong, be for the right reasons. Forgive us the lives lost to achieve peace." The governor bows their head for a moment.

"Murderer," one of the Triade men says loud enough for everyone to hear. Governor Suri ignores the comment and retakes their seat.

"What was that about?" Saul whispers.

"Perhaps we should get started on these policy documents," Vice Governor Jaarid says. "We have a lot to get through today."

"We will not be managed by the Destroyer!" The Triade king stands suddenly, his chair falling backwards.

He marches out of the room followed by his advisors. Only two Triade men remain in the room and they sneer at Governor Suri.

"Does someone want to explain what is going on?" Vice Governor Jaarid asks.

"Our people worked the moon mine in the Lordinia System. You murdered them." The man points a finger at Governor Suri.

"The Lordinia Black Hole formed almost a thousand years ago. Why is this relevant?" Vice Governor asks.

"Because the Destroyer sits before us. You will pay for the lives of our people you stole."

Governor Suri stands and locks eyes with the men. "The destruction of the moon base was caused by Warlord Kllrarn's illegal weapons dump. Your people wouldn't have died if they hadn't accepted bribes to keep it a secret."

Someone taps my arm and I jerk back from the rail. One of Saul's Peace Keepers stands beside us. The other people up on the balcony make their way quickly towards the stairs.

"The Perceptives have ordered everyone to leave the building quietly," the Peace Keeper whispers. She stands back out of sight of the people below us.

"You can't make us leave because someone challenges Governor Suri," Stev says. "There are cameras down there. You can't keep these accusations quiet."

"I need you to lower your voice, sir," the woman says. "The Perceptives believe an attack may be attempted. We've been asked to evacuate everyone quietly, to be safe."

"There are no Perceptives down there," Stev says.

'Cassie, you need to leave.' Dennian's voice sounds in my mind. I peer over the balcony, but he hasn't moved from his position below us. At the meeting tables, the two tigers have moved into position behind the higher ranking members.

The Triade man speaks again. "We demand you release our planet from your federation of lies."

"We should go." I touch Saul's shoulder and nod towards the stairs. "Where's Farray?"

The moody prince no longer sits with our group.

"I don't know," Stev replies. "He left after his guards did. Assumed he needed the bathroom."

"Come on, let's get outside." I tug on Saul's hand and Stev follows us still arguing. Saul and Stev's Peace Keepers surround us in a loose circle.

As we head down the steps, Governor Suri speaks again. "We accept your proposal to reintroduce warlord rule to Triade. You will be restricted to your star-system and will need to seek approval from ourself to leave. As none of you have a current warlord

217

rank, you will be under the rule of Class One Warlord Tarsh –"

"You're talking about a Warlord who lived a millennium ago."

We reach the bottom of the steps and I turn to see Governor Suri smile at the man.

"We were and always will be Warlord Tarsh," Governor Suri says.

Saul grabs my hand and tugs me out the door. I blink in the bright sunshine. Dozens of Perceptive and Protector Peace Keepers roam the open court yard checking everyone's belongings.

"Head for the hovercraft," Stev's Peace Keeper says.

We walk quickly towards the sculptures we passed on our way from the landing pad. A person in a yellow and black hooded cape steps into the centre of the courtyard and hands shove me.

I tumble sideways taking Saul and Stev with me. As I fall, I catch a brief glance of Dennian dashing past me. We land in a trench under one of the blast protectors in a pile of limbs.

The ground rocks with the first explosion. Glass and metal shards from the building shower down around us. My ears ring.

Peace Keeper

Dennian – Present

The vision hits me moments after I tell the Protectors to evacuate the building. The images explode in my brain and I fight the urge to draw what I see. There isn't time, so I project what I see; two detonations inside the building and three outside in the courtyard.

Lucei and Thylace rear up, placing paws on the nearest delegates, and vanish from the room. Cassie reaches the doorway and steps into the courtyard. I sprint in her direction. Behind me, power surges as Governor Suri throws up a shield of energy moments before the first blast detonates.

I reach Cassie and shove her towards the nearest blast protector. She falls, taking Saul and Stev down with her. I skid to a halt, searching out the three terrorists.

The first stands in the centre of the courtyard that's filled with Peace Keepers and people evacuating the conference building. The ground rocks with the first explosion inside the building. My ears ring, but I pick out the other two locations from my vision.

Screams fill the air, the public's panic threatening to overwhelm me. I create a quick illusion of a man in a hooded cloak with the gold and silver dragons across the back.

I feel the three Triades. Their explosive devices are internal. Their final moments contain joy. They believe the governor and vice governor will die along with those escaping from the building.

I suck energy from my dragon stone and throw out three shields. The power detaches from me and I hold each in place by a thin thread. In training, a Perceptive is taught never to allow their power out of their grasp. A loss of concentration will bring it all back at me in a force stronger than a lightning strike.

One of the men turns to look at my illusion of the Keeper and grins as they detonate. The blast erupts against my shields, tearing at me as I dig my heels into the ground. With nowhere else to go the explosions shoot into the air, funnelling upward like rockets. People scatter in all directions.

The Perceptives throw up their own energy shields as they put themselves between the fleeing public and my shields. I wait for the blast energy to dissipate before I pull my own power back to me safely.

Something hits me in the side. I catch a glimpse of yellow and black robes before I lose control. My shields ripple and snap back towards me. The Keeper illusion vanishes.

'Get down!' I project to everyone in the vicinity.

The Perceptives drop to the ground, strengthening the shields they hide behind. The explosion rips over the top of the Peace Keepers and I'm thrown backwards.

I hit the edge of a blast protector and Farray lands on top of me, his hand closing around my throat. Whatever he's about to say is cut off as my power hits us. Farray's eyes open wide as blood vessels burst. Red fern-like patterns spread across his skin, then his body goes rigid and he collapses on top of me.

Pain fills my body and I can't breathe. The mythical creatures on my armband light up in a variety of colours. White lights appear in my vision. The dragon stone around my neck shatters.

Injuries

Booom! I feel rather than hear the final explosion. My ears ache in the silence that follows. Stev's elbow digs into my ribs. I try to shift my position, but he's curled in a ball with his arms over his head while lying on the layers of my dusty dress.

"Help me up," I say.

"What?" Saul yells back.

I reach a hand out to the other prince and he helps me stand. Stev sits suddenly, grabbing my ankle as I pull myself out of the ditch beneath the curved sculpture of the blast protector. Stev's mouth moves, but all I hear is the ringing in my ears.

As I turn back around, I catch sight of a limp hand covered in red fern-like patterns. I heave myself from the ditch, tripping on my skirt in the process. The hand belongs to Saul's female Peace Keeper.

I swallow back the bile rising in my throat and scan the area. Peace Keepers struggle to their feet and hurry to check anyone still in the courtyard. Three blackened craters in perfectly contained circles litter the open space.

I step forward and nearly trip over Farray. His exposed skin has the same fern-like pattern and his red-shot eyes stare blankly up at me. His body shifts and I smother a scream behind my hand before I realise there's a person beneath him.

"Dennian!" I throw myself to the ground dragging Farray's body away.

Dennian's face is pale and his body is still as though he holds his breath. His blue uniform is covered in dirt and sweat. He opens his eyes and his fingers curl into the gravel at his sides.

"Is he alright?" Saul asks loudly from beside me.

"Fine." Dennian's voice is rough.

A few stragglers run out of the building. The moment Governor Suri follows, the convention centre caves in with a massive rumble. I crouch over Dennian until the dust cloud settles. I sit up and wipe a hand over my face leaving a dirt smudge in its wake. Governor Suri turns in a circle surveying the destruction. Their hair and face paint remain perfect.

"Milord," a Perceptive calls out. "Our dragon stones are depleted from the blast."

Governor Suri looks at their own dragon stone bracelet. "Mine too," they say. "We've called the remaining Perceptives to assist. Tidy up here. We're going to retrieve King Mercardi."

"Yes, Milord," the man replies.

Governor Suri vanishes into thin air. The Peace Keepers return to checking on anyone left in the courtyard.

"Where are my guards, my father?" Stev presses his back against the blast protector as he edges towards us.

"The tigers took the delegates to the *Brinthiss Malla*," Dennian pauses, sucking in shallow breaths before speaking again. "If your guards had teleportation devices on them, they'll be there too."

"What's the *Brinthiss Malla*?" I ask.

"Governor Suri's spaceship," Stev replies.

I glance over my shoulder towards the hovercraft. "Do you think you can make it over to the transport?" I ask Dennian. I feel exposed in the courtyard despite the Peace Keepers roaming around.

Dennian nods his head and lifts his arms slightly so Saul and I can get under each side of him. The three of us stagger to our feet. Saul rests his hand against Dennian's side before yanking his hand away. It's comes away bloody and Saul's face turns an odd shade of green.

"You Perceptives know how to heal, don't you? Some sort of energy transfer from your dragon stone?" Saul asks.

"Yes." Dennian takes another shallow breath.

"That's good, but let's get you back to the medics at the mansion anyway," Saul says.

Stev shadows us as though we're a shield protecting him from the world. We make our way slowly up the flight of stairs towards the hovercraft. The pilot edges a door open as we approach. He looks around warily.

"Where are the others?" he asks.

"They won't be joining us," I say.

"The other Prince?"

"Dead," Saul says.

"Get in. You're lucky I waited. Thought the whole place was going up." The pilot grabs the controls while Saul and I help Dennian climb in. Stev pushes in past us and huddles in a corner. I haul myself up beside him and Saul closes the door behind us.

As the ground falls away beneath us, I look out over the collapsed convention building and the black circles in the courtyard. A shudder rolls over me and I dig my fingers into the seat.

"Help me get his shirt off." Saul drags my attention back to the inside of the hovercraft. He's pulled a small first aid box out from under a seat and undoes Dennian's shirt buttons with trembling fingers.

I slide over and help Dennian sit upright. He squeezes his eyes shut as we remove his Peace Keeper shirt leaving him in the t-shirt underneath. Blood drips down his side and pools on the seat beneath him.

"That's not good," Saul mutters.

"I've seen Dennian heal himself before." I keep my voice low so only Saul can hear.

"No, I mean this." Saul lifts the leather band from around Dennian's neck. The remains of a powdery rock clings to metal dragon claw.

"Do you have another stone, Dennian?" Saul asks.

"Cassie has one," Dennian mumbles.

I reach up to my neck, but the necklace is gone. "Delegate Shan took it." I look at Saul in alarm.

"Stev, what about you? Any dragon stones we should know about?" There's an edge to Saul's voice as he starts pulling bandages from the first aid kit.

"I gave it to Cassie." Stev remains huddled in his corner.

"Where is it?" Saul looks back at me.

"In my room at the mansion, but it's not like the others. It's dull. I don't think it will work."

"I can use it." Dennian's words are barely audible. A trail of blood trickles from the corner of his mouth. My throat constricts.

"Right, let's get this bandage on so he survives the flight," Saul says. "As soon as we land, get that stone."

I hold the edge of a bandage while Saul wraps it around Dennian's middle in an attempt to stem the flow of blood. Dennian's face is drained of colour and he slides down into a horizontal position as soon as we're done.

As we near the mansion, I slip my shoes off. We touch the ground with a gentle bump and I have the

225

door open before the motor stops. Then I hitch up my skirt and run. Trev waits by the landing pad and yells as I dash past.

"We need a medic," Saul calls out, distracting Trev long enough for me to make my escape.

My breathing comes in long ragged gasps. I burst through the doors and take the steps two at a time. In my room, I drag out my suitcase and start throwing items out. I know I tossed the rock in there somewhere.

I pull the last shirt out and upend my suitcase giving it a shake. Nothing else falls out. I'm scrabbling through my belongings when Mum bursts into my room.

"Cassie!" She throws her arms around me. "I heard about the attack on the Conference Centre. Are you all right?"

She backs up, clutching my arms as she looks me up and down, taking in my filthy dress and dirt smeared across my face. I see the dull dragon stone where it's rolled under the edge of the bed. I lunge for it and grip it tightly in my hand.

"Dennian's hurt." I lurch to my feet. Mum grasps my hand, but I pull away and dash back down the stairs on bare feet.

Dusk settles over the mansion while bright lights flood the landing pad. People swarm around a stretcher. Four hover-cams hang above the scene. As I draw closer, Eric and one of the medics grab hold of me, preventing me getting closer.

"I need to get to Dennian!"

"We're doing everything we can for him," the medic says. "You'll only be in the way.

I struggle against their arms. "Saul," I yell.

The prince appears from the chaos and reaches for my hand. I slip the stone into his palm.

"I'll get it to him," Saul promises. He pushes his way back through the crowd as Eric pulls me further away.

"Damn," Trev mutters as he dashes past. "We're going to have to change up the whole week's programing."

I stand still, blinking back tears as the medics haul Dennian away on the stretcher. I continue to stand there after Eric releases my arms and the spotlights turn off. Eventually Eric departs and I sink to the ground.

"Everyone's looking for you." Sometime later Nathan appears by my side in the near darkness guided by his torchlight.

"I haven't gone anywhere," I say.

"Saul said to tell you the stone lit up when Dennian touched it. Apparently that's a good thing? They've let Saul stay with him, but the rest of us had to get out of the way." Nathan sinks to the ground beside me and switches off his torch. "I didn't know Dennian was even with you guys today."

"He's a Peace Keeper," I say dully.

Nathan nods and we sit in silence for several moments.

"Come on." Nathan stands suddenly and holds out a hand to me.

"Where are you going?"

"If we can't wait by Dennian, I'm going to take our minds off everything."

I stand and allow Nathan to guide me through the darkness lit only by his torch. We skirt around the mansion and head towards the field where we had our picnic date, before Dennian came back into my life.

Nathan drops my hand and waves an arm at the blanket laid out across the grass. A telescope points at the stars, its viewer image displayed on the screen mounted at its base.

Nathan kneels on the blanket and I sink down beside him.

"I've already set it up. See, that's the Lordinia Star." Nathan points to the image on the screen.

"When will it die?" I ask.

Nathan checks the time on the screen. "In about half an hour."

We lie side by side in silence as we wait for the death of a star that happened almost a thousand years earlier. There's a bright flash on the screen then the star folds in on itself.

"Farray's father blamed Governor Suri for the black hole," I say.

"How many people do you think were there when it happened?" I feel like every death is happening in this very moment and the pain crushes my chest. Tears spill from my eyes.

"Not many according to the history book I read. The planet was evacuated beforehand for a meeting of high ranking warlords." Nathan pulls me to his chest and I sob as Farray's ancestors die in a fiery explosion in the night sky above us and Dennian lies injured somewhere inside the mansion.

The moon rises before Saul finds us. He sinks onto the rug beside me and Nathan, before pulling me into a hug.

"He's going to be fine," Saul whispers into my hair.

"Can I go see him?" I ask.

Saul shakes his head "Trev banned us all from the room and Dennian needs to rest. I'm sure he'll come find you once his wounds have healed fully."

"Are you okay?" I ask.

"Father contacted me. Mother made it safely aboard the *Brinthiss Malla*. He wants me to come home."

"Are you going to leave?" I ask.

"I haven't decided yet."

Bad Spirits

It's three days before the next challenge. Dennian shows no sign of his injuries beside tiredness around his green eyes, and the rock Stev gave me now glimmers from the metal claw on Dennian's leather necklace. Besides a brief moment alone when he assures me he's fine, Dennian's prevented from interacting with the rest of the group.

Jayne told me Trev blamed him for the mess of what was meant to be a group date with the princes. No one mentions Farray, and Stev wanders the mansion looking pensive after having a massive row with his two Peace Keepers when they return. Saul's guard also returns with a new companion to replace the woman who died at the conference centre.

We stand in yet another sprawling garden, although this one has a mound of dirt set off to one side and what look like trapdoors and a narrow tunnel leading beneath the surface.

I wear flats and trousers matched with a red, fitted V-neck top. Beside me, Mum and Jayne wear dresses. The remaining contestants stand on Sara's far side, while Trev lurks behind the bushes, monitoring the scene.

"For the next challenge, we're going to need Dennian and Shane to accompany Cassie." Sara smiles brightly at the hover-cam.

I lean over to Jayne. "Who's Shane? Have I met a Shane? Are they sneaking extra contestants onto the show when I'm not looking?"

"He's the medical student," Jayne whispers in my ear. "He wants a wife so he won't be distracted by dating while he's studying." She nods to where the mysterious Shane stands at the edge of the group.

"He's a contestant? I thought he was part of the show's medical team." I stare at the guy who treated Nathan's dislocated shoulder, Stev's poisoning, and held me back while Dennian was wheeled away on a stretcher several days ago.

Before I have time to dwell on the extra contestant, Sara waves me forward to stand with the selected guys.

I stand between the men as the three of us stare down at the tiny timber hatch cover set into the ground beside Sara's feet.

"There'd better not be bugs down there," Shane mutters.

I glance at Dennian, but he continues to study the slightly disturbed ground around our feet.

Nathan, Eric, Saul, and Stev stand to one side watching us. Stev's mouth turns up in a smirk as though he knows what is about to happen.

"As you have probably guessed, we will be looking at more fears today," Sara says. "The three of you will use this hatch to make your way into an underground space where we will see how long you can stay down there. We will of course be monitoring you the whole time and there is an escape hatch to get you out if needed."

Sara ushers Shane forward first. The camera pods come in close as Shane struggles through the small gap and sweat forms on his forehead. After a few minutes, he disappears below the surface.

"How are you with small, underground spaces?" I ask Dennian.

"Not something I enjoy," he replies quietly.

231

Sara calls me and I walk over to the edge of the hole. The tunnel looks tiny and I smear dirt over my designer slacks and flats as I lower myself into the entrance. I drop to my knees and feel around in the darkness. There's a short tunnel ahead of me that opens into what feels like a larger space designed for the three of us to lie side by side. Shane shifts in the darkness.

"Where are you?" I hit my head on the timber roof above me. I crouch down lower.

"Over here," Shane replies. I move towards his voice.

"Well this is cosy," I mutter as I twist around so I can lie on my back on the dirt floor.

"As least there are no bugs," Shane mutters.

"That's your fear?"

"Yeah. Do you know what Dennian's is?"

"Not sure. Maybe being in a small space underground."

A snort of laughter escapes Shane's mouth. "At least it's nothing extra they're going to do to us down here."

I turn at the sound behind me and I glance towards where I think the tunnel entrance is. For a moment I catch the reflection off two cat-like eyes. My heart rate spikes before the reflection disappears.

"Dennian?" I whisper.

"Yes, it's me." His hand brushes against my hip and I have to shuffle towards Shane to make room for Dennian to lie beside me. After some moments, the three of us are in position with our arms brushing in the confined space.

"Well this is fun." I say dryly as I wriggle to get into a more comfortable position. "How long do you think they'll make us wait?"

A slight noise above us is followed by what sounds like hundreds of small pebbles being poured down a tube. Moments later bugs pour down over us.

Shane screams and jerks his body wildly trying to shake the bugs off. I cop an elbow to my ear and curse as I try to wriggle closer to Dennian in the confined space.

"Watch out, Shane!" I curse again as he thrashes beside me. Bugs crawl down my shirt making me want to shake them out, but I lie as still as possible and put up with the sensation.

Dennian throws his leg over me and reaches for Shane. He grabs hold of Shane's flailing arm while lying on top of me. I turn my head towards Shane, but I can't see anything. I can only feel Dennian pressed against me and Shane's slowly stilling movement.

"It's a trick. There're no bugs." Dennian's voice murmurs beside my ear.

"I can feel them. They're crawling all over me," Shane whimpers.

"All in your mind," Dennian replies softly. "You're safe here. Nothing can hurt you."

Shane goes still beside me although he continues to whimper. Dennian rolls off me back into his space. Several bugs make squishy sounds as he moves. I grope for his hand and give it a squeeze when he places it in mine.

"You're ruining our scenario, Dennian." Trev voice comes through a speaker near my head. "I suggest you don't do that again. Lie back and get comfortable because Stev has arranged a special surprise for the three of you."

A low chanting begins through the speaker and Dennian tenses.

"What's wrong?" I ask.

"Spirit summoners," Dennian hisses. "They aren't allowed to perform outside Atlas."

"What—"

'Cassie?' The voice is quiet and wraps around me like a familiar blanket.

"Dad?" I whisper.

'Yes it's me, Sweetheart.'

Tears prick at my eyes. Beside me, Shane mutters to himself in a softly whispered conversation that I can't quite make out.

'Tar?' A young boy's voice cries out. *'It's dark, Tar.'*

"Zeth." The name slips from Dennian's tongue as though he can't quite believe it.

'Are you looking after your mother?' Dad speaks again, drawing me away from the scared child. The air cools like a mild breeze on an early spring morning.

'You know I always—' Dad says.

'He's coming for you,' the child cries. Dennian goes rigid beside me.

"Dennian?" I reach for his hand. The child has gone silent.

'Spirits of Aurumargent, protect me from the dead who seek to harm me,' Dennian mutters to himself. *'Spirits of Aurumargent, protect me—'*

'Cass—' Dad's voice fades away as Shane also calls out to whoever he had been speaking to. An icy chill creeps over me and I shiver.

"I warned you I'd come back, boy." The gravelly male voice sends shivers down my spine. It sounds like he's in the hole with us instead of speaking in our minds. Dennian makes a strangled noise and stops chanting.

"Dennian? What's going on?" I say.

"I want my hand back," the voice continues. "I want my eye back, and I want my life back." The last two words are growled. Dennian rips his hand from mine as he lifts his arm. He struggles beside me.

I reach for him and my hand passes through something icy cold. It burns the skin of my hand, but I find Dennian's hands. They're clasped in front of his neck as though holding an invisible hand away from his throat. I jerk my numb hand away.

"Get us out of here!" I yell.

Beside me, Dennian jerks again. Then, in a swift movement, he lifts his hips and slams his feet into the covered hatch above us. One half of the cover flies open, sending sunlight and dirt streaming down on us. As I avert my eyes from the falling debris, I catch sight of the ghostly figure struggling with Dennian.

The man's body is transparent, almost misty, but the claw marks are visible across one side of his face. His one good hand is clasped around Dennian's neck. The stump presses against Dennian's chest.

I scream, scurrying backwards into Shane. As the sunlight hits them, the man from Dennian's fear drawing loses consistency. Dennian throws himself through the hatch opening and the man fades from my sight.

I haul myself out of the hole. My heart pounds and my limbs shake. Dennian sprints towards the mansion, ignoring the three cloaked figures with clasped hands standing beside the remaining guys. They continue the chant I'd heard while in the hole.

"Stop it!" I scream.

I run at them, shoving the one in the centre. The figure stumbles, breaking the connection with the other two and the chant trails off.

Someone grabs me from behind, pinning my arms to my sides. I struggle for a moment then throw my head back.

"Oomph," the person grunts as they release me. I turn around to see Stev with a hand over his nose.

"What is wrong with you?" he yells at me. "No one is allowed to touch the Spirit Priests."

"This was your idea?" I scream. "That spirit attacked Dennian!"

Trev steps between me and Stev. "Calm down. It hasn't hurt anyone. Everyone else has to face their fears."

Trev waves a hand at where Shane dances around in his underpants trying to shake the last of the bugs from his hair. His shirt and trousers lie on the ground at his feet.

Nathan steps forward, holding my trembling body to his chest. I glance at the others. Saul isn't present.

"That *harmless spirit*, the one from Dennian's fear drawing, just tried to strangle him!"

"Dennian's drawing is of the Keeper," Stev says. "Takarna isn't dead. It couldn't have been him."

"He certainly looked dead when he was in that hole with us." I rub the back of my hand. It's red with cold.

"Excuse me," Stev says. "I need to speak to my father." He turns on his heel and marches off towards the boys' rooms.

"Wait, we haven't finished the scene," Trev calls out.

"Yes, you have." Saul stops in front of us. His two Peace Keepers flank him along with two additional Perceptives who weren't here earlier. "Atlas Spirit Summoners are forbidden on Terra. Yuri, Mara, arrest those men." Saul points at the three cloaked figures.

"You can't do that," Trev protests.

"I'm the prince of Terra! I will not have them here!" Saul pulls himself up to his full height. "You think your program is important? Well, manage this – I'm leaving."

Saul spins on his heel and walks up to me. He gives me a small smile. Nathan releases me and steps back.

"It would never have worked between us. I want you to give something to Dennian for me." Saul steps forward and kisses me full on the lips before pulling back. "Goodbye."

Saul strides off towards the landing pad on the other side of the mansion.

"I need to check on Dennian," I say.

Trev grabs my arm, halting my escape. "You need to get ready for the elimination ceremony." Trev glances down at my dirt-covered clothing.

"Saul just walked out. Isn't that dramatic enough for you?" I say.

"I planned an elimination. There will be an elimination." Trev waves over several of the crew who come to stand with us boxing me in.

"Make sure Cassie gets ready for the next scene," he says before turning to Nathan, Eric and Shane. "Get changed for the ceremony. You have half an hour."

Nathan shoots me a concerned look before following after Shane and Eric. I'm marched up to my room by the program security. While I have a quick shower, Lori and Carter arrive to pick out a new outfit for me. Five minutes later I'm back in the chair having my hair re-styled and fresh make-up applied. There's no time to find Dennian.

Sara pokes her head around the door. "Two minutes."

I pull on a new off-the-shoulder dress in pale purple and slip on the heels in a matching shade. Lori zips up the back of the dress. Lori and Carter head out of the room, leaving me to take several deep breaths before making my way downstairs. Mum meets me at the bottom.

"What were you thinking earlier?" she hisses under her breath. "Stev is threatening to leave."

Butterflies fill my stomach. "So Dennian will be the last one standing?" Maybe I won't need my backup plan.

"I hardly think so after his performance today. Trev says it will be between Shane and Nathan if Stev walks out on you."

The butterflies turn to stone. "I'll speak to Stev," I say. "Did anyone check on Dennian?"

"Oh, he's fine." Mum waves a dismissive hand and gives me a gentle shove towards the doors where Sara waits to open them for me.

I fix a smile on my face and step through the doorway into the function room. The furniture has been rearranged now there are only six – five guys left in the house. I scan the room quickly, but Dennian isn't here. My footsteps falter.

I glance over to where Nathan lounges with a drink. Where is he? I mouth. Nathan shrugs his shoulder with a concerned look on his face.

I hesitate for a moment and almost turn around and walk out when my eyes land on Stev. His face is turned into a scowl and he wears make-up, possibly to hide the fact I head-butted him earlier.

I take a deep breath and walk over to Stev. I sit down on the edge of the seat beside him and wait for him to look at me.

"I want to apologise for earlier." I try to sound sincere. "I was scared and didn't realise it was you who had grabbed me. I hope you can find it in your heart to forgive me."

"You embarrassed me in front of the priests," Stev says.

"I'm really sorry about that—"

"I expect you to behave more appropriately when we visit my family."

I suck in a sharp breath. "Of course, I'll be on my best behaviour." I beam at Stev.

Stev launches into a long winded history of the spirit priest while I keep my smile frozen in place and wait for an opening to excuse myself with the pretence of needing to be seen speaking to the others before the elimination.

"Excuse me," Nathan interrupts. "Do you mind if I steal Cassie away for a moment?"

"It's no matter to me. She'll be mine in the end whether you spend time with her or not." Stev waves a hand dismissively.

I struggle to keep a smile fixed on my face as I stand and take Nathan's arm.

"I thought we could take a moment out in the garden?" Nathan suggests.

"Sounds great," I force out.

We step out into the flowering garden with its shrub-lined low brick wall and a little nook with a garden seat. Nathan leads me out of view of the doors we exited. A single hover-cam follows us.

"You look beautiful tonight." Nathan leans in to kiss my cheek. "Dennian hasn't come out of his room," he whispers in my ear. "I asked if they'd let me stay with him, but they wouldn't let me."

"Where's his room?" I keep my voice low as I smile flirtatiously at Nathan for the camera.

"We have a great view of this garden from our bedroom windows." Nathan speaks loud enough for the camera this time. I glance over his shoulder towards the chest-height wall and the wing of the house behind it.

"That must be lovely," I reply.

"Don't those shoes hurt your feet?" Nathan asks. "You look like you could sprain an ankle in them."

"You're right. I'd love to take them off for a few minutes."

Nathan leads me over to the garden bench and makes a show of removing each of my shoes and giving my feet a brief rub.

"Oh ohh, here comes Eric to steal you away," Nathan says. "You ready?"

"Yes."

"Okay...go." Nathan leaps up off the bench and runs at the wall before vaulting over it. I hitch my long skirt up and throw myself after him. The tail end of my dress catches as I go over. Nathan grabs me, pulling the fabric free.

"Run." He reaches for my free hand while I hold my dress with the other.

The grass is springy and well-kept under my bare feet as we run across the lawn. Nathan reaches the door first and tugs it open. I dart through and he follows behind me. The closing door halts the hover-cam trailing after us.

"This way," he whispers.

I follow him up a staircase similar to the one leading to my own room. We reach the top of the stairs without encountering anyone. The hall to our right has a number of doors with a chalkboard on each. Nathan taps on the one with Dennian's name on it.

"Dennian?" he calls out softly. When there's no answer, I push the door open and squeeze past Nathan.

Two single beds line the walls of the room, although only one appears to have been slept in. Besides the desk in the corner and a small pile of clothes beside one bed, the room is empty.

I walk through to the ensuite door and rap my knuckles against it. "Dennian?"

I turn the handle and ease the door open. Dennian crouches on the tiles in the corner behind the shower screen with his arms wrapped around his head.

I squat and reach towards him, but before I can touch him, my fingers touch what feels like an invisible but solid wall, and I receive a sharp shock of static electricity. I jerk my hand away.

"You okay?" Nathan asks from behind me.

"Yeah, I just got a shock," I say. "Dennian? Can you hear me?"

I reach for him again receiving another shock before I touch Dennian's arm. His hand lashes out and wraps around my wrist. I stumble forward until I'm on my knees inches from Dennian face. He blinks a few times before his grip eases.

'Cassie?' His body trembles.

"Yeah, it's me." I flex my fingers to restore circulation to my wrist. "Saul sent the spirit summoners away. The spirit can't hurt you now."

'He will come for me.' Dennian wraps his arms around his body and stares at the wall. With his arms no longer in front of his face, red finger marks show on his neck. 'He will always come for me until an apprentice replaces him.'

"The man from your fear drawing, the one who attacked you today, Stev says that's the Keeper of the Dragon Temple," I say.

Dennian doesn't respond, continuing to stare at the wall. Nathan shuffles from foot to foot behind me.

"Dennian," Nathan says. "It wasn't real. The Keeper can't die until an apprentice has been trained to replace him and he can't be a spirit unless he's dead."

'And as the world reaches its end, the Sabre Horn Tigers shall guard the temple.' Dennian's mind voice says. 'It was written on Takarn's stone at the museum.'

"I've never heard of a Sabre Horn Tiger," I say.

"A what?" Nathan looks at us with an odd look and I realise Dennian only spoke to me.

'It's the dragon name for the Temple Tigers.'

"I think we should get him to bed," Nathan suggests.

'I couldn't save him.' I'm hit by a wave of emotion so strong, I stumble back and sit abruptly. Tears well in my eyes at the overwhelming loss and terror.

"The Keeper?" I ask in confusion. Dennian shakes his head.

"The child?" I guess. I'd heard a young boy when we were in the hole.

'Zeth.' My chest constricts at the emotion attached to his silent word.

"Who's Zeth, Dennian?"

He squeezes his eyes shut and tears leak from the corners. I wriggle up against the wall beside him and he leans into me, pressing his face into my shoulder as I hold him.

'The Atlas prince.'

I suck in a breath recalling the name Zeth Shen on both Stev's family tree and Dennian's fear drawing. Dennian knew one of Stev's cousins; an Atlas prince.

'He should have replaced the King of Atlas. If I couldn't protect Zeth, how can I protect anyone?'

"You saved Nathan from falling to his death, me from drowning, and the people at the conference centre. I'd say you're pretty good at saving people."

'I don't want to have to choose. I can't lose you,' he whispers in my mind.

"I'm not going anywhere."

Dennian's pain still washes over me. I close my eyes and focus on my own feelings. I recall the time at the zoological park when Dennian held his hand almost to mine and showed me how he felt. I move on to our first kiss after he rescued Prince, the electric feeling flowing through me as our lips touched.

I pull forth each memory of him and me and force them at Dennian. His fingers loosen against the fabric of my shirt and his tears slow. I continue to hold him.

"Why did the spirit try to strangle you?" I ask. "He said he wanted his eye, hand and life back."

'I never took his hand,' Dennian says dully. *'Governor Suri did.'*

243

"Why would they do that?" I ask. He'd said something similar at the museum, but I'd assumed he was joking.

"Are you just going to ask him random questions until he speaks?" Nathan leans against the wall as he watches us.

"He did...oh, never mind," I say.

The bedroom door bangs open. Trev storms into the room followed by Mum and Jayne.

"What are you doing in here?" Trev demands. I look up at him from my position on the bathroom floor.

"Nathan and I are checking on Dennian like you said you would." I glare at him.

"You can't be alone with the boys in their room," Mum says.

"You need to stop showing favouritism," Trev says.

"Favouritism! I sat with Stev and then Nathan and now I'm here with Dennian."

'I'll be fine, Cassie.' Dennian lifts his head from my shoulder and huddles into the corner of the room.

"You need to leave this room right now," Trev demands.

"I can stay with him, Cassie," Nathan offers.

"Fine." I touch Nathan's arm briefly and march out of the room without looking back.

Jayne holds out my shoes as I pass. I take them but don't stop to put them on. She jogs after me as I head towards my room in the other wing of the house.

"Is Dennian okay?" she asks. I stop and turn on her.

"He had some dead guy try to strangle him because someone thought it would make good viewing to summon random spirits while we were stuck in a hole! I didn't even know spirits could be summoned!"

"There's no need to shout at me, Cassie. I had no idea it was planned."

"Sorry." I sigh and run a hand through my hair, but my fingers tangle among all the pins used to keep it in place.

"I eavesdropped on Stev's conversation with his father..." Jayne bites the corner of her lip.

"What happened to not being allowed to talk to people outside the house while we're filming?" I say.

"Apparently that rule doesn't apply to princes." Jayne pauses to glance around us. We're alone in the hallway leading to the next wing of the house. "You know how the Keeper is Governor Suri's chief advisor?"

"Yes."

"Stev thinks he's dead." Jayne looks at me like she's told a planetary secret.

"I think he is too. I put my hand through him earlier today." I rub the skin on the back of my hand at the memory.

"You don't understand. The Keeper can't die unless he has an apprentice to replace him. So if he's dead, someone else must be pretending to be Keeper."

"Don't you think Governor Suri would have noticed the loss of the chief advisor?" I raise my eyebrows.

"Exactly! Stev's father apparently thinks the governor is hiding the disappearance from the delegates," Jayne says.

"How important can one guy be?" I ask. "The governors have been running the universe for a thousand years already. Surely they know what they're doing? If I was the governor, I wouldn't want to be advised by that guy." A shudder rolls over me.

"Yeah, but this guy predicts the future or something. He tells Governor Suri what the best course of action is, where problems or natural disasters might happen. Stev says the government only exists because of the Keeper."

"I'm sure it's nothing. It's not like the world is going to end."

"I think you need to distance yourself from Dennian if the Keeper's spirit is really after him. You should pursue Nathan. He's much safer and he's from Terra. I don't think Dennian is. I don't want to lose my best friend, Cassie." Jayne reaches for my hand.

"There you are, girl." Sara appears in the corridor. "We need you in the elimination room."

"Dennian and Nathan aren't there and Saul already walked out. Trev has enough footage of me reading out the guys' names. If he wants an elimination, tell him to stage one and let me know who I get rid of."

Keep Still

Dennian – age five

"Please give him back. He's not broken. He's allowed to be a boy." I tugged on Master Carlen's arm that held Zeth to his side.

"Are there any more of you?" Master Carlen turned his eyes on me and I took a step back. I shook my head vigorously and tried not to think about Lucei. Master Carlen said he could see into people's heads.

"Myaa," Zeth cried, waving his chubby little arms.

"You'll see your Ma soon enough," Carlen sneered at my brother.

"No. Don't give him back to the parents. The tigers can keep him," I begged.

Master Carlen grabbed my shoulder with his free hand and thrust his face into mine. "The world is going to end in the next couple of decades and I will live to see it happen." He shook me. "I won't have you little chimaeras running around under my feet or trying to replace me."

I didn't understand what he meant. I only wanted Zeth back so we could return to Myaa and her tiger streak. But since I got the mark on my back, I belonged to Master Carlen. I'd tried scratching it off, but no matter how much I bled, it wouldn't go away.

Master Carlen stopped beside the edge of the forest closest to the people places. The rows of stones with our names on them were on the other side of Master Carlen.

I took a deep breath, but no tigers were in the forest nearby. A fresh, damp dirt smell filled my nose instead. There would be a new stone in the spirit place.

"Stay here and don't move." Master Carlen thrust me against a tree and walked out into the open with Zeth still under his arm.

"No…" I whimpered. "Don't take him."

I blinked back tears as Master Carlen approached the place the parents live. Myaa always told me to stay away from the big place. The bad parents lived there and they didn't like children who looked different. My colours looked more like Myaa than the king and queen who lived in the big people place.

Master Carlen slipped inside the gate and left Zeth alone by the door. He turned and walked back towards me. I sank to the ground and put my fist into my mouth. Myaa said we had to stay away from that place. I was meant to look after my little brother, but it was harder than with Lucei. She wanted to be a tiger. Zeth preferred being a boy.

Master Carlen kicked my leg when he came back. "This is what happens to unwanted children." He raised his hands and waved them around in the air while looking back at the house. Zeth crawled in our direction and tumbled off a step.

The door opened and the parents came out. The mother screamed and I leaned forward wanting to grab Zeth, but Master Carlen held me back.

"I'm not ready to replace you yet. There are so many years I can still take from you."

The king disappeared and returned with a big stick capped with a shiny stone. He raised it above his head and brought it down on top of Zeth. My little brother screamed and I covered my ears, cowering against the tree.

The smell of blood clogged my nose even when I held my breath, but I couldn't move in case they did the same to me. The parents couldn't see us at the moment, but if we took a single step forward, they would know we were there at the edge of the forest. Zeth stopped screaming. I wanted to scream myself, but I was choked by fear. If I made a sound, I would die like Zeth. Then Lucei would have no family.

Master Carlen placed his hand firmly on my back and I received my first ever vision from Aurumargent. In my mind I had a sudden flash of the future; Master Carlen shoving me and me stumbling forward in the very moment my mother looked up from her gruesome task…

I wet my pants. For a moment I was frozen in place then a tiger called out from deep in the forest.

When Master Carlen was away and I was alone with the tigers, Myaa had told me of the secret way to travel; focus on where you want to go, picture the fabric of the world, pull the edges apart in your mind, and step through the gap to where you want to be.

Master Carlen said it took years to learn how to step out of existence. He probably only told me because he wanted me to know how much more powerful than me he was. It was different to materialisation, he said, which is how the portal to the island worked and the devices the Peace Keepers carried. That relied on a direct path for the material to flow from one point to the other, which is why the portal only worked when the planets looked at each other.

The fabric was different. It was the way the dragons used to travel. A person momentarily stepped out of existence to a place like the path to the Otherside. There was no light, sound, or feeling. It was easy to lose focus and never make it out. It required complete concentration. Myaa said it came naturally to the tiger cubs when they were old enough.

I closed my eyes and focused my thoughts on the Dragon Temple, the murals on the walls and the cool stone floor, instead of the bloody scene in front of me. I felt for the fabric of existence in front of me. For a second I thought I almost had it.

I was concentrating so hard that I yelped when Carlen pushed me in the back, sending me stumbling forward. The fabric tore open, everything turned black and I landed on my hands and knees on the stone floor of the temple. I threw up the greens I'd eaten for breakfast.

Family

And then there were four.

Trev took my suggestion seriously. He had Eric, Stev, and Shane line up as usual then cut together footage from previous weeks to make it look like Nathan, Dennian, and I were all there. I briefly pondered asking if he could do that for the rest of the series and I'll rock up on the final day in my wedding dress to marry Dennian.

Eric leaves the house and Shane is substituted into the family date line-up in lieu of Prince Saul.

Mum and I head to Shane's family first. He lives several hours away, so we have plenty of time to memorise the questions and responses Trev wants.

Shane meets us at the front path leading to a two-storey detached dwelling.

"Three people live here alone?" Mum whispers, her eyes wide.

"Four, actually." Shane steps forward to take my hand. "My older brother is currently away at medical residence, where I'll be headed in a few weeks. Come inside and meet my parents."

We pause on the doorstep for the hover-cam to record Shane knocking on his front door. I plaster a smile onto my face as his parents open the door together. A second hover-cam loiters inside with them.

"Welcome to our home." Shane's mother greets me with a hug.

We enter a grand living room filled with antique furniture and awards lined up on shelves. Shane tells us both his parents are also doctors. I try to remember my cue cards and act like I've been interested in Shane from the moment I laid eyes on him.

When I think I can't take any more without saying something inappropriate, the comms on both Shane's parent's wrists beep.

"No rest for the heroes," Shane's dad jokes. "We're needed at the hospital."

They grab their bags, kiss Shane's cheek, wave to me and head out the door.

After they've gone, Shane sits with his hands in his lap looking mildly uncomfortable. "More tea?" he eventually asks to break the silence.

"I think it might be time for us to go." I stand abruptly.

"Thanks for having us," Mum adds.

Shane follows us to the door and watches while we get back into the transport.

"What an incredible house." Mum stares wistfully out of the window as we drive away.

"I'm not marrying the house," I reply.

*

Two days later, Mum, Jayne, and I arrive at Nathan's family home on the other side of the continent. Nathan meets us at the front door of an average modular family home similar to the one I grew up in.

He leans in to give me a hug and a kiss on the cheek.

"Ready to meet the family?" he asks with a grin.

I smile back at him. "Lead the way."

252

Nathan reaches out to take my hand and leads me into the house without waiting for the hover-cam. Mum follows behind.

We enter the average living area that feels almost cramped after being in the mansion for weeks. Family photos line the walls and several children's toys are piled in a corner.

Two small children sit swinging their heels against the couch, while a woman with a strong facial resemblance to Nathan rushes forward with arms outstretched.

"This must be Cassie." She grasps my hands and kisses both my cheeks. "I'm so excited to meet the girl who's going to secure Nathan's place at SuriTech."

Heat floods my face, but she has already moved on to Mum.

"I'm so sorry my husband couldn't be here to meet you. He has an extended shift at the plant and we couldn't refuse the extra money what with the two little ones in school. It was such a relief when we found out Nathan had been conditionally accepted into SuriTech–"

"Mum, let them sit down for a moment before you talk their ears off," Nathan interrupts with a smile.

"Of course, so sorry. Here I've got drinks prepared in the kitchen." She disappears out a door.

"This is my sister Kylan. She's nine and the little one is Trant."

"I'm five." Trant holds up four fingers and Nathan reaches over to ruffle his hair.

I take a seat on the couch opposite the kids and Mum sits beside me. Nathan perches on the arm of the lounge his siblings occupy.

"Here we go." Nathan's mother returns with a tray of drinks and a stack of cue cards in one hand. She hands us each a glass then sits there grinning at me. "You two will have such beautiful children."

"Mum!" Nathan shoots her a look. "There are three other guys still in the competition."

The smile slips from her face. "But what about your apprenticeship? They said you have to be married."

"It'll be fine, Mum. Aren't you meant to ask Cassie some questions?"

"Of course." She glances at the cards in her hands before looking back at me with the smile in place again. "What draws you to my son?"

My stomach turns nervously. I forget what my response is meant to me, so I tell the truth.

"Nathan is a very genuine, smart, funny, and caring guy. I'd be proud to have him as a husband..." *If I'd never met Dennian.* My smile wavers.

"Cecilia," Nathan's mum looks at Mum then at the cards again. "What qualities are you looking for in a future son-in-law?"

While Mum answers with a pre-prepared response, I focus on maintaining my expression. Inside, my stomach churns. I like Nathan. I don't want to ruin his chances at a career, but I love Dennian. I already have a backup plan in place in case Stev looks like he might be the winner. Could I carry through with it if Nathan is the one chosen for me?

"Cassie?"

I glance up to see everyone watching me. "I'm sorry, could you repeat the question."

"I was asking what you want to do with yourself once you're married, career-wise?" Nathan's mum asks.

"I'm going to make documentaries, about the unusual animals of the universe," I say.

"Nathan loves to travel." She beams at me.

"SuriTech is huge. What are you planning to study there?" Mum asks.

"My passion is the stars and what makes up our universe. I played around with some genetics as well to increase my chance of getting the apprenticeship," Nathan replies. "That was Sci. Suri's passion."

"Sci. Suri?" Mum asks.

"SuriTech was established by a scientist called Suri. He lived about a thousand years ago and was the father of the first Governor Suri," Nathan explains.

"Genetics? Do you know anything about chimaera?" I ask.

"Chimaeras are seriously awesome." Nathan leans forward, his face lighting up as he prepares to impart his knowledge. "Sci. Suri devised a way of combining animal and human DNA to create a type of hybrid person."

"Like a shapeshifter?" I stare at him.

"Not exactly. Apparently most of the participants only took on the vague appearance of the animal. So they might have eye or hair colour of their animal DNA. There were rumours that a couple managed to switch between forms, but I don't know if it's true or not. Why do you ask?"

"Dennian said Stev's family are all chimaeras," I say.

"Seriously? That must be why he refused the blood test for the fitness assessment," Nathan says. "Atlas had a massacre decades ago where a group of people killed anyone they suspected of being chimaera."

"Dennian also refused the blood test," I say.

"Yeah, but I think most of the test subjects were Atlasian. The reports I've seen claimed the descendants of Mellakai had a better chance of the procedure taking."

"Tell Cassie about your admissions assignment," his mum says.

"I'm sure she doesn't need to hear about that," Nathan protests.

"No, tell me," I say.

"I was looking into whether being chimaera would cause diseases to mutate between animal and human." At my blank expression, he explains further. "Take the Owl Flu as an example. It can't be contracted by a human, but what if the person has owl DNA, would it mutate into a human disease?"

"That sounds dangerous," I say.

"It would be, except every sample I looked at showed the chimaera genes blocking both human and animal diseases. They don't get either," Nathan says.

"I think it's time for your mother and I to have a private chat." Mum stands with a look at Nathan then follows Nathan's mum into the kitchen. One of the hover-cams follows.

"You're very deep in thought there," Nathan says as his siblings decide they're bored and scurry off to the toy corner.

"I was wondering what animal Dennian would be if he was chimaera."

"Well don't suggest that to Stev. He's likely to challenge Dennian to a duel or some such if he thought chimaera genes were involved," Nathan replies.

He stands and moves over to the couch beside me before taking hold of my hand. He stares at our entwined fingers for several moments before speaking.

"You're not going to choose me, are you?"

I blink back tears. "I really like you, Nathan. We would have made a great couple, but I'm in love with Dennian."

Nathan nods his head although his smile is forced. "You'd be happy with me. I'd give you the freedom to chase your dreams. If for whatever reason it doesn't work out with Dennian, I'll be here for you."

I pull one hand away and dash a tear from my cheek. "What are you going to do?" I ask.

"Keep learning, keep applying to SuriTech. Maybe one day they'll see what they're missing and snap me up." His smile is sad.

"They'd be silly not to."

"Do you want to play a game?" Nathan's sister Kylan appears by my side holding a board game.

"Sure." I force the reply out. I'm already playing a game. Maybe hers will be more fun.

*

The transport pulls up in front of a large family home in the same district as the mansion. I stare out of the window at the neatly kept garden flanking either side of the path to the front door.

A second vehicle pulls up behind us. I twist around to watch Dennian climb out followed by a hover-cam. He walks over to the gate and wipes his palms nervously against his trousers.

The vehicle door finally clicks and slides open. I step out and wrap my skirt around my legs. To mark the end of Governor Suri's visit to our planet, Lori has dressed me in a soft fabric printed with fire-breathing dragons. My top is fitted with a black and red flame pattern. I glance at Dennian's plain shirt, pants, and bare feet and feel overdressed.

I take Dennian's hand when I reach the entrance gate. He squeezes my hand and gives me a nervous smile. Mum stands several steps behind me.

"Who are you introducing us to today, Dennian?" I recite. Dennian glances towards the house quickly then back at me.

"Star," he replies briefly.

"Your sister?" I ask.

"Yes. She cleared her schedule so she could meet you in person."

Butterflies flap their way around my stomach. "What if she doesn't like me?" I break away from my cue cards.

Dennian gives my hands a reassuring squeeze. "You'll be fine. As long as she doesn't refer to herself in third person," he adds.

Dennian opens the gate and Mum hurries after us. At the door, Dennian doesn't knock or wait for the hover-cams. The door opens under his touch and we step into a pristine hallway with an artistic style but no personal touches.

"You don't actually live here, do you?" I ask.

"Rented for filming. Star travels and I live elsewhere," Dennian replies.

Before he can elaborate, a young woman around Dennian's age approaches us from the living room. She flicks her long brunette braid over her shoulder as she reaches for Dennian. She looks how I remember her from the day I saw her watching me at the zoo.

She steps forward and touches her forehead briefly to Dennian's. She releases him and looks us over.

"I'm Dennian's sister, Star. It's a pleasure to finally meet you, Cassie. Dennian's revealed much about you." She pulls me in for a hug.

"I see you don't have the same issue with touching that Dennian has," I say.

She laughs. Her grey eyes have an intensity to them like I'm being sucked into a whirlpool.

"Touching reveals a lot about a person." Star winks at me then reaches a hand out to Mum.

"You must be Cassie's mother." Star beams at Mum. "I've been curious to meet you. You can't imagine how surprised I was when I found out Dennian was in love with your daughter. Come into the living room and we can get to know each other better." Star finally drops Mum's hand and gestures towards the lounges in the spacious living room off the hallway.

My mother pulls me down into the seat beside her and Dennian sits opposite us beside his sister.

"You don't look alike." Mum says.

"We adopted Dennian when he was ten. We have different parents." Star smiles at us.

"Your parents aren't here with you today?" Mum says.

"They've both passed away," Star replies.

"How old are you?" Mum asks.

Star pauses for a moment as though calculating the years. "Eighteen I suppose. I don't really keep track of these things."

"You live alone?" Mum frowns.

"Hardly. I always seem to be surrounded by people wanting something," Star replies.

I glance at the small stack of cue cards on the drinks table between us, but Star ignores them.

"Tell us about your family?" Mum asks one of her cues instead. "One of Cassie's suitors is the nephew of the Atlas King."

Star tilts her head to one side and studies Mum. "You care for your daughter, but you care for your own comfort more." The playful tone slips from Star's voice. "You're too busy chasing perceived power to recognise true strength."

"Nonsense," Mum says.

"You could be in a room with the governor and the Keeper and would never notice because you'd be so busy looking for a person who appeared older, more influential," Star adds.

"It's not like either of us would ever meet the Governor of the Universe and the Keeper's dead. I've seen his ghost. I didn't like him," I say.

Star's assessing gaze locks on mine before turning to her brother. The pair have a silent conversation for a moment before Star relaxes and turns back to Mum and me.

"And if you did meet the governor, what would you ask them?" Star says.

"If the governor is born with their parents memories, do they recall their own conception? Because that would be weird," Mum says.

"It's not something I've ever dwelled upon." Star's expression is baffled.

"I'd want to know why my friend's SuriTech apprenticeship is conditional on him being married. SuriTech is Governor Suri's company, isn't it?" I ask.

"Excuse me?" Anger crosses Star's face and she glances at Dennian again. I can't hear what they say, but then her smile returns.

260

"Whoever specified that condition will want to hope Governor Suri doesn't find out or they will have a lot of explaining to do. The governor is obsessive about having the best candidates based purely on merit," Star says.

A weird tension spreads through the room despite Star's return to her friendly demeanour. Mum shifts in her seat and glances at her own set of cards. "As Cassie's mother, I expect her to find someone who will always put her first."

Star laughs. "Perhaps Cassie should have used a more traditional method of finding a life partner. Do you really think Stev Shan would consider anyone else before himself?"

"Of course he would. He's a Prince and a well brought up young man," Mum says.

"The boy is being groomed to take a leadership position on Atlas. He's not going to put a girl first, especially one from a different planet. You're selling your daughter as a brood mare and you'll want to hope the children look like they're from Atlas." Star locks eyes with Mum.

"I suppose you're going to claim that your brother will put Cassie first?"

"No. Dennian's job must always take priority."

I glance between Star and Dennian, but neither look at me. Dennian leans forward suddenly and glances towards the back of the house. He shoots Star a puzzled look but remains silent. He hasn't spoken since we entered the house.

"Looks like the kids have arrived." Star claps her hands together with a grin.

A flash of colour erupts into the room as a small child dashes in and throws herself at Dennian. She

261

scrambles up his back until she clings to his shoulders like a little monkey. She appears to be around five years of age.

"This is Lyri," Star says. Lyri's long hair hangs in streaks of ebony, blonde, and ginger.

"Wow! You look like Dennian's little monkey, Zeke," I say.

"Zeke's my br–" Dennian's hand covers Lyri's mouth, cutting off her words.

With his free hand, Dennian makes a series of hand signals. When she nods her head, he lowers his hand.

"Zeke's a monkey, not a boy," Lyri says carefully as Dennian squeezes his eyes shut in a pained expression. "I'm allowed to look after him sometimes."

"Is she adopted too?' Mum asks eyeing the young girl.

"Lyri's our cousin." A young boy steps in the room.

He looks to be around thirteen years old. His facial features resemble Dennian's although the boy's hair is darker. The various shades of brown are offset by thin streaks of white, giving the appearance of downy feathers on a young bird of prey. If Jayne were here she might hold these children captive until they divulge who their hairdresser is.

"This is Tryce, my half-brother." Dennian speaks for the first time since entering the house. Tryce reaches out and touches his fingertips briefly to Dennian's. The boy lowers himself into a vacant seat and studies each of us in turn.

"Dennian hasn't mentioned either of you," I say.

"I don't suppose he would have." Tryce glances at his brother. "Dennian's quite protective of us."

262

"Are you going to be a Peace Keeper like your brother or do you have grander ambitions?" Mum asks with a hint of patronisation.

"Being a Peace Keeper is a worthy career," Star says. "They've existed for longer than the government. Without them, there would be no government."

"You're wrong," Mum says. "The government came first and then the Peace Keepers were created afterwards. You should Suri® it before throwing false facts around."

Star bursts into uncontrollable laughter. "Suri® it?" she gasps in between ragged breaths.

"Yes," Mum says indignantly. "Surely you've heard of the Suri® database used for fact checking?"

"Of course we have, but that would be the first time in our entire life anyone has told us to Suri® something." Star's laughter becomes more manageable. Dennian and Tryce's faces sport their own amused grins.

"Dennian isn't a Peace Keeper. He lives on the island with us, and all the orphan babies, and Myaa's streak," Lyri says, her fingers weaving through Dennian's short locks.

Dennian does a few hand signals which Lyri watches from over his shoulder. She replies with a couple of her own. Tryce catches me watching the exchange and leans forward to whisper.

"She's mentally deaf, can't hear telepathy," he says. I nod my head.

Star's laughter dies down and Mum glances around the room awkwardly.

"What do you want to do when you grow up, Tryce?" I ask.

"I'm going to become the next King of Atlas."

I stare at him, waiting for the punchline of the joke, but it doesn't come.

"King Niko Shan, Delegate Glar Shan, and Senator Kel will pay for their crimes," he continues.

"What crimes?" I ask hesitantly.

"All of them," Tryce says.

Lyri climbs down off Dennian and crawls onto my lap, startling me out of the weird silence that has fallen over the room.

"What do you do for work?" I ask Star.

"A bit of everything really." She waves a hand vaguely. "But we're here to talk about you. Tell me about the dress you want for your wedding."

My mind immediately goes to the embroidered tunic dress in the display case at the dress shop. The one I'm never going to have. I try to picture one of the dresses Sara selected, but they're all a blur of pale greens and pinks.

"We've picked out a few possibilities, but haven't settled on the final dress yet," I reply. Star nods her head as she studies me.

"It must be time for me to have a word with Star in private," Mum says.

Star stands gracefully. "Actually, I'd love a chat with my future sister-in-law." She reaches out and takes my hand, pulling me up off the couch while smiling at Mum.

Star tows me into the kitchen before Mum can object. A single hover-cam follows after us. Star drops my hand and turns to face the camera.

"Leave us." Her voice has lost the young, giggly tone of earlier. The hover-cam drifts out of the room. I turn to stare at Dennian's sister.

"My brother is in love with you," she says.

"You make that sound like a bad thing." I cross my arms over my chest and she sighs.

"Tell me, Cassie, if you had to choose the person you love, or saving the world from destruction, which would you select?"

"I'd choose saving everyone. I couldn't be happy if everyone I knew had died and I'd had the ability to change that," I say. Star nods her head.

"You have the ability to alter the path your life will take. Dennian doesn't. His path was chosen for him before he was old enough to know what happened," Star says.

"It doesn't feel like I have much choice at the moment."

"I didn't say they were good choices, only that you have them, and if Dennian is what you want, you need to choose him. The choice isn't his to make." She stares at me intently with her serious grey eyes.

"Okay…" I say.

"Good, ready to head back in?"

"Don't you want to get to know me, ask some questions, that sort of thing?" I ask.

"No." Star taps the back of my hand. "I know everything I need to."

Star doesn't wait for me to respond. She steps past me and by the time I follow she has donned the innocent persona of earlier.

"Time for us to go," Mum says when I step back into the room.

Lyri throws herself at me. "I like you."

"I like you too," I say. She kisses my cheek and scrambles down to take Tryce's hand. He gives me a little wave.

"I guess we'll see you around when Dennian shows you the island," Tryce says.

Mum says a brief goodbye to everyone and I'm left alone with Dennian for a moment. He leans in and hugs me.

"The Temple Tigers guard the Children's cemetery during the festival," he says.

"What festival?"

"Stev will tell you about it on the way to Atlas. Be careful," Dennian whispers in my ear.

"You said the tigers wouldn't hurt me."

"They won't. But the people will kill to protect their secrets." He brushes a kiss across my check and steps away.

As I'm about to leave, he pulls off his shirt and hands it to me.

"To fix my smell?" I ask with a smile.

"More of an introduction."

I walk out of the house and join Mum outside. The next time I'll see Dennian will be at the semi-final elimination. From here on I need to focus on my backup plan in case this program doesn't end the way I want it to. I lift his shirt to my nose. It smells of him.

"Did you think they were a bit weird?" Mum asks as we slide into the waiting vehicle and head towards the Interplanetary Airport.

Atlas

It takes two and a half days to reach Atlas on Delegate Shan's shuttle. I don't see much of Stev or his father during that time. Mum and I spend our waking hours learning Atlas etiquette such as how to greet Atlia City royalty and their strict no touching rules.

When I ask about my dragon stone that Glar Shan took during the conference, I receive a hand-written note from the delegate. Inside is an apology as the stone was damaged during the attack. I'm a bit surprised. I saw Dennian's destroyed stone, but I thought Glar Shan had been evacuated before the blasts.

When I mention it to Mum, she tells me to drop it. One doesn't upset the rulers of the planet they are visiting, especially when the prince has shown an interest in me.

In any spare moment I can find, I play around with Guya's old hover-cam controller to learn the finer details of the night vision settings that I'd never had a chance to learn before.

Before we enter the atmosphere of Atlas, servants arrive to prep us for our first appearances. Lori and Carter stayed behind on Terra, as did Trev although he left me with a hefty stack of cue cards. Mum and I travel alone with a single camera operator.

The Atlas servants put a black wash through my hair despite my objection then stain my skin with a white cream. By the time they're done, I could almost pass as an Atlas born.

I frown at myself in the mirror. If I'm forced to stay with Stev, I may have to look like this for the rest of my life.

When the vessel docks, I join Mum in the departure room. Servants collect our bags to send to the arrival lounge, and Stev and his father join us.

"Ready for your visit to the centre of the universe?" Stev asks.

"Can't wait." I turn the corners of my mouth up in something that resembles a smile and stroke Guya's hover-cam stashed in the folds of my long skirt.

Mum and I walk down the ramp into a large entrance hall, keeping the required distance behind the Atlas born. Dark haired people walk to and fro as though they all have important destinations to get to. A pair of uniformed men approach and speak to Glar Shan. They disappear into a private room leaving the rest of us to wait with Stev. The servants line up our luggage for inspection.

I let my gaze wander the international space port of Atlas's largest city of Atlia. Shops line the hallways, filled with every last minute purchase a traveller could ever need.

The entrance doors slide open and a Temple Tiger prowls into the building. I stare in shock as she lifts her horned head and sniffs the room before heading towards the baggage.

Someone screams and several people dart out of the nearest door while others back away. Stev moves so that I'm between him and the tiger.

I don't take my eyes off her as she circles the luggage then lies down on her belly with her paws stretched out in front of her and her yellow eyes scanning the crowd. Her tawny fur looks like it was once a similar colour to Dennian's hair, but now has a whiter hue of old age.

I fumble with the hover-cam and manage to switch it on. The camera operator has all his gear packed up in bags after being told he would only be allowed to film where the Atlas rulers give permission.

"What is it doing?" Mum hisses in my ear. She tugs on my arm to pull me backwards while staying behind me.

"I don't know," I say.

"This way." Security guards usher Stev towards the room his father entered. Mum, the camera operator, and servants hurry to follow. In the panic, they don't notice me pull away.

The immediate area has emptied of everyone except the bravest security guards who keep their distance from the massive animal. I send the hover-cam ahead of me as I creep slowly forward. The tiger turns her yellow eyes on me.

"That's my bag you're lying on," I say.

She studies me for a moment before a very clear image of Dennian appears in my mind. He sits at the edge of a crystal clear lake with this tiger by his side. I blink several times. Did she send me that image?

"I know Dennian. He gave me his shirt. It's in my bag." I point to my bag.

She stretches slowly and rises to all fours, before approaching me. I freeze in place trying to remember what to do around wild predators. I glance quickly at my hover-cam then back at the tiger. Is looking in her eyes considered a challenge? Don't run. They can smell fear.

She pauses in front of me and I meet her eyes, unable to look away. She lifts her nose and sniffs the air around me. Out of the corner of my eye, I catch two security guards creeping towards us with shock-batons. The tiger whips her head around and snarls at them. I take a small step back as the guards turn pale with terror. After staring them down, she brushes against my leg and leaves the building through the front doors. My legs give way and I sink to the floor.

"We thought you were a goner," one of the guards says, leaning shakily against a wall. I don't have the strength to respond.

The servants find me still seated on the floor sometime after the tiger's departure. They collect the luggage and help me to my feet.

"Where have you been?' Mum wraps me in her arms when we re-join the others.

"I wanted to see the tiger."

The hover-cam comes back to me with a quick command on the controller.

"Whatever for?" Stev says dismissively before following his father out of the building.

Vehicles pull up to the curb and I slide into one vehicle beside Mum, while Stev, Glar, and their guards take the other vehicle. As we pull away, we pass the tiger lying under a tree watching us. I twist around in my seat to see if she will try to follow us, but instead she vanishes.

"I don't think I like this place," Mum mutters.

I glance down at the hover-cam still in my hand and smile to myself. Perhaps Atlas won't be so bad after all.

The vehicles travel around the edge of the modern city of glass and metal buildings towering over the ocean views.

We pull up to a large gated compound. To one side stand more buildings while the other direction leads to a cleared hill that backs onto the edge of a forest that stretches as far as the eye can see.

The gate swings open and we follow the other vehicle into the compound. We pull up at the front of the palace and I step out of the vehicle.

The tiger lies on her belly beside a row of hedges as though waiting for us to arrive.

A servant touches my arm alerting me to the fact I've been standing in the driveway staring at the tiger while the others hurried inside. I back away slowly before stepping inside. The woman fastens the door behind us and sighs in relief.

"I don't care what the governor says. A tiger wouldn't be wandering around like that if Takarna was around," Glar Shan says to a well-dressed man who has come to greet him.

"What do you expect when Suri allows them to wander around freely," the man replies, stroking the large ruby gemstone mounted at the top of his carved timber staff. "Stev, welcome back. I trust your journey has been productive?"

"Yes, Uncle Niko. This is my future wife, Cassie." Stev waves me over.

"You haven't won the competition yet," I say.

"A mere detail. Cassie, this is my uncle, King Niko Shen of Atlas."

Mum gasps while I stare at the tall man before me. He's taller than his cousin, Glar Shan, although he has the same dark hair and blue eyes of the Atlasian race.

No one had mentioned we'd be meeting the king although the etiquette of such a meeting may have been covered during the journey to Atlas – I hadn't really been paying attention.

Mum manages a low bow, reminding me that I'm meant to do the same. No one here shakes hands in case they happen across a mind reader. I'm not sure how often this might occur as so far the only person I know who seems able to do that is Dennian.

King Shen gives us a small nod of acknowledgement.

"She looks like she'll do." He claps his hands together and several servants appear, before I can say anything inappropriate. "Show our visitors to their rooms." He walks out of the room followed by Glar Shan.

One servant leads Mum away while I follow an old woman down a hallway. I step on her heels when she stops suddenly. She drops to the floor and bows, touching her forehead to the polished floor while chanting. In front of us, the tiger lies on the floor watching us.

"Welcome to our house, grand lady," the woman mutters as she rises to her knees.

"Aren't you afraid of it?" I ask in a hushed whisper so not to startle the animal.

"Temple Tigers are the blessed pets of the dragons who once lived in the cliff caves on the far side of the forest," she says.

"But Stev keeps telling me how he is a descendant of Mellakai the dragon slayer."

"He is. The Shens, Shans, Kels, and many other prominent families are proud descendants of the dragon slayer," she replies.

My brows furrow. "So are the Atlasian people for the dragons or against the dragons?"

"Yes," she replies with a nod.

"I don't understand. Which one are they?"

"Both," she says as though it should be obvious. "They support whomever gives them power."

I ponder that for a moment while the tiger watches me through half closed eyes. "Do the tigers normally come inside?"

"Oh no. They never come near the city. There have been reports of them in the forest by the Children's Graveyard, but never closer. We are blessed by their presence."

"I didn't get the impression anyone else felt blessed," I say.

"King Niko and his wife don't like the tigers," the old woman says.

"Why?"

The tiger blinks slowly at us and the woman speaks again.

"The Tiger Prince took the princes and princess away. The Demon Festival tonight is for parents to banish the animal spirits from taking the children." The woman climbs to her feet.

"Who's the Tiger Prince?"

"You'd have to ask her." She waves a hand at the tiger before showing me into the room opposite the tiger's position. The yellow eyes continue to watch me.

*

We eat dinner in a long dining hall where I sit between Mum and Stev. King Niko sits at the head of the table with his wife Queen Lari on one side, and his cousin Glar Shan on the other. Another man introduced as Senator Kel rounds out our number.

The group talks about me as though I'm not in the room. I pick at my food while glancing at the royals. My thoughts wander back to the meeting with Dennian's family. His half-brother, Tryce, named the three men in this room as those he wanted to bring down. I watch them trying to see what would make a thirteen year old boy want to take on Atlas nobility.

A servant enters and places a covered dish in front of Stev. At Delegate Glar's urging, Stev stands and places the dish in front of me before lifting the cover. Beneath is a small decorated cake with an odd sickly citrus scent to it.

"I hope you will honour me by sampling this desert." Stev steps back from the table.

"Doesn't everyone else get some?" I glance at the empty places in front of everyone else.

"This is just for you," Stev says.

I look at the dish. As I lift the fork, a massive paw swipes the plate from the table. Queen Lari screams and pushes away from the table and I'm left with a growling tiger on top of the table in front of me. She opens her mouth and snarls at Stev.

"Stay still," the old servant woman hisses at me from a short distance away.

Everyone else has backed away from the table, but I remain still in my seat.

"She ruined Cassie's commitment cake!" Stev points an accusing finger at the horned animal. A shiver rolls down my back. I haven't committed to anything.

The tiger stares at each person in turn then extends her claws. She swipes at the table leaving a pattern of gouges.

"Someone get this thing out of my house," King Niko demands.

The tiger turns in a slow circle and snarls at him. A very clear image of the tiger nuzzling a cub enters my mind as though someone has shown me a film clip. I can almost smell the greenery of the forest surrounding them. King Niko's face drains of colour and beside him, the queen faints. With one final look around the room, the tiger vanishes.

"Are you okay?" Mum hurries forward and grabs my shoulder.

"I'm fine." I reach out to trace the marks left in the table. It looks like a crown.

"You could have been eaten alive!" Mum exclaims.

I stand up slowly. "I don't think she wants to hurt me."

Glar Shan grabs the servant and shoves her towards the table. "What does the beast's message say?"

"It's the symbol of the Tiger Prince," the old woman says, looking at the mark on the table. "The girl is protected."

Glar backhands her and she falls to the floor clutching her face. I step towards the woman, but Stev grabs my wrist.

"Stev, show your girl the menagerie," King Niko says, having recovered and checked on his wife now the tiger has left the room.

"I don't feel particularly well." Mum raises a hand to her forehead. "I think I may go lie down."

"Will you be okay, Mum?"

She nods her head and follows a servant from the room. Stev gestures for me to follow him. The remaining servants lead Queen Lari away, leaving King Shen, Delegate Shan, and Senator Kel to accompany us. I stay close to Stev's side, putting distance between me and the three older men with their secrets.

"What was that about?" I whisper.

"The Tiger Prince is an evil spirit. He stole my cousin, Prince Tarla, away. The Tiger Prince then used Tarla's spirit to lure his siblings away. Now he is trying to prevent our marriage." Stev leans in close to my ear so no one else can hear.

"I haven't agreed to marry you."

"You will. Father doesn't have time to find someone with genetics similar enough to an Atlas born without being related to us," he replies.

"This is about genetics?" I come to a stop in the garden suddenly reminded of Dennian and Nathan's comments about chimaera.

"I'm not going to discuss this further." Stev continues walking.

I glance around me as I follow the men outside into the walled compound, but the tiger is nowhere to be seen. Over the wall, the hill rises up to the forest edge. To one side, I think I can make out stones in rows on a flattened section butted up against the dense trees.

"What's that up there?" I ask Stev.

"That's the Children's graveyard."

"Can I go see it?" I ask.

"Why would you want to do that? It's full of bad spirits. Tonight's the Demon Festival where we drive the demons from the dead. You'll enjoy that."

"Wow, sounds fun." I force a smile onto my face as I glance at the graveyard again.

We step onto a path winding between fenced animal enclosures. Some of the creatures I've seen before at the zoological park and as far as enclosures go, these

276

are relatively spacious and looked after. I make what I hope are appropriately appreciative noises while King Niko talks about his collection, but my mind wanders to Dennian and the time we spent together before I was forced into this show.

"And here we have the latest addition to my menagerie. The tri-colour monkey is native to the Southern Island Group," the king explains.

My feet stop moving as I stare into the enclosure. Three small, miserable monkeys huddle together on a platform. Their fur consist of streaks of ebony, blonde, and copper exactly like Dennian's cousin, Lyri, and little Zeke.

"I don't know why you insist on keeping the things," Senator Kel says to King Niko. "Terrible clingy creatures, they are." He shudders.

"What do you think of the place, girl?" King Niko asks.

"Impressive." I school my features. The weeks of filming have been good practice.

"The children should probably go prepare themselves for tonight's festival while we have that discussion I mentioned earlier," Glar Shan says.

King Niko nods his head. "Of course. Let us go to my office."

He leads the other two men down another path in the direction of one wing of the mansion without another word to me or Stev. Stev stares after them longingly.

"In a few years I'll be joining in on those meetings," Stev says almost to himself.

"Have you ever met a young boy by the name of Tryce?" I ask.

Stev ponders the question for a few moments. "King Niko's youngest child was named Tryce, but he died as a baby."

"How did he die?"

"I don't know. He was sickly like his older siblings and he didn't survive."

We reach the house and Stev points me in the direction of my room.

"You should get ready for tonight's festival. It will be very impressive." He walks off in the opposite direction.

On the way to my room, I hear the muted voices of Mum and the camera operator. I pause and knock on the door to the room and Mum opens it. She wraps her arms around me in a smothering hug.

"I'm so sorry, honey," she whispers into my hair.

"What's going on?" I ask. The camera man leans against one wall with his arms crossed.

"We're leaving. This place isn't safe what with that tiger roaming around and that King gives off a really weird vibe. I'm sorry I dragged you into this program." Mum pulls me into another hug, but I pull away.

"Trev's not going to like this," the man mutters. "He gave me strict instructions."

"We can't leave now," I protest. "There's something strange going on and I want to find out what it is. Also I need to get footage of the tigers." I give Mum a look hoping to remind her of my backup plan. Plus now I've seen a Temple Tiger, I want to film more.

"You filmed the thing when we arrived," Mum says. "Isn't that good enough?"

"Not really. I need to capture them in their natural habitat."

278

The camera operator studies me, but doesn't say anything.

"But you could die!" Mum moans.

"I'll be fine. The servant woman says the tiger is protecting me. If the tiger was going to attack, she would have done it already."

"I don't know. I still think we need to get out of here. We'll tell Trev that it's not going to work out with Stev," Mum says.

"Fine, but we leave in the morning. We're staying for the festival," I say.

"There's a festival?" the camera operator asks.

"Sure is. Should provide some good footage," I say.

"I think I'll stay here. Will you be safe with Stev?" Mum asks."

"Of course, he's a prince." I back out of the room. Now I only have to give Stev the slip and make my way to the Children's Graveyard. In the dark. On my own. With other tigers somewhere in the forest.

I find my own room and rummage through the outfits the film crew packed for me. I find a forest green dress with a layered shirt that obscures the deep pockets set into the side. I pull it on over Dennian's shirt and tuck the hover-cam and controller into the pockets.

I don't bother doing makeup as I'm not planning on hanging around at the festival for long. I slip on the sturdiest shoes in my bag and open the door. A stream of servants storm the room.

"This won't do," one says. "You're going to be in public with the prince. You don't want to shame him by looking like a peasant."

"I'm not changing my outfit." I put my hands on my hips as I stare them down.

"Hmmm, it's not exactly fashionable." A woman looks me up and down as I stand there in my flowing green dress.

"It's a bit quaint, but we can work with it. It would save us tailoring any of the dresses we have to fit her figure," another says as she forces me into a chair and attacks my face with makeup.

A third woman takes my flats and replaces them with a pointed toe wedge that squeezes my foot in all the wrong places.

"You can't expect me to walk in these?"

"Don't worry, girlie. All you need to do is stand next to the prince and try to look Atlas born." The second woman spins me around to face the mirror.

Makeup layers my face and contrasts with the black rinse through my hair. I touch a hand to my locks and my fingers come away stained. Someone drapes heavy jewelled chains over my shoulders.

"Don't keep the prince waiting, now girlie." They pull me to my feet and throw open the door. I do a quick sweep of the room but can't see what they did with my sensible shoes.

I teeter in the wedges for a moment before making a slow escape, my feet protesting with each step.

Demons

Half a dozen guards take Stev and me into the brightly lit city as dusk begins to fall. I glance over my shoulder trying to keep the direction of the Children's Graveyard in sight while hoping we don't drive too far away from it.

We end up circling around to a massive park surrounded by modern city buildings rising up into the air. The park itself is littered with lanterns and bonfires with crowds of dark haired adults and children hovering around them. Not a single person here differs from the dark-haired, blue-eyed appearance associated with the Atlas people. Even with my hair coloured, I don't quite look like I fit in.

"Are your parents and uncle coming?" I follow Stev into the crowd with tiny, painful footsteps as we head towards the lanterns. His guards trail behind.

"They'll be here later," he replies as a man begins a chant and the crowd joins in.

"What are they saying?" I ask, unable to make out the Atlas words.

"They're calling for the demons to leave the children and be banished to the graveyard," Stev says. "When I was younger, one of my friends dared me to enter the Children's Graveyard during the festival. I crept right up to the oldest row of stones and then ran away before any of the demons saw me." Stev laughs.

"Sounds terrifying," I reply for lack of anything better to say.

"It was. There's a drinks stand over there. You can go get us a cup each while I get a good position by the central bonfire." Stev waves his hand in the direction of the drinks stand then towards the bonfire in the centre of the park.

"Sure," I say.

I take a lantern and make my way towards the drinks stand. Two guards peel away to follow me. I grind my teeth and join the beverage line.

My little toes throb where they rub against the shoes. I squat to undo the buckles. When I step forward to receive two drinks, I slip the shoes off. The hem of my dress obscures the abandoned footwear and my bare feet that curl into the soft grass.

A group gathers around a tall, hand-cuffed man being led by a leash around his neck. The restrained man can only be described as patchy. He has the black hair of Atlas except for a large light-brown clump on one side. One eye is blue, the other brown. His fingers appear to have been formed without the top two knuckles, which has the effect of making his thumbs look extraordinarily long. His head repeatedly twitches to one side, giving him the appearance of a crazed bear.

"Beware the chimaera for he shall steal your children from their beds!" The man's handler pulls him through the throng of people.

The bear-man lunges against the lead and I shove the drinks table with my hip. Liquid sloshes over everyone standing nearby as the table crashes to the ground. I bolt.

"Grab the girl. She has palace jewels." One guard reaches for me but trips over my abandoned shoes.

I slip into the crowd and cover my lantern. I slow to a casual walk. With my dark hair, I blend in. Running would give me away. My heart pounds as sounds of a search reach my ears, but I don't look back.

When I reach the edge of the park, I look up towards the forested hill and start along the street leading in that general direction. I uncover the lantern so I can see where I step. The grass ends, replaced by a rougher human-made surface.

I pass a few people to begin with. They give me odd looks as I head away from the festivities, but most ignore me. I've been walking for some time when three young men appear ahead of me. I move to the side of the path expecting them to ignore me as the other have done, but they stop in front of me blocking the path.

"What's a non-Atlas doing wandering around our street on the night of our festival?" one of them says.

"Do you think it's a demon?" another asks.

"Of course I'm not a demon," I say. "I'm here visiting Delegate Shan's family."

"I think the demon's lying to us. It's stolen Atlas jewels," the first boy says.

I touch a hand to the weighty chains around my neck. The boys crowd towards me and I take a step back, glancing around for an escape. Perhaps wandering around a strange city on my own isn't the best plan I've ever had.

A growl erupts behind me and I twist towards my tiger stalking towards us. The boys make a variety of squawking noises and scatter. The tiger stares after them.

I don't want to be out on the street anymore. I set off at a brisk walk which turns into a run as soon as I judge that I'm far enough away from the tiger that it won't mistake me for prey. My bare feet pound the ground, but it's still less painful than the shoes. The hover-cam in my pocket slaps against my hip.

After some minutes, I turn at the sound of breathing. The tiger lopes along beside me. I stumble but catch myself before I fall to the ground. Seems like my protector is going to follow me all the way.

Towards the edge of the city, the streets split into several directions. I slow down to work out which direction is best. The tiger pushes past a hedge into a narrow laneway I hadn't noticed.

I hold my lantern up, but I can't see much other than the glow of her eyes as she turns to wait for me. I pull the hover-cam out and use the controller to set it to follow the tiger.

"I hope you know where we're going," I mutter as I follow her. In response, I receive a clear image of rows of headstones up on a hill. The tiger turns back around, and I jog to keep up with her.

The buildings stop some time before we reach the base of the hill, as though no one wants to live too close to the forest. To my right the lights of the king's compound glow in the darkness, the closest dwelling to the graveyard.

The tiger leads the way, with me holding my lantern high to see the ground in front of me. We're back on grass, easing the discomfort from the soles of my feet. I stop as we reach the tree line. The graveyard is some distance to our left. When I turn in that direction, the tiger steps in front of me.

"I want to see the graves." I point over her shoulder to the graveyard.

She looks at the tip of my finger as though that is what I'm trying to draw her attention to then an image appears in my head of me following the tiger into the forest.

"Why should I follow you into a dark forest?" I place my free hand on my hip and glare at her in the light of my lantern. Behind her a full moon rises, bathing the landscape in a silvery glow and casting shadows around me.

The tiger sits and blinks her eyes slowly at me.

"Fine. What do you want to show me?"

She leads me into the forest. The moonlight filters through the treetops adding to the light from my lantern. I follow in the tiger's paw prints for some way before more tigers appear up ahead.

I'll either be the first person to capture footage of the Temple Tigers in their natural habitat, or get eaten.

A couple of animals glance at the hover-cam moving towards them, but most continue to crouch down and press their chins to the ground at various locations among the trees.

I jump at what sounds like a rocket launching somewhere behind me. Flames shoot into the sky from the direction of the city park, followed by brightly coloured fireworks that send sprinkles of coloured lights through the forest. More follow and the sounds echo through the forest.

One of the tigers walks towards me and my heart pounds in my chest. Dennian might be able to handle wild animals, but I'm not really sure what I'm doing. My tiger presses against my leg and the other one pauses to sniff the air before turning away and joining the others. As the fireworks die out, the tigers begin a low keening noise and move deeper into the forest.

My tiger moves forward and crouches down as the other had done. I step closer. In front of her lies a tiny pile of human bones. I move deeper into the trees finding several similar piles.

"Why are there bones in the forest?" I keep my voice low. It feels disrespectful to speak loudly in front of the dead babies.

In response I receive a series of images, the first being a dark-haired adult hurrying into the forest and leaving a crying baby beneath the trees before hurrying off again.

The next is of my tiger approaching a tiny bundle that has turned stiff and blue with cold. It's followed by another young child slightly more alive that turns stiff with shock when the tiger approaches.

After that death, the tiger watches on helplessly over the abandoned babies until she comes across what I first think is a tiger cub. It uncurls as though sensing the tiger among the trees and I realise it's a baby with hair the colour of tiger fur. The baby crawls towards the tiger and reaches out a tiny hand to clutch at her fur as he looks up at her with bright green eyes. The images end and I blink several times in the gloom.

"Was that Dennian?"

The tiger nods her head.

"You rescue the abandoned children?"

She nods again before moving through the forest. I hurry after her, not wanting to get lost in the dark. My camera hovers in front of me.

We emerge from the trees at one end of the graveyard. The light of the full moon casts shadows among the headstones, the inscriptions on the nearest stones indicating I'm in the older area.

My tiger joins the others lying on the grassy slope like a line of gargoyles guarding the spirits from the people below in the city. I program the hover-cam to watch them.

I tread carefully over the springy grass rows making my way to what I hope is the newer section. When I reach the other end, I shine my lantern over the inscriptions again. Some graves have flowers or toys arranged around them and I glance over my shoulder towards the festival fires around the city below me.

"Are you looking for someone in particular?"

I scream. A girl leans against a headstone one row back from where I stand. She's younger than me, I'd guess around fifteen years old. The moonlight reflects off her fair hair that's the same shade as the Temple Tigers' fur. In fact, in the moonlight she looks remarkably like a younger female version of Dennian.

"I thought you were one of the demons." I giggle nervously.

"Oh no. The evil demons all live down there." She waves a hand towards King Niko Shen's mansion. "The tigers make sure none of them bother the spirits during the *festival*." She scrunches up her face on the last word.

"What makes them demons?"

"They kill their own children if they don't look the right colour."

"You're not dead," I point out.

"Dennian keeps us safe."

"He lives nearby?" I ask.

"On the island like the rest of us." She doesn't elaborate. "Whose grave are you looking for?" the girl asks again.

"It's silly really. I doubt Lyri actually has a grave here."

"She's at the end of that row," the girl says.

I stare at her for a moment then walk towards the stone she indicated. The engraving reads 'Lyri Kel' and the date matches her age.

"Kel," I say. "Is she related to Senator Kel?"

"Senator Kel is her father." The girl watches for my reaction.

"But the grave is empty." It's more of a statement than a question. I know Lyri is alive.

"Most of them are. Myaa showed you where the parents abandon their babies. Most of them die, but we look after the ones who can be saved."

"Myaa's the tiger who has been following me?"

"Yes, she's the leader of our tiger streak." The girl waves a hand in the direction of the other tigers.

"What should I call you?" I ask.

"I'm Lucei."

I glance at the headstone beside Lyri's. *Zeke Kel.* "Dennian has a little monkey called Zeke."

"He gets the names from headstones," Lucei says.

"Does Dennian have a grave?" I ask.

"You won't find that name on a headstone. It was given to him by Carlen."

"What are the symbols on the stone covers?" I ask.

"They're to stop the spirits escaping," Lucei says. At my look, she elaborates. "The symbols block teleportation and stepping out of existence. If you're put in the grave, you can't escape."

"Where is Zeth's grave?" I ask.

The girl reaches out a hand and gently brushes a hand over the stone beside her.

"He's here," she says, a note of sadness in her voice. "At least most of him is. Dennian hasn't found Zeth's right leg yet."

When she doesn't elaborate, I pick my way over to Zeth's headstone and shine my lantern over it.

ZETH SHEN
SECOND CHILD OF
NIKO SHEN AND LARI SHEN
AGE SEVEN MONTHS
CAUSE OF DEATH UNKNOWN

I shine my torch over the stones beside it. On one side is 'Tarla Shen' like in Dennian's fear drawing. Lucei's name marks the stone she leans against.

"You're the princess?" I ask.

She laughs. "A dead princess if King Niko or Queen Lari knew I was alive. Dennian saw them kill Zeth, you know? I felt my twin die."

I follow the row further along. The grave beside Lucei's belongs to Tryce Shen.

"Why do the Atlas people abandon their children?"

"They're worried we're active chimaera because we look like our animal genetics," Lucei says.

"Active?" I ask.

"Most only carry two sets of DNA, but an active chimaera can shift between human and animal."

"My friend Nathan says it isn't possible to switch," I say.

"Of course it's *possible*. The dragons did it all the time."

"Dragons don't exist," I say.

"They exist. They just aren't here anymore," Lucei says.

"How can you be so sure?"

"There's a pictorial history of the dragons at the temple, Governor Suri has Mellakai's collection of dragon scales, and..." she pauses for a moment as though deciding whether to tell me the final reason, "Dennian saw a dragon when he was younger."

"Don't you think someone would have noticed if there was a dragon around?" I ask.

"Dennian thinks she took human form. Are you going to choose Dennian? Stev isn't very nice. He's too much like the rest of the Atlas nobles," Lucei says in an abrupt change of topic.

"It's not really my choice, but I'd like it to be Dennian."

"You'll like our island. It's very pretty. You should probably get back to the palace compound before they realise you've been up here."

"What about you?" I ask.

"I'll stay here with my family until the festival is over." Lucei waves a hand towards the line of tigers watching the city. I nod my head, collect my hover-cam and head back down the hill towards the palace.

By the time the sun begins to rise over Atlia City, Mum and I are on a shuttle home. I arrange the film edit to show the behaviour of the tigers during the festival. I may still need to sell it to the other network as a backup plan.

I send a message to Jayne about what I discovered, although I don't mention meeting Lucei.

Semi-Final Elimination

I pause on the landing outside my room at the mansion two days after Mum and I return to Terra. The long window overlooks one of the more secluded gardens that surround the house. Dennian prowls the small patch of grass, alternating between studying the page in his hand and staring at the sky. A smile creeps over my face and I slip quietly downstairs.

I push the door open onto the garden and Dennian's head whips around to face me as soon as I step out. He looks over my current outfit and I twirl on the spot.

"What do you think?" The white dress is sleeveless with strips of black lace at the top of the bodice, the waist, and two strips around the knee-length skirt.

A line of black ivy winds up one side of my face courtesy of Jayne who is currently getting ready for the second to last elimination. I finally managed to remove the black dye from my hair and the white stain from my skin.

When Dennian continues to stare at me without speaking, I point to the plastic-paper in his hand.

"Have they given you a script?" My brows pull together. Trev said the last three guys will declare their feeling and intentions for me before one of them faces elimination.

My night was sleepless, wondering if it would be kinder to let Nathan go rather than give him false hope, or if I should do what I'd wanted to from the beginning and send Stev home.

"I wrote my thoughts." Dennian swallows nervously. "To help me speak."

"You can practice with me now before we're in front of the cameras." I smile and reach out to hold his free hand. He takes a deep breath and looks at the words. I glance down, but he's used the scratch marks instead of Common.

"I was raised to believe I'd always be alone." Dennian pauses and I give his hand a squeeze. "But then you walked into my life and insisted I teach you. With each moment together, I saw possibilities. My soul belongs to you and no destiny can change that. So here I stand offering you every part of me I have to give. You have my heart, always."

"That's beautiful. See? There's no need to be nervous," I say.

Dennian rubs the tattoo between his shoulder blades. "I feel like something is about to happen."

"Like what?"

"I don't know," he replies.

"Cassie!" Jayne's voice echoes through the house.

"I should go. They'll be expecting you in a moment too," I say.

He nods his head. I lean in to kiss him quickly on the lips.

"I love you." I pull away and dash inside.

'I love you.'

I follow Jayne as she leads me to the location Trev selected for this scene.

"It's beautiful." Jayne skips ahead of me. "It looks like a trial run for the final."

"I doubt the person leaving with their dreams shattered will see it that way," I say.

"Think positively. As soon as this is over, we'll be free. Carter has already offered me an apprenticeship. He says I could teach a few people how to do my designs. And you will be famous. You can get a job, or sell the footage of those tigers to pay for your own editing equipment. This is what we always dreamed of," Jayne says.

"Then why do I feel like I'm trading my dreams for Nathan's?" I mutter.

"There you are," Trev calls out as we turn the corner. "Get up on the stage."

I stand on a raised dais while Lori smooths out my skirt and Carter frowns as he re-applies my lipstick. Mum and Jayne flank me as they will on the wedding day. The hover-cams focus on me and the final four men walking into the scene to stand several paces away. This is their chance to tell me why they should be chosen. Trev wants the audience to believe this is my decision.

I look across at the guys. Stev's expression is cocky as though he expects his position will mean he's the last one standing. Beside him, Nathan rubs his hands down the side of his trousers. He grins at me nervously when he catches me looking. Dennian stands on Stev's other side clutching his speech in his hand. Shane's pose is relaxed.

Sara steps forward. "Before we give you the opportunity to convince Cassie why you should remain, Mrs Brooke has selected one of you to go home after the family meeting. If she says your name, please say your goodbyes."

Sara steps back and Mum moves forward clutching her cue cards. I curl my fingers into my skirt as I wait to see who is going home first. In half an hour, only two of the four guys will remain. My stomach churns.

"…and so I chose Shane."

I snap my head up as I catch the last of Mum's words. I wasn't aware I'd tuned out her speech. Shane clasps arms with Nathan, says a quick goodbye to Stev and Dennian, then approaches the dais.

"It was great to meet you, Cassie. I hope you find what you're looking for." He pulls me in for a brief hugs.

"I hope so too," I whisper as he leaves the scene.

On Trev's cue, Nathan steps forward and comes to stand before me. He reaches out and takes one of my hands in his. I keep my eyes on him, acting like the other two aren't standing behind him and his hand isn't sweaty.

"Cassie, during our time together in the mansion, I have come to respect and care greatly for you. Heading forward with my SuriTech apprenticeship, I know I will be able to provide a happy life for you. We'll make a great team. I stand here, waiting for you to choose me," Nathan says.

"Thank you, Nathan." I lean forward and kiss his cheek.

Nathan steps down from the dais. Trev signals for Stev to approach next. The Atlas prince strides forward. I try to find a resemblance between him and his cousins, Lucei and Tryce, but they look much more like Dennian.

Stev steps up in front of me but doesn't take my hand. I focus on his face and keep my smile in place. If the audience can tell who I want to win and who I don't, Trev will make me re-do the scene.

"Cassie, you are faced with a simple choice. With me you will be a princess, with anyone else, you will be nothing–"

An eagle swoops through the setting, dropping a square of black cloth on the ground in front of Dennian, before it lands on the flower arbour. The bird ruffles its white-tipped, brown feathers.

Dennian doubles over as though racked with pain. He scrapes one hand over the tattoo on his back and stares at the item on the ground.

"What in Kllrarn's name is going on? We need to keep moving with this shoot. Stev, repeat your speech," Trev calls out.

"Cassie, you are–"

The eagle screeches loudly. It tilts its head as it eyes Stev.

"Why is the bird grinning?" Jayne whispers in my ear.

I glance back at Dennian still crouched on the ground. His eyes are closed and his expression pained. The bird takes flight, landing on the grass. It picks up the scrap of black cloth and hops forward to place the item closer to Dennian's feet. It squawks at him and ruffles its feathers as though waiting for a response. Dennian opens his eyes and looks at me.

"This is my scene." Stev glares at everyone.

Dennian breaks eye contact then reaches out and runs the black cloth through his fingers. The eagle chirps softly.

"We don't have all day, people," Trev calls out. "Let's get this scene done."

Dennian stands abruptly. His fist clenches around the cloth and he rips the mic transformer pack out from under his shirt. He throws it to the ground, where it breaks into pieces, and strides away. The eagle takes flight, swoops low over Stev's head and follows in the direction Dennian has taken.

"Dennian!" I push past Stev and jump off the dais.

My heel breaks off in the grass and I spend precious moments tearing my shoes from my feet. I look up as Dennian disappears around behind the hedge. He holds an arm aloft and the eagle lands on it. I sprint across the grass on bare feet.

I tear around the corner and skid to a stop. The garden opens out after I round the hedge. Dennian and the eagle have vanished. A hover-cam catches up with me and we turn in circles trying to convince ourselves he's not here. My chest constricts and I run back to the stage.

"Did you pay him to leave?" I yell at Trev who has emerged from the scenery to take control of the unravelling scene.

"That wasn't scripted. We had no idea he was going to walk out." Sara reaches for my arm, but I pull away glaring at the faces around me.

"No! He wouldn't leave. He wrote down what he was going to say for his speech." My body trembles. Jayne and Nathan's faces are a mix of worry and confusion.

"Control yourself, Cassie. He was about to be eliminated anyway," Stev says.

"What?" I look at the faces around me before making a grab for the two cards Mum was meant to hand me once the three boys had finished their speeches. Nathan is written across the first one, Stev on the second. It had already been decided.

I sink to the ground as tears stream down my face. A single black and brown feather with a thin white edge lies on the ground beside me. I run it through my fingers focusing on its similarity to Tryce's hair.

Keep the Dead

Dennian – Present

Water drips from my hair and rolls down the back of my neck as I sit at the edge of Takarn Lake, staring at the skull balanced in my hand, but my mind only sees the square of black summoning cloth Tryce dropped at my feet and the look on Cassie's face as I walked out.

Atlas wanes into a crescent above me in the sky. The bushes rustle and Lucei appears with Myaa and Thylace at her heels. In one hand she holds a bottle of black ink and a pair of black pants.

"I'm sorry, Dennian. We all liked Cassie," Lucei says.

"Governor Suri had to announce the Keeper's death. It couldn't be hidden any longer." Tryce appears beside me in human-form although he still smells like an eagle.

I nod my head. Even if I was allowed to speak, no words could make their way past the lump in my throat. Lucei holds out the clothing. Tryce takes the skull from my hand and places it in a sack.

I drop my wet shirt on the sand and change into the black, loose fitting trousers. I drop to my knees facing the lake and rock pinnacle rising from the centre. The clear water sparkles with the discarded gemstones of the long ago departed inhabitants. If I tilt my head back, the dragon statues of Aurum and Argentum come into sight, their outstretched wings forming the roof of the dragon temple as they perch atop the pinnacle of rock.

297

Lucei wipes a tear from my face and I close my eyes against the morning sun. I try to block out the world as I kneel motionlessly in the sand, but I still sense Lucei pouring ink into the palm of her hand.

She marks my chest, the backs of my hands and my feet. Lucei leans in to kiss my forehead before departing with Tryce, leaving me to meditate in the shadow of the dragon temple as the ink dries into skin.

When the sun is high in the sky, I open my eyes. I have eighteen more dead apprentices to retrieve so the Keeper trials can begin. This next one is at the bottom of the lake with his feet attached to a large rock.

Brinthiss Malla

My bedroom door clicks opens. I pull my pillow over my head and curl further under the blankets.

"I know you've told me to go away the last dozen times I've come in, but this time I actually have something worth getting out of bed for."

Jayne's voice is muffled by the pillow over my ears. The bed dips as she bounces on the edge.

"Seriously, this is literally the most exciting thing that will ever happen in our entire lives... Are you even listening to me?" She tugs on my pillow leaving me clinging to one corner.

"I was trying not to," I mumble.

"Governor Suri has announced the death of the Keeper. Stev's arranged – "

"I don't want to know about Stev!" I grab the second pillow off the bed and throw it against the wall.

"You don't understand," Jayne says. "The selection of the new Keeper has always been done in private by the current Takarna, but Delegate Shan and Atlas King Shen have accused Governor Suri of hiding the failing health of Takarna. They've agreed for the Keeper trials to be held in front of witnesses..."

"So?"

"So, Stev has got an invite to the trial. You get to see the apprentices compete to replace the most powerful man in the entire universe! You could film it!" Jayne exclaims.

I sit up. "Where is this happening?"

"On Governor Suri's vessel." Jayne bounces on the edge of the bed again.

"When do we leave?"

"Wait, that's all it takes to get you out of bed?"

I swing my legs to the ground. "Dennian was with Governor Suri's Peace Keepers when we went to the convention centre. Let Trev know I'm ready to go as soon as he is."

Jayne locks eyes with me briefly then walks out of the room. I stand up and head for the bathroom. I'm long overdue for a shower and change of clothes.

*

The *Brinthiss Malla*, Governor Suri's flagship, hangs in orbit around Terra. I've seen images of it close up on the news with its sleek grey lines, and the gold and silver dragons of the Temple painted down each side.

The Peace Keepers who meet Stev, Nathan, and me at the space station inform us the vessel is named after a butterfly. I guess it's a fitting name for the ruler of a mostly Pacifist federation.

I expect us to be shown to a shuttle to take us into orbit, but instead they lead the four of us to a circle painted on the pavement that transports us directly on board the vessel. There's a brief tugging on my skin and my mind goes blank. When my vision returns, we're standing on the metallic floor of the entrance room of Governor Suri's vessel.

Delegate Glar Shan steps forward to greet Stev and orders one of his Peace Keepers to take our luggage to our quarters. I brush my fingers against the hover-cam in my pocket but leave it hidden. Having insisted on going up first, Trev lurks beside the camera operator giving directions. Delegate Shan ignores the men so we get away without repeating the introduction.

300

An alarm sounds. "Prepare to exit orbit," a voice sounds through the vessel's intercom.

A mild vibration runs through the floor and I stumble at the tugging sensation that vanishes almost as soon as it begins.

"We'll be in orbit around Atlas within a day," Glar Shan says. "My poor little shuttle will have to catch up with us there. I'm starving. Let's see what's on offer for lunch."

Glar Shan leads the way and I look at every person we pass, but few of them are Peace Keepers and none are Dennian. Nathan falls into step beside me.

"Are you sure Dennian will be here?" he asks. I nod my head. I don't know what I'll do if he's not.

The cafeteria is large with a variety of tables in different sizes and heights to compensate for the different races aboard the vessel. Spongy mushroom-like stools complete the set up and when we sit in them, they expand to support our shapes. I find myself seated opposite Delegate Glar and Stev, and next to Nathan. Trev and the camera operator sit at another table while the hover-cam circles us.

"You are about to witness history, my children," Glar Shan says.

"I'm sure it will be very exciting." I crane my neck to search the room. A handful of people sit at tables around the room, including two Peace Keepers. I'm fairly sure the fair-haired one was at the conference centre.

"You don't understand." Glar Shan leans forward and lowers his voice. "Both my brother and Niko's brother are candidates for the position of Keeper. Governor Suri has lied to the delegates about the

Keeper's health. By the end of this day, the Shens and Shans will control the Keeper and the government."

My mouth drops open, but Nathan speaks before I can. "We were told there are nineteen apprentices, so your brothers only have a ten percent chance of one of them to become the Keeper."

"You are going to be married into the most successful family in the universe," Glar Shan addresses me as though Nathan hasn't spoken.

"Stev hasn't won the competition yet." Nathan glares at Stev and his father.

"He will." Glar waves a hand dismissively.

I grab hold of Nathan's arm to stop him rising, but before I can form a satisfactory reply, Star strides into the room.

I grip Nathan's arm. "That's Dennian's sister," I whisper.

Star pauses, her eyes narrowing as she looks in our direction. She heads towards us and drops into the vacant seat beside Delegate Glar, her expression relaxed once more. He flinches and leans away as though afraid of being touched.

"Do you know where Dennian is?" I ask.

"He's busy," Star says abruptly. "Who gave permission for these people to come aboard?" Star asks conversationally. Her eyes flicker over to Trev and the camera operator.

"I did." Glar Shan's voice is patronising. "This is my son and his future wife, and a couple of her friends. They're here to witness the Keeper trials."

I cringe, fighting the urge to explain the situation to Star.

"You brought them on board without permission. I suggest you send them home immediately." Star ignores Delegate Glar's tone.

"That's not possible. They're from Terra. We must have already left their star system," Delegate Shan says.

Star thrusts her hand out towards Trev and the camera operator. They vanish along with the hover-cam. I stare at the empty table.

"Nothing is impossible," Star says.

"What did you do to him?" I ask. Beside me, Nathan and Stev remain perfectly still as though expecting to also disappear.

"I sent them home." Star turns to Glar Shan. "I inspected Terra SuriTech the other day," Star continues, "I was particularly interested in the processes of the General Admissions Selector and I discovered that *you* had recommended her."

"Caro Lyne is excellent at her job." Glar Shan's eyes refuse to meet Star's. He looks over my shoulder like he's searching for someone to rescue him. I lean forward watching the interaction.

"And what job would that be?" Star asks casually. Glar's eyes flick up to hers quickly then dart away.

"I don't know what you mean," he mutters.

"The last person who attempted to interfere with SuriTech met an unfortunate end." Star's voice sounds like a warning.

"Now, Star –" Glar begins.

"Have we ever given you permission to utilise our individual name?" Star's raised voice sends shivers down my spine and Glar gulps.

"Of course not, Governor Suri."

Nathan chokes on his drink and my jaw drops. I'm still trying to form a coherent sentence when the two Peace Keepers approach our table.

"You summoned us, Milord?" the darker of the two asks.

"*Ex*-Delegate Shan will be leaving us today," Star says. The eyes of the two men open wide.

"You can't do that. I'm appointed by the people of Atlas as their representative," Glar Shan snarls.

"A delegate must have a clean record. They may be dismissed by the governor, which would be me, or the vice governor, if they have charges brought against them.

"What are these charges?" Stev demands while his father glares at the governor.

"I'm so glad you asked. Glar Shan has multiple reprimands for overstepping his position such as inviting guests aboard my vessel without permission." They wave their hand at the four of us sitting at the table.

"That's hardly–"

Star cuts Stev off. "There's the new matter of tampering with SuriTech admissions."

"You can't prove I had anything to do with that," Glar Shan says.

Governor Suri moves their hand towards his and he jerks his away before contact can be made.

"I could if I wanted to. I could also prove that you're attempting to overthrow my government..."

The Peace Keeper I don't recognise reaches forward and grabs Glar Shan's hand.

"You think you can destroy the Atlas government with this?" Glar demands. "Our people won't stand for it."

Governor Suri stands from their seat.

"By tomorrow, a Shan will be the new Keeper and he can challenge your decisions," Glar Shan threatens.

"You'd do better to bet on a Shen becoming Keeper. Yumi, escort Glar Shan off my vessel," Star says.

"Yes, Milord," the Peace Keeper says. He grabs Glar's arm and pulls him upright.

"You think your Peace Keepers will stand by you when they realise you have been lying about the Keeper's health? You thought you could hide his disappearance from us, but you forget that Atlas has a close relationship with the Dragon Temple and its Keeper. We noticed the instant something happened to him," Glar Shan hisses.

Governor Suri laughs. "Ignorant little man. Takarna Carlen's been deceased for eight years."

"But...I've seen..." Glar Shan stumbles over his words.

"We attended the Keeper's anniversary celebrations," Stev says. "He was there."

"No, the temporary Keeper was there. I'm surprised you couldn't tell the difference considering your close relationship. Take him away, Yumi," Star says.

"What about my son?" Glar Shan demands. Star Suri glances at Stev.

"He may stay to witness the trials so he can see what true power looks like," they reply.

Raising the Dead

Nathan meets me outside my temporary quarters the following morning. My dress is simple with pockets big enough to hold my hover-cam and controller. Nathan looks me over with a sad smile.

"Everything all right?" I ask.

"I was wondering how I could ever compete against the future King of Atlas, and Governor Suri's brother." He shrugs his shoulders.

"You're way better than Stev will ever be." I reach out to take Nathan's hand.

"I wouldn't mind, you know," Nathan pauses before continuing. "If you met up with Dennian while we were married. I owe the guy my life after all."

"Let's go watch Stev's uncles fail miserably at these challenges," I say. "I'm sure that will cheer us up."

We pass through an elaborately carved doorway with every mythical creature imaginable including several I've only ever seen on Dennian's armband. The central creature is a dragon.

The arch leads to the temple room where the Keeper trials will begin. Creepers cover the walls and various plants grow wild in their allotted spaces. An eagle perches on the branch of a larger plant at the rear of the room.

We weave our way through people already gathering on the cushions scattered across the polished stone floor. Nathan points out space beside Stev near the raised platform at the back of the room.

A statue of the gold and silver dragons sits in the centre of the platform. At the base lies a large piece of jagged crystal that looks like it was once part of an undamaged sphere. Two cauldrons sit on either side of the statue, the flames making shadows dance across the walls. A hooded figure stands statue-like in the shadows. His black cloak is split up both sides revealing bare arms clasped behind his back in the Perceptive Peace Keeper stance.

As we reach the vacant cushions near the stage, Nathan stops suddenly in front of me. I peer around his shoulder. A row of human skulls line the stage. I count nineteen.

"Are they the apprentices?" Nathan asks with a note of horror in his voice as we kneel on our cushions beside Stev. I pull the hover-cam from my pocket.

"Which one is your uncle, Stev?" I ask straight-faced. "They all look the same to me."

Stev glares at me as I set my camera to film the row of skulls.

Governor Suri steps up onto the platform, having changed their outfit into a dark blue dress with the two dragons elaborately stitched into the material. When they walk forward, the splits in the skirt reveals trousers and lengths of fabric to appear dress-like but not impede the movement of the wearer.

My eyes drop to the belt hanging loosely over their hips and supporting two knife sheaths. They glance at my hover-cam but don't say anything.

The room fills up quickly with Vice Governor Jaarid and the Planetary Delegates taking the centre cushions along with King Niko Shen and his wife.

Peace Keepers take their positions along the walls. I sit up straight, searching the Perceptives, but they all wear boots. Several Temple Tigers appear by the stage and lie down on their stomachs. Star Suri pauses halfway along the row of skulls and waits for the room to fall silent.

"The Keepers have guarded the temple since the departure of the dragons. At the end of his life, each Keeper selects an apprentice to train and take the name Takarna. If the boy fails, another will be selected. It's rare for the Keeper to select more than three boys to train."

Governor Suri pauses and glances at the row of skulls as my camera follows their movements.

"Takarna will live for as long as it takes to train a boy," the governor continues. "Which brings us to our current situation. The last Keeper has caused the deaths of twenty boys in an attempt to live forever."

Several gasps and mutters break forth at Governor Suri's announcement.

"There are only nineteen skulls," I whisper. Stev shushes me.

"The Keeper trials have never been witnessed by an outsider before, however the people of Atlas have accused me of hiding the Keeper's demise. In the interest of transparency, we hold the trials publicly."

Governor Suri picks up a black cloak from a pile beside the broken crystal orb and drops the hood over the first skull. I nudge the camera around for a better view.

"Each apprentice shall be recalled and offered the chance to compete. Should they refuse, they will cross permanently to the Otherside." A small wooden box appears in Governor Suri's hands. They place it at the front of the stage.

The figure steps out of the shadows at the back of the stage. He pads silently across the stage on bare feet marked with black ink in stripes giving the appearance of claws. The same pattern repeats on his hands.

I gasp and grab Nathan's arm. "That's Dennian," I whisper.

"How can you tell?" Nathan whispers back.

"Everyone else has shoes on."

Governor Suri waves Dennian forward and he crouches beside the first skull in the long row. The front of his cape parts revealing glimpses of his toned and inked bare chest although from my position on the floor, I can't make out the design. He places a hand over the cloaked skull and sparks jump from his inked hand.

Dennian steps back and the cape over the skull billows up into a crouched human shape. Hands land on the floor and the cloaked figure chokes, spewing a mouthful of water onto the floor.

"He just raised the dead!" Nathan exclaims.

"What did you think would happen? Have a bunch of bones complete the trials?" Stev sneers as Governor Suri walks the line, depositing a cloak over each skull.

"But it was just a skull," Nathan mutters.

Dennian moves down the row, repeating the process. The sixth apprentice also spews up water when he is revived. When Dennian reaches the end, nineteen cloaked and hooded figures kneel in a silent row. Dennian stands and returns to the back of the stage.

"As none of the apprentices survived long enough to complete the training, I am required to recall Takarna Carlen as well." Governor Suri flicks open the catch on the small wooden box set on the stage and tosses a black cloak over the top. They step back behind the row of hooded boys, their hand palming a knife from their belt.

A cloud of dust billows upwards, filling the cloak. The figure stands and a flesh hand rises up from the box and attaches itself to the swirling dust cloud of inside the sleeve.

The crowd in the room lean away from the grotesque figure and I realise I'm holding my breath. In the shadows, Dennian tenses behind his own hood.

The Keeper's fleshy hand detaches from the dust and launches itself across the room. Dennian lunges to the side as Governor Suri's knife flies from their hand in a flash of movement.

The blade pierces the back of the disconnected hand and embeds itself in the wall where Dennian's head had been. The knife vibrates for several long moments as the fingers twitch. The dusty remains of the old Keeper collapse to the floor.

Dennian pulls his cloak back around himself but not before the raised scar across the left side of his ribs is revealed, confirming my suspicious around his identity. Dennian turns his head in my direction although his eyes remain hidden behind the shadow of his hood. My hands shake as I clutch the hover-cam controller.

Governor Suri strides over to the hand and yanks the knife from the wall. They shake the dying appendage free over the cauldron beside the dragon statue and hold the blade in the flames for several moments before returning it to its sheath.

"As Carlen is no longer capable of holding the position, we will continue the trials with the apprentices," the governor says calmly.

I scan the room of shocked faces, but no one challenges Governor Suri. Dennian has returned to his position at the back of the stage. Two tigers press into his legs and nuzzle him reassuringly.

A Peace Keeper carries a small round table onto the stage and places a stack of shot glasses and a dark corked bottle on top before backing away. Governor Suri uncorks the bottle and pours a pale green liquid into each of the glasses before turning to face us.

"Dragons' Bane." They hold up one shot glass. "This liquid causes hallucinations and interferes with hearing, sight, and concentration. The Keeper is required to carry out their role under all circumstances and so the trials are completed under the influence of Dragons' Bane."

Governor Suri approaches the first hooded figure, the one who'd choked up water, and holds out the glass.

"Will you compete in the trials?" the governor asks.

The figure doesn't move. After a moment, Star rests a hand on his shoulder and the cloak collapses to the ground as a ghostly figure rises up then dissipates.

Star steps up to the next figure. "Will you compete in the trials?"

The young man climbs to his feet and takes the shot glass. He throws his head back and downs the green liquid. His hood falls away from his face revealing the dark hair of the Atlas born.

"That's my uncle, Charn," Stev whispers. "He's going to win."

Star takes another shot glass from the table and repeats the process. By the time they make it to the end of the row, eleven young men remain standing and only one filled shot glass remains on the table.

"Looks like Governor Suri miscalculated how many would compete," Stev jokes. I don't reply.

Of the eleven, half appear to be from Atlas, including two Stev has pointed out as uncles. They're aged from late teens to early twenties. Several sway under the influence of the drug and one stares at his hand like he has never seen it before.

"You will undergo a series of trials. In the past, this has been to traverse the path to the dragon cavern overlooking Takarn Island, however for the benefit of our audience, the tests will be conducted on the *Brinthiss Malla*. At no point can an outsider interfere with an initiate. This includes myself. A fail will result in death and you won't be given another chance at life."

"Death!" Nathan mutters. "What the hell do they have to do?"

"They have to prove they have the skills of a dragon," Stev replies.

Governor Suri utters a word I don't understand and two tigers rise to their feet. They walk out of the room and the boys follow. One wall of the room flickers and turns into a holographic screen. The image displayed is of another section of the vessel where a long pool takes up most of the room.

"To enter the dragon cavern, an apprentice must first traverse a flooded tunnel. A strong, slender swimmer can make it through in approximately twelve minutes before reaching a locked door. The tunnels are narrow and don't allow for breathing apparatus to be used. Each apprentice must stay under water for this time."

Governor Suri pauses as the display shows the boys reaching the pool. Each one drops his cloak to the floor revealing a dragon tattoo on his back the same as Dennian's. My stomach churns.

They step onto platforms floating on the surface of the water. Manacles close around their feet and hands.

"Once twelve minutes have past, they may unlock their chains and surface. This will test their focus as they need to telekinetically unlock the chain without losing focus on their breathing." As Star finishes speaking the platforms drop out from under the boys and they plummet to the bottom of the pool amid varying amounts of thrashing. A mesh cover snaps into place over the surface.

A few of the boys stand still, the chains weighing them to the bottom, while others struggle slightly under the water. A slow, intermittent pattern of bubbles rises to the surface. I grip Nathan's arm and hold my breath, while Stev chants his uncles' names softly.

I glance at the time on my camera monitoring screen. At three minutes I've taken a breath four times and the first of the boys start to struggle wildly before his body goes limp. Moments later his wispy spirit rises to the surface and disappears.

"He's dead." Numbness spreads over me. Memories of my own near drowning flood back and I press my trembling hands together in my lap. I glance at Dennian. He stands motionless behind his hood facing towards the screen.

"He was already dead," Stev says.

The minutes tick by and another boy loses his fight, leaving nine still underwater when the grate folds back into the wall. Another minute passes and one of Stev's uncles makes it to the surface and flops onto the floor with his arms spread out across the floor. A third boy drowns and two more complete the task. A handful of people get up from their cushions and hurry out of the room, hands pressed to their mouths and tears welling in their eyes.

I dig my fingers into Nathan's arm. The final three make it out of the pool. As they kneel on the tiled floor dripping wet and gasping for breath, a cover locks into place over the pool and the lights dim except for one shining on the door at the far end of the room. The boys scrabble to their feet.

An obstacle flies out from the wall and the eight guys throw themselves out of the way. They make a run for the lit doorway as a variety of obstacles erupt from the walls, floor, ceiling, or swing suddenly towards them.

One young man trips over Charn's foot. On the screen it looks deliberate. The guy falls to the ground and is crushed by a swinging hammer. His spirit and body dissipates as the others have done. Dennian's fingers curl into his legs, but he doesn't move. Governor Suri's face darkens, but they don't interfere.

"Did he just kill that other guy?" Nathan whispers in my ear. I nod, my reply stuck in my throat.

Five make it to the door, including both Stev's uncles. When I look around the room, I'm greeted by a sea of shocked faces many of which are turned away from the screen. The two tigers return with the remaining apprentices.

"I told you one of my uncles will become Keeper," Stev says, the only one in the room who doesn't appear bothered by the deaths of the six other men.

"There's still a sixty percent chance they won't," Nathan mutters beside me.

Governor Suri waves a hand and a metal coffin appears at each end of the stage. One has a lid and the other doesn't.

"Dragons travel by stepping out of existence. Each person will be sealed within this first box and must make their way to the second box. A clear head is needed so as not to be lost in the nothingness. Who will go first?"

Charn shoves one of the others forward. The young man paces back and forth between the two boxes as though counting his steps. He wipes his palms on his dark trousers and sits in the first box, taking one final glance at his destination before lying down.

"You can go as soon as the lid is in place. Are you ready?" Governor Suri asks. There's a slight pause then they step back letting the lid lock into place.

I nudge my camera forward and catch the moment the young man appears white and shaking in the open box. He sits up and drags himself out of the box.

Governor Suri repeats the process for Charn, slamming the lid in place as soon as he lies down. Nothing happens for several long moments, then he appears and Stev cheers. The next young man never makes it to the second box. His spirit rising though the lid our only indication he's left the competition. Daric Shen, Stev's other uncle, goes next.

"You're last, Goyer." Star opens the lid again once Daric climbs out of the other box.

The last young man steps confidently into the box and Star drops the lid back in place. With the camera focused on the boxes, I glance at Dennian. He clenches his hands as the tigers growl low in their throats.

I turn my gaze in the direction of his stare. Daric and Charn clasp hands and focus on the box. Star yanks the lid open, but the first box is empty.

A thump sounds in the second box and Goyer struggles with his hands at his throat.

"Enough!" Governor Suri demands.

Goyer's body goes limp and moments later his spirit comes flying out of the box. Instead of dissipating as the others have, he launches himself at Charn and Daric yelling obscenities.

"Murderer!" he yells. "They cheated!"

Goyer's spirit wraps his hand ineffectively around Daric's neck who tries to brush him away.

"What are you going to do about it?" Charn laughs. "It's already been prophesied that the next Keeper will be a son of the Shan-Shen twins."

Goyer jerks backward and turns to face Governor Suri. "Do something," he demands.

"We're forbidden from interfering in the trial," Governor Suri snaps.

"There's nothing anyone can do," Daric points out. Goyer's spirit whips around in frenzied circles.

"The Temple Tigers don't accept these candidates. Hayka doesn't have the strength required of a Keeper, and Daric and Charn are no better than Carlen was." Lucei steps out from the side of the room and jumps onto the stage. Several tigers crowd around her. "We nominate the Tiger Prince to continue as Keeper," she says.

"What is the meaning of this?" Niko Shen stands up and points at Governor Suri. "The Tiger Prince isn't real. It was a story made up when my son was taken by the beasts." He glares at the tigers.

"If the name upsets you, I'll use his birth name –
Prince Tarla Shen." Governor Suri says. There's an
intake of breath around the room.

"My son was sickly and died as a baby. Show me
where this imposter is. I'll have him arrested." King
Niko scans the crowd.

Several Atlas Peace Keepers step forward but
hesitate when no one reveals themselves as the lost
prince.

"I wouldn't advise that course of action." Governor
Suri monitors the scene but makes no move to
interfere.

King Niko laughs. "And why not?"

"Because Tarla isn't the only one here today,
Father," Lucei says.

A huge male Temple Tiger presses against her side.
Tryce strides across the stage from the other side and
stands facing the Atlas king with his arms crossed.

"What's going on?" Nathan whispers.

"They're chimaera," I reply quietly as I turn my
hover-cam to look at the Atlas king.

King Niko's face has turned an odd shade of white
as his fingers grip the Staff of Office. The tigers rise as
one to their feet with their attention on the king. Niko
turns on his heel and pushes through the people seated
on the floor, striding quickly from the room.

After a moment of indecision, his Peace Keepers
follow. Up on stage, Dennian's shoulders relax. Lucei
and Tryce scan the crowd a final time, their gaze
pausing on Stev who sits trembling beside me. The
siblings head back to each side of the room.

"Are you all right?" I ask Stev.

He blinks at me and shakes his head before
replying. "Of course. As soon as one of my uncles

becomes Takarna, he can fix this mess." He glares at his cousins, Lucei and Tryce.

Governor Suri picks up the remaining shot of Dragon's Bane and holds it out.

"Whoever is selected, bears the burden of the universe upon their shoulders. The wrong candidate will doom us all. Will you accept your destiny, Tarla Shen?"

Keep Living

Dennian – Present

I release the breath I'm holding when Niko Shen leaves the room. He didn't look at me behind my hood, but he's now seen the faces of Lucei and Tryce. They constantly remind me they are old enough to protect themselves, but Zeth's murder still haunts my nightmares.

"Will you accept your destiny, Tarla Shen?" Star doesn't look at me as she holds out the glass.

'They cheat like the evil-smelling one did to become Takarna.' Myaa growls low in her throat as she stares at Daric and Charn.

I glance at my uncle, Daric, and his cousin, Charn. Having been dead for decades, they're now not many years older than me. Hayka is the only other contestant remaining and he never mastered the next challenge. I know because that's where I collected his skull yesterday.

Star's fury rolls over her in charcoal-scented waves, although her outward appearance is calm. We both noted Daric and Charn's interference in the pool, then Charn tripping Vosh in the obstacle course, and finally the pair of them suffocating Goyer when he stepped back into existence. Governor Star Suri will not tolerate another Keeper like Carlen.

My heart pounds as I step forward. I reach out and take the drug from Star's hand, throwing off my hooded cloak as I do, and revealing the Tiger Prince crown Lucei inked on my chest after she drew the claw-lines on my hands and feet. My eyes meet Cassie's.

"No." She shakes her head frantically. I would attempt to reassure her, but the rules forbid talking until inside the cavern which in this case will be after surviving the water trial.

I pull my necklace over my head and hold the dragon stone in my hand for a moment, drawing as much energy in as I can. My blood tingles as I hand the stone to Star. Dragon stones are forbidden during the trials.

Goyer's ghost starts laughing. He points at Daric and Charn. "You're both going to die!"

"Not if we get him first," Daric replies.

I've never had a choice. This was always my fate. I lock eyes with Cassie and lift the glass to my lips. The bitter liquid burns in my throat and I sway on my feet.

I blink several times as my vision blurs. Angry spirits whizz around the room, their cries muffled to my suddenly blocked ears. I flinch and raise an arm as Carlen flies at me.

'Not real. Use your other senses.' Myaa steps in front of me.

I squeeze my eyes closed and breathe deeply. Carlen has gone. Only the faintest hint of decay lingers near the caldron where Star tossed his hand. I pick out the individual tiger scents, as well as Lucei and Tryce. On the floor in front of the stage, my cousin Stev, sits beside Cassie. Fear taints her scent. Four of us now compete for the position of Takarna and only the winner will live.

'Come.' Myaa weaves her way through the people towards the door. I move after her with my eyes still

closed. I can't trust my sight or hearing until the Dragon's Bane wears off.

A body of water appears in front of me. Myaa is no longer beside me. My mind tries to recall the twists and turns of the underwater cavern with the secret marks to point the way in the labyrinth of submerged tunnels, but this is different.

I stumble forward onto a platform and metal bands lock around my ankles and wrists. My heart rate increases and I drop underwater.

I was three when Carlen first did this to me. I'd loved the water before then. Myaa had taught me the tiger underwater breathing trick before Carlen had stolen me from the streak.

I'd panicked when I realised my hands and feet were locked into place and I couldn't break free. Myaa dived under with me while the streak distracted Carlen. Myaa didn't touch my locks, saying I needed to learn how to free myself, but she reminded me to breathe. Water was made from oxygen. As long as I remembered that, I could stay underwater indefinitely.

I hadn't succeeded in telekinetically opening the locks like I was meant to, I'd clawed them open instead. The next time Carlen did it to me, I was prepared. When I realised he was afraid of the water, it became a safe place once more for me.

I rest my hands and head against the wall of the pool and slow my breathing. The Dragon's Bane flows through my bloodstream and I struggle to focus on the present. My mind keeps darting back to the past.

The spirits of the dead apprentices whisper to me. Some are the ones who died today, whispering stories of their earlier deaths, while two appear to be from

Carlen's training days, whispering about how he caused their deaths to make Keeper.

"You can do this." Goyer gets up into my face. "Don't let those bastards win. I gave you the curse to destroy Carlen, now you owe it to me to avenge my death."

The water ripples as the grate above my head folds back and another presence folds itself around me, wrapping itself into the gaps of the cuff locks. I cringe away from the minds of my uncles. They did this earlier thinking no one noticed, but Star and I had. I wait. I can stay underwater indefinitely.

Aurumargent whispers to me, flashes of images entering my mind. My fingers itch to draw, but nothing is clear enough yet, just snippets of dragons, medallions, and black holes.

"Are you going to get out of the water?" Goyer asks, snapping my muddled brain back to the present. I have no idea how much time has passed.

I nod my head. Daric and Charn have retreated and the four metal cuffs fall open to my mental prod. I push off the bottom of the pool and haul myself out of the water. A floor snaps into place and I roll away from the wall as the first obstacle appears.

I close my eyes again knowing I can't trust my vision while drugged. The movement of the air around me, the electric tang of triggers activating, and the shouted directions from Goyer are all I need.

As I roll across the floor to avoid an obstacle punching down from the ceiling, I recognise the pattern as the same from the dragon cavern. In a moment, I'll reach the sweeping stone hammer that gave me the scar on my side.

Something grabs my ankle and I fall to the floor. I kick out, but Daric and Charn's presence hold me. As the hammer swings towards me, I raise both my arms in front of my body and pull forth energy to shield me from the impact.

The explosion feels like lightning striking the ground in front of me. Sparks ripple over my body. My uncles' presence snaps back and my ankle is free. I open my eyes to the stone shank hanging above me and the lower hammer section in shards around me. I scramble to my feet and stagger sideways as light-headedness overcomes me. I lunge forward.

I slam into the doorframe and realise it's over. I stumble forward and Myaa appears in front of me. I drop to my knees as a wave of dizziness washes over me. I use the wall to pull myself to my feet and follow her back to the main room.

My feet bring me to a stop in front of a body-sized box and for a moment I see my headstone above it. It sits in a row beside Zeth's, Lucei's and Tryce's. Zeth is the only one there though. The only one I failed to save. If I fail today, maybe I'll see my baby brother again.

I close my eyes and breathe. Lucei crouches beside Thylace and the other tigers of Myaa's streak. Tryce loiters on the other side of the room, most likely watching his half-brother, Stev. Fear still wraps itself around Cassie, along with relief. I have one more challenge before I catch up to Daric, Charn, and Hayka.

"Whenever you're ready," Star says behind me.

I step into the box and lie down. The lid drops into place, plunging the tiny space into darkness. Images flood my mind again. I'm lying in a hole beside Cassie with bugs crawling over us while Carlen wraps his hand around my neck. I throw my hand out, but it hits the lid of the box. Then I'm six, lying in my grave struggling to breathe as the air slowly runs out.

Aurumargent whispers to me and in my mind I'm standing beside a crystal clear lake with mountains and caves rising up before me.

"Once upon a time, we dragons lived peacefully among the humans..." A young, dark-haired man, who smells like charcoal and sage, faces a small child playing in the sand.

"Why did he do it, Bron?" the girl asks. A gentle breeze ruffles her blonde hair and the scent of charcoal and violets fills my nose.

I reach for her, but I'm still in the sealed box. My fingers ache for my drawing materials, but instead I feel for the fabric of the universe. It opens in front of me and I fall out of existence. For the briefest moment I'm surrounded by nothing then I'm sitting up in the second box. There are two trials left to complete.

Star waves her hand over the stage and the boxes disappear. Four thick transparent panels appear in their place. In front of each sits a pedestal with a piece of coal on top. Daric, Charn, and Hayka step up beside me.

"If Governor Suri can make things appear and disappear, why do they need a Keeper?" Cassie asks from somewhere behind me. I don't hear the response as Star continues speaking.

"On entering the dragon caverns, you are on a timeline. You have reached the glass room. The only way out is through the panel before you and the room is booby trapped. You have seventy-five seconds to make it through. If you fail, you will die. Time starts now."

"Ready to watch Dennian die?" Stev asks Cassie.

Her fear mixes with anger as I take the coal from the pedestal in front of me, and cover it with my hands. My eyes drift closed as my mind sinks into the molecular level of the coal. I channel energy into the coal, forcing the atoms to rearrange. When I open my eyes, a diamond rests in the palm of my hand.

I look up. Charn runs his hands over his panel. Daric smashes his pedestal against his section of panel, but it remains intact. Hayka attempts to copy me although all his coal does is crumble in his hands.

"Thirty seconds," Star says, pacing slowing back and forth just outside the space.

I step up to the panel and dig a corner of the diamond into the surface. As I drag the diamond around in a circle, Daric throws himself at me and I drop the rock. We fall to the ground and my head hits the floor. Blackness claims me.

Dennian lies still with his eyes closed. Adrenalin floods my body. I sit up on my heels, ready to run forward, but Governor Suri's look halts me. We're not allowed to interfere.

Daric searches Dennian for the diamond, but it's rolled away. Charn lunges for it and frantically cuts into his panel. Daric grabs at his cousin, but Charn kicks him in the head and continues cutting a hole in the panel with the diamond. The fourth man beats his fists against his panel having given up on the crumbled coal.

"Twenty seconds," Governor Suri bites out. They stop pacing and stare at their brother lying on the floor.

"Do something!" I yell at them.

"If I interfere, it voids the trials," Star snaps. Their mouth moves silently, repeating 'wake up, Dennian'. He stirs. Charn is nearly through his panel.

"Fifteen seconds!" Governor Suri says.

"Dennian, get up!" I yell.

I lurch forward dragging Nathan and Tryce with me, but Stev grabs me around the waist and we all tumble backwards.

"You're not going to help him beat my uncle," Stev hisses in my ear.

Nathan throws himself at us as we struggle on the floor. Nathan throws a punch at Stev while Tryce tries to pull me away. Several Peace Keepers descend and pull us apart. I twist in the arms of the woman holding me until I can see Dennian.

"Get up," I yell again.

The ghost boy settles on the ground and sticks his face up close to Dennian's.

"You can do this. Don't let them win," the ghost says.

Dennian opens his eyes and looks at me groggily through the transparent ghost. I reach out a hand in his direction and he rolls onto his knees. Blood drips down the side of his face as he searches the floor for coal, but the remaining pieces have been reduced to black dust in the fight. Dennian stares at his blackened fingers and my heart hammers in my chest. I want to call out to him again, but the words are stuck in my throat.

"Five seconds!" Governor Suri calls.

Daric lies on the floor, and the fourth man continues to beat his fists against his panel. Daric rises groggily to one knee. Charn's centre panel piece falls out and he climbs through the gap taking the diamond with him. The hole closes up behind him as though it was never cut.

Dennian lunges at his panel. He slashes his hands across the surface horizontally then vertically. A piece of panel falls out, leaving claw marks on the edges and Dennian dives through. The instant Dennian hits the floor, Daric and the other man left on the other side of the panels drop to the floor. Their spirits rise out of their bodies. My knees buckle and I collapse to the floor.

"Demon! He cheated," Stev shouts.

Charn throws himself on top of Dennian, pinning Dennian's hands under his body. Charn wraps his arm around Dennian's neck, choking him as they struggle on the floor. Governor Suri takes a step forward then stops, their fingers drumming against their leg as they scowl.

Dennian throws his head back as fur ripples over his body and his limbs morph. A set of swept-back horns erupt from his head and connect with Charn's forehead with a loud thunk. Charn falls backwards and I gasp. Dennian has been replaced by a large horned Temple Tiger.

"He's a shifter," Nathan whispers.

Tiger Dennian spins around, landing with giant paws of either side of Charn's body. Dennian roars and the other tigers in the room add their voices to his. Charn crawls backwards as blood drips from two wounds on his forehead.

"Enough!" Governor Suri bellows. "If you die, we have to start the trials again and neither of you are strong enough to pass a second time. We move on to the next task."

The governor waves their hand and two huge boulders appear hanging by chains above the stage. A shimmering barrier activates between the new trial and the people sitting on the cushions watching.

The tiger collapses onto his side and the hair and fur vanish, leaving a bare-chested Dennian crouched on the floor wheezing and rubbing at the bruising on his neck. Charn staggers to his feet wiping blood from his face.

"Shouldn't you let them rest?" one of the delegates calls out.

"Anyone who enters the dragon caverns is on a timer. They stop, they die," Governor Suri says. "The next trial is one of endurance. Each initiate must hold the equivalent weight of an adult dragon off the ground until the dragons, Aurumargent, provide a vision, which the initiate must sketch. Once complete, the apprentice may remove himself and reveal what he has seen. This tests the ability to focus on Aurumargent while being otherwise occupied telekinetically."

Dennian crawls forward and wriggles underneath one boulder, placing his feet staggered under the rock as though he will take the weight in his legs. He lies back with his arms outstretched and eyes closed. Paper and pencils appear on the floor beside him. Charn slides into position under the other boulder and holds his hands up without touching it.

"Charn Shan and Tarla Shen, at the end of this trial, one of you shall become the new Keeper. Take the weight," Governor Suri calls out and the chains holding the boulders snap. I gasp, but both remain suspended above Dennian and Charn.

"Okay, now I know how he beat everyone in the weight lifting completion," Nathan whispers.

"I knew he cheated," Stev hisses.

"He looks like he's fallen asleep." I watch Dennian lying under the boulder with his eyes closed. His hand lies beside the paper.

Charn repositions himself, putting one arm up against the boulder and then a leg. Stev shifts nervously beside us muttering to himself.

"How long do you think this will go for?" I ask as the time ticks over to ten minutes.

"Until Dennian fails," Stev replies. Nathan pulls me into a hug as we watch Dennian's final trial.

Dennian's fingers reach out and take the pencil. Without opening his eyes or moving the rest of his body, he starts drawing.

Charn wipes one hand across his brow, sprinkling drops of blood on the floor. The boulder tilts momentarily. He glances at Dennian and grabs his own pencil. He repositions so he is in a similar position to

Dennian but places the page against his legs where he can see it as he scribbles furiously.

Dennian flips his page over, still without looking at it, and draws on the other side.

Charn rolls out and his boulder drops to the floor, narrowly missing him and sending a tremor through the floor. Stev cheers as bile rises in my throat. Governor Suri reaches out a hand and Charn's boulder disappears before it can crush Dennian.

Charn sinks to his knees and presses a hand to his chest as he offers up his drawing. Governor Suri waves a hand and the sketch projects onto the screen that appears behind her. My chest constricts. Dennian hasn't moved from under his boulder, still drawing on his page as though he hasn't noticed Charn finishing.

"Maybe it's not about who is fastest," Nathan whispers.

Charn's drawing is rough and spotted in blood from his head wound. In it, two people stand on the stage in this room. One looks like it may be female and the other is dressed in black pants and cape. Various other people sit around them in a semi-circle.

"Explain it to us." Star Suri's tone remains neutral.

"I would have thought it was obvious." Charn looks up at Governor Suri, who stares at him silently. "It's an image of the delegation meeting to be held tomorrow. I'm the one standing beside you in the position as your chief advisor." Charn grins.

Governor Suri steps forward and places their hand on the physical drawing as they look at Charn.

"The world is about to end and Aurumargent offers up a vision of you winning a position?"

I flinch at the thump as Dennian rolls away from his boulder. He pauses on the floor to rub at his bruised

330

throat before heaving himself to his feet. He drops to his knees beside his surviving uncle.

"Perhaps I should have mentioned to the gathering that Aurumargent provides the same image to each apprentice. Shall we see if Dennian's sketch matches your own?" Governor Suri asks. Charn's grin falters.

Governor Suri takes the drawing from Dennian and projects it on the screen. The drawing shows three males who emanate superiority. The oldest in the centre appears to be the leader. He stands straight and tall despite appearing to have lived at least eighty years. The next looks to be around my father's age and has a completely expressionless face. The youngest could be in his early twenties, his expression a cheeky grin. Around his neck hangs the circular medallion I've seen Dennian draw previously. In one hand the young man holds a large scroll of paper. The three men wear dark trousers like the apprentices and matching shirts in red for the eldest, amber for the second man, and bronze for the youngest.

Governor Suri flips the drawing to the other side. The scroll of paper is spread out to reveal the writing, the same scratchy kind Dennian writes. There are two columns with headings, but only one has writing below it.

"Explain your vision." Star Suri holds out two black capes and both boys take one. They throw them over their shoulders, leaving the hoods off.

"The dragons will bring the contract. They hope if you concede to the gods they will be merciful and not destroy the world as promised." Dennian's voice is rough. "Aurumargent believes you should nominate a challenger to fight for the right to keep our world."

"Who will challenge?" Governor Suri asks.

"The dragon Sapphia," Dennian replies.

"He lies," Charn cries. "The dragons are long gone."

"Sapphia came to the temple many years ago." Dennian doesn't look at his uncle.

"Who are the dragon riders in your drawing?" Governor Suri points to the three men.

"The dragon elder, Rubyss, and his son, Ambress..." Dennian pauses as I stare at the picture wondering why he refers to the men as dragons. "The young one is the Story Keeper," he finishes.

'The final task to become the new Keeper – speak what is necessary, regardless of cost,' an eerie voice whispers through the room.

'I promised...' Dennian whispers.

'Say the name.'

Dennian lifts his head and looks straight at his sister. "Forgive me, Star...The Story Keeper is Bronzrr."

The dragon symbol matching his tattoo appears on the back of his cape.

Charn collapses to the floor. His spirit rises up from his body leaving only the black cape behind.

"Takarna." People chant the name from the crowd.

Star's face drains of colour and she presses a hand to her chest. As Vice Governor Jaarid moves to join them on the stage, Star Suri steps backwards and vanishes from the room. Dennian lunges afterwards, his hand closing around empty air. He presses his forehead to the floor and covers his head with his hands. Several tigers vanish from the room.

I push forward, trying to reach Dennian, but the Peace Keepers surround the stage.

"Thank you all for attending the trials today." Vice Governor Jaarid surveys the scene before him. "I now request all guests to depart. Delegates can remain behind. We have much to discuss with the new Keeper."

Between the shoulders of several Peace Keepers, I watch Jaarid place a hand on Dennian's shoulder and lean forward to say something. Dennian pushes himself up from the floor. He wipes tears from his cheeks as he reaches out a trembling hand for the dragon stone Jaarid holds out.

"Everybody out." Several Peace Keepers push forward. The room has already begun to empty.

"I need to speak to Dennian," I say as one of them takes me by the arm and tugs me towards the exit.

"Takarna will be occupied for some time," the man replies.

"Hey!" Stev struggles against the men attempting to lead him out the door. "I'm Delegate Shan's son. I should be able to attend in his absence."

The man hesitates for a moment before replying. "The Keeper says a Shen sibling will attend as acting delegate."

We're herded from the room and I lose sight of Dennian. One of the Peace Keepers thrusts my hover-cam towards me and the door closes behind us.

"Now what?" Nathan asks.

"We head back to Terra and finish this game." Stev clenches his fists and storms off. I turn away from Nathan to go pack my bags.

"Cassie, wait!" Lucei runs up to me as I reach my temporary quarters. I pause.

"Dennian never had a choice," she says. "We tried to see where Star went, but none of us can sense her in the universe. Dennian has to step into Governor Suri's role alongside Jaarid until she returns."

"Star tried to warn me this would happen." I turn away before anyone sees the tears in my eyes. Lucei and Nathan don't follow me.

Wedding

I replay the clip again of Dennian transforming into a Temple Tiger. Fur, horns, claws. The same claws that saved Nathan on the cliff face and marked the old Keeper's face.

"There you are." Jayne flicks on the lights of the media room and I quickly close my screen.

"What's going on?" Jayne asks. "Trev has been trying to interview Stev and Nathan about the trials, but they aren't saying much other than the new guy is called Takarna Tarla. Did you get footage or not?"

"Just finishing the editing now." I rotate my seat as I stare at the black screen.

"Can I see it?"

"I, ah… need to fix some things first," I say.

Everyone in that room saw him transform. Would it bother him that I filmed it? The final cut wouldn't make sense if I left the footage out.

"Cassie, you've seen the new advisor to the governor. No one seems to have heard of him before. Tell me what he's like. Is he as powerful as they say a Keeper is?" Jayne pleads.

"He's Stev's cousin," I say. "And yes, he's powerful."

"Oh wow! Why didn't Stev say so? Trev and your mum are going to love this. You could be marrying the Keeper's cousin! Lord, Cassie, if you go to Atlas, I might never see you again. I really think Nathan's the way to go." Jayne wraps me in a hug.

"You could always tell Trev that Governor Suri fired Stev's father from his position as delegate. I'm sure that would be great for ratings," I say. "If they're all so concerned with fixing me up with someone of status, I'm surprised they haven't tried marrying me to the new Keeper."

"Why? Is he single?" Jayne asks.

"I was being sarcastic. The Keeper doesn't have time for a relationship." I remove my edited footage of the trials onto my screen and walk out of the door.

*

The tunic dress lies across my bed beside a pair of flowing white trousers. The tunic is almost identical to the one I'd admired in the dress shop, although instead of the pale green embroidery, a rainbow of threads weave through the fabric leaving only the shoulder caps completely white.

I trace my fingers over a tri-colour monkey in a green leafy tree above a horned tiger prowling the forest floor. A variety of other animals and plants complete the design.

I undress and slip the wedding outfit on. It clings to me as though designed for my body. A tiny metal ring is sewn into the left shoulder, but there are no accessories on the bed so I ignore it. I'm standing in front of the mirror when Lori and Carter step into my room.

Lori dumps an armful of pale green fabric on my bed. "Where did that dress come from? Sara told us we were going with this one."

"It was on my bed," I say.

"I wish Trev would tell us when he changes things," Carter mutters. "Never mind, I can change the makeup colour palette. Jayne was going to do the finishing touches to the design anyway. She said she'd be here as soon as she's dressed."

I sink into the chair by the dresser and Carter begins on my face while Lori braids my hair into a crown around my head. By the time they finish, Jayne appears in a lilac floor-length dress with pale green trim. Her hair sits in deep brown curls in top of her head. Several lilac streaks add to her look.

"Wow! You got the dress you wanted! So many pretty colours. Let me at that face of yours. I have so many ideas," she exclaims.

Lori and Carter pack up their tools and slip out of the room. When Jayne's finished, I stare at my face in the mirror. Jayne has copied part of the dress' design along the side of my face including a miniature tiger.

"It's beautiful," I say.

"Carter said when people see my designs on your face, we'll be raking in the business." Jayne beams at me. "I can start the apprenticeship as soon as this program wraps."

"Good for you," I say.

"Aren't you excited?" Jayne frowns at me. "We're about to embark on the rest of our lives."

"I guess I imagined it would be with Dennian." I trace a finger over the tiger at my waist.

"He walked out, Cassie. That's not the type of guy you want. Nathan would be way more reliable."

"I don't think Dennian had a choice. Let's get this over with."

I stand abruptly, pushing my chair backwards. A pair of soft flats sit on the floor beside my bed and I slip them on, ignoring the pale green heels Lori brought in. I stride out of the room with Jayne hurrying after.

Sara waits in the foyer with Mum. Both are dressed in wedding finery and Mum tugs at her midnight blue jacket as we approach.

"That's not the dress we chose." Sara frowns.

"I can't change now. It would ruin my hair and makeup. Could cost us hours before we start the scene." I try to look concerned. "But if you really want me to…"

"No, no, if that's the dress Trev wanted, that's what we'll go with," Sara says. "As we rehearsed yesterday, Cassie will walk down the aisle towards the stage and Jayne will follow. Stev and Nathan will already be there and their families and the eliminated contestants, most of them anyway, will be in the rows."

Sara hands me the cue cards and I glance through them quickly. She hasn't given me the final one with who they've chosen for me.

"Say your part to each of the finalists then we'll give you the winner's name."

I nod my head as I read over my lines again so I can make it look natural for the cameras. Mum gives me a quick hug and hurries off to her position in the front row of the gathering.

"What's this?" Trev storms over to me and holds up a screen. He taps it and my teaser of the Takarna trials plays. I used a few snippets from my footage although none of it shows Dennian. Jayne leans over my shoulder to watch.

"The trials, of course. Is your network planning on making a bid for the whole footage?" I say.

"Don't forget you and your mother belong to us," he says.

I step up into his space and look him in the eyes. "I have exclusive footage of the Temple Tigers during a

338

festival on Atlas as well as the Keeper trials. I can pay our way out of the contract if needed. You however, have invested a lot in me. It would be unfortunate if I chose not to go through with the wedding."

"I expect you to make the right decision up on the stage." Trev leans towards me in a vaguely threatening manner, but I hold my ground.

"Don't worry, I will."

"Sara will lead you into position. Start walking when you hear the music and look at both men equally." He stares at me for a moment. "Is that the dress we chose?"

"Of course."

Trev gives me one last look before turning on his heel and marching off.

"Let's go." Sara walks ahead of Jayne and me. We head outside and stop behind a hedge at the edge of a large manicured garden.

I peer through the greenery. Yesterday it had consisted of a stage and seats on either side of an aisle. Now flowers and ribbons adorn every surface, including the arbour above, where I'll be standing in a few moments.

The music starts and I take a deep breath, unsure what decision I'll make. I walk slowly down the aisle with a smile fixed in place and my eye line focused on a point between Stev and Nathan. As I get closer, I look at each of them in turn.

Stev wears the traditional flowing Atlas robes like the ones on the mannequin at the dress shop. A golden crown perches on his black hair to match his cocky grin.

Nathan wears a deep green tailored suit. His galaxy print tie peeks out from the V of his jacket. He shifts nervously from one foot to the other.

I reach the steps taking me up to the stage. A small piece of tape marks the place Trev wants me to stand opposite the two guys. Jayne follows behind me and takes her place at the back of the stage.

I face the gathering for a moment. Mum sits in the front row as do Nathan's family and two Atlas women. One is Stev's aunt, Queen Lari Shen. I guess the other to be Stev's mother. Half a dozen Atlas Peace Keepers stand close by.

I turn to face Stev first. "Prince Stev, I've had the most amazing time getting to know you over the last few weeks. We've had moments of real connection. I can see myself…" I pause, forcing myself to recite the remaining words on the cue card, "standing beside you as you take your place in the Atlas government."

My smile twists into a grimace and I re-set my expression before turning to face Nathan.

"Nathan, I feel like we've become such close friends during this journey together. Your intelligence shines through and I know you'll be an asset to SuriTech."

Nathan's hesitant smile slips slowly from his face as I recite the words. They sound like a rejection to both of us. Jayne steps forward and slips the remaining cue cards into my hand.

I read the first one as I step back into a position where I can see both Nathan and Stev while facing the crowd and hover-cams. *Pause and aim for a conflicted expression.*

"This is one of the hardest decisions I've ever had to make." I read out the second card. Stev grins at me.

On my other side, Nathan wipes his palms nervously on his deep green dress pants.

I turn over the final cue card and look at the name. *Stev.* I place my hands together and rest them against my face with my eyes closed. Looking conflicted is not difficult.

I open my eyes and look out over the crowd wondering if Mum will forgive me for what I'm about to do. A Temple Tiger appears by the hedge at the back of the garden. My heart skips a beat, but the tiger loiters and I don't think it's Dennian.

Something small and furry leaps off its back and dashes up the aisle in a blur of copper, blonde, and ebony. A few people scream and stand as the monkey bounds past.

The tri-colour monkey scurries up the steps and into my arms. It's larger than Zeke but smaller than the adults in the Atlas menagerie.

"Lyri?" I ask.

The monkey chirps what sounds like agreement and hands me a scroll of paper she clasps in her claws. As soon as I take it, she leaps down and runs back to the tiger.

"What on Terra is going on?" Trev marches towards the stage. "Say your lines."

I open the scroll and a grin spreads across my face. The document has been signed by Takarna Tarla on behalf of Governor Suri. I turn to face Nathan.

"Nathan, I'm sorry but my heart lies elsewhere. Good luck with your apprenticeship. You're going to rock it." My grin widens as I hand him the scroll.

A range of emotions wash over his face as he looks at the documents.

"This is unconditional acceptance into SuriTech," he whispers.

"Congratulations." I step forward and hug him.

At Trev's annoyed waving, I pull away and face Stev. The Atlas faux prince smirks at me.

"Stev," I pause for the camera. "I wouldn't marry you if you were the last person in the galaxy."

"What are you doing?" Trev bellows. Behind me a laugh escapes from Nathan. Stev's face is a mixture of shock and fury.

"You can't do this to me," he hisses. "I won't let you embarrass me like this." Stev grabs my arm and leans in to whisper in my ear. "You will marry me here and now or I'll have my Peace Keepers arrest you."

"Let go of my arm unless you want that Temple Tiger to make your face look like the old Keeper's," I whisper back.

Stev jerks away from me and looks back down the aisle. The Temple Tiger is no longer there. Damn. I leap off the stage and run. Behind me, Stev crashes to the floor as he trips over Nathan's outstretched foot.

Two Atlas Peace Keepers step in front of me before I reach the final row of chairs. I skid to a stop leaving grass stains on my white slippers. I turn to face Stev who brushes himself off and glares at Nathan.

"Get back here, girl," Stev demands. "We paid good money for you."

"What?" Nathan gets his objection in before I can.

"Cassie." Mum stands and reaches a hand out to me. "We signed an agreement. Come back up on stage and everything will be fine. You're marrying a prince."

"No, you signed the contract." My hands fist by my sides. "Stev isn't a real prince. Three of his cousins are still alive. And his father is no longer delegate. Governor Suri fired him."

"Shut her up," Stev yells.

I back away from the Peace Keepers behind me, but two more converge on me from the other direction. I glance at the rows of people seated either side of me. Saul sits in the middle of one row talking into his wristband. I hope he has his own Peace Keepers nearby.

The hair on my arms stands on end as the air crackles with energy and a dozen government Peace Keepers appear moments before Saul's three run into the clearing. They're a mix of Protectors and Perceptives.

"I'm Yumi," the lead Peace Keeper says. "I require all Atlas Peace Keepers to stand aside and the Atlas noble to accompany us back to the *Brinthiss Malla.*"

"What is the meaning of this?" Queen Lari stands and glares at the newcomers who flank the gathering.

"There's been a change of leadership on Atlas and the new prince wants his crown." Yumi glances at Stev who grips the crown tightly with one hand.

"On what grounds?" Queen Lari demands.

"King Niko Shen and Queen Lari stand accused of the murder of Zeth Shen, as well as the attempted murder of Tarla, Lucei, and Tryce Shen. Various other members of the current leadership also stand accused of abandonment to commit murder, including the Shans and the Kels." Yumi reads off the screen in his hand.

"Lies! I demand you reveal the identity of our accuser," the queen demands. Stev stares at them wide-eyed.

"The murder of Zeth Shen was witnessed by Takarna Carlen and Takarna Tarla," Yumi replies. "The Keeper has submitted a sketch as evidence."

Queen Lari signals her Peace Keepers and they surround her and the woman beside her, as well as Stev still up on the stage. The two hooded Atlas Peace Keepers lift their arms towards the newcomers. Yumi falls to his knees, his hands clutching at his throat.

'Enough!' Dennian's voice echoes through our minds and all the Atlas Peace Keepers crumple to the ground unconscious.

A blue hooded cape darkens into black as Dennian steps forward. He lowers his hand while the government Peace Keepers restrain the Atlas guards. They vanish, taking the accused with them. Two government Protectors remain with Dennian. On the stage, Stev, the only Atlas born remaining, clutches the crown to his chest.

I run up to Dennian, pulling the black hood from his head. The green of his eyes is somewhere between Atlas blue and tiger yellow. I thread the fingers of one hand up the back of his neck and into hair as soft as fur. I press my lips to his. His mouth explores mine as his hands wrap around my waist pulling me against his body.

I pull my mouth away to whisper in his ear. "I choose you."

He studies me without speaking and I wonder what he sees.

"The Keeper is not allowed to be distracted by relationships," he says.

"You looked like you managed fine while competing on the show," I reply. The corner of his mouth twitches up. "Are we worth bending the rules for?" I ask.

'Would you still choose me if our time together will be brief?'

"Yes. I'll have you for as long as I'm given," I say.

'Then, yes.'

"Do I call you Tarla, now? Or Takarna?" I ask.

'Always Dennian. I'd rather be a nobody than King Niko's son.'

"You'll never be nobody." I lean into him and our lips meet again.

When we pull apart, Dennian tucks something into my hand. I look down at the dragon stone Glar Shan took from me.

"He said it was destroyed!"

'He lied.'

"Stop, stop, stop!" Trev marches up to us. "You walked out and despite making a great scene, you don't get to come back and interfere with my final act."

"My exit was unavoidable." Dennian keeps a hand on my waist. "Governor Suri required my attendance at the Keeper trials. But I have a free half hour at the moment to marry Cassie. Once I relieve Stev of the Atlas crown."

"It's mine. You can't hold two positions," Stev says.

"The crown is not for me. Lucei prefers to remain with the tigers and Zeth is dead. That leaves our half-brother as the remaining prince. He's keen to take the position," Dennian says.

"Tryce Shen can't be more than thirteen years old even if he is still alive," Stev says. "I won't hand over the Atlas crown to a child."

"Lucei Shen and I have agreed to mentor Tryce until he is capable of ruling on his own." Dennian holds out a hand towards Stev.

The crown vanishes, leaving Stev grasping at empty air. Dennian closes his hand around the crown. The tiger from earlier reappears and gasps come from the wedding guests. Vice Governor Jaarid stands beside the tiger.

"I heard there was going to be a wedding?" Jaarid says.

"Cassie has asked me to marry her." Dennian smiles down at me.

"In that case, it is my duty, in the absence of your sister, to officiate the ceremony," Jaarid says.

The tiger nudges up against Dennian's leg and he places the crown on its head. The tiger vanishes.

"I trust there's no objection to the Vice Governor of the Universe marrying me to the Keeper?" I ask Trev.

The director's mouth opens and closes several times, but no words come out. I take hold of Dennian's hand and lead him up the steps to the stage. Nathan steps forward to welcome Dennian.

"You have a lot of explaining to do," Jayne whispers as Vice Governor Jaarid steps onto the stage after us.

Trev waves Nathan and Stev from the stage. Nathan leans in to give me a quick hug while Stev stalks off the stage, all the way down the aisle and out of the garden.

The hover-cams reposition and Jaarid faces us. Dennian clasps my left forearm with his so our arms are held between our bodies.

Jaarid pulls a ball of gold thread from the pouch at his waist. He pins one end to Dennian's shoulder before winding the fine metallic thread around our clasped hands. He fastens it to the tiny ring set into the left shoulder of my dress. He repeats the process with silver thread.

"Jayne has the rings when you're ready," Trev interrupts.

"That won't be necessary," Jaarid says. "Takarna Tarla and Cassie Brooke, do you agree to this union?" Jaarid asks.

"Yes," we repeat.

"Dennian, you can do the honours," Jaarid says.

"Close your eyes," Dennian whispers.

I do as he says. The threads binding our arms fizzle. Heat travels along my arm, but it doesn't burn. Bright light reaches my eyes behind my closed lids.

It lasts only a few moments. I open my eyes to Dennian's smiles. I glance down at our joined arms. The thread has vanished, leaving a gold and silver entwined band around each of our ring fingers.

I glance at the tiny hook on my shoulder. A silver dragon is embroidered into the shoulder cap where there wasn't one before. The other side has the golden dragon.

"Takarna, Cassie, you are now joined. May your love transcend death into eternity," Jaarid says.

I step forward and kiss Dennian. He wraps his arms around my waist as I thread my fingers into the hair at the back of his neck. Nathan's cheer rises up above those of the other wedding guests.

Dennian presses his forehead against mine. *'I need to leave. Star hasn't come back yet. Jaarid and I have to meet with the Atlas delegation to cement Tryce's position as the new Atlas king.'*

What about us?" I whisper.

'Will you come with me? Stay on Brinthiss Malla *until I'm finished with these meetings?'*

"Yes."

'Lucei will come collect you when you're ready.' Dennian steps away and holds his hand out to Jaarid. The Vice Governor places his hand in Dennian's and they both vanish, leaving me alone on the stage with Jayne.

"Did he just walk out on you again?" Jayne asks.

I look out over the people gathered. Several seats in the front row are now vacant thanks to the Atlas group leaving. Mum cries into a handkerchief. Nathan has taken one of the vacated seats clasping his acceptance letter. The other contestants sit together in the middle rows. Only Stev and Farray are missing.

"Get over here." Trev waves a hand at me. I step down off the stage and walk over to him.

"Well, that's going to be exciting for your viewers," I say. "The vice governor and Keeper both at my wedding."

Trev glares at me. "How long have you known?"

"That Dennian's the new Keeper? I found out halfway through the trials like everyone else. You'll get to see it too if your network is the highest bidder for my footage."

"You've broken the contact. I should make you and your mother pay every credit in penalties," Trev says.

"I just guaranteed you the best ratings you could ever imagine," I say. "You won't do anything to me – or Takarna Dennian."

"Get inside. Sara has questions to ask you for the final wrap-up." Trev storms off.

I slip back into the mansion after Sara while the guests mill around wondering if congratulations are in order or not.

Sara's questioning goes on for an hour although for many of the responses I merely tell them to bid for my footage of the Keeper trials.

I finally make it back to my room and drag my bag out from under the bed. It doesn't take long to pack my belongings into it. Most of the outfits I've worn since coming to the mansion don't belong to me. The only thing I keep is the wedding dress. I'm staring at my packed bag when Mum and Jayne enter the room.

"Why didn't you tell us Dennian is the Keeper?" Jayne's voice rises into a squeal as she wraps me in a hug.

"Didn't want to spoil the footage before the final bids are in," I say.

"How's that going?" she asks.

"Deadline's any moment now."

My screen pings and Jayne releases me. I scan the message including the final offer for my footage.

"Wow!" Jayne leans over my shoulder. "Have they added in an extra zero?"

"Looks like Trev's bid wasn't high enough." A grin spreads across my face. "He'll have to watch the trials on another network. He might not even get that promotion he was chasing."

"I can't believe my daughter is married to the Keeper and making her own money," Mum says.

"Any other surprises you've been keeping from us?" Jayne asks.

I pause and look at the pair of them. "Probably one other thing you should know. Dennian's sister, Star, is the Governor of the Universe."

Jayne's mouth drops open and Mum stares at me blankly.

"Star, the weird girl we met?" Mum asks. I nod and catch sight of Lucei leaning against the doorframe.

"Ready to go, sister?" she asks.

"Where did you come from?" Jayne asks.

"Atlas." Lucei pushes off the wall and prowls into the room. "We should get going. I don't want to miss father's murder trial." A grin spreads over her face.

"Murder?" Mum repeats.

"Mother and Father killed my twin, Zeth," Lucei says.

"This is Lucei. She's Dennian biological sister," I say.

"Maybe you should stay here for a while?" Mum looks at me in alarm. "Trev said the property will be transferred into my name by the end of the day."

"I'm going with Dennian." I give Jayne a final hug. "Thanks for being such a great friend. I'll visit you," I promise.

"You better or I'll come looking for you." Tears stream down her cheeks.

Sara raps on the doorframe. "Mrs Brooke, Jayne, we need you both in the garden for the final camera scene."

Jayne rushes back over to me for a final hug and Mum kisses my cheek before they both leave with Sara. I pick up my bag and sling one strap over a shoulder.

"Ready?" Lucei asks.

"You're not going anywhere until I have that footage." Trev walks into the room flanked by three security guards.

"I've already sold the recording. You should have offered more. It was a once in a lifetime opportunity, after all."

Trev waves the security forward.

"I wouldn't do that if I were you." Lucei stalks forward. The men look at her.

"Why's that?" Trev demands.

"Because you're out numbered," she replies.

Trev laughs. "Two little girls against my three guards? I don't think so."

"I never said I was a girl." Lucei folds over, fur and horns erupting from her skin. Her front paws hit the ground as her claws dig into the carpet. She bares her teeth.

Trev squeals and bolts from the room. The three guards push each other to be the first out of the door.

Lucei turns to look at me with her yellow eyes. An image form in my mind of me reaching out and holding onto one of her horns.

As soon as my hand wraps around the horn, we vanish from the room. Everything goes silent. I open my eyes to complete darkness. There's no light, sound or smell. It's neither hot nor cold, only complete sensory deprivation. I open and shut my eyes several times, but I can't tell the difference either way. I move my feet, but I'm not standing on anything. There's no resistance except for when my knee collides with Lucei's furry side. I feel like time has stopped.

Light assaults me and I blink several times to find us back on the *Brinthiss Malla*.

'This way.' My new sister-in-law leads me to my room aboard Governor Suri's spacecraft.

Takarn Island

I sit on the floor of a viewing room aboard the *Brinthiss Malla*. The vessel hangs in orbit above the watery Atlas. Night creeps across the surface of the planet.

My eye is drawn to the barren landscape of the half-crescent moon. If I move my head quickly, the surface shimmers into blues and greens before returning to its original grey.

I'm still darting my head from side to side when Dennian's reflection appears in the transparent surface in front of me. I reach up a hand and tug him down beside me. Fatigue shows on his face and he closes his eyes briefly as he rests his head against my shoulder.

"There's something odd about that moon," I say.

Dennian opens his eyes. "It's an illusion."

"The whole planet?"

"No, it's there, but not barren. That's where Takarn Island is," Dennian says.

"Stev said the island was on Atlas."

Dennian nods his head. "It was there a long time ago. The dragons moved it."

I raise my eyebrows, but he doesn't appear to be joking.

"You look exhausted," I say. He nods his head.

"Using a lot of energy." He looks at the planets below. "Come. I'll teach you about the dragons."

Dennian takes my hand and hauls me to my feet. We head up several decks and along a couple of corridors, before stepping into a museum.

Portraits of previous governors line the walls. The most recent is of a man leaning against a tree trunk.

The caption below it reads: Governor Aden Suri, 924 – 967 AG.

I circle the room until I find Star. In the painting she wears a dark leather mini skirt slit up both sides and studded with tiny dragon stones stitched into the hem. Her sleeveless top is of the same blue material as the Peace Keepers' clothes. A silver dragon is painted on her left arm and a gold one on her right. She smiles down at the single red long stem rose in her hand as she faces a full length mirror.

The reflection in the mirror is of a tall, muscular warrior holding a heavy sword with an ornate swirling hilt designed to protect the hand. On his bare chest is a large circular tattoo with a complex swirling pattern like the mark on the Government Peace Keepers' shirts. The man has an assortment of weapons strapped to various parts of his body and eyes that follow the viewer.

The caption reads: Governor Tarish "Risha" Suri, 18 BG – 36 AG.

"She looks exactly like Star." I point to the portrait of Risha Suri, the first governor.

"Star's chosen to look like Risha," Dennian replies. "The man in the mirror is Warlord Tarsh, the Destroyer and Risha's alter ego," Dennian adds before I can ask.

I nod my head as though I know what he's talking about and scan the rest of the room. Beneath the artwork sit a series of glass cabinets containing a few paper books under glass although most appeared to be some form of plastic.

I make my way over to the glass case in the centre of the room. A forked sword with an eerie green edge lies on the padded base of the case. Twelve names are etched into the blade. Around the sword lie a dozen different coloured scales big enough to have come from a dragon.

"A scale for every dragon Mellakai killed," Dennian says.

"Why is it here?" I peer closer at the sword.

"The Suris are descendant from Mellakai. The sword belongs to Star."

I turn to look at Dennian. "So you're the Keeper of the Dragon Temple and give guidance to Governor Suri who keeps the sword that killed the dragons. Are the dragons good or bad?"

"Are humans good or bad?"

I cover up my lack of logical response by pointing to a piece of cloth inside the case. "What's under that?"

Dennian waves his hand over the case and the cloth slides off an amethyst scale with a glossy, melted edge.

"That's from the dragon in your drawing," I say. "Why is it covered?"

Dennian shrugs and tugs the cloth back over it. "Star doesn't like to see it."

"Come, I'll show you where I live." Dennian takes my hand and the nothingness envelops us. It lasts a fraction of a second before sunlight warms my skin.

"Welcome to Takarn Island," Dennian says.

We stand on a sandy beach on the edge of a sparkling blue lake. In the centre of the lake, a jagged rock rises from the water. At the very top, two dragons perch, their emerald eyes twinkling in a life-like manner.

Dennian pulls his leather necklace off. The dragon stone is dull although the colours are still present. "I need to get a fresh stone. Then I'll show you the temple."

Dennian pulls off his shirt and dives into the lake. He moves smoothly through the clear water before eventually disappearing from sight in the deeper water.

I wade out into a shallow section off the beach. The water is warm and rocks sparkle in a rainbow of colours beneath the surface. I scoop up a handful revealing precious gemstones.

"The dragons liked the shiny things." Lyri stands on the bank watching me.

"Hello again." I wade out of the lake to join the young girl on the bank. A tiny ball of fur launches itself at me.

"Zeke!" Lyri yells as her baby monkey brother burrows into my hair and wraps his tail loosely around my neck.

"Where did you go, Zeke?" Voices come from the greenery before four children stumble onto the beach.

They stare at me and the youngest, a child around Lyri's age, hides behind a young teen. They all have the unusual colouring of chimaeras.

""This is the girl Dennian likes?" The second tallest tilts her head as she studies me.

"Do you reckon she scares easy?" The oldest asks his cousins.

The kids all grin at each other, before they all transform. The oldest boy dives into the water and becomes a turtle. The girl morphs into a grey-footed tree-hopper. A lizard takes the place of the shy child and the final girl takes to the air as a brightly coloured parrot. They each disappear in a different direction.

"Wait for me!" Lyri grabs her brother from my shoulder and chases after the tree-hopper.

355

"Dennian's animal is scarier," I call after them.

The surface of the lake ripples and Dennian emerges. He hangs his necklace back around his neck. A new, glowing stone hangs from the dragon claw clasp.

"Can you swim over to the temple?" Dennian asks.

I gauge the distance. "I guess we'll see."

I strip down to my underwear and join Dennian in the water. I set a slow pace through the water. Sunlight sparkles off the water and warms the back of my head. Dennian swims beside me. Every now and again I look up at the towering rock formation and the dragon statues perched at the peak so similar to Dennian's tattoo.

When we reach the island, I grasp hold of a rocky edge and look up. Dennian might be able to climb that with the help of his claws, but I won't be able to.

"This way." Dennian swims a short distance around the rock formation. He rests a hand near a series of the scratch-mark language. "There is a cave below us. You'll need to hold your breath."

Dennian takes my hand and as soon as I take a deep breath, he pulls me under the water. We swim under the rock ledge and surface in a dark cavern. Dennian leads me out of the water and we stand by the edge of the underwater lake.

"Can you see it?" he asks.

A speck of light appears a few metres away, followed by another and another. The walls light up as my eyes adjust to the darkness. We stand in an ancient lava tube marked with luminescent images.

"What is it?" I ask.

"A record of the birth of the universe."

Dennian takes my hand as we begin the climb though the painted rock tunnel to the temple above us. As we walk, planets form from dust and the dragons appear. They rule the universe and then Aurum and Argentum, the gold and silver dragons, arrive.

At one point, humans appear beside each dragon. Aurum and Argentum pass away and the temple appears in their place, only the island is on Atlas instead of here.

Wars begin, dragons die. One man holds a twin-pronged sword with a glowing green edge. Eventually all the dragons depart, leaving a single yellow dragon behind to guard the temple.

These last few images have slash marks through them, as if a crazed warrior was let loose with a sword. I run my fingers over the deep grooves cutting through the ancient images.

We step out into the light beneath a cavernous room, the ceiling created by the dragons' outstretched wings. In the centre of the room sit several hollow crystal spheres. The closest to us is broken. It matches the piece on board the *Brinthiss Malla* present at the Takarna trials.

"What's with the damage?" I point to the sphere and back towards the passageway.

"It's always been like that. Carlen didn't know why. The tigers say it happened a long time ago."

"Governor Suri has a long memory. Have you ever asked Star what happened?"

"I asked." Dennian nods.

"What did they say?"

"If a person doesn't change their direction, they'll end up where they are headed."

"That doesn't really answer the question," I reply.

357

"I don't think it was meant to."

I look through the gaps formed by the Dragons' wings and legs. "Where do you live?"

"Down there," he points out over the lake. There's a flat grassy area surrounded by forest. Behind that are rocky outcrops. I can't see any dwellings.

I walk around the edge of the temple, peering through gaps. The forest covers the island and reaches out in the distance towards the ocean.

When I turn away, Dennian's expression is blank. He blinks several times then rummages through a glass cabinet in the centre of the floor. He pulls out a dozen sketches and spreads them across the floor in a circle around him.

"Everything okay?" I ask.

He looks up as though he's forgotten I'm there.

"Sorry. Sometimes Aurumargent speaks to me and I have to interpret what it means." He waves a hand at the dragon statues above us.

I peer over his shoulder at the drawings. Several I've seen before such as the ones he presented at the trials. I recognise the bronze medallion, the black hole, and the library with the amethyst scales melted to the floor.

One I haven't seen before is of a baby sapphire dragon in this temple. By the less developed pencil strokes, I suspect Dennian made this drawing a long time ago.

"Perhaps it will help if you explain it to me?" I suggest.

"When the world ends, we will be given a choice whether to challenge a god for our lives or concede this world to them and hope the gods have mercy on us."

Dennian taps a finger against the two-columned scroll and then the same scroll held in the hand of the young dragon rider.

"We suspect the world will end either way." Dennian shrugs.

"So we all die and I didn't need to worry about the ending of the tele-program?" I ask hesitantly.

"Possibly." Dennian looks over his sketches. "Star wants to create a new world using the building blocks of this one. They suspect if we can create it at the same time this one dies, no one will notice."

"Won't that kill us anyway?" I ask.

"We've recorded the current arrangement of the universe and predicted how it will be on the day the world ends. Star just has to work out how to get everything from here to there."

"Is that the purpose of the black hole?"

Dennian pulls the drawing towards him. Galaxies are sucked into the black hole exactly as I remember.

"It would require an unimaginable amount of power." Dennian glances at the image of the medallion. Faint lines surround it as though absorbing energy from the universe. I look over the sketch of the three men.

"So this guy has the medallion that Star needs. He's the one you called Bronzrr."

"He's a dragon." Dennian nods.

"They're chimaera, like you?"

"Star's ancestor, Sci. Suri, believed the dragons and dragon riders were the same. That's where he got the idea to genetically engineer human chimaera."

"So these human-dragons are coming to ask if we challenge or concede to the gods and the medallion stores power that can be used to create a black hole to make a new world? What's with the little blue dragon?" I ask.

"That's Sapphia. She will challenge the god."

"But she's so little," I say.

"This was twelve years ago," Dennian says. "She came to the temple, but Carlen didn't believe me."

"Where is she now?"

"It's not my place to say. She'll reveal herself when the time is right." Dennian looks out over his island.

"What about the last drawing?" I point to the library.

"I think that's Sapphia's mother." Dennian runs a finger over the melted scales. "There are two books on the shelf that she was after. They hold the answer to how to make Star's plan work."

"Do you know where the books are?" I ask.

"I think Star might know."

"So to save the world, we need two books, a medallion, and a dragon?"

"You make it sound simple." Dennian laughs. "Perhaps we'll live a long married life after all."

Library of the Gods

Star

Having close to a thousand years of memories in our head, déjà vu is a regular occurrence, but stepping into that library hits me like a blow to my solar plexus.

I ease the door closed behind me and I shut my eyes briefly. When I open them again, I see the room afresh. A single book sticks out from one row, but it's on a lower shelf than I remember. Pieces of furniture are scattered around the room and I bend down to pick up a small stuffed toy tiger from behind an oversized armchair.

One horn hangs loosely from the Temple Tiger's head and when I raise the toy to my nose, I'm assailed by the charcoal scents of dragons, drowning out the stuffy, seared smell of the library.

Keeping hold of the toy, I kneel on the floor and run my hand over the gap in the amethyst dragon shape melted onto the floor. The missing scale lies in the glass case containing Mellakai's sword, Slayer, and the dozen other dragon scales on board *Brinthiss Malla*.

Footsteps sound in the corridor and I freeze in position. They continue past the closed door and I release the breath I'm holding.

I twist on the balls of my feet as I move to stand, but my eye catches a discrepancy on the smooth strip of tiled floor next to the nearest bookshelf. I crouch low on the floor and look at it from a different angle.

A magical sensor stretches from the bookshelves right up to Amethyss' melted foot scales. I turn carefully in a circle checking the rest of the floor, but the sensor only surrounds the shelving. If I trip it, I could end up scorched into the floor beside the dragon.

I push myself to my feet and edge up as close to the sensor as I can without touching it. The book from Dennian's drawing sits out from the others, its spine labelled 'The Book of Creation' taunting me from beyond the reach of my outstretched hand. Beside it, another title catches my eye – 'The Book of Myth'.

I focus on the shelf and mentally grab for the books. They hit my chest and I fumble for a moment as I try not to drop the two books or the toy tiger still in my other hand.

Footsteps pound down the corridor, alerted by my use of energy. I clutch my items to my chest and step out of existence as the door to the library is thrown open.

The End
Book 1

*

If you enjoyed this book, please leave a review at the place of purchase or on Goodreads. Reviews help authors get noticed, and help readers find the next book they'll fall in love with.

About the Author

Nikki Moyes writes YA fiction and her first book, 'If I Wake' was published in 2016. She was born in Victoria and has moved around Australia amassing an eclectic range of occupations including tall- ship watch leader, apiarist, rose farm hand, and sandwich artist. In her spare time she learns tissu, static trapeze, and aerial hoop (she couldn't decide on one) in case she needs to run off and join the circus.

You can find her here:

www.facebook.com/moyes.nikki/

@nikkimoyesauthor

@NikkiNovelist

Other books by Nikki Moyes

<u>Young Adult Fiction:</u>

If I Wake

<u>Suri Series:</u>
The Castle
The Halfling
The Keeper: Book 1
The Challenger: Book 2 (coming soon)
The Destroyer: Prequel (coming soon)

<u>Non-fiction:</u>

Kokoda Trek

A Suri Series short story
A thousand years before the events of The Keeper, Risha Suri is the first successful child to be born with her father's memories. To avoid an alliance with a brutal warlord, she enters the virtual-reality game to seek help from the first warlord who resides at Castle One.

A Suri Series short story
The dragon Bronzrr dreams of becoming the next Story Keeper for his clan, but to do so he'll have to destroy the friendship he has with the little halfling outcast, Sapphia.

Sign up to my newsletter to receive a free copy.
http://nikkimoyes.com/index.php/newsletter/

On the 75th anniversary of the campaign between Australian and Japanese troops, author Nikki Moyes trckked the 96km of track where her grandfather acted as a translator. This is what it is like to hike the Kokoda Track.

Lucy and Will's lives intersect in dreams, where destiny pulls them together through different times in history, but Lucy is uncertain if Will exists outside her mind. When school bullying goes too far and Lucy considers ending her life, only Will can reach her. But how do you live when the only person who can save you doesn't exist?